Jerry O

Anthony Graham

Jerry O

First published in Australia by Anthony Graham 2026

A catalogue record for this book is available from the National Library of Australia

ISBN: 978-0-646-73676-1 (pbk)

Artwork and photography by Horatio Saitis © Anthony Graham 2026

Typesetting and design by Publicious Book Publishing
Published in collaboration with Publicious Book Publishing
www.publicious.com.au

God is concerned about the state of the human condition. He sends his son, formerly known as Jesus and now known as Jerry O' back to Earth to read the world the riot act. Despite our great advances in technology, we have become coarsened and narcissistic. This time the son returns to Earth with company. The novel describes the fantastic odyssey of Jerry O' and his troupe. The novel veers between ribald fantasy, adventure and sharp commentary. The climax is stunning and dramatic.

One
PARADISE

Wilfred stood at the rear of his electric golf cart measuring the distance to the hole. His drive had been competent. He was on the fairway. He leant into his bag and took out a six iron. He replaced it with a five iron. He took his stance and prepared to strike the ball. He forward pressed slightly and swung. The ball left the club with a pleasing thwack. It was slightly long and faintly sliced to the right. Wilfred replaced the club and got into the cart. He drove towards the green. He pondered on the vagaries of the game of golf. How long had he been playing it? On and off, he thought to himself, for two hundred years and still he was not its master. His father had never showed the slightest interest in the game. Still, he was busy enough, with his seven universes with their fiery suns and the often-troubling comportment of the various planetary occupants. Wilfred drove to the side of the green and alighted. He was playing alone. This was how he liked it. He had time to contemplate between shots. The Three Moons Golf Club was one of many courses in Paradise. Yet there were comparatively few golfers. This was because it was a game limited to being played on the little planet Earth and those humans who played it were often consumed with sins of pride, envy and greed. Paradise had accordingly been denied them. Wilfred smiled to himself thinking of the funny tartan pants the human men wore when playing golf and the strange and inconsequential dress code which tony clubs clung to. It was different in Paradise. Here all inhabitants were civilized and considerate to one another. It was, after all, how they got to Paradise in the first place. Earth was still the only planet that Wilfred's father had colonized with fully rational beings. Wilfred doubted that his father would try it again. Humans, he mused, had shown that given the choice of good and bad, they usually took the wrong path. Wilfred ruefully thought of the various dictators that Earth had produced, the calamities brought by humans on themselves and the Crusades, allegedly fought, in the name of his father.

Yet Paradise was changing. Wilfred's father had authorized the building of fifty thousand homes in a new suburb of Paradise One called Earthly Meadows. There would be shops, sporting facilities and theaters. Wilfred expected this was due to the population explosion on Earth. More humans must surely mean more inhabitants of Paradise. There were similar sub-divisions being developed in each of the other six Paradises.

The son was always the loyal right-hand man to his father. He knew one day his destiny would again overtake him. He knew his father would one day inform him of the second coming to earth. He still had the punctures in his hands to remind him of his first visit over two thousand years ago when he called himself Jesus.

Wilfred took a pitching wedge and walked to his Titleist Pro V. He paused to stand on the ridge where his ball was perched and enjoy his view of the three over-lapping lakes which dominate the course and which were the 'three moons' of the Club's name. It was late afternoon in Paradise, and its two suns were starting to dip towards the North. The day had been fine and clear. The temperature was a balmy 23 degrees. It was just another pretty day in Paradise. Wilfred was a tall man. He was dark and slim. His beard was neat and trimmed. He wore a dark blue Three Moons Golf Club golf shirt with khaki tailored shorts, ankle socks and tan leather golf shoes. He stood over the ball. The Fifteenth was a par four. He was going to lob the ball to the green and wait for the dip and borrow to run the Pro V to the hole.

He heard a voice and turned to see a golf cart driving towards him. It had a single occupant. He knew him. It was Mohammed, his father's aide de camp.

The cart pulled up just short of where Wilfred was standing.

'Wilfred', Mohammed said, 'the Big Feller wants to see you.'

'Mary Mags and I are having supper with him.' Wilfred replied, 'don't tell me he's forgotten. I would like to finish my round. I am seven over with three to play and I expect to par this hole. I am having a good round.'

'Sorry,' said Mohammed, 'he told me it was urgent.'

It must be a new crisis, thought Wilfred, perhaps an out-of-control Asteroid or a war between the two factions of the sub-human Grillabies on Pluto.

He followed Mohammed back down the Fifteenth fairway to the path that cut behind the green to the Seventh hole and led to the clubhouse and car park. A pro shop attendant was waiting to take the golf cart.

Wilfred packed his golf bag into his white Mini and headed through the gates into Atlantic Boulevard. Mohammed was leading the way in his SUV.

The trusted aide had been with the Big Feller since before Wilfred was born on Earth as Jesus of Nazareth. When Muslims entered Paradise and came upon Mohammed, they sometimes took him to be God. He quickly disabused them, pointing out that the Big Fellow had a variety of names which included Mohammed and he was merely Mohammed Zim, a former Abyssinian tailor and minor politician who had been accepted into Paradise and who became the confidante and aide to the Creator by dint of his hard work, loyalty and good works in Paradise. Mohammed would confidently twirl his handlebar mo. and show a mouthful of sparkling white teeth to the Muslims. They would be disarmed and relieved.

The two vehicles entered the grounds of the Big Feller's residence and administration center. The red brick office block which housed the bureaucrats was starting to empty as the workers went home. The white cement angel's block, known as The Citadel, on the other side of the residence, on the other hand, never slept as angels travelled between Paradise and Earth carrying out their work as agents of the Creator. Between the office block and The Citadel was the simple, single story red brick bungalow where the Big Feller lived with his wife another Mary.

Mohammed and Wilfred entered the house. The Big Feller was waiting. He ushered his son into the small ante room which served as his front office.

'Thanks for being so prompt,' he said, 'there is something that has been troubling me for months. I now believe it requires our urgent attention.'

The Big Feller sat in his old tan leather armchair and lit up his briar pipe. Facing him was his white board wall showing the present state of the seven Universes. Wilfred sat next to him, perched on the arm of the chair.

'You know son I will not interfere with nature.' The Big Feller had clearly rehearsed what he was going to say, 'if I was to even clip a dove's wing or shake a monkey's paw the course of nature would be affected. The human condition is at the very essence of nature. Goodness knows, when Adolf Hitler was born, I thought long and hard about it. In the end nature triumphed and the modern world was born. However, Calliope has been reporting to me of recent developments and his accounts become more disturbing by the day'.

Calliope was one of the lesser-known angels. He was a particular favorite of the Big Feller. He often went to Earth delivering messages for Him. He was a source of information about Earth and its troublesome inhabitants. Gabriel and some of the other high-profile angels seemed, to Wilfred, to be put out by the fact that Calliope had the Big Feller's ear. Not that they would ever say much. After all they were angels. They answered to Wilfred's father. However, Wilfred saw angels as being like the Roman Senators he had come up against two thousand years ago. At heart both groups were roosters who enjoyed their finery and their positions. Still, Wilfred would never utter a word against an angel. After all they were his father's messengers and agents. They served Paradise daily in a meaningful way.

Tea had arrived. His mother Mary walked in carrying a tray. She gave Wilfred a peck on the cheek. 'I have sent Mohammed to pick up Mary Mags,' she told the pair before retreating.

The Big Feller had a sip of his Ceylon Blend and puffed his briar. Wilfred remained silent. He waited to hear the news.

The Big Feller resumed speaking.

'It seems that Iran now has numerous nuclear weapons. I have no doubt that it will use them in my name against Israel. North Booga will then launch against the South. China will invade Taiwan and while this is going on, the USA is engulfed by absurd notions of sex, gender and race. They all claim that they fight on my behalf. But this is not all. Computer technology has only further sapped the good qualities of humans. You can add an eighth deadly sin. It is the sin of narcissism. Humans are now obsessed with themselves. They somehow think others are interested in their every facile thought and deed on this foolish X technology. Women think they are men and men do not know whether they are Arthur or Martha. There is little or no contemplation or sensible self-assessment. The leaders are generally egocentric. The hoi polloi has become dumbed down and feral. This is all the fault of the worst generation of earthlings ever, those foolish baby boomers. They taught the later generations in the schools and universities. The children have learned no logic. They have not been taught the fundamentals. The so-called Baby Boomers are now sucking the intellectual stimuli out of the world with their thick half formed theories. Climate change is just one of the nonsensical pseudo-scientific clap trap accepted as a reality on earth. There are still good humans, but they are frightened to speak out because the Baby Boomer chatterers have snatched control of the media. It is a tragedy, my son, and I am going to do something about it. Now I know you are going to say, but what about nature and I tell you I am still determined to let nature take its course. There are, however, other steps that can be taken.'

'The angels,' Wilfred chimed in.

'No, not the angels! They have enough to do. Gabriel complains constantly that his army is overworked. The angels will play their part, no more, no less. No son, I am going to send you back to earth in human form to warn the hominids of their impending disaster.'

'You mean it is the second coming,' Wilfred knew his fate required him at some time to return once more to earth to shepherd the flock to Paradise at the end of time. Had this time now come. He glanced ruefully at his hands. He was not looking forward to being on another cross, pinned with nails or worse.

'I did not say that.' replied his father, 'I want you to return to earth with information to impart to the earthlings. You are simply to tickle their ears. Give them choices. Ask them to renew their faith. The churches should be doing this, but they are beset by corruption, pedophilia and terrorism.'

'But' said the son, 'can't I make an approach as the son of the creator to the Pope or the Archbishop of Canterbury or what about the Ayatollah.?

'No, no,' said the Big Fellow, 'if you went to the Vatican, you would be caught up in arcane Papal politics. The Archbishop of Canterbury would have you locked in a mental institution and the Ayatollah would see that you are beheaded. Even the good Buddhists would graciously smile, offer you herbal tea and show you the door. No, you will go to the planet Earth under an assumed name and let the humans deduct who you are. Last year fourteen hundred and thirty-eight people went to St Paul's Cathedral in London claiming to be Jesus, the son of God. Over two thousand charlatans turned up at the steps of the Vatican making the same assertion. You will make actions speak louder than words. You leave tomorrow, but I do not expect you to be gone long. Your mother is informing Mary Mags as we speak. She is being prepared for your departure.'

'Ok,' said Wilfred, girding himself for the challenges ahead. The slight fade, in his golf swing, that he wished to turn to a draw, would just have to wait to be analyzed and re-worked.

'You will be known on earth as Jerry O.'

'O,' queried Wilfred.

'There is an Earthling expression 'God is an Irishman' - the name feeds this gentle misconception. It will not be difficult for the humans to divine who you really are. Even the Baby Boomers will understand through their haze of Marijuana and misconceptions. Calliope is also going to be with you. He will generally remain in spirit form and will assist you in your task.'

Wilfred sipped his tea. He did not smoke but now wished for the comfort of a hooked meerschaum. He tried to take in the sudden change in his comfortable peaceful life.

'And by the way,' the Big Fellow leaned forward and touched his son's arm affectionately, "you will have company. I am going to send a scribe and an adventurer to keep you company. The scribe will notate the journey in preparation of a third Book of Revelations being written by one of the Gospel writers and the adventurer will look after your back. I would have preferred that your traveling companions were more recent inhabitants of Earth, but that would have involved using a provisional resident. I decided against this. I have assigned Charles Dickens to be your scribe. He is presently in charge of the front desk at admissions".

'And the adventurer,' Wilfred was pleased at having company for his journey.

'Vasco De Gama,' replied God, 'he is now our sword swallower at BigFellerWorld. He will enjoy a change of diet.'

Two

The arrivals reception center of Heaven was never shut. There were no actual pearly gates. Nor was St Peter in charge. Peter was now a fisherman running a string of skiffs in the Apollon Sea catching, the never-ending supply of, tuna and snapper upon which the residents of Paradise dined. Michaelangelo, who daubed from his studio in the foothills of Heaven, painted a mural of his vision of St Peter and the gates. The painting hung behind the reception desk in the spacious welcoming lobby.

Charles Dickens enjoyed his work as front office manager. He still wrote daily. His new books were received enthusiastically. His latest tome was Lush House, the story of a family who were happy and agreeable and never squabbled over money or property. He added piquant touches of irony which artfully differentiated the nuances of the many characters that peopled his story. It was his first novel set in Paradise. All his previous works were set in Nineteenth Century England? It had taken him time to realize that contented people could be rich fictional subjects.

When Wilfred was being told of the forthcoming trip to Earth, Dickens was standing quietly in the rear of the reception corral watching a young trainee clerk dealing with a new customer. There was a lengthy spiel which accompanied every arrival.

"Yes Sir, you have made it to Heaven. We call it Paradise. No there is no Hell, there is simply death or Paradise. No, no Purgatory either. Yes, I understand you were an Agnostic on Earth. That has made no difference. You led a good life. You were honest. You cared for your family. You did not harm others. You knew your own failings. You are now at the entrance to Paradise. You are accepted as a provisional resident. Yes, I understand that you are eighty-seven years of age. You will remain that age for one hundred years. If after that time you wish to continue to live you will be accepted as a full resident. You will then become thirty-five years old. This is the age of all permanent residents. Your grandson who was killed in an accident is here. He attends school and will continue to age until he is thirty-five. He will then remain that age. I am sorry to tell you that your wife did not make it. I am afraid she was a sinner. You can find more information about her iniquity from your assigned mentor after you have settled in. There is no crime in Paradise, no sickness, no drugs [other than tobacco which has been found to be harmless] and no political parties. There are no computers, phones, radios or televisions. Paradisians, as we call one another, communicate directly with each other. Your sex drive has been removed. Yes, I understand you are eighty-seven, but you will be thirty five soon enough. You will make many friends of both sexes. You will enjoy hobbies, crafts and sports. You will also find work that both sustains you and enriches your life.

There are less than forty million residents within the seven universes of Paradise after all the many thousands of years of life on earth. You are to be congratulated. Your acceptance is an honor well deserved".

Charles Dickens was pleased by the young clerk's accuracy and brevity. She would be a fine acquisition to the front office staff. The old man was being escorted out the building by his mentor to a waiting SUV to be taken to his temporary accommodation whilst his induction continued. Charles Dickens congratulated the trainee before returning to his back office. When he got there, he was surprised to find the Big Feller's aide de camp Mohammed sitting on couch twirling his mustache.

Mohammed did not stay long. He had another visit to make.

BigFellerWorld was a relatively new development in the Provisional Colony. The Creator got the idea from the reports he received about Disneyland on Earth. There were rides and stalls. There was even a jungle cruise and an old-fashioned giggle palace. The children accepted as provisionals loved and used the park. Adults too, enjoyed its simple pleasures. Vasco De Gama knew he had made Heaven by the skin of his teeth. He guessed his mammoth expedition from Portugal to Africa and India in 1497 was the sealer. Vasco was the commander of the four sailing ships which made the voyage. Two were lost, but Vasco somehow managed to steer the remaining ships home to Portugal. Sure, there were scandals, Vasco's cruelty to pilgrims is well documented, but he restored his reputation by the good advice given to the young King John 111.

The hundred provisional years were difficult for Vasco. It was hard for him to forget his former life of power and privilege. However, as time passed, he became sanguine. There are no viceroys in Paradise. Every Paradisian is recognized for their singularity.

De Gama, after he got settled in Paradise, became a ship's captain taking passengers between the seven Paradises across the Celestial Ocean, but when the Big Feller began establishing his theme park, Vasco applied for a job. Sword Swallowing is an ancient Indian practice. Vasco had learned the art whilst in the sub-continent in the early sixteenth century. The swallower passes the sword through the mouth and down the esophagus towards the stomach. The art requires great concentration and skill, but most of all requires courage and that was the aspect of the craft which appealed to the Portuguese adventurer.

At the time Mohammed arrived to inform Vasco of his new assignment he had finished performing for the day and was busy polishing his swords. De Gama sat on a wooden three-legged stool in the performers recreation area rubbing a rapier furiously with a chamois which he dipped from time to time into a bottle of steel polish. Vasco had not previously met Mohammed, but he knew of him and appreciated that he was an emissary from the Creator himself.

'The Big Feller is sending young Wilfred to Earth. You are to accompany him,' said Mohammed.

This got Vasço's attention. He carefully laid down the rapier and stood up waiting for further information. Mohammed continued:

'The writer Charles Dickens will be accompanying you. He will be the scribe. The three of you will all take human form. You and Dickens will resume your old body forms. Wilfred will be known as Jerry O.'

'Jerry O' what?' Vasco interposed.

'It does not matter,' Mohammed replied, 'his real persona will soon be exposed. Do not trouble yourself with detail, your role has been clearly defined.'

'And my role is?'

'You are Vasco De Gama the great adventurer and protector of our Wilfred.'

Irony was not the Portuguese sailor's strong point, but for what it is worth, he detected not a hint of causticity in Mohammed's tone, inflection or demeanor.

Three

CHARLES DICKENS JOURNAL

I have always resisted, some would say defied, the temptation to write an autobiography. There are those amongst my many critics who would say: 'Oh yes, Dickens, of course he would not write a memoir. He is too subsumed by self-indulgence and greed to write of a subject without a ready audience for weekly serialization.' Others would claim my life was not worthy of biography. It is too ordinary, too devoid of interest, too mundane. Finally, there have always been a minority of scurrilous chinwags who maintained all my books have been personal histories. The latter repulsive claim arose largely after Martin Chuzzlewit. Let me assure all you dear readers that I am not and have never been anything like Martin Chuzzlewit. Do you not perceive that, by his very name, I am distancing myself from him.

Since arriving in Heaven and settling into the wonderful pattern of peace and sanguinity that exudes from every lustrous pore of every plant, seed and breath of wind, my writing has changed. In my first manifestation on Earth I was consumed by an overwhelming hankering to inform the world of the injustices, inequality and almost, but not quite, insuperable impediments that stood in the way of a poor man to achieve advancement. In that old world of mine, I observed men and women who chose to be horrid. They were often confronted by the simple ready choice of good and evil and yet always opted for evil. My books sought to elucidate this odd manifestation of the frailty of the human spirit. Was there really a devil? Was Beelzebub working with teams of swarming demons to infect and snowball the decrepitude of mortal beings? It turns out that there is no Hades, people create their own hell on earth. It is only the just who obtain the ultimate reward. That is the cause and effect of the laws of nature. Upon reflection it is fair indeed.

Now I live amongst only the good and decent that have been panned and quarried by the creator. This has provided me with many challenges. Yet I have, I think, found a fresh voice. The minuscule differences in paradisal behavior provides me with abundant and profuse fodder for novelization.

I have been content with my lot. No more than content - overjoyed. Yet when Mohammed told me of my new mission, it provided me with a bright and unfamiliar task. I appreciate, of course, I am simply the scribe. I must confront the ghost of long-gone pride. I am no biblical scholar or psalm writer. I am the scribbler, the chronicler of whatever incidents occur, the recorder of all the conversations and the registrar of events. Oh yes, my good readers, it is indeed a satisfying venture that awaits me.

Four

CALLIOPE'S EPISTLE

Angels are not authors. We are spirits, no more no less. It is true we come in different guises. There are healers and agents, tempters and guardians, arbiters and singers. There is one scrivener Metatron, but he is the accountant of the Universes, recording the daily deeds like entries in a ledger. There is no nuance in Metatron's penmanship. He is our dry dusty angel.

I am different in that I write surreptitiously. We angels have our tasks rigorously allocated by our CEO Gabriel. He watches from his cubicle within the Citadel. He is our eagle-eyed overseer, always ready to censure and proscribe.

It is probable there will be only one reader of my epistle. I am being presumptuous. This is not an epistle. It is only a pre-cursor to the task of some saintly man of letters who may find some Skerik of substance in amongst my piffle. I hope so.

I trust it is John who reads my work. He is so sharply focused and steady of hand. His gospels are as fresh as this morning's catch of snapper and as bright and gleaming as the buttons on a Field Marshall's dress tunic. If it is Matthew, Mark or Luke, I do not complain. Of course I do not complain. I am simply puffed that any holy writer should scan my scratching.

There is no pecking order in Paradise. Saints have no right to jump a queue or take precedence over other Paradisians. They have their Saint's Picnics and second last suppers and so on, but that is just giving them the opportunities to share past glories, wins, losses and travails. Nobody would want to deny them these privileges, if you can call them that. On the other hand, though the saints live and breathe the same air [well there is no actual air, but you know what I mean] as angels, I realize that it is only the Big Feller and Wilfred who totally understand what the angels are all about.

First let me dispel a myth. There is no Holy Ghost. He is simply a manifestation of the Creator. I am not too sure about Wilfred. He seems to have always been around. The Big Feller is married to Mary, but she arrived in Heaven after Wilfred returned after the crucifixion. There are many different opinions about the meaning of the trinity. It is not appropriate for me to seek to explain something which I find inexplicable.

Getting back to the angels. Remember reader, we do not come here by dint of the natural selection of good people. We have always, yes always, been around. We are the other universal creatures. To repeat my thesis. The Creator is universal. The angels are universal. I am not sure about Wilfred, but Mary is a recent arrival. However Gabriel is coming towards my desk, I must stop writing and hide the parchment under my cloak.

Gabriel has gone. He is suspicious of me today. Then again he is always suspicious of me. As I started to say before I was interrupted, we angels are not necessarily good. We are also not necessarily evil. Michael is brave and just, but he is proud and full of himself. He is our male model who won Paradise Survivor. Gabriel is the eponymous managing director of angels. He controls our work with freakish energy. Raphael is called the healer, but as the Big Feller frequently says, it is nature that heals. It is Raphael who brings back the messages of recovery. He is, therefore, always content and composed. The humorists amongst us call him the Person Whisperer. Uriel, well Uriel is Uriel. According to historical reports he is supposed to lead us all to destiny. Fortunately, the Big Feller is not upset by this nonsense. It is just angel spin. Uriel is our prankster.

Rumor has it that there are different breeds of angels. Seraphims sing and praise the Creator, Ophanim guard him and Chayot are living beings. This is just baloney. All angels are Malachims and proud of it. We travel at will through space and time. We can pass through solid surfaces. If we need to, we can adopt any earthly or other form to suit the circumstances. I frequently transform into an elderly black woman from the American deep south, but not always. I have been a wasp [not the human variety], a lizard and a towering gum tree.

For some reason the Big Feller likes my messaging. Perhaps it is because I am succinct. Gabriel is not happy that I seem to be favored by the Big Feller. I am sure that he does what he can to poison the well with head office. Mohammed has as good as said so. Gabriel is particularly put out about my new assignment. It is a feather in my cap. I will wear it proudly.

Now I know angels do not usually get to write biblical tomes. I hasten to add that I do not know whether the forthcoming trip will even bring forth a further testament. I have merely guessed that it will. I have also figured that this odyssey is the first step towards the rolling up of earthly existence. I may be wrong, but it is with this theory that I leave you dear saint with this first fumbling attempt at helping you to draft the epistle of the angel Calliope. The new book might be the sequel to the New Testament. On the other hand, it might be a Book of Revelation. Perhaps it might be called the Post-Modern Book of Revelations.

I will update the manuscript as the trip progresses, but my first verse could read something like this:

CH. 1 V. 1 The son of the creator has been requested to return to earth. He will be accompanied by a learned scribe and a great adventurer. His care is entrusted to a humble angel. The mission of the son is to preach to the people on earth and warn them that they are sinking into a swampland of sinning.

Dear saint, I hope my first effort is not too embarrassing. You can see that I have made changes to exclude my name from the verse.

Five

Mohammed had been busy organizing a meeting with the selected travelers. The Big Feller, no doubt, wanted to fill in the gaps, give some directions and make sure the mission was ready to roll.

There had been some annoying interruptions to Mohammed's meticulous planning. The angel Uriel turned up first. He claimed that he was to be Calliope's assistant in the assignment. He said he had a particular feel for humans and had on several occasions entered the human form to perform what he described as 'stand up' at comedy clubs in Berlin and New York. He also shimmered around the room giggling and calling out that his bent was burlesque. Fortunately, Mohammed knew Uriel of old. He was ever the joker. Mohammed told Uriel to buzz off, and he did with a last cheeky spin of his glimmer.

Next to arrive was the Angel Metatron. He was more difficult for Mohammed to get rid of. Metatron was a pedant at the best of times, but today he was positively casuistic.

'I am the keeper of the Angel's books,' he commented, 'it is important that I record the events that will take place on earth for posterity'.

'That is why Charles Dickens is going along, 'replied Mohammed.

'But Dickens, though a good, no great writer I grant is not experienced in the form and constituents of a proper report to the Archangel Gabriel. He is a fastidious angel. I am answerable to him. I know he is most concerned that the trip is formally diarized. I wish to simply attend all meetings and be briefed regularly by Calliope. I know Calliope is a paragon, but can he be expected to record daily events. This has never been his occupation. He is untrained and ill equipped for this project.'

Mohammed took it for a while. He was reluctant to get into a squabble with angels, but he had work to do.

'In the first place Metatron, you are answerable to the Creator, as is Gabriel. Secondly the Creator has appointed Charles Dickens to be the scribe. He will accompany Wilfred on the trip and will note up the events that transpire as they occur. You will no doubt get a chance to de-brief Calliope after he returns. In the meantime, you can go back and tell Gabriel that I know he has urged you to make this representation and it is rejected.'

Metatron left. An angel has no tail, but at least metaphorically it was between his legs.

This was not the end of the matter. Mohammed was unsurprised when Gabriel flounced in.

'Look Mohammed, this really is not good enough' he said. 'Angels are entitled to a modicum of respect. I am their eternal leader, and I believe I have done well. I do not ask much, just that our Angel Recorder goes on the journey to assist Calliope with projects that are probably beyond his capabilities. It will be better for all.'

'In a word, no,' replied Mohammed, 'speak to your parrot Metatron, I have given him chapter and verse. Now Gabriel would you mind letting me get on with organizing the forthcoming meeting. There are places to set and an agenda to prepare. You can tell your angels that you have made all the protestations that your arcane politics allows you and that I was absurdly stubborn. Call me a mule if you like. For my part I will not tell the Big Feller of your shenanigans this morning. Though as you are aware he is all knowing.'

This seemed to, if not satisfy, at least pacify Gabriel who left without losing a single trace of his accustomed hauteur.

At last Mohammed was free to prepare the seating and leave out paper and pens and copies of the agenda.

The time arrived all too soon and the group sat at the board room table in the Creator's small meeting room. The Big Feller was at the head. Mohammed sat on his right, ready to write up the meeting, get refreshments and perform chores. Next to Mohammed was Calliope who had added a few shades to his usual glimmer and could be therefore discerned as a humanoid shape. On the other side sat the three journeymen, Wilfred, Dickens and De Gama. They had been formally introduced outside by Mohammed and were taking each other's bearings.

The Big Feller raised his hand for attention and commenced:

'Wilfred has been told the purpose of the forthcoming trip, but I will repeat my explanation so that the rest of you know where you are going, why you are going there and what form the trip will take.'

He continued:

'As you are aware the human race is my most complex creation. The human body is as intricate as it is composite. Yet nature itself trumps anatomy. I carefully enabled nature to evolve, and this has happened. Humans at first were little more than simians. They resembled those annoying sub-human Grillabies on Pluto, who incidentally continue to fight endlessly amongst themselves. As time has passed humans capacity for learning has increased by a hundred fold. Their life span has more than doubled due to great men and women mastering ways of curing illness and disease. Others have grasped the significance of diet and exercise and taught humans' ways to extend and improve their conditions. Nature itself has also evolved as humans digest how to use their environment. Yet for all this they somehow never learn. Calliope has been my eyes and ears. Let me tell you of the small things first. They may seem unimportant but are symptomatic of the whole human enigma. It starts with the children. The teachers are often ignorant themselves. The basic tenets of learning are no longer being taught. The parents are often of no use. They treat the children as if they are small adults. Childhood itself is being denied to them. These children, unless something is done, will grow up to be even worse than the foolish, narcissistic baby boomers who are now teachers, lawyers and world leaders. Large canines which were bred over centuries to be hunters and runners are being cooped up in tiny enclosures called yards and kept as trophy pets by humans. The dogs are becoming as neurotic as their owners. Tribes of poorly educated people called counsellors now are paid by other humans to give them half-baked advice as to how they should live their lives. Though the middle classes in the first human world wring their hands endlessly about the state of the planet, they continue to drive huge petrol guzzling vehicles called SUV's and talk constantly on portable powered phones. There is a new cult of celebrity which involves humans seeking fame for its own sake even if it is for a fleeting moment. As part of this odd phenomenon, they use their computers and phones to constantly inform the world of what they had for breakfast, where they are standing, who they are looking at and other minutiae. However, what I have just detailed to you is small potatoes compared to the more important dilemmas facing humanity. Some of the priests are pedophiles and the churches have either failed to act or covered up the evil. Some Muslims claim that they must eliminate all Christians and create an Islamic caliphate across the world. In the pursuance of this object, they encourage young men to act as suicide weapons in the belief that they will be transported to here where they will find fifty virgins waiting for them. Though it is difficult to comprehend, there are takers to this monstrous offer. W existhole societies where the starving outnumbers the fed and the homeless outnumber the housed. Wars still break out constantly. Yet I guess you may say to me, but you do nothing. Yes, this is true, I created a whole system of nature and allowed it to evolve without my interference. This will continue. However, I want a warning given to humanity. The priests must be told they need to be good as well as pious. The Muslims must be told they should drag themselves into the new century. The first world must re-learn the basic tenets. Children must be allowed to be children. Hypocrisy must first be exposed and then excised from the human condition. There is plenty to be done. You are designated to be my messengers. Wilfred, you shall be my spokesman, Charles Dickens you shall be the scribe and Vasco De Gama you shall be my son's protector.'

'I will need an army, 'exclaimed De Gama.

'You will have no army, you will have your sword, and you will have Calliope.' replied the Big Feller.

Vasco looked at Calliope. One could see he was less than impressed, but he said nothing.

'There is much we need to know,' said Dickens, 'though I see newcomers to Paradise on their way through the front office, my experiences are fleeting and unsubstantial. I have been told of computers, my confrere WMT is more knowledgeable of modern man than I am.'

'WMT?' Mohammed queried.

'William Makepeace Thackeray.' responded Dickens.

'Well, he did write Vanity Fair,'interposed Calliope.

The Big Feller laughed and smiled at Calliope. It was fortunate Gabriel was not present; he would have been furious.

Dickens continued, 'Only recently a man was admitted as a provisional and he commented on our lack of computers. In fact, he told me he could supply me with some, which he called Apples. His name was Jobs.'

'Job,' exclaimed Mohammed.

'No Jobs,' answered Charles Dickens.

'You will have no computers, no small phones nor other twenty first century devices. Dickens you shall be a writer from the nineteenth century. You shall speak in the language of your time. You shall be dressed in your velvet frock coat with leggings and stockings. On your feet you shall have black patent leather shoes with silver buckles. You will have a trimmed beard and carry spectacles. De Gama you will speak accented English. You shall wear a ruffled white shirt, belted scarlet doublet tight at the waist, hose and thigh boots of the best Portuguese leather. You will have a black silk robe as an outer-garment, and you will be topped off with a tall crowned black chapeau upon which the red steel cross of the De Gama family crest shall be fastened. You will also both be supplied with changes of clothing.'

Vasco seemed pleased by the finery he was to wear, but Charles Dickens was less enthusiastic.

'And I?' said Wilfred.

'You, son, shall be a smallish Irishman in a modern tailored black suit designed by a Monsieur Armani. You will have a white shirt without a tie and black leather shoes. You will be the epitome of the successful Irishman. In many corners of the earth there are such men. They have gravitated towards airlines and are either Presidents or the Chief Executives of many of the large travel companies on Earth. They are not necessarily particularly talented, but they are usually ruthless and efficient. However, Wilfred, do not trouble yourself about this. You will merely look like one. You shall still be my son. It is simply part of my plan.'

Wilfred nodded, but he was still not quite sure what was expected of him.

'Calliope,' the Creator continued, 'you shall generally be invisible to humans or simply be a shimmer to the travelers. However from time to time, you may assume human form. I know you enjoy your physical embodiment as the fat black woman and for the purposes of the trip this shall be your human guise. This will enable Wilfred and the others to know you. You shall be called Dora, a maid who comes from Alabama.'

Calliope nodded happily.

There followed further discussion as to the minutiae of the trip. Credit cards were supplied. Dollars were handed over by Mohammed and the group dispersed to gather themselves for the journey ahead.

Six

CHARLES DICKENS JOURNAL

I write the next excerpt of my journal immediately following my meeting with the Creator, Mohammed and my fellow travelers. I want to get my impressions down while they are fresh in my mind and before I eat a light repast and rest up for the enterprise that lies ahead.

But first there are some weighty matters that I have considered and should commit to print. Who, dear reader, are you? When I was on earth so many years ago, I knew my readers well. My books, remember, were serialized, a bit like this journal. Every week young cockney boys would take to the busiest intersections in London and sell my week's output. I tried to write a longish chapter to give them their money's worth. I knew my readers because I could see them walking the pavements of Putney, Elephant and Castle and Camden Town. They would line up to buy my latest offering and place the bound up new chapter in their leather carry bags or in a pocket of their greatcoat. The young ruffians who were the sellers fought like rats in the Soho sewers to bag and keep a prized territory. I used to often travel the streets in my carriage observing my readers. I claimed it was for research purposes, but my real reason was to watch the pennies accumulate. My deadly sin was greed, but I knew it was the cancer of my soul and I fought it off and became a better person.

So, I say again, who are you my reader? I have cogitated on this puzzle since I was first given the task of compiling this document. In the end I have appreciated that it can only be the residents of Paradise. I have no brief to publish my jottings on earth. The Big Fellow has not raised this with me, and I accept that this must only mean that if it is published at all it will be in Paradise where my fee is my satisfaction at the knowledge, I have a happy reader. I simply compile the journal, and do not put it out for distribution and sale.

Having come to this weighty conclusion I address my dear fellow Paradisians. If you are my readers, think now of my anxiety. I contemplate too much and write too many words. I know this of myself, but to leave Paradise for even a moment is a worrying notion. We are indeed fortunate spirits to live eternally in Paradise. We are all early middle age. We have no illness or disease, the seven deadly sins cannot afflict us, and we are comforted not bored by our daily life of work, friendship and play. We have vast libraries of books and songs. There are sports to play and pastimes to enjoy. As some of you know I still write.

I have read my critics on Earth. They were few and far between at the time my books were written, but huge tomes have since been published by scholars claiming to know the meaning of my words. They parse sentences with the same pernickety precision of a saucier straining cucumbers to prepare the perfect vichyssoise. They criticize my verbosity and flowery linguistics. As they are entitled, oh yes, as they are entitled. In my defense I simply point out, dear reader, that my audience were poor put upon Londoners without much fuel or thick clothing to ward off the awful English winters, lacking food and money and most of all lacking any hope of advancement beyond their allotted station. Many of them could read but only slowly and others could not read at all. At times at night, I would have my driver take my carriage through Tottenham and Notting Hill and watch small groups of people sitting in their tiny gas lit sitting rooms in a circle being read to by the best educated in the family or by a poorly paid reader. I used to imagine it was my newest chapter of David Copperfield or Nicholas Nickleby and I believe I was often right. The betters, the upper classes read me as well, but they saw my work as misplaced social commentary, or worse still, as satire. I was going to add God help them, but he did not and nor did they deserve it. I have tried my best to write with less prolixity, but alas I am unable. I have read modern writers. I wonder how Raymond Carver could encapsulate raw emotion and tell a twisted tale in so few words, but that was his talent and it is not mine. I praise the wondrous adjective.

Now to our meeting! I have not been to the Big Feller's house before. It is surprisingly modest. The administrative block is a substantial edifice but lacking in pretense. I cannot say the same for the Citadel. The angels' headquarters are a beacon of opulence within the Creator's grounds. Calliope, our angel, is an odd one. He shimmers around in what I would say is a showy way. He certainly bears the confidence of the Creator and for that reason alone I must trust him. I cannot say I am impressed by Vasco De Gama. I have never liked the Portuguese. I have always thought of them as nothing much more than inbred Galicians. Nothing I saw from De Gama has caused me to change my opinion. Do not misunderstand my meandering assessment. I have read of Vasco's great deeds and his bravery. He qualified for Paradise and saw off his provisional hundred years so he must be a good man. It is just that when I was on earth I read of his travels, his victories and his rises and falls. He was not my hero, but I believed his deeds to be heroic. There were portrait paintings of the man, not least of all by De Fonseca, but they bear little or no likeness to the Vasco De Gama I met. He is not the tall, elegant figure depicted by De Fonseca, but a short, squat man with more the mien of a barbary ape than a nobleman. Am I being spiteful, I think not, I am being truthful. Mohammed was as efficient and well organized as usual. The Big Feller was everything and more than expected. His calm demeanor is only matched by the sharp focus of his mind. You are saying, ha-ha, Dickens is oft and away groveling at the bootstraps of the Creator, but I am not. I have said what I believe. I have left Wilfred until last. This is for a reason. Why is there a son of the Creator? How did he arrive? Is Mary his natural mother? What is his purpose? If the Creator lives for eternity is Wilfred, the eternal son? I cannot answer any of these vexed uncertainties, but the questions run through my head like Scottish salmon leaping from rock to froth as they head down the lochs to the open sea beyond. I am but the poor fisherman without the correct tackle. I glimpse the shiny pink fish momentarily as they fly past but cannot ever catch one.

Whatever Wilfred's reason for being, he takes on his mighty new task with humor and aplomb. He will be a worthy leader. He has the experience. On his last visit to earth, he was crucified and resurrected.

Now it comes to me, Wilfred is the Creator's link with the planets beyond Paradise. The Christians talk of a holy ghost as well. I have never come across such a creature. But, dear reader, I must stop contemplating. My head is becoming painful, I must be ready for the journey of the morrow.

Seven

CALLIOPE'S EPISTLE

CH. 1 V. 2 'And the Creator met with his son and the fellow travelers, the scribe Dickens and the adventurer De Gama, to discuss their journey. Their wont was ministered to by the loyal servant Mohammed and the Angel Calliope was present to accept his responsibility.'

There I have recorded my second draft verse. I hope it passes muster.

I can assure you that the events prior to the meeting were stressful. Gabriel hovered in the vicinity of my cubicle. He pretended to interrogate my neighboring angels, but his questions were innocuous and the subjects inconsequential. All the while Gabriel kept his cold black eyes firmly fastened on me. Even when I turned to face the wall, I could feel his glare on my back. He was also shimmering in an unnerving way. His gold sheen would suddenly turn to chocolate brown and then back to silver. He was trying to intimidate me and he was succeeding.

Metatron was also hanging about with his account sheets. He would sidle up silently to me with one or another question about my forthcoming expenses. A heavy shroud of skepticism lingered over every inquiry.

I was glad to be free of them, when the time came to attend the conference.

The Creator stirred me with his powerful analysis of the state of humanity on earth. Even though I was the source of much of the information, the Big Feller's dissection of the situation was nothing short of masterful.

I have to say I was impressed by De Gama. It is true he was quiet, but I could imagine his power and strength if it ever came to pass that he needed to act to protect Wilfred. I was not so sure about Dickens. I expected such a famous author to have a robust personality, but he seemed too concerned with detail and straw splitting. He reminded me of a human Metatron. Perhaps all scriveners are masters of fine points and niceties. Perhaps my humble self ought to be digesting his erudition.

After the conference was over Mohammed sat down with me and discussed rhyme and reason. He told me that the Creator would trust me to shift from shimmer to human form to invisibility as the occasion demanded. He said I was to use my discretion. Discretion, I like the sound of that word. It must mean that I have an important, no make that helpful, role to play.

I mentioned to Mohammed that Gabriel seemed to be a trifle put out. I was careful to make my comments in a bland way. I do not want repercussions. Mohammed said that he would placate Gabriel. He reassured me.

I will go back to my cubicle in the Citadel to rest. I will adopt the human form of the black maid Dora from Alabama. She will snore loudly with her mouth wide open. She will have three gold teeth. Metatron and Gabriel will not like this vision, but they will keep their distance. Uriel will enjoy my affectation.

I have a long and variegated trip ahead. Even angels require rest.

Eight

It was the day of departure. The travelers assembled in the circular colonnade which abounded the administrative block, the angel's Citadel and the Big Feller's house. The news had got out. Many paradisians had made their way to the parklands in front of the buildings and were setting up picnic tables, laying out food and drink and making a day of it. After all, it was not every day that Wilfred journeyed to the planet earth.

Socrates and Plato stood together near the rear of the crowd, munching grapes and talking quietly. They were amongst the few paradisians who still wore their old raiment. They apparently found their robes comfortable and neither of them was much for sport which would have required them to dress differently. They found golf particularly abhorrent and often enjoyed the company of G K Chesterton who famously once said while still on Earth that golf spoils a good walk. This comment never failed to amuse the two Greek philosophers. They were in paradise when Wilfred had gone to earth as Jesus of Nazareth and returned after the bloody crucifixion and splendid resurrection. They hoped that Wilfred would not have to endure misery to spread the Big Feller's message.

'They say this is merely a fact finding mission,' said Plato.

'I doubt it,' replied Socrates, 'if that is all that was required an angel could have done the job. Anyway, who is "they". I see there is a scribe. You must have been in the running, Plato.'

'I think not,' responded Plato, the Big Feller wants a report, I gather, not an hypothesis or tract. He has picked the right man in Charles Dickens. I doubt The Republic has sold more copies in its existence than Great Expectations sold in a single week in London in 1861.'

'Ah,' said Socrates, 'but has it.'

'Has it what?' said Plato.

'Great expectations,' Socrates replied, slapping his spindly thigh.

The crowd was now increasing in number, and the two Greeks were gathered up in the throng. Most paradisians were dressed in simple twentieth century threads of shirts, jeans and sneakers, but there were no rules or protocols and amongst the crowd were professional clowns in full getup, a British Hussar in his scarlet livery, surfers in board shorts and a Texas Ranger wearing leathers and wide brimmed black hat.

There were cheers when Wilfred arrived in his Mini with his wife Mary Mags. She hugged him briefly and stepped into the crowd where she was greeted by her friends warmly. Some were puzzled. Wilfred's face was as always, but he appeared shorter with frizzy black hair and was dressed in a fitted navy suit with open neck white shirt and tan dress shoes.

'I wonder what he is supposed to be,' muttered Socrates.

'A film star, perhaps,' said Plato, 'the men actors are often much shorter than they look and wear built up heels,'

'And how exactly do you know of such matters,' Socrates queried, "it is not as if film actors are thick on the ground in paradise."

'I have read of it, Socrates,' Plato replied huffily, 'anyway we will find out soon enough.'

Mohammed had now come from the Creator's house and was standing in the colonnade talking to Wilfred. Charles Dickens and Vasco De Gama arrived at about the same time. Vasco looked striking in his red doublet, black leggings and thigh boots made of the best tan leather. He seemed larger than usual, and his clothing and posture gave him a dignity that belied his usual unprepossessing mien. Dickens noticed and muttered to himself under his breath that Mark Twain was right. He was referring, probably to the Twain quote 'clothes maketh the man. Naked people have little or no influence on society'. Charles wondered if Twain had been considered for the position he now occupied. He thought the American would have been an ideal choice. Little did he know that the Big Feller had carefully considered the merits of the two writers and decided on Dickens mainly because he lived and wrote during Victorian times and was therefore removed from most of the splendors of the new world and more attuned to the human miseries endured by the penniless and uneducated masses. It was what humans needed to hear now. Dickens himself cut a fine figure in his velvet long coat, leggings and patent leather shoes.

The front door of the angel's building opened and out waddled a black woman of late middle age. She was as tall as she was round. To highlight her girth, she wore an ankle length bustled skirt which billowed in the slight breeze created when she walked. She had a curled semicircular head of the blackest hair one could imagine and carried a string shopping bag full of apples. Yet, despite her curious appearance she carried herself with a special, rare dignity that left even the strutting Vasco De Gama a mere shadow in her wake.

'What on earth are we seeing, Plato,' exclaimed Socrates, 'is this some bizarre tableau that the Creator has in mind? Is there to be music dancing and comedy as well?'

'Rest easy, my old friend,' replied Plato, 'you should know by now that the Big Feller knows what he is about. Behind every picture there is a purpose.'

'Who said that?' asked Socrates.

'I just did,' was Plato's reply. He enjoyed his verbal jousts with Socrates and believed that he held his own.

The Creator appeared from his house. Mary could be seen within, standing framed in a front window.

The Big Feller said nothing to his travelers. He had said it all at the meeting. The crowd was now hushed and expectant. Even the large host of angels who were gathered in motley legionss at the windows of the Citadel seemed still and awed.

Then from the side path between the administrative red brick office block and the Creator's dwelling emerged a slender young woman. She was dressed in a chain mail halter worn over a rough sewn hessian robe. Her dark hair was encased in a fur hood, and she bore a sword aloft proudly.

The Big Fellow welcomed her and gestured to the travelers to gather round.

'Make welcome Joan,' he said, 'she is accompanying you on your journey. She will be your strategist. She is better known as the Maid of Orleans.'

Nine
EARTH

CHARLES DICKENS JOURNAL

I have a confession to make dear reader. Though I write this episode as a precursor to leaving Paradise. We are two days into our journey. We have already had some exciting times. I am nothing if not an accurate narrator. Therefore, I feel absolutely obligated to scribble in chronological order. I am, however, unable to resist telling you about my present circumstances.

Let me set the scene. My desk is framed by a large window facing Central Park in New York. Joan of Arc is not only our strategist but is our de facto organizer. She allocated the central room of the hotel suite we occupy to me, knowing that I am the scrivener of the group. I write in Helvetica script on a small black tablet called an iPad. My typing, as it is called, is infantile, but with one finger I am telling my tale. I am enjoying the experience. I doubt if the Big Feller will permit the introduction of iPads to Paradise. He rightly believes that simplicity breeds contentment. Nevertheless, when in Rome one must do what Romans do and I guess when on Manhattan Island one must fit in with the local customs. We are in the Royal Plaza Suite of the hotel. It has three bedrooms. I share a room with Vasco De Gama. Fortunately, it is a large room with two beds and I can cope with the Portuguese sailor's guttural mutterings, sonorous snoring and occasional ripe fart. It is not ideal, but I have never needed much sleep and spend most of my spare time looking at, what are called, Apps on this tablet and writing this memoir.

Wilfred naturally occupies the master suite, and Joan is in the third bedroom. Each bedroom has a large separate bathing area. There is a dining room with a massive twelve-seater oak table. It has twelve matching chairs. The whole apartment is furnished in an ornate and baroque manner. The suite comes with a butler, but, unfortunately, he was swiftly sent on his way. We are serviced by the angel Calliope, in his manifestation as the black woman Dora. He claims to be our maid. Calliope is a scamp and I have not noticed him doing any servile duty. He is eager to spend time chatting with any or all of us, but so far that is the extent of his domestic service. Each day a team of black frocked hotel parlor maids march through the suite sweeping, vacuuming (a new word for me) and polishing. It is luxury beyond my belief.

On the other side of the apartment are expansive views of Fifth Avenue. The toffee-nosed butler, just before he was sent on his way, told us that this street is one of the finest shopping strips in the world. I prefer the green bustling raffish beauty of the park. During the day, there are hundreds of walkers and cyclists who pass along the wide, spacious paths which sinuously meander through the greenery. At night, the lighting is subdued and dim. Hansom cabs improbably clip clop their way in and out of Central Park with their drivers dressed in Nineteenth Century garb. It sends a warm glow through me as I recall my old London Town. I have noticed that many of the bicycles are identical. It has occurred to me that these bicycles must be rented by the hour or day. There are other cyclists dressed in strange loud skintight clothing called Lycra. Their helmets, shirts and even pants advertise certain products. Often these names have a European heritage. The bicycles they ride are narrow with slim wheels. Strangely many of these comically suited creatures are lumpen and ugly. These humans do not seem to realize they look ludicrous as they ride through and out of the park with their bundles of fat shaking and slopping over the sides of their narrow leather cycle seats. The runners also tend to wear uniforms. They wear black tights and long sleeve singlets set off by shiny rubber shoes. The walkers generally dress in normal street clothes, however I am puzzled to notice that there are a large number of men who mince along the path leading packs of dogs. Calliope, nee Dora, told me they are gay dog walkers. He then explained the modern usage of the word 'gay'. It has apparently been purloined by the homosexual community. This seems to me a pity, as it is a fine and expressive word. I have laughed to myself imagining that I am sitting in my old club in 1852 talking to perhaps a cabinet minister or retired general. He asks me if I have seen anything interesting and I tell him the Serpentine is being circled by many gay dog walkers. The cabinet minister or general may say, but why are they gay and I would reply that they are only gay in the sense that they are buggers. I doubt if the Reform Club would tolerate me after that remark and I would soon find myself trotting down the Strand to the Garrick Club where buggers were welcome even then. Calliope also told me that dog walking is a paid occupation. The dogs come in all shapes and sizes. There are some small house dogs, but I saw large spaniels, graceful Dalmatians and even hounds and bull terriers. Where would these dogs spend the rest of their day? Surely, they must be cooped up in apartments on Manhattan Island. This gave weight to the Big Feller's observation that humans were thoughtless and narcissistic. A human person or family which houses a large dog with hunting genes in an apartment is keeping the dog for the human's sake and not the sake of the poor canine. I now see a man in a bright pink sweater and a matching woolen cap carting along seven dogs. He is certainly striking as he is wearing black corduroy pants tucked into black thigh boots. My guess is that he is a bugger. There is a small rat like dog which seems to be the leader. There is an angry German Shepherd, two sad retrievers, a large hound, a waddling corgi and a tiny fluffy shiatsu wearing foolish baby blue booties. I feel like rushing to the elevator, running across the road and into the park where I would rest the leashes from the homosexual and free the dogs. I will not do so. I am a measured scribe and not a hero. It is perhaps fortunate for the pink sweatered man that Joan of Arc is not watching the tableau below. I doubt if she would tolerate such insensitive handling of fine animals.

I must return to our departure I have been sidetracked by the view.

It was heartwarming to observe the large and, I might say, motley crew of Paradisians who turned out to see us off. It came as a huge surprise when Joan of Arc was introduced by the Creator. She is a worthy addition to the troupe with her proven bravery and strategical skill. Calliope is still somewhat of a mystery to me. There is much an angel can do with his ability to dematerialize at will and carry out instructions direct from the Big Feller. He certainly made our arrival interesting. I will not say he smoothed the path, that would be an over-statement. But more of this in the next chapter. So far however, since we have settled in, all our Calliope has done is to flounce around the suite chatting merrily about everything and nothing or complaining about Gabriel.

'Gabriel certainly knows how to blow his own trumpet,' said Calliope to me, 'but that does not mean he is Satchmo.'.

I did not understand this allusion until I looked up Wikipedia on my IPad and found that Satchmo is a Mr Louis Armstrong who conducted an orchestra. He was a leader of men unlike, according to Calliope, Gabriel. I should add that I have met Mr Armstrong, as I admitted him to Paradise as a provisional not so long ago. He seemed a generous and friendly soul.

The trip itself to Earth was uneventful. It turns out the Big Fellow simply adjusts time and space so that one moment we are seated in the departure lounge in the angels retreat and the next milli-second we arrive on Earth. More of our first moments on Earth later.

Ten

CALLIOPE'S EPISTLE

Look I should be proud as the clown Punch. My troupe is on earth. They are all alive, almost too much alive some would say and here am I writing my next verse of my epistle. Nobody may read it. Alas! I say though the scribe Dickens is a man of many [too many] words, I write the small and certain script. Well, this is my wont.

I realize that for there to be a valid epistle it must be contiguous and continual. I must disclose that I have diverted from my orderly pathway. Charles Dickens is presently closeted in the study of our magnificent apartment overlooking Fifth Avenue scribbling his logbook of our voyage. He is using a black electronic tablet as a writing tool. I am envious of his capacity to adjust and make use of Twenty First Century technology. There are a number of these tablets strewn around the suite. They open curtains, turn on televisions and order food. I am, of course, well versed in their usage through my numerous visits to this planet, but in my role of Dora it would seem incongruous to be tapping away on an iPad. My designated role is as the servant of the others, and I should at this moment be sweeping up and gathering clothes for the laundry basket. Instead, I lie prone on a couch as a shimmer writing the next verse of my epistle in my mind diary which will travel instantaneously to my corral in the Citadel in Paradise. I agree, however, that I have cheated. I use the sitting room iPad to 'divine' new words to explain my scripture. Divine! what a word it is. But this is not all, reader, please forgive me for what I have done. When Dickens was performing his toilette yesterday, I shimmered into his study and began to read his work. Please believe me I only read a paragraph or two. I then became overtaken by my perfidy and left the room. I read enough, however, to know my scribblings are no more than a travesty of the art of composition. I considered bearing my soul to Dickens but have thought better of it. I will try and forget it. But can you Biblical scholar, can you?

It was the latest addition to our team [mob. menage, group - IPad words] who gave me the order to be a maidservant. Joan D'Arc is her given name, but she gives few clues that she was born a humble peasant in Domremy in France. Far from it: she is headstrong and formidable. She has the measure of the rascal De Gama and Dickens is polite but cautious in her presence. Even Wilfred treats the young lady with a measure of respect that I [so humbly] feel is not in keeping with his stature as the Big Feller's son [if not heir].

Still the Creator told us upon departure that Joan of Arc would be our strategist. I only wish she was an angel. She would surely frighten Metatron no end and even the bumptious Gabriel would be wary of her.

I should probably write my mind notes whilst in Paradise, but events overtook me. It was my job to herd the group into the departure hall and ready them for their journey. Whilst doing this I had to keep an eye out for Gabriel, or one of his toadies, particularly Metatron [the officious sleuth] who had been hanging around outside the hall trying to ascertain what was going on. I am concerned that there may be interference run by Metatron on the orders of Gabriel, but I am ready. I work for the Big Feller. He has my loyalty not Gabriel and his angelic bootlickers. He has given me the power to carry out what humans would call miracles to advance the operation. I guess Metatron will be careful not to jeopardize the mission. I suspect he will simply be a meddlesome auditor of my expenses and critic and informer of any missteps that I make.

The Big Feller has set some limits. He has warned me to be circumspect. I find this a difficult concept, but I am trying. I hope you are sympathetic, my dear John. Well, I hope it is John who is my reader. I hope it is he who turns my diffident script into powerful scripture. If it is Matthew, Mark or Luke I will still be honored. Paul too is welcome to digest my ignoble offerings [more iPad dictionary words I confess].

I have already carried out some important tasks to smooth the path of the visitors. They have been interesting and unnatural, and they have astonished the human beings who have observed my work. Some of it has even gone to plan.

I hear voices. People are coming, it is Joan and Vasco De Gama.

'Look Vasco,' she says in her high-pitched voice, 'we shall make our next move when the orders come through. Jerry O' gets his orders from the Big Feller, probably via Calliope and it is then and only then when we move.'

I was puzzled for a moment, 'Jerry O' and then I realized she was talking of Wilfred. She is right, of course, to call him by his adopted name. To call him Wilfred would be simply confusing.

'I am sick of hanging around this suite of rooms I am a man of action.' replies Vasco.

'Yes,' Joan says, 'I have known action too.'

'And it got you burned at the stake in Rouen, at the behest of the Bishop of Beauvais so I am told,' growls the Portuguese sailor.

'There are no French bishops here. Sir,' Joan haughtily responds, 'and I am in charge of the stratagems of the visit. Like it or lump it.'

It was her final word and De Gama wandered off still muttering, imprecations I suspect, about the nature of the young Frenchwoman.

Joan of Arc sat on an easy chair in the large sitting room of the great Plaza Suite [which I organized]. I lie comfortably on the couch composing my verse. Joan watches my shimmer. She knows I am here but does not seek to engage me.

CH. 1 V. 3

And so the Creator led his two disciples headed by his only son to travel forth unto Earth and shortly before their departure he introduced to them Saint Joan of Arc who will accompany them and manage their journey. The humble angel who was allocated the task of accompanying the flock arranged for the egress from Paradise and so the odyssey began.

Eleven

The arrival is complete.

Wilfred, Vasco, Charles and Joan of Arc are standing in the center island of Times Square in New York. Calliope, though invisible, is with them. Wilfred wondered if their sudden appearance would cause a disturbance. However as Wilfred surveys the scene he appreciates that Times Square is home to all manner of oddballs and that a Portuguese sailor, a girl warrior dressed for battle, a Nineteenth Century novelist on his way to his club and a Irish businessman traveling together were just another slightly fruity part of the ever shifting kooky diorama of Manhattan.

The Big Feller had ensured that each of the troupe would act and speak in accord with their identity, time and appearance. Wilfred found his own Irish brogue pleasurable. It was a lilting musical tongue. De Gama spoke English with a thick accent. He cannot say 'TH' s so that a word such as 'theatre' became 'seatre'. De Gama may have been a great adventurer, but Wilfred was of the opinion he was a somewhat smelly and gauche companion. Dickens was a pleasant and careful man. He spoke as he wrote. Precision trumped emotion and fiction was masked by truth. Joan D'Arc was a fiery and aggressive young woman. Though she was quite small, she held the floor whenever she saw fit.

Wilfred thought of the then invisible angel Calliope. Wilfred regarded him as a scamp. Though the angel was invisible, Wilfred knew he was nearby. This was his vocation. Calliope would always be close by.

Joan was standing on the edge of the curb examining the scene as if she was still the general, she once was. Since traffic had been removed from Broadway, the roadway had become a teeming mass of humanity.

'Lack of humanity' thought Joan watching the crowd jostling as they roamed apparently aimlessly around and about the wide boulevard taking in the sights. Joan was a neophyte to the Twenty First Century, but she could tell that most of the swarm were as dumbstruck as she was at being in the famous square. Joan had died young. It seemed so long ago that the cruel Bishop of Beauvais had ordered her to be tied to a stake and burned alive. Though the Bishop purported to be the servant of the Creator, she had not run across him in Paradise. She doubted if many of the protagonists of the Hundred Year War were basking in Paradise. The chevauchee tactics adopted by the British were brutal and murderous. It would be called 'scorched earth' tactics today. Joan knew the British were not alone in the use of such stratagems. When Joan decided to act, the invaders had nearly succeeded in their aim of conquering France. Not that the French ruling caste helped. Charles VI of France was a lunatic and his brother the Duke of Orleans was assassinated on the orders of the King's cousin, the Duke of Burgundy. Joan had grown up in the village of Domremy. Her parents were loyal to the French crown, though the village was surrounded by Burgundian traitors. It was the burning of the village that spurred the then sixteen-year-old Joan to take action. Joan persuaded her Uncle Durand to take her to see the nearest French battle commandant Count Robert de Baudricourt. He was dismissive of this slip of a girl claiming to have a warrant from God to fight the invaders and Burgundian turncoats. Joan was not deterred and returned a few months later supported by two men of stature, Jean de Metz and Bertrand de Paulengy. Joan predicted to the commandant the exact nature of a military reversal near Orleans.

The commandant took Joan to meet the new King Charles VII. He was impressed by Joan. She became the standard bearer of the French army. Though only sixteen she possessed an acute understanding of the tactics of war. It was at her insistence that the army attacked the main English stronghold at Tourelles and with only a small force captured the fortress of St Augustine. This was not her only victory but eventually Joan was captured by Burgundians who sold her to British partisans. Then came her 'trial' and death.

Joan was sainted whilst still a 'provisional' in Paradise. This honor did not serve to reduce her hundred years, but once ensconced as a permanent, she found that Sainthood brought some fringe benefits. The saints have their own area within Paradise. Joan lives with her parents who had both lived on after her death and were later accepted in Paradise. There is a party for the saints each year at the Big Feller's home. And most importantly angels are allocated to saints to perform good works or miracles on earth and keep the saints informed of happenings on the planet. Joan's angel is Sandalphon. Joan had not discussed Sandalphon's role in the trip with the Creator. She was not sure if he would play any part at all in her odyssey. Joan got on well with her angel. At first, he had bridled when she called him 'Sandals', but he had come to respect and cherish his tiny charge. Sandalphon was a cautious angel who, Joan thought, was ill equipped to aid a saintly warrior, but well qualified to serve a diplomat or preacher. And this was Joan's quandary. The Big Feller had simply told her she was to be the strategist, but what was to be the strategy she must adopt and more importantly what exactly required tactical initiative. Joan sighed, she guessed time would tell. The Big Feller knew what he was about, of that, she was sure.

The party moved from the curb into the Broadway throng. Wilfred was looking around for Calliope. He knew that they were booked into the Plaza Hotel, but he did not have the faintest notion how far away the hotel was. Could they walk it? Which direction was it? Joan of Arc was by his side.

"Were you given instructions", asked Wilfred, "how we get to the hotel".

"No", she replied, "we can ask someone. The Plaza is apparently a famous landmark".

There were people walking in every direction, and Joan singled out a man in a neat blue suit.

"Excuse me Sir, can you direct these lost souls to the Plaza", she said to the man.

He looked the group over and as he passed said "use your phone, use your GPS".

He hurried away fearfully.

"What does he mean, Wilfred", asked Joan.

Wilfred shook his head. He had little or no understanding of human technology other than the appreciation of the advantages of the titanium shafts in his golf irons.

Charles Dickens spoke up:

"I have been told that humans now use small mobile phones which are not connected by wires. These phones incorporate maps which are hooked into the satellite metal canisters that circle the earth. Look around you every person has one. I will ask somebody".

Dickens approached a middle-aged man carrying a brief case.

"Privee kind Sir, can you inform our party of the whereabouts of the illustrious Plaza Hotel. I am afraid to say we are quite disorientated".

The man put his head down and started to scurry away. Charles followed him calling out.

"Some brief help sir that is all I ask".

As Dickens headed North up Broadway in the wake of the man the others followed. The fellow with the briefcase began shouting "help. help". He ran furiously away. The group let him go.

Wilfred looked around uneasily. He could see no police, but he did not want the group to spend their first night in jail in New York. He gathered his team and they ducked down Forty Second Street. They walked east on the narrow footpath. Other pedestrians cringed against windows or doorways as they passed. Some even ran across the street as they saw them coming.

Three black youths in their late teens were approaching. They wore hooded jackets with baggy pants and white sneaker shoes. They each had both hands in the side pockets of their jackets. As they advanced, they watched the party from paradise with unconcealed interest.

Charles Dickens observed their curiosity. He moved to the front of the team and spread out his arms.

"Kind sirs", he began, "can you help this poor little tribe who are lost in the wilderness of Manhattan Island. We are expected at the Plaza Hotel. Can you give us the benefit of your knowledge"?

The youths looked at each other with amazement.

"Go fuck yourself you creep", said the biggest of the boys.

Dickens turned to Wilfred, apparently pleased by the exchange. He pivoted back to face the boys.

"You are Chaucerian by your idiom, young man. This is a revelation to me. I did not realize there were Twenty First Century men who were Chaucerian. This is a wonderful surprise".

The three young men muttered to each other apprehensively. The boy who spoke first stepped forward.

"Don't chosser me, you fucking creep. Ey yo if you don't fuck off we'll crip you".

"Crip us, you will need to provide some derivation and an explanation for your remarks. Also you may be Chaucerian linguistically, but your first remark to me asking me to fuck myself is a physical impossibility".

The young gang bangers had reached the limit of their patience. They now all had their hands out of their pockets. Two of the three were holding tapered knives. The third wore sharply contoured metal rings on every finger.

Two events then occurred. Joan of Arc and Vasco stepped forward. Their fists were raised in a pugilistic mode. Secondly Calliope emerged as Dora. She materialized between the two groups.

"Hey Auntie, where da fuck you come from", said the largest gang banger.

Dora spoke softly but with a certain conviction

"Don't you talk to me like that, you insolent lowlife. I will give the three of you five seconds to move off, otherwise I will start knocking your heads together".

The youths shambled off.

"You're lucky this time you cock suckers", was the leader's final attempt at bravado.

Dora held back Vasco, who apparently heard and understood the nature of the boy's final insult.

Dora then led the way down Forty Second Street to Fifth Avenue. "I think we had better find you a cab before you get into real trouble", she said as they approached the intersection of 42nd and 5th Avenue. Upon reaching the corner Dora was gone and Calliope was the faintest burnished shimmer.

Joan, a girl of no experience, was still trying to fathom the gang banger's last remark. A cock she knew was a rooster, but how could someone suck a rooster and more importantly why did the man Vasco De Gama become so enraged when the youth said the words. "Suck upon a rooster", she repeated to herself. "Suck upon a rooster, what could it possibly mean and why was it so much an affront to the Portuguese man".

However, as they came onto 5th Avenue Joan forgot about the enigma.

The four visitors gasped in awe at the teeming procession of passing southbound traffic and the crowded footpaths where a mass of humans walked at almost trotting pace in both directions.

Twelve

Wilfred led his team North along 5th Avenue. He was taking a gamble. He knew the Plaza Hotel was on or close to 5th Avenue. It was either North or South of where they were. Wilfred chose North.

Southbound pedestrians kept to the right and Northbound pedestrians kept to the left. Provided you walked quickly you could keep pace with the crowd. Calliope was now totally invisible, but he was wafting along at Wilfred's elbow. He could pass through solid substances invisibly, but if he chose, he could glow and shimmer. He could enter a human body. This would cause the pierced human being to feel heat and discomfort. As Calliope kept pace with the others every so often, he would brush a pedestrian traveling in the opposite direction. Occasionally a punctured or brushed person would turn back in a startled manner. However, the glance would be no more than momentary once the pedestrian saw the motley crew which he had just passed.

Generally, once pedestrians saw a dark-haired modern business type leading a Nineteenth Century commoner, a thickset gaudily dressed ancient Portuguese mariner and a small, ferocious metal plated girl warrior they quickly looked away. Some, no doubt, thought it was an advertisement for a Broadway show, others might have seen it as just another crazy stunt, but every passer-by avoided eye contact. On the other hand, Vasco De Gama and Joan of Arc watched the parade of pedestrians with undisguised curiosity. Dickens averted his eyes as a British gentleman should. It was early afternoon so most of the walkers were shoppers, but they were the usual disparate assortment of locals plus visitors from every corner of the globe.

Calliope whispered into Wilfred's ear. The Big Feller wants you to announce our arrival. It will be subtle, oh so subtle, but it will be a Lilliputian message to humans that something is up.

Wilfred turned to the invisible Calliope and asked him what was expected of him. The fact that the small business type, leading the odd bod gang, was apparently talking to himself did not surprise the pedestrians in the vicinity. What more could one expect from this rag tag crew.

Calliope told Wilfred to cross the road.

Take your team, Wilfred, and walk directly across 5th Avenue. Do not wait until you reach the lights. 'Just cross'.

Wilfred looked out at 5th Avenue in alarm where a continual stream of cars, taxis and motor bikes headed south.

'Don't worry, Wilfred, you will all be safe,' said Calliope.

Wilfred obeyed his instructions. He led the others to the curb and without adieu they walked across 5th Avenue. As they began walking the traffic died down and halted. From one end of 5th Avenue to the other vehicles simply stopped dead in their tracks.

At the instant the travelers reached the opposite curb the traffic began moving again as if the event had never happened. Vehicles seemed to be traveling at the same speed as they were moving immediately before the phenomenon.

Seventeen pedestrians and eleven motorists took still photos of the incident on their phones and five were alert enough to film a video.

Carl Martinez in the Central Manhattan Traffic Department oversaw the 5th Avenue CCTV. He called in his supervisor to view the footage, but the supervisor was unimpressed.

'Proof our drivers are the best in the world', the supervisor said, 'I hope the police arrest the freaks.'

There were two policemen who had been walking behind Wilfred and the others. They had been keeping an eye on them, but the group seemed to be doing nothing much wrong. The man in the suit was talking to himself, but if you arrested every person in 5th Avenue who had a conversation with himself, the jails would be overflowing by eight AM each day. The girl in the chain mail looked a bit fierce, but she was behaving herself and the swarthy man in the military regalia scratched his arse from time to time in a conspicuous manner, but so do politicians.

When the group set off across 5th Avenue, however, the two police leapt into action. Jay walking is taken seriously in New York. The officers cut across the pedestrians and reached the curb at about the time the travelers had arrived at the opposite side of the road, but by then the traffic was moving again. There was nothing the officers could do. They ran back towards

42nd Street to catch the lights. After all, the rag bag gang was going to be easy enough to find.

Calliope had noticed the two police running towards the traffic light corner.

'Quick,' he whispered to Wilfred, 'I will get us that taxi.'

Most of the vehicles in 5th Avenue were taxis, but none would have stopped voluntarily to pick up Wilfred, Vasco, Charles and Joan of Arc. Calliope used his power to stop one. It simply pulled up dead adjacent to where the group was then situated.

Calliope had selected a stretch cab so that the four could sit in the back. The driver was dumbstruck when his vehicle simply came to a standstill. Wilfred and the others hopped into the back of the taxi.

'The Plaza Hotel,' said Wilfred.

The cabbie who was an illegal immigrant from Montenegro was impelled by Calliope to drive. He continued south until he could turn left and circle back towards Central Park.

Calliope was invisible but was sitting on the front seat next to the driver.

Back on 5th Avenue the two police officers were standing helplessly at the lights on the corner of 42nd and 5th watching the cab. One of the police officers shrugged his shoulders.

'Jay walking, big deal,' he said to the other. They resumed their beat.

The new trendy Zara store is on 5th Avenue between 42nd and 43rd Streets. Pressed against the window was a slight shimmer. It was Joan of Arc's angel Sandalphon. He shook his head in bemusement.

He was not sure what to make of it. Also, Sandalphon was torn between two moral imperatives as they seemed to be in direct competition. Sandalphon admired his charge Joan of Arc. She was a plucky, spirited young woman. She was a saint for a damned good reason. On the other hand, he was obligated to his CEO Gabriel. Sandalphon was not the brightest bulb in the Creator's stable of heavenly creatures, and he was grappling with his problem. He had the responsibility of looking out for Joan, but Gabriel had told him he should report the travelers every move to him. A more savvy being would have taken the problem to Mohammed or discussed it with another angel - such as a free spirit like Calliope, but Sandalphon was no Calliope and he remained glistening at the window of the Spanish clothing store pondering on what he should do next.

As the taxi headed up Madison Avenue towards the Hotel, there was a hubbub of noise in the back as the group sought to digest the exciting experiences that had already ensued. Vasco boasted of the injuries he would have inflicted on the baby gang bangers they had encountered in 42nd Street.

'I would have taken their knives and cut them up like a fisherman would fillet a cod. Their entrails would have been exposed, and their mouths would have been puckered and gasping for life,' he said.

Charles Dickens took note of De Gama's words. It would be a useful addition to his account of their first day on earth. Wilfred was silent. He was now in the form of a human being once again. He realized the enormity of the mission which confronted him.

He also grasped the problems which would beset the other members of the team. As humans they would be confronted by all the temptations of the flesh. They may succumb to strong drink or drugs or the steamy stimulus of the flesh. He worried about little Joan who may have been a great warrior but was surely quite unworldly when it came to matters libidinous. Dickens would probably cope, but then there was Vasco De Gama. Wilfred shuddered a little as he looked at the beefy little Portuguese, who was at that very instant scratching the broad expanse of his arse. Joan was also silent. Should she ask the others about the 'rooster sucking' insult? As she contemplated this matter the stretch taxi turned left into East 60th Street before switching back into 5th Avenue. The Plaza Hotel is officially on the corner of 59th Street and 5th Avenue. The latter avenue borders Central Park to the East. It is the only street bordering the great park which retains its name.

Calliope decided that it was time to materialize, so suddenly the Montenegrin driver found a buxom black woman sitting next to him in the front passenger seat.

'I need a receipt,' said Dora.

'You get out of here, who you are, where you come from,' shouted the frightened driver.

'I see the toll is now eighteen dollars. I will give you fifteen per cent gratuity, so your fare totals in round figures twenty-one dollars. You are nearly at the Plaza so if I give you twenty-five dollars you can keep the change. But I need a receipt,' Dora nee Calliope was polite but insistent. Gabriel had warned Calliope she must keep proper accounts and he would comply with this directive. Calliope took the driver's receipt book from where it sat on the glovebox and tore out a page before replacing it

'I will make out my own receipt,' he said to the driver.

'You cannot be here, what you do, where you come from, get out of my cab,' the driver was almost at the Plaza but he was becoming frantic and hysterical.

Suddenly Vasco leaned over the front seat

'Be quiet vassal, or I shall bite off your nose,' he snarled at the driver.

Fortunately, the cab at that moment pulled into the portico of the hotel and stopped. Dora left twenty-five dollars on the front seat before disappearing. Calliope could not resist passing through the driver for a split second, leaving him quietly heaving and retching. Later that day the taxi driver sought counseling from his brother a Montenegrin Orthodox priest. His brother must have been prescient, because he told the man to express his appreciation to God in his prayers as he may have been granted a mystic experience.

The travelers alighted from the cab in their disorderly way.

'Checking in,' asked a somewhat confounded bellman.

'You betcha,' replied Wilfred in his best Irish, come transatlantic accent.

Thirteen

Jerry O', formerly known as Wilfred the son of the Big Fellow, led his team up the steep Plaza escalators to the lobby. There had been some confusion at the portico. Jerry O' had been asked by the bellman the name under which the booking had been made. Jerry O' was already a little flustered and disquieted by the contretemps that had occurred first in 42nd Street and later in the taxi. Without thinking he said:

'The booking is probably in the name of the Big Feller.'

'Trump,' the bellman replied, with more than a little derision.

Calliope, out of sight but present, whispered into Jerry O's ear.

Jerry O' quickly corrected himself.

'We have three rooms booked. Two singles and a double twin. The booking is in the name O.'

'How do you spell that?' the bellman was used to rock stars, African cannibal kings and drug addled Hollywood actresses so the four travelers were odd, but not that odd. He lost interest as he wrote the name O down and radioed the front desk to tell the clerk that the O party was on its way.

The four visitors gasped in awe as they reached the top of the escalator and saw the vast expanse of marble that lay before them. Finely dressed men and women sat at well-spaced low chairs working on lap tops and talking in ever so hushed tones. Coffee and petit fours were being served to others at a corner bar. The concierge desk was busy with a large group of Japanese tourists fresh from a city bus tour and eager to have every second of tomorrow organized. The reception counter was clear. It was manned by three chic young men. They were clad in black fine wool morning coats, grey waistcoats, striped pants and black and silver spun silk ties. They watched the arrival of the party without much enthusiasm.

Jerry O' and Charles were walking purposefully towards the reception corral, but Vasco De Gama had taken the long route. He skirted the room taking in the sumptuous surrounds. Joan on the other hand, scurried to and fro like a little savage mouse. She oohed and aahed at each new discovery, but onlookers nevertheless seemed to appreciate that beneath the surface of the girl lay streaks of violence. The chain mail helped to encourage this discernment. As the four travelers made their way the undercurrent buzz of voices and tinkling coffee cups turned to utter silence. Calliope was invisible but was here and there at the side of Vasco and Joan rounding them up and moving them in the direction of reception.

'Yes sir, I am Clive how can I help you.' asked a somewhat puffed up young man behind the counter addressing Jerry O' who responded:

'We have a booking; it is under the name of Jerry O'. The booking is in my name.'

Reception clerks exercise discretion to decline bookings when they are sure that to admit the guests may cause the hotel misery. The clerk after taking a good look at the four would be customers determined that this was just such a case. Three were in fancy dress. There had been an unfortunate incident in the portico which he had observed on CCTV. The clerk was not sure quite what the problem was, but a cab driver had been left doubled up in apparent physical pain. In addition, when the taxi pulled up there was a fifth passenger, a fat black woman, who seemed now to have disappeared. The clerk did not know how correct he was, because Calliope was at that moment standing at the young man's elbow watching the check in process carefully. Calliope personally had made the booking after obtaining a gold MasterCard for Jerry O' and regular Visa cards for Charles, Vasco and Joan, if there was a screw up it would be on Calliope's head. Gabriel would be beside himself.

'I am sorry Sir, are you sure you have got the right hotel? This is the Plaza. I am afraid there is no reservation in your name. We are heavily booked. In fact, we are quite full. I am sorry we cannot help you', the man said this in a self-satisfied way. He was perfectly polite, but Calliope knew that shortly the deference would turn to disrespect.

Calliope began rifling through the small box of cards beside the clerk. He readily found the booking. He removed the card and flicked it across the counter so that it was facing Jerry O'.

"But you seem to have found the booking", said Jerry O' looking at the card.

The clerk visibly colored. He looked for help from his two fellow desk officers. They both kept their heads turned away as they pretended to busy themselves with other tasks. This was Clive's baby and he would have to carry it.

'Yes, you are right here it is.' he replied, gasping a little for breath as he examined the card. Clive had annoyed Calliope, so he entered him for an instant causing him moderate discomfort.

'Let us see what we can do for you. I will see if I can find you an upgrade. You have reservations for three rooms. I will see if we have high floor rooms available.'

Clive had not taken the booking in the first place and if something went awry, he could lay the blame firmly at the door of the reservations clerk. Well, they looked a little odd, he would say, three of them were in fancy dress, but they may be going to a party. They were perfectly well behaved. This was not strictly accurate as the burly swarthy man had blown his nose in a thuggish way against the cloth of his tunic and the small woman had leapt onto the counter and was now sitting facing the lobby shaking her legs backwards and forwards. There was also the question of the guest card. It seemed to have just materialized in front of the Irishman. There was no opportunity for any of the group to have looked in the box of cards. This was simply a mystery.

Whilst Clive was searching the computer for rooms, Calliope leaned over his shoulder and began making his own exploration. Clive was mystified by what seemed to be the oddest computer glitch he had ever come across. The computer appeared to be acting of its own accord. Clive moved to the spare computer at the rear of the corral.

"We seem to have a small computer issue", he said, "I am sorry to hold you up".

Calliope found the Royal Plaza Suite in his search. It was presently vacant. Calliope could see that the tariff for the suite was considerably more than his budget, but the rosy cheeked clerk had said he would try and find them an upgrade. Calliope went ahead with the booking. He printed out the hotel account and manufactured four room key cards. He got Jerry O's credit card from him and took an imprint. Calliope then went over to Clive and perforated him briefly to get his attention. He also brushed his shoulder gently causing the man to look back at the counter. The clerk, when he had recovered from being entered, immediately saw the room key cards, the imprint and account. He looked dubiously at Jerry O' and the others, but Jerry O' was still standing at the counter watching him. The other three were now together some distance away pointing at and apparently discussing the sweeping gracious marble staircase which was a feature of the lobby. Clive looked over at the other clerks, but they were both now serving other customers.

"Have you found us accommodation", asked Jerry O'. He spoke quietly but firmly.

Clive had enough. "Yes Sir, we seem to have upgraded you to the Royal Plaza Suite. It is our finest suite. The Prince of Wales stays here whenever he is in New York".

'And the Prince of Darkness,' replied Jerry O', speaking of the ongoing myth that was alive and well amongst humans that there was an evil being wandering around tempting them. 'Talking about not taking personal responsibility,' the Big Feller would often say about the fiction of Lucifer.

Clive knew he was going to be hard put to explain why he upgraded four weirdoes from a three-room minimum price reservation to the most expensive suite in the house. He could see his prospects of eventually rising to be front office manager evaporating. However, Clive had reached breaking point. He was feeling ill. He seemed to be having odd spasms of heat and discomfort. He just wanted the freaks to be gone.

'Now do you have luggage Mr O,' Clive asked.

Calliope realized he had forgotten to summon the bags. He did so immediately, loading a trolley which stood next to the bellman's elevator. It was manned by a young porter. Calliope arrived and began pushing the trolley towards the reception counter. The young porter slipped and almost fell, but then followed the trolley as it proceeded rapidly and apparently of its own accord.

Clive had been completing his duties by putting the key cards into envelopes. He noticed that Jerry O' had given an odd-looking Irish address, but he was not going to challenge him. For all he knew there may be a place called O'Paradise in Ireland and Jerry O' may possess Post Office Box Two. Clive looked up and saw the trolley rushing towards the counter apparently unmanned followed by a running porter. On the trolley was a Samsonite duffel containing Jerry O's travel needs, an ancient leather portmanteau which belonged to Charles Dickens, a heavy red metal steamer case inscribed with the Portuguese Coat of Arms owned by Vasco De Gama and a large cane box the property of Joan of Arc. Upon the cane box was a large cage containing a live and angry Faverolles Clair rooster.

Clive fell to the floor in a faint. Though he returned to work the next day, he was never the same again and was promoted to front office manager, where he had little or no direct contact with the public.

The porter arrived shortly after the luggage and escorted the group to the separate entrance to the suite. He was not too sure about the rooster, but he had once seen an arab with a small goat at the hotel and many American widows travelled with dogs. The party [including the invisible Calliope] entered the elevator to the suite with the eager porter extolling the Hotel's virtues. The elevator door smoothly shut.

On the other side of the lobby there was the barest glimmer. Sandalphon watched the scene in satisfaction. He believed that Joan of Arc, his young charge, was going to force an enemy to suck a rooster. She had stated as much. Well, if that was so, she would need a rooster and if she was going to get a rooster it should be a fine French rooster. Sandalphon was not sure of the mechanics of such a punishment, but he knew Joan was a girl of her word. Sandalphon had much to report, but he was still torn between a mistress and a master. Perhaps tomorrow he would work out what to do. He was confident that Calliope had not spied him yet and Sandalphon vowed to keep to the shadows.

Meanwhile the elevator arrived at the Royal Suite and the group were disgorged.

Fourteen

CHARLES DICKENS JOURNAL

In that first moment of landing, gaining our earth legs, surveying the milieu and shaking ourselves like enthusiastic gun retrievers waiting for the call "Fox", our world was phantasmagorical.

I soon realized that a call of "Fox" in Times Square would simply herald the arrival of a television crew from the well-known news channel. Not that the arrival of a television crew at this early juncture in our odyssey could be anything but a bad thing. I am sure Wilfred - no stop he is no longer Wilfred. Our leader the son of the Big Feller now bears the peculiar tag of Jerry O'. This appellation is, between you and I reader, surprisingly simplistic and facile. It requires little or no imagination for even a modern human being to translate 'Jerry' to 'Jesus' and appreciate that 'O' means 'of'. However, the Creator is neither simplistic nor facile. He must know what is required.

Words are my life. I hope my scribblings have already made this palpable. When I wrote my novels it was with the intention of feeding the imagination of the poor masses. Oh yes, there was the underlying intention of making myself rich. And I say, why should that not be so. After all I created a whole industry of readers who spent their days reciting my writings to the illiterate at the cost of a penny a chapter.

Yes, words are my life, and I expected upon my arrival on earth to see groups of highly educated erudite humans discussing the metaphysical and the philosophical with all the erudition of the learned thinkers in Nineteenth Century salons in London. Alas, this has not been my conclusion. It seems that the language has not evolved and compounded. Rather it has been debased and polluted by Twenty First Century human beings. There may, of course, be parlors where the language is dissected and scrutinized, but I somehow doubt it. In the short time I have been back on earth I have concluded that the modern technology of phones, pads and computers has diluted the hominid capacity to contemplate and deduce. Plato and Socrates may rest easy [and I know they do, having seen them at our sendoff]. They can argue, submit and discuss to their hearts content. I wish Fox Television was able to show the two Greek thinkers talking the talk. Then again the inane viewers may prefer the latest cooking show or a weekly insight into the lives of other bird brains. From the above, my reader, you will realize I have watched television from time to time since arriving in Manhattan.

But enough pontificating let me take you back to our arrival on Earth.

We are standing on an island in the middle of Times Square which is better known than the Square of St Peter's Basilica and infinitely better known than other great public places such as St Marks, Trafalgar or even the Grande Place. It seems Rome, Venice, London and Brussels are all loci of historical interest but no longer spaces for the public to congregate, enjoy and relish.

I fully expected that we would be viewed with, at least shock, and perhaps derision. This was not the case. The crowd was a mélange of color and discordance. Many of the swarm were obviously tourists. Brightly clad Africans in their full-length robes mingled with small Boogers with brawny arms wearing sleeveless round top shirts [they are called Tee Shirts] with the words 'Tommy Hilfiger' on them. There were Muslim women in burkhas and other females who seemed to be clad in little other than undergarments. Businessmen wore fine wool suits and other men wore torn blue slacks [known as Jeans] and hooded tops. The Jeans often had slipped south and from time one could see the exposed upper cleavage of a bottom and even an occasional curling butt hair strand.

Yet there was one common denominator! Phones, my reader, phones, they all carried phones. They are tiny phones, but extremely versatile. They can make images, play music, send messages in font and make calls.

This was the communal universality. The whole throng were engaged in photographing, sending messages and telephoning and while doing so they listened to [I imagine] music through minuscule earpieces. For a moment, pray the merest moment, I imagined my books being broadcast through the ear buds. But then looking at the flock, I realized that such a thought was a fantasy left unthought, let alone unspoken.

I was a little surprised that Wilf—, I must say Jerry O' had not been informed of the location of the Plaza Hotel. Odder still was the fact that our strategist Joan of Arc was not given directions. I am not so surprised that Calliope was of little assistance. He is a strangely muddled angel, who works on the basis that last minute redemption is a more propitious culmination than careful forethought. So far, his modus operandi has been successful - so far!

Though we approached some passers-by they were less than helpful. I suppose it may have been our appearance. I single out De Gama. He is a rapscallion, of that there is no doubt. However, my friends, I suspect he will be a useful rapscallion.

The momentary confrontation with the three youths was most interesting. They were clearly feral and illiterate. They spoke in a strange guttural dialect of English. I have come across South Sea Islanders who speak a language known as "Pidgin". The youths spoke in similar vein. Their vocabulary is minimal, their comprehension apparently infinitesimal and their cross-communication skills hidden in some crevasse of their cerebrums. To add gravitas to their language they use profanity as an emphasis. This phenomenon reminded me of the language of Chaucer, but when I tried to investigate the etiology of their syntax, they became angry and threatening. I was glad when Calliope finally appeared as the black woman Dora and saved the day. I suspect if it had been left to Vasco De Gama, he would have seen the drawing of blood to be the preferred method of problem solving.

The first miracle, if I am permitted to call it that, was the crossing of 5th Avenue. I would not be surprised if one day in the distant future, it is called just that. I shall certainly name a chapter in my forthcoming book after our strut. 'The Crossing of 5th Avenue', it has a feel to it, does it not. I can tell that you agree. A writer must know what a reader will think of a passage before the reader has scanned it.

I had been aware of a police presence in 5th Avenue and I was sure that though we were never in danger, our parting of the traffic was surely illegal. It was obviously more than just good fortune that caused the taxi to halt and pick us up. It was not so fortuitous when Calliope suddenly appeared in the front passenger seat and demanded a receipt. It seemed a gauche thing to do. I would have thought that Calliope would have a better method of proving expenses were incurred than by simply materializing in the front seat of a cab as a fat negress and demanding a receipt. Even the most equable amongst the human species are likely to be unnerved by such an incident. It is not, however, my place to speak of ethics or courtesies to an angel. I am the scrivener. That is why I am here and penciling. It is what I do.

I am not entirely sure what occurred during the check-in process, but I do admit that apparently Calliope excelled himself. I write this chapter in the opulence of my study at the Plaza. I appreciate this is the work of our angel. It is just how he did it that puzzles me.

The arrival of the luggage was also clearly Calliope's doing. Not that this seemed to have been planned. My guess is that he simply forgot and when the pretentious clerk Clive asked Jerry O' if we had bags, the invisible Calliope rushed off and started pushing the trolley. This was under the very nose of a rosy cheeked young porter who nearly went head over heels.

The luggage was generally what we expected, except for the Rooster. I had heard Joan muttering something about sucking Roosters in the taxi. I did not follow the connotations of her remark. In fact, I thought

I had misheard her. I thought she may have said the taxi driver could 'muck up Massachusetts', thinking this was probably some idiomatic observation, based on Joan's misapprehension of local geography.

In any event Joan strongly denied the rooster was hers and it made a rapid and ignominious exit from our suite carried off by our bellman

Fifteen

CALLIOPE'S EPISTLE

It is one thing to be a messenger for the Big Fellah, it is another thing altogether to be looking after four visitors to earth from Paradise, including the son Wilfred now known as Jerry O'.

It has been very stressful. I regret to say that I am not well suited for the task. I am doing my best, do not get me wrong. I will take it on the chin if things go up the spout. It will be Gabriel meting out my punishment. I confess this may be hard to take.

But this bleating is not what I should be writing. You, John [or Matthew or Luke or Mark] are not interested in my troubles. I should remember your travails all those years ago.

I must concentrate on what I am doing while I am writing this stuff and nonsense, though I sincerely hope it is more stuff than nonsense.

We are still here at the Plaza cooling our heels. I am masquerading as a maid. I am not proud, but I am not and never will be a scrubber or polisher. The Plaza has a team of such people who breeze through the suite twice every day with their trolley, brushes and implements. I keep well out of their way. I generally disappear (actually) while they are about, in case they quiz me about my experience and practices as a cleaner.

I should tell you that I have been doing some soul searching. Well, angels do not have souls, but I expect that you know what I mean. I have seriously thought of abandoning my labored, amateurish attempt at an epistle. The scribe Charles Dickens is a professional writer. I have now sneaked two looks at his jottings. He seems to always have a beginning a middle and an end. I have none of these things. I remember once being asked to deliver a message from the Big Fellah to an Irish writer James Joyce. Joyce was lost for the title to a huge novel he was writing. I was to whisper the word Ulysses in his ear until he received my message. Unfortunately, I misunderstood the instructions and gave the message to a woman in Dublin called Joyce James. I whispered Ulysses in her ears for days until, unhappily, she went mad and was hospitalized. The Big Fellah had to use a nun who was being considered for sainthood to cure her. In the end this was a good thing as it gave the nun her final miracle, but I had some nervous moments, and Gabriel made a number of submissions to Mohammed to have me restricted to desk duties. Fortunately, Mohammed told Gabriel that he would reprimand me and that would be the extent of my punishment.

'You have a mind like an unmade bed,' Mohammed said to me, 'please Calliope try and put some order into your work.'

And I have tried. I also do not like giving up on something I have started. I will continue with my writings. If in the end you find it useless at least, I will have done no harm, but if you find even a line, an idea, a word perhaps - I think more than a word, useful then It has all been worthwhile.

I have referred to Metatron before. I fully expected Gabriel to send him after me as his spy. We angels can see each other even when we are invisible to others, but with some skill an angel can keep out of the line of sight of other heavenly spirits. Goodness knows there have been many occasions I have avoided Gabriel, by keeping out of his line of sight.

In any event, when we got to Times Square I kept an eagle eye out for Metatron. He was not there, but to my surprise there was Sandalphon lurking in the shadows outside an Adult Book Shop. I thought it may be a coincidence but then I realized he was a saint angel. I put two and two together. He was looking out for Joan of Arc. She was his saint. I gave further thought to this. After all, if Sandalphon was hanging around so he could provide services to Joan, there was no reason why he should not make himself known to me. Then I realized two things. First of all, Mohammed said nothing to me about

Sandalphon coming along to help me out and secondly why was Sandalphon trying to hide from me. He is an angel that means well, but frankly he is not the smartest of creatures. Uriel once jokingly said of Sandalphon that he was two good deeds short of a plenary indulgence.

I have decided the clueless Sandalphon has been sent here to look after Joan, but to report to Gabriel as to the events that transpire.

Things did not go quite as smoothly as I would have liked in the taxi and at the check-in so Sandalphon will have much to report. I think I will watch and wait to see how our plans progress before deciding whether to confront him and perhaps try to recruit him.

I suppose I should have known that the Plaza Hotel is a fair walk North of the theatre district, but I am used to just arriving at destinations. I am no mapping expert or guide. The problem that I did not work out in advance was that I had four human beings (at least temporary human beings) with me who would have to proceed in a physical and temporal way. This is an issue that I have addressed for future excursions.

Here I go again writing my defense to Gabriel's allegations, when all you are interested in are the blunt, cold hard facts.

I realize that Wilfred (I will follow Dickens and call Wilfred, Jerry O' and yes this proves I am perusing his work) is a little overawed, but he will find his feet. Dickens is somewhat of a nuisance. He must understand that the rest of humankind are not just specimens to be examined under glass. His nonsensical comments to the three gang bangers about Geoffrey Chaucer only incited them. They did not have the faintest idea what Dickens was talking about but they certainly knew he was not being complimentary. Vasco De Gama certainly looks fierce and he talks fierce. My question is can he act fierce? Time will tell. Joan is going to be an asset, but if she is really a strategist it should have included the strategy for knowing how to get from Times Square to Central Park. I nearly said something to her, but it was not my place.

The crossing of 5th Avenue was exciting. I had to call on all my powers to stop both lines of cars. The approaching armada of cars had to be stopped as had the cars that had just passed the pathway I had chosen. The walk was to be the modern parting of the Red Sea. I must admit this last conclusion is mine. I was not told this by Mohammed. I leave it to my scholarly reader, of course, to come to his own conclusion.

I make absolutely no apologies for materializing in the taxi. I expect there will be ramifications. I have checked and the cab driver is suffering from post-traumatic stress disorder. This will no doubt be sheeted home to me. I was told that I had to keep proper books. There was no possibility the driver would have given a receipt to any of the others. Anyway, it was not their problem. They have enough things to do, what with trying to understand what was being said to them and trying to understand the local customs. The cabbie is an illegal immigrant. Receipts are anathema to him. I needed to be in the front seat to get the receipt. Again, I seem to be answering critics before they surface. I am sorry. sir.

I also agree that the check in at the Plaza could have been handled better, but I was not to know that Clive the foolish desk clerk would pretend to lose the reservation. The upgrade may have been a touch overkill, but the group is happy and the Suite itself draws attention to its occupants.

I guess I should have brought the luggage along earlier and I am sorry the porter was pushed off balance, but it all worked out in the end.

I wondered when I was invisibly pushing the luggage trolly along why there was a rooster in a cage on the pile. Sandalphon must have put it there. However, Joan did not want it and it was removed.

My epistle is below:

CH1 V4

5th Avenue was crossed by parting the cars as Moses parted the Red Sea and the Son and his small party made their way to a local hostelry for refreshments and rest. The humble angel accompanying them assisted the team in their trek across the great city.

Sixteen

At 9.45 on a Tuesday morning the newsroom of the Daily Standard in central Manhattan was buzzing with its usual high level of energy. It was known affectionately by the reporters as the Bear Pit. The forty odd news hounds in the Bear Pit were either on their phones, yapping to each other across the room or scanning their desk top computer screens.

The offices were simply partitioned with floor to ceiling glass. This was planned by the decorators to make the offices look bigger than they were. The idea did not work. Each office was barely large enough for a desk, a couple of chairs and a steel filing cabinet.

Gordon Robert Checker, the city editor, was sitting behind his desk watching the other editors in their offices. He was universally known as Chub. He checked his watch. Fifteen minutes to go. Every morning at 10.00 AM, the foul-mouthed Australian Editor-in-chief Bear Grizzard met with the various departmental editors to map out the early afternoon edition of the paper. These days the Standard was more an on-line news source than a hard copy daily broadsheet. As news happened it was written up and posted on-line. Twice a day, at 1.00 PM and 1.00 AM hard copies were produced. Grizzard ran two editorial meetings a day. The 10.00 AM meeting was the first and later at 7.00 PM the group met again to sort out the early morning edition. All editors were expected to be generally present for both meetings, though senior journalists like Chub could and often did delegate attendance to one of the city desk reporters who worked under him. There were many occasions that Chub was in no fit condition to attend the later meeting. On these occasions the desk reporters would note the boss' s absence and take over. Chub was a journalist of the old school. He drank hard but had a reporter's nose for a story. He possessed a source in most of the big hotels and many of the fancy night spots. He knew some high placed police officers and had a snitch in the mayor's office. Chub's expense account was a masterful work of fiction, disguising as it did the many pay offs he made.

Chub noticed the new Travel and Leisure editor Joanne Rixti was carefully punching holes in sheets of A4 and placing the sheets in an expensive looking leather binder. Stuck up ivy league bitch, thought Chub, as he took in her tailored blue suit matched carefully with dark navy heels.

The English Arts and Literature editor Roger Sebastian Keats was looking into his man bag. Probably checking that he has got his make-up stored away, surmised Chub. Keats claimed to be related to the great poet, but Chub noticed his accent wavered under stress. More some outer county than Westminster was Chub's opinion and as for being related to Keats, that was a fantasy. The man's forebears were more likely to be barrow boys than bards.

Checker could see the Foreign Affairs Editor Bruce Gotby also readying himself for the meeting. He was Chub's particular bete noir. The man always dressed as if he was about to go on an undercover overseas assignment, but as far as Chub could ascertain he rarely ventured out of Greenwich Village. South of SoHo was foreign territory to Gotby. Chub's sources told him Gotby spent his nights snorting cocaine with other journalists in his posh warehouse conversion in the Village. Today the man was dressed in a long sheepskin coat topped off by a red Fez. Chub snorted in derision, but he was reminded of something.

Five minutes to go and Chub Checker remembered the incident in 5th Avenue yesterday. There were three separate videos on UTube showing four weirdos crossing 5th Avenue illegally. There were also several still photos posted and numerous pathetic tweets. Two people had rung the city desk yesterday trying to sell the videos. Chub had their names, but the trouble was that nobody had got the weirdos commencing their walk. This was significant as it might explain why the pathway the walkers took seemed to be so even. The videos and stills showed the odd bods passage was past four stationary cars with their front grilles exactly parallel to one another. In addition, the rears of the stationary cars ahead were exactly parallel to one another. Chub took another look. It could be explained by the fact that 5th Avenue traffic may have been bumper to bumper and almost stationary to begin with. In other words, the break in traffic simply existed because the whole army of cars was barely moving. Goodness knows 5th Avenue was often banked up.

If there was nothing else Chub's nose would not have been twitching, but there were two other pieces to the puzzle. Brian, a porter at the Plaza and paid source to Chub, had rung with some garbled story about four people booking in to the Plaza Suite. Three of the four were in fancy dress. There was a pirate, a girl in some ancient army costume and a man wearing an outfit from ye olde England. Brian had gone on to say that the freak show's luggage trolley had moved through the lobby without human assistance and one of the items of luggage was a live rooster in a cage. Brian claimed that some of the other items of luggage were of ancient origin. Chub took the story about the self-propelling trolley with a grain of salt, but the fancy dress, the strange luggage and the rooster interested him. Were these the same kooks who had crossed 5th Avenue. Finally, there was a strange message from a taxi driver informant named Abdul that one of his fellow drivers had been threatened by a freak in some strange old-time costume. The driver had sustained some physical injury, but he was also rambling about a black woman materializing into the front seat of the cab. Again this last story seemed fanciful to Chub, but the screwballs had certainly made an impact. Chub decided to take the strange tale to the editorial meeting. He grabbed a couple of copies of still photos of Jerry O' and the team and made his shambling way to the meeting.

Chub was last to arrive as usual. He sat in the remaining seat of the small round boardroom table in the annex to the managing editor's office. Predictably the brown noses were as close to Bear as possible. On his right was the British phony Keats and on his left was the dope fiend Gotby. Joanne Rixti was all bright eyed and eager. She was sitting forward as if she was about to commence an exam paper that she was ready to kill stone dead.

'All right Keats,' said Bear, 'what do we have.'

'The Warhol Retrospective is showing at MOMA. The Great Gatsby is opening at the Shubert and there is a reading by an Australian poet at the Samuel J Friedman sponsored by the Manhattan Theatre Company. There will be a season of readings by several poets from around the world.'

'Well, whacky fucking do,' said Bear with little or no interest, 'you have plenty to go on with and Gotby what is happening out there.'

'Perhaps the lead story should be the new North Booga missile test our military is monitoring, 'replied Gotby adjusting his fez somewhat.

'No more fuck North Booga missile tests,' said Bear Grizzard, those little fuckers test missiles every other day. It will be news when that little fat arsehole Moon Moon or whatever he calls himself changes his pants suit. Isn't there some war somewhere. What about a fucking famine that is always news, but not those little fucking roundheads in North Booga.'

Gotby was making notes on a pad. No doubt he was dreaming up a war or a famine or better still a war and a famine combined.

Grizzard surveyed the table. Joanne Rixti was leaning forward expectantly. She had opened her leather folder in readiness. But Bear looked over at Chub.

'And what about you, Chub, you drunken fucker what have you got.'

'Well bos,' Chub spoke with equanimity, he was used to Editors-in-chief. They came and they went. Those who were not carried out feet first usually were escorted from the building by security. Working journalists were the constant at the Standard not Editors-in-chief.

Chub passed over the still photos of Jerry O' and his three companions to Bear. The editor-in-chief looked at the photos briefly.

'And just what the fuck is this, Chub. Have you completely lost your fucking marbles. Are you suggesting the city desk leads with a story about four jay walkers?'

'No there is more to it, Boss. I think the same four threatened a cabbie and then checked into the Plaza. They are in the Royal Suite. That costs $8000 a night. Their luggage was odd. They had a live rooster in a cage. There is a story here boss, I am not sure what story, but I would like to follow up.'

'No fuck you, Chub, this is bullshit. Four freaks jaywalk across 5th Avenue and threaten a cabbie. So, fucking what. And they are staying in a suite at the Plaza. For all we know it is the King of Liberia traveling with his palace guard. The rooster may be his father-in-law.'

'I think Liberia is a republic, Mr Grizzard,' interposed Joanne helpfully.

'I do not fucking care if Liberia is a fucking West Indian anarchy. Forget fucking Liberia and, Chub, forget this bullshit story. Find out if that fucker of a mayor of ours is chiseling his expenses or porking his personal assistant. In other words, do something useful.'

Joanne Grixti could not help herself. She was a former valedictorian at Wellesley and a world class saxophonist as well as possessing a Journalism major.

'I believe Liberia is in West Africa, Mr Grizzard, not the West Indies,' she said.

'Didn't I tell you not to fucking mention Liberia. I could not give a flying fuck if it is on Jupiter. Mention it again Joanne, and even though you are a fucking gamma, fucking delta fucking sigma or whatever, mention fucking Liberia again and I will tip you out of here on your pretty little arse.'

Chub could see that Joanne was suppressing a comment, but he could not resist.

'I think Joanne was in the Alpha. Gamma Delta sorority chief,' he said happily, waiting for Bear to blow up.

Fortunately, at that moment Bear's personal assistant walked in.

'There is a volcano erupting in Bulgaria,' he said, 'tens of thousands dead.'

'Great,' said Bear, 'hands to the wheel everybody.'

Seventeen

After the editorial meeting broke up, Chub Checker made his way back to his office to collect his cell phone and notebook. It was time for Chub to commence his investigation. But he needed sustenance first.

As Chub left the Bear Pit, he observed a group of young women news hounds congregated around Joanne Rixti as she regaled them with her account of the editorial meeting. He could hear them muttering imprecations directed against their esteemed editor Bear Grizzard. The words 'sexual harassment' seemed to be their catch cry. A fat lot of good that will do them, thought Chub as he passed them, this is a newspaper not a sheltered workshop. He winked at Joanne who glared back as if he Chub was somehow responsible for the events that had occurred. Chub made his lumbering way to the lift station. Bruce Gotby was already in the elevator. Chub squeezed in through the closing doors. He noted that though Gotby was nearest the door he had made no effort to press the 'door open' sign. Chub looked Gotby up and down and punched him solidly on the arm.

'Trying out for the Village People, Bruce,' he said.

Gotby ignored him, but two young cadet reporters in the rear of the elevator sniggered.

Chub left the building and headed towards Times Square. He walked in a purposeful manner and at a relatively fast gait. He turned into W. 44th and walked into the Algonquin Hotel. He entered the gloomy little front parlor bar and sat on a corner stool. The rest of the hotel had been elegantly restored, but fortunately the hotel owners had left the shabby little forward saloon relatively untouched.

'Breakfast, Chub,' asked the bartender.

'Thanks Brigitte,' Chub replied.

Brigitte made Chub a Bloody Bullshot. She mixed Belvedere Vodka, iced Court Bouillon and tomato juice in a cocktail shaker. She added ice, a squeeze of lemon, salt, pepper and Worcestershire Sauce. She shook then poured into a long highball glass. She completed her masterpiece, by adding a swizzle stick, a cardboard umbrella and a stick of celery. She passed the drink to Chub who removed the swizzle stick and brolly. He put these items on the bar counter. Brigitte collected them and threw them into a bin. Chub took a deep draft of the drink and took a bite of the celery. He felt the fire of life enter his body. Becoming used to the low lighting he looked around the bar. There were a couple of other dinosaurs nursing drinks. Chub nodded to them. There was no time for idle conversation though as Chub felt his journalistic nose metaphorically twitching.

He rang the mayor's office from his cell phone:

'Hi Arnold, Chub here,' he said to his snitch, the press aide to the mayor.

'What's new, my man,' replied the press attaché, who once played in an all-white hip hop band which had one minor hit, but still talked as if he was Dr Dre.

'I need to get a look at the CCTV footage for 5th Avenue. This would be an easy task for someone of your great power and influence,' Chub knew his sarcasm would be lost on Arnold.

'Bro, that lookee is not readily available. My white arse would be set on fire if I let every honky who comes along see the city's CCTV flickers, the aide replied.

'One I am not 'every honky' Arnold, but your trusted associate and two let me quote you word for word what my Managing Editor Bear Grizzard said to me this morning at an editorial meeting. "Find out if that fucker of a mayor of ours is chiseling his expenses or porking his personal assistant". That is what Bear said to me Arnold, but I am not presently doing his bidding. I want to see the CCTV for reasons that have nothing to do with the mayor, his swindle sheets or his sexual proclivities.' Chub spoke quietly but with authority.

'Give me an hour,' replied Arnold without even the hint of his usual pathetic excuse for ghetto talk.

An hour and a quarter later Chub Checker was sitting in the control room of the Central Manhattan Traffic Department with traffic controller Carl Martinez looking at the footage of Jerry O', Vasco, Charles and Joan walk across 5th Avenue. Carl was helpful and interested.

'The thing is Mr Checker,' he said, 'the traffic was traveling at seventeen miles per hour before it came to a stop. As you can see when the four people commenced crossing the vehicles stopped dead. The four lanes of cars are exactly parallel. If you look at the front cars, they are also parallel. It makes no sense. If one person, let alone four just walked across a road occupied by four moving lanes of autos doing seventeen miles per hour, there would have been injuries, nose to tails, angry drivers and probably incidents of road rage. Here there is none of this. The cars just stop dead and when the pedestrians have crossed start moving as if nothing has happened. It makes no sense. Also, the four pedestrians cross single file. That seems to me to be strange. And the pedestrians.' Carl stopped speaking, raising his eyebrows.

'Yes,' Chub replied, 'I guess you see some pretty weird sights in Manhattan, but these freaks are right up there.'

The two men watched the video a number of times, but Chub was still none the wiser.

'Can we check the weirdos movements after they crossed 5th,' he asked.

'Yes they got into a stretch cab. I will show you the footage. I can get you the plate number.'

They watched the footage of Jerry O' and his team entering the cab and the cab taking off.

'Do you want me to try and plot the route of the cab,' asked the traffic controller.

'No, you have been very helpful,' replied Chub. He did not want the controller to become too interested. Checker was eager to retain exclusivity. If there was a story, he wanted it to be his story.

'There was no police report?' Chub had noticed two police officers on the western side of 5th Avenue after the group had walked to the eastern side.

'No, I guess the problem is Mr Checker, when you boil it all down it is still just jay walking. But I should have asked, why are you so interested?'

The penny had dropped with Carl Martinez that there may be more to the story than he realized.

'I am thinking of a human-interest story, about the fine work your department does monitoring traffic in New York, these four crazies are just a hook. Do you mind if I take your photo?' Chub had taken out his iPhone and was opening the camera App.

'Aren't you going to get a camera guy?' asked Carl.

'No, these days the phone is our cameraman. Modern technology,' lied Chub.

The taxi was readily traceable, but the driver had gone to ground. Chub went to the cab depot and started asking questions. He found the driver had probably been working under a false name. If he did not want to be found he would not be.

He waited at the depot until Abdul the man who had rung the paper turned up. He confirmed to Chub that the missing driver claimed to have been menaced by some freaks in strange costume. One of the freaks had threatened to bite his nose off. The man had suffered injury in an inexplicable way, but the major cause of his stress was that a black woman materialized into the front seat of the cab.

'Materialized,' asked Chub, 'what could he have meant?'

Abdul told him that in the first place, cabbies did not take front seat passengers, and this driver was alleging that when the journey started there was nobody in the front seat.

'I see,' said Chub, 'he is saying that during the journey the black woman materialized.'

Though Chub said he could see, he meant he could see what was being claimed. He could not see at all, what was claimed to have happened.

He made his goodbyes to Abdul. It seemed that all roads led to the Plaza Hotel and that was his next stop.

Eighteen

Chub Checker took a cab from the taxi depot to the Plaza Hotel. He realized that he needed more sustenance. He walked over to Central Park and bought two Hot Dogs which he wolfed down with a can of full-strength Coca Cola. He walked back to the portico of the Plaza.

Checker lived alone in a one bedroom roach farm in Lower Manhattan. He could only afford it because it was rent controlled. He had no wife. There was no girlfriend either. He enjoyed occasional congress with Molly who lived downstairs. This was the extent of his romantic life. She was a decrepit fifty-five-year-old spinster waitress at a grease joint on 43rd Street down near the Hudson. The Chub Checker roach farm was always a substantial mess. Chub had engaged cleaners from time to time, but they did not last. He did not know whether he was happy, fulfilled or sad as he was generally either drunk, hungover or both. However, there was something about these four weirdos that energised Chub. The way they walked single file across 5th Avenue was subversive. It appealed to the Checker sensibilities. It asked to be investigated. Not that there was a story. Not that there was even the hint of a story. 'Yet,' said Chub to himself, 'yet.'

Chub looked around the lobby of the Plaza and by chance saw his source standing guard at a trolley load of luggage. A large group, probably a family, of very obese Texans were at reception talking to each other in loud drawls.

'Brian,' said Chub, walking up to the porter, 'I need to see you.'

He passed a hundred-dollar bill to the porter. As if by magic, upon some unseen sign by Brian, another porter arrived. Chub guessed the bags belonged to the Texans. There would be a big tip involved, some of which would not make its way to the share pot.

Brian led Chub out of the hotel front door and across the portico to the luggage storage area.

'You want to find out about the freaks, Chub,' asked Brian.

'Tell me from the beginning,' said Chub.

'Well, they turned up in a cab. It was a stretch and there were four of them.'

'Not five,' asked Chub.

'No, I only saw four. There was a guy with an Irish accent in an Armani Suit.'

Plaza porters see so much fashion they all become experts.

'There was a brown, ugly one in a pirate suit, another guy who looked like something out of a Jack the Ripper movie.'

'What, he had blood on him, what do you mean?' asked Chub.

'No,' said Brian, 'it was just the clothes. I cannot explain it, but it was his clothes. Then there was a pretty young gal dressed up with so much armor, she looked as if she was about to invade Poland.'

'When did you first see them?' asked Chub.

'I was standing beside my trolley. It was empty but suddenly it filled with luggage,' said Brian.

'What do you mean, suddenly filled with luggage. Did other porters arrive?' asked Chub. Incorporeal activities were not features of the Checker repertoire.

'No, I tell you Chub, the bags just appeared, and there was a rooster, a live rooster,' Brian became red faced and sweaty at the memory.

'Ok, tell me about the bags,' Chub was worried that Brian was becoming too edgy. He did not want him to either rush off or ask for more money.

'There was a duffel that belonged to the Irishman. There was a stained old leather bag which belonged to Jack the Ripper. The pirate had a great big metal case. Have you seen the Titanic, it was like the luggage the rich dudes brought on aboard,' Brian was now animated and apparently, at least temporarily, over his fears.

'And the girl?' queried Chub.

'She had, like a bamboo box and the rooster was in a cage on top of the box. But she denied it was hers. I finished up selling it over in the park, but that is another story.'

'How do you know what bag belonged to which particular person?' Chub was not sure where this was going, but it was an interesting story and he wanted to get to the bottom of it.

'Easy, peasy Chub,' said Brian, 'I took them up to the suite.'

'You saw them, check in?'

'Check in, oh Chub that was a complete shemozzle. The desk clerk Clive is a snotty nosed prick at the best of times and apparently when he saw them coming he decided to lose their booking. And this is the funny part. Clive claims the booking card suddenly appeared on the counter.'

Chub was becoming interested despite himself. Now there was luggage appearing on a trolley and a booking card appearing on a counter to add to the strange traffic movements in 5th Avenue and the black woman apparition reported by the cabbie. But what did it all mean?

'There is something else odd, Clive said he did not upgrade them to the Royal Suite, but the computer did it on its own.'

This last revelation did not surprise Chub so much. He had never mastered technology, and he found computers often seemed to act contrary to his instructions.

'You took them up to the suite' pressed Chub, 'anything strange happen?'

'Only that they talk funny.'

'What do you mean, talk funny?' asked Chub.

'It's just that they talk the way they look,' replied Brian.

Chub decided to let this pass. 'I see you have CCTV in the portico. Any chance of me seeing it?' asked Chub.

'It will cost you, another hundred for me and fifty for security.'

'Make it hundred and you give security what you like,' Chub knew when to barter.

'Ok,' said Brian and the two of them went to the security office which was directly behind the lobby. Brian had a quick chat to the security officer and left Chub to it.

'I had better get back on duty,' he said, 'see me before you go.'

The video was readily retrievable as the check in time had been recorded. Chub sat back and watched the footage. He watched the cab pull up at the hotel. He could see the four odd balls alight. There was no clear view of the driver, but you could see the shape of his body rising and falling as if he was writhing and heaving.

When the cab drove off it was empty save for the driver, but as the four back seat passengers alighted one could see a large dark person occupying the front seat. Chub watched the film several times, but there was no getting away from it. At first there was nobody in the front seat, then there was somebody, then she [he thought she] was gone again. Chub remained cool and detached throughout the viewing. The security officer was controlling the movie upon Chub's direction. He did not show any interest in the viewing. Chub wanted it to remain that way.

Chub went back to the lobby. Brian was busy with some South Americans. When he became free, Chub approached him.

'The names, Brian, what are the names of the freak show members?'

'Only one name was given to the front desk,' replied Brian, 'this is against the rules, but Clive the clerk's head was messed up. The Irishman is checked in as Jerry O.'

'Spell that,' asked Chub and Brian did just that.

'I was going to tell you about the rooster Chub. The girl said it wasn't hers and I was given it. Well, I took it over to the park and I sold it to a guy for fifty dollars. This morning, he came over here looking for me wanting his money back,' Brian was sweating again.

'Reason,' asked Chub.

"The rooster disappeared", answered Brian.

'It may not have liked its new owner and decided to find a better home,' replied Chub.

Chub Checker had enough, more than enough. He needed now to evaluate and apply the evidence he had accumulated. 'What in all hell did it mean?'

Nineteen

Chub hopped into a cab and headed back to the Standard office. He still had not filed any copy today. He was in no position to report on the freaks. So far there was no story, just a farrago of miscellany which would be laughed out of an editorial meeting by Bear Grizzard, who, in the first place, had told Chub not to pursue the story.

When Chub got back to the Bear Pit, there were a few reporters working phones and a few others peering at computer screens. The majority had filed for the day. Soon the second shift would turn up. These were the night beasts who worked through the hours of darkness to sparrow fart, honing old news and reporting on events that occurred through the night. Most of these journalists were conduits of overseas news agencies. The only features editor still on board, predictably, was Joanne Rixti. She sat in her office applying a particularly deep shade of purple nail polish. She appeared to have changed her clothes and was now wearing a sheer black evening gown. She studiously ignored Chub as he passed.

When he settled into his office Chub opened a desk drawer and brought out a sheaf of papers. He decided to use one of his already written back up stories. He called them his insurance policies. He always had about six of such stories in the case of an emergency such as acute drunkenness or a woman falling out of the sky. Though he would concede in recent years the latter event was highly unlikely. Chub looked over at Joanne. It was not a look of lust, but rather curiosity. Was she getting any, he thought? Joanne must have sensed something, and she looked up and stared grimly at Chub, shaking her head slightly in disgust. Chub gave her the finger as he looked back. He doubted that she was being bonked. There would have to be rose petals wafting on the air, Yo Yo Ma playing Mozart outside in the soft twilight and two white doves ready to fly off with her panties but even then, Chub thought, Joanne would still be a Wellesley Alpha Gamma Delta Valedictorian. Chub shuddered slightly.

He went back to his insurance policies. Only his two most trusted hacks knew of their existence. He found the very thing for the occasion. It was a story he had written a few months ago, but it was still as current as the fresh punnet of plums he had noticed on the barrow of a vendor downstairs.

The St Patrick's Day march was one of New York's great traditions. It had started as a Roman Catholic event, but in time it had become ecumenical. This did not please some traditionalists, particularly those with an IRA bent. When Muslims joined in the march this was almost too much for these troglodytes to bear. Chub had gone to the most conservative Mosque in New York and found a Mullah prepared to make a few ill-chosen anti Catholic comments. Amongst other things he had suggested that American Catholics were simply puppets of Rome, prepared to serve Vatican masters who were corrupt and treacherous. Chub then went to an old and cantankerous priest in Brooklyn who claimed Muslims were barbarous primitives practicing an obsolete religion. Chub rounded out the story with some brief comments from moderates on both sides, a compressed history of the March and an oft quoted verse from the poet Alfred Percival Graves.

When after the Winter alarmin',
The Spring steps in so charmin',
So fresh and arch
In the middle of March,
Wid her hand St. Patrick's arm on...

Chub read the article and scanned it into his computer. He delivered the piece electronically to the sub-editors who were busy fashioning headlines and by-lines on the floor above.

He left the floor. He noticed Joanne was still at her desk. She was now pursing her lips in front of her hand-held mirror. She looked up briefly as Chub passed and raised a purple nailed middle finger. He smiled happily back. Perhaps there was more to the girl than he first thought.

It was time for sustenance. Chub walked down the stairs into the Galleon Steak House. He was greeted warmly by the Maitre'D.

'Mr Checker, it is so good to see you. Your usual table?'

Chub nodded. He dined at the Galleon three or four evenings a week. He always sat at the same table. It was a table for two which sat under the broad staircase that led to the private dining room upstairs. Chub always had the same meal. Two scotches and a bottle of Valpolicella accompanied by a medium rare steak served with pommes frites and creamed spinach. The spinach is for my health Chub said to the waiter, every time he ordered the repast.

During his meal Chub recapped the day's events. His first conclusion was that the freaks wanted to be found. Probably it was a weird publicity stunt, perhaps for a new movie or a boy band. Then again, if this was the case, it was not very well orchestrated. They were a day and a half into it and he seemed to be the only journo with the hint of a sniff. And Chub had no illusions about himself. Twenty years ago, editors in chief said he would go a long way and now they just wished he would. Then he had a future and now Chub well knew he simply had a past.

The odd thing about these freaks was the consistency of the narratives from everybody. Every historian was clear there had been an inexplicable event. Chub himself had seen the footage of 5th Avenue and the shape in the taxi. These were puzzling. But what about the self-propelling luggage, the front desk shenanigans and the disappearing rooster, something odd was going on in New York City and Chub Checker wanted to know what it was.

Chub finished his red wine with a gulp and ordered a cafe noir and the check. He took out his notebook and read and reread the name of the Irishman who was the master of the Royal Suite, Jerry O'. Chub would ring Jerry O' first thing tomorrow. He looked up for a moment. The dim front bar was now filled with journalists, detectives, lawyers and other drunks. As Chub looked away, he noticed that at the end of the bar there was a fat black woman. He quickly looked again but now she was gone.

Chub's check had not arrived. He waved to the Maitre D' who came straight over.

'My check please Alfred;'

'It has been taken care of Mr Checker,' Alfred replied.

'Taken care of, by who—?'

Alfred interrupted, 'the lady at the bar. The black lady, she seemed to know you. She knew your name.'

'The fat lady?' said Chub.

'Well, I cannot call her fat Sir, none of our patrons are fat. Let us say she is well proportioned.'

Chub rubbed his hand across his eyes. He laid a hand on the Maître D's arm.

'Has she been in here before? Do you know her name? Did she pay by credit card? What did she have to drink?'

'I can answer all your questions, Mr Checker. I have never seen her before. I do not know her and she paid by cash. She did order an unusual drink - a Paradise Cocktail - the barman had to look it up in his mixer book. She left most of it.'

Chub staggered out into the street. He was followed by a shimmer of silver.

Calliope wondered if he had done the right thing in paying for the man's meal. The angel could not blame the cocktail. He drank only a tiny amount. He found the blend of Gin, Apricot Brandy, Orange Juice and Lemon Juice to be disgusting. Cheek, Calliope thought, calling such a drink a Paradise Cocktail.

Twenty

The first day and a half of Jerry O's return to earth were relatively uneventful. The Big Fellow had urged him to exercise discretion.

'I do not want a big splash,' he said to Jerry O'. 'Let the humans find you. If you land on the planet and perform some major miracle everything that follows shall be an anticlimax. Calliope on my orders will assist the process. Stay in your hotel until Calliope gives you the say so. I know it will be difficult to keep the others cooped up but believe me it is necessary'.

Jerry O' was not so sure that Calliope was assisting the process. He was a slovenly maid in his guise of Dora, and he had so far given Jerry O' no hint of what was expected of him. Dickens appeared comfortable. He spent much of his time writing his jottings in his airy little study. Joan was a treasure. She had discovered daytime television, and she watched the antics of the Jersey Girls and the Kardashian Family with apparent pleasure. Vasco De Gama was the problem. He was like a caged beast. He ate ravenously. He had practically exhausted every option on the room service menu. His table manners were disgusting, but fortunately the maids cleaned up with equanimity. Jerry O' guessed that some of the humans who occupied the Royal Suite in the past were worse behaved than the Portuguese sailor.

A minor crisis was averted in the first hour after the party arrived when the butler turned up. He was a tall, thin, hollow-cheeked man appropriately named Mr Gaunt. He said he came with the suite. Fortunately, Calliope turned into Dora and told the man to vamoose. She claimed to be Jerry O's personal butler and maid. Unfortunately, Calliope was tardy as usual and Dora did not appear until Mr Gaunt was in the living room of the suite informing the group of the duties he would perform. Dora suddenly appeared behind the butler and tapped him on the shoulder.

'You are not needed Sir, I am the general factotum of my master Mr Jerry O' and his acolytes. We thank you for your offer, but you must go now.'

Dora escorted the bewildered Mr Gaunt out of the suite and when she returned, she seemed very self-satisfied. Jerry O' was not sure. He thought Dora would only have raised suspicion with her belated appearance, odd language and strange manner. Still the man went and has not been seen since.

Calliope was sent for by Mohammed. As he received his wave message he shimmered and glinted in a quite alarming manner. He later took Jerry O' aside and told him.

'I will be gone for a short time, Wilf – I mean Jerry O.' The Big Fellow wants to see me. I trust he just wants me to bring him up to date. I hope he is satisfied with my efforts. I may need your reference. I hope I don't need to call on you, but who knows. There are angels and angels, but that's all I will say. I have already said too much.'

Jerry O' gave Calliope some solace, but privately he thought that though Calliope probably delivered a good message, when it came to concentrating on more than one task at a time, his skill sets were sorely tested. The Big Feller liked Calliope. Jerry O' knew that. He would leave it in his father's omnipotent hands. Jerry O' was always content to do his father's bidding but he was missing his daily round of golf. He wondered if he would get a chance to play one of the great courses on earth. This was, after all, where the game was invented. St Andrews, Ballybunion and Augusta National came to mind.

Calliope was apprehensive. He had no brief to buy Chub Checker dinner. Calliope wondered if Gabriel and Metatron had reported him to Mohammed for breaching guidelines or some other bureaucratic infraction. The angel was nothing if not brave. He would take his medicine. Calliope returned to Paradise.

Calliope was back in the Citadel sitting in his corral waiting for a summons from Mohammed. He had been correct in his assumption that his expenses were under scrutiny. Metatron had marched over with his large red accounting ledger.

'What is this Paradise Cocktail, Steak, Fries, Creamed Spinach, Red Wine, Whisky and coffee, Calliope? I do not recall any authority from Mohammed to permit you to make such purchases. And the taxi fare. It seems excessive and the receipt is poorly written and incomplete. It is quite unsatisfactory, Calliope, quite unsatisfactory.'

Gabriel was standing at Metatron's shoulder nodding in agreement.

'Quite unsatisfactory,' he parroted.

Calliope decided that he would not be tempted to argue or respond. He bowed his head and raised his hands in apparent abject regret.

'I will rectify the paperwork, Metatron, I am seeing the Big Feller this morning.'

This revelation shut them up and they wandered off huffily muttering to each other.

Uriel had been watching with obvious relish. He fluttered over in his merry way.

'Naughty angel, Calliope, you have got up the pointy nose of Metatron and better still the turned up schnozz of Gabriel. If you are not careful you will be asked to ensure in future your spinach is never creamed. Remember Popeye, remember Popeye. His spinach was never creamed.'

'I haven't the faintest idea what you are talking about Uriel, Popeye is a cartoon character, not a real person and I have never eaten spinach in any form,' Calliope was trying to enter into the spirit of Uriel's odd humor, but banter was not his strong point.

Uriel, nevertheless, seemed to enjoy the riposte and he wandered off chuckling.

As Uriel passed Sandalphon's corral, he called out to him.

'Sandalphon, did you know Popeye is a cartoon person? What do you think of that Sandalphon?'

Sandalphon ignored Uriel. He had been watching Calliope since he arrived with undisguised interest. Calliope had noticed this, but he decided to let things lie. He doubted that Sandalphon appreciated that

Calliope knew he was following him around. Better he leaves things that way.

But then the message came through from Mohammed that the Big Feller was ready for him.

Far from being critical, the Big Feller was pleased with the progress of the expedition.

'Everything is going to plan, Calliope. Buying dinner for Chub Checker was an inspired decision. It is a small sign to the doubter that he may need to reconsider and contemplate, the way to the Checker soul is through his ample stomach. So well, done my old friend, well done. There are a couple of things you should appreciate and reinforce with the party on my behalf. In the first place the three former humans accompanying Wilfred each now bear the age of their greatest achievement when on the planet before. Joan is sixteen. This was her age in 1429 when she led the French Army to victory against the Burgundians at Orleans. Some say she was merely the standard bearer, but this view is wrong. Joan was a fighter and master tactician. De Gama is thirty years old. This was his age when he arrived in India in 1498 with the Portuguese fleet. Dickens is forty-nine years old which was his age in 1861 the year of the publication of Great Expectations his finest novel. The three of them must also be totally aware that they are returned as human beings. They have the same emotions and will meet the same temptations as humans. If they succumb, they will not return to Paradise. I appreciate that they have not been given any choice in the matter, but frankly they are all in Paradise by the skin of their teeth. De Gama was a savage man who put his sailors at risk for his own ends. He has been rewarded, notwithstanding, for his great enterprise and resourcefulness. Dickens was an avaricious fellow who made a great deal of money from his writings. He got to Paradise because of the comfort he gave to poor Londoners who lived without any money, creature comforts or education. Dickens' novels educated and influenced them. He gave them hope, where previously there was none. Now I know young Joan of Arc is a saint, but if there was a more bloodthirsty violent female saint, I know not her name. Joan however fought when grown men were afraid to fight. She was a great example to the French people when they were wracked by division and internal conflict.'

The Big Feller paused and took a puff of his pipe.

'And Wilfred or Jerry O' as he is now known,' queried Calliope.

'No Calliope, Wilfred is my son. He is in human form, but he is not human. He will look like an Irish Airline executive, but he will act as the son of the Creator.'

'As before,' echoed Mohammed.

'Exactly,' said the Big Feller, 'as before.'

'Now let us turn to Mr Chub Checker,' the Big Feller said, 'he may seem an unlikely vehicle for our message to be delivered, but in the world that he lives he is an exception. Modern Manhattan is awash with humans who are shameless and corrupted. Checker is a reprobate. I have no doubt of that, but he is an honest man amongst a nest of thieves. Calliope you are to tell Wilfred or Jerry O', as he is now known, to grant Checker access and inform him of the identity of the party. You may use your angelic talents to achieve this end.'

The Big Feller said his goodbyes and Mohammed escorted Calliope out. Mohammed was not as full of praise as his master.

'I do suggest you try and think things through, Calliope. You have a worrying tendency to act after or during an event, when with only minor planning hiccups could easily be avoided.'

'I know, Mohammed, I will try harder,' Calliope meant it at the time, but he was by nature a disorderly angel and nature was immutable. Calliope knew that too.

He avoided the Citadel and went back to the Plaza. As he left, he observed three windows of the Citadel were framed by the faces of angels.

Gabriel and Metatron were together at one window watching with pursed lips. In the second was Sandalphon taking note of the time of departure. In the third was merry Uriel singing to himself.

'Popeye is a cartoon person, noshing spinach, his diversion.'

Twenty-One

Stir crazy! That phrase was not one that was within the De Gama vocabulary, but it described perfectly the way the seafarer felt.

'It is worse than sailing around Africa in the Sao Gabriel, I feel like a sea rat,' he shouted to nobody. The Sao Gabriel was the flag ship of his old fleet. It was a twenty-seven-meter-long carrack that was not named after the angel.

De Gama was exaggerating. He had seen worse, much worse. He lived at sea through months of boredom only to suddenly stumble into moments of panic and danger. Though he was a brave and resourceful sailor, he was a risk taker. On his way home from Calicut, half his fleet was lost after De Gama had gone to sea despite monsoon warnings from local fishermen. Still Vasco had felt that he needed to leave. Vasco's relationship with the local sovereign was sorely tested by the Portuguese Captain's obduracy and blunt bargaining. King Zamorin, in the end, asked for twenty gold escudos as customs duty which so angered De Gama that he kidnapped sixteen Calicut fishermen. The expedition to Calicut had exacted a large cost. Over half De Gama's men died. It also failed in its principal mission of securing a commercial treaty with

Calicut. Nonetheless, the spices brought back on the remaining two ships were sold at an enormous profit to the crown of Portugal. Vasco da Gama was justly celebrated for opening a direct sea route to Asia. His journey would be repeated thereafter by yearly trips to Africa and India.

And here he was centuries later this great man of the sea cooped up in an airless palace accompanied only by the hermit writer Dickens, a strip of a girl and Jerry O' who so far had been a disappointment to Vasco.

'When do we embark on our great mission? The present-day humans are sallow and cowering vassals. I could smite them all without any need for supporting troops. My hot breath would be the fire of the dragon that would have the mortals trembling like insects faced with a Bengal tiger,; hollered Vasco.

Jerry O' ignored him. He saw no point in arguing with the wild Portuguese hero. Charles Dickens heard some muffled noise from the comfort of his study and accurately deduced it was De Gama raving. He disregarded the noise and continued writing his journal.

On the other hand, Joan of Arc was not unsympathetic. She had taken to watching a British reality TV series called 'The Only Way is Essex', which chronicled the gauche exploits of a group of boorish young Brits who lived in Basildon. She was particularly taken by a nightclub singer called Arg and his friend Mark. But Joan too needed fresh air. She had asked Jerry O' if she could take a walk and he had simply told her to be patient. We will make our presence felt soon enough, he had told her. Joan had no choice but to listen to the rackety De Gama. He was in the same room.

'We could go for a walk, Vasco.' she helpfully suggested. 'We could stroll in the park across the way. The weather is clement and it is only a short walk from here. I can see no harm that could come from this. We are not prisoners.'

If Calliope had been on Earth, he would have appeared as Dora and read them the riot act, but Calliope was in Paradise at his briefing.

So the two travelers left the Royal Suite and made their way downstairs. They passed through the lobby without incident. Other guests either averted their eyes or shrank back into recesses. Brian the porter had his cell phone out and was ringing Chub Checker. The desk clerks busied themselves hoping against hope that the two would not approach. Vasco and Joan walked out of the Hotel and crossed the road and entered Central Park. They made their way down one of the snaking pathways. Joggers veered away and cyclists sped up when they saw them. Vasco was singing 'Spires that in the Sunset Rise,' a haunting Portuguese sea shanty and Joan was skipping along like any happy sixteen year old out on a jaunt on a fine day. Today Vasco wore a dark green doublet with shiny black hose topped off by his tall, crowned chapeau. Joan was in her favorite chain mail battle dress.

Most pedestrians simply ignored them. The dog walkers tried to herd their flocks. The leashed flea taxis seemed to appreciate De Gama and Joan and woofed friskily.

The trouble occurred when a man began following them. He was clad in a skintight black track suit with wide white side stripes. His hair was orange and pompadoured in an alarming way as if he had just been given a great fright. He stayed close behind them. Vasco stopped singing and whispered to Joan.

'We are being followed Joan. He appears to be a poltroon. I will call him out.'

Joan stole a glance back and did not disagree. The man was, at the very least, a posturer.

Vasco turned back. faced the man and squared his shoulders.

'What is your wont, swain? Are you following us? Desist or there will be trouble.'

The man laughed in contempt.

'Look at the pair of you,' he retorted. 'you are a couple of circus freaks. I will say this, pal, you have a fine arse under your frock, and your little girl friend would be pretty as a picture if she took off her chastity belt.'

'What is this fine arse, you say fine arse, you make comment about my arse you miserable Americano cock sucker,' Vasco was angry. He remembered the young men who confronted them upon their arrival and their cries of 'cock sucker.' It suited the present circumstances.

Joan now wished they had not gone for a walk. It was better Vasco was angry inside the suite at the Plaza than here in Central Park.

The large man had now come up to them. He looked down at Vasco and with one hand casually lifted the front of the De Gama tunic. He whistled with apparent incredulity at the size of the mound covered in its black hose. The American with the other hand momentarily grabbed a handful of Portuguese pubis.

'I reckon you may be the one who would like his cock sucked, you ugly little monkey. Hop off now before I put you in New York Presbyterian.'

Joan was the first to react. She had watched the contretemps unfold with interest, but when the large man took hold of a handful of Vasco's manhood, she reacted swiftly and kicked the man just below the kneecap with all the force she could muster. The man hopped in pain and Vasco clenched his hands and struck the back of the man's neck with a violent chopping motion. The man fell to his knees and both Vasco and Joan began raining blows on him.

By now a crowd had gathered and was watching the mauling with apparent enjoyment.

Then two things happened. First three mounted police officers arrived, alighted and rushed into the melee. Second Joan was transported from the scene.

She found herself back in the Plaza Suite. Sandalphon was with her.

'You are here Sandals, I did not know you were here. You should not have taken me from the park. What will become of De Gama?'

Sandalphon took his time to reply.

'I was sent here by Gabriel, young madam, to care for you in case of emergency. This was just such an emergency. I am your angel, young madam, it is only fit and proper I should be here. You are after all a saint. It is true to say that Calliope does not know of my presence. I would be grateful young madam, if we kept it that way. He is back in Paradise, but he will soon return. Vasco will be arrested. I have no doubt of this. You must tell Jerry O'. He will know what to do.'

Voices could be heard. Charles Dickens and Jerry O' walked in. Sandalphon was gone. If Joan was abashed, she did not show it.

'I have to tell you Jerry O', that Vasco is probably presently in jail. He and I took a constitutional in Central Park when a large thug accosted us. He assaulted Vasco in a disgusting way and accused him of the vilest deviation. Vasco and I reacted. The police arrived, but I was able to escape.'

Joan of Arc now obviously knew a 'cock' for the purposes of a particular insult was not a rooster.

Jerry O' was silent. Dickens was twittering about prison life in England and wondering how American jails compared to London Nineteenth Century penitentiaries. He seemed pleased. It gave more life, perhaps, to his scribblings.

Fortunately, Calliope then returned and appeared as Dora.

'He shall be bailed Jerry O', but leave him in until tomorrow. It will settle him down.'

The phone rang. Dora answered.

'Yes Mr. Checker, we would look forward to meeting you,' she said, 'we have been waiting for your call. 9.00 AM will be fine.'

Twenty-Two

Chub Checker was so flummoxed by the phone call to the Plaza Suite that he had a health night. Instead of visiting The Galleon or the Cambodian grease factory which were his preferred haunts, he bought a large Margherita Pizza from his local Dominos and took it back to the roach farm where he ate it out of the box and washed it down with three Peroni beers. He filed the pizza box and empty bottles under the couch and tried to get a handle on the story.

'What story,' he kept saying to himself, 'what story.'

Brian, the Plaza porter, informed him two of the freaks had gone for a walk. Brian rang him back later with news of the fight in the park. Little escapes the front of house staff at a great hotel. Gossip, innuendo and guest misbehavior runs through a lobby like wildfire burns up dry leaves in the heat of an Alabama summer.

Chub subsequently made enquiries of his best police source. An arrest had been made. There would be an arraignment tomorrow.

Chub decided against coffee in favor of two fingers of Jamesons. He wanted to be fighting fit for tomorrow.

At 9.00 AM sharp Chub knocked on the door of the Royal Suite at the Plaza. The door was opened by a pleasant looking well-groomed youngish man in a beautifully cut suit and a crisp white open necked shirt. He was alone.

'Come in, you must be Mr. Checker. What a pleasure to meet you sir, I believe you are one of the city's most distinguished journalists. Have a seat can I get you anything?'

Chub dearly wanted a stiff drink, but it could wait. He sat perched on the edge of a deep armchair.

And you are Mr. O?' he asked.

'Call me Jerry O,' was the reply.

Chub noticed the man had a rich southern Irish brogue. When Jerry O' sat down his suit coat opened to reveal a bright flowered pattern lining. Paul Smith, thought Chub, Three Thousand Dollars plus.

'Are you here alone, Jerry O?' Checker asked disingenuously.

'Oh no you will meet the others later, but I suspect you have some questions for me,' said Jerry O'.

Chub noticed the man did not seem to be the least bit fazed in having a reporter on his doorstop. He appeared pleased and acted as if he was expecting Chub.

'Frankly Jerry O', I am not sure why I am here. Your group, your entourage has caused quite a stir. Your friends' clothes are odd, perhaps they are in fancy dress or in character for a play or movie. I have seen your walk across 5th Avenue, and it puzzled me. Then there was the problem in the taxi, the check in procedure, the luggage trolley which seemed to be self-propelled and then there was the contretemps in Central Park.'

Chub ruefully stopped his narrative. When you boil it down it is two pennies worth of nothing. This man is probably just a business type with weird friends. If all he did was hang out with people in fancy dress that would make him less freaky than most Manhattan executive hotshots.

'You are most perspicacious, Mr. Checker, you see I am really Wilfred the son of the Big Feller, I suppose you are surprised, no astonished, you probably do not for a moment believe me.'

'The Big Feller,' Chub asked, 'who is the Big Feller?'

Jerry O' laughed and slapped his thigh.

'Of course, you humans mostly call him God, at least the Christians amongst you. The Muslims seem to have got their apostles mixed up. They claim somebody called Mohammed has precedence. Strangely enough there is a Mohammed who is close to Dad, but he is his servant. I do not think it is the one the Muslims worship. Nobody worships our Mohammed. He is well liked that I grant you but not worshipped.'

Jerry O' laughed again. Now Chub really needed that drink. Jerry O' at that very instant divined this.

'Can I get you a tipple, Mr. Checker, or Chub may I call you Chub, the hotel has supplied a couple of fine Scottish single malts, but it is hard to go past our Irish whisky. I have a bottle of Ballykeefe. It is an Irish single malt. Do you know it, have you tried it?'

'Call me Chub, and yes I would like to try an Irish.' Chub regained his composure at the prospect of a stiff drink.

Jerry O' poured him a generous measure and a tumbler of water for himself from a cut glass pitcher.

'Your health, Chub, your very good health,' Jerry O' lifted his glass and they both took a drink. Chub enjoyed the smooth velvety warmth of the single malt aged Irish dram as it ran down his throat.

'Now you were saying you were the son of God or the Big Feller. Where do you actually come from Jerry O' and why are you are here.'

'I come from the place we call Paradise. Some call it Heaven. Others call it Nirvana, Elysium. Valhalla or the hereafter. There is only one place, Chub, just Paradise. I am here because the Big Feller is concerned about your future. Not yours particularly, but all the hominids. Small dangerous countries with large chips on their shoulders have weapons that could cause the destruction of whole societies. Wars are being fought in several countries where both sides claim to have God on their side. This is impossible as the Big Feller is the only God and he has taken no sides. But worse the human condition has been corrupted by narcissism. Both sexes are obsessed by worldly goods, appearance and most of all themselves. The new technology only encourages this folly. Television is another cause of the debasement. My little friend Joan who you will meet soon has been watching a group of ugly Saxons living puerile lives on television. Yet it is not shown as drama or comedy. It is real life. I have been meaning to warn her about it. I do not want her infected by the squalid values portrayed in this show. It is something about the county of Essex in England. Do you know the show?'

Chub did not know of the series, but he made a note of it in his little notebook.

'I do not want to be offensive Jerry O', but how do you expect me to believe you. I mean you say you are from Paradise. That is a tough ask and why Irish, why the accent and the expensive clobber. That suit is a Paul Smith. It is big money.'

'The Irish concept is just the Big Feller's sense of humor. He says that in Ireland there is a saying that God comes from Ireland so he would humor them with the name. The clothing represents the new breed of Irish business types who run airlines, own newspapers and dress with studied nonchalance. They are his words, Chub, my father has quite a sense of humor.'

'I still don't get it, why not go to a church. It is your natural home. Why the Plaza, why me - and your friends, who are they and why are they here.'

Chub finished the remainder of his drink and placed the glass down on the ornate coffee table at his hand.

'The churches are corrupt. There are some good leaders, but my exhortation is going to be directly to the people. As for my friends, the Big Feller has sent Charles Dickens with me. He is to write a journal of the trip. He is engaged in this task as we speak. Joan of Arc, the saint, is also here. She is our strategist. This leaves my supposed protector Vasco De Gama. He is not here currently.'

'Yeah,' interrupted Chub, 'as it happens, I know about Vasco, he is in Manhattan lock up. There is a bail hearing at noon.'

Jerry O' left the room and returned with Joan and Charles. He introduced them. Chub was beyond shock but was manfully trying to cope.

'What a pleasure it is to meet a New York journalist. I look forward to discussing syntax.'

Charles spoke to Chub as if to an equal. The man was, after all another scribe. Joan was not sure what to make of the man. She was obviously jumpy. The last big plug ugly men she knew who smelt so strongly of hard liquor were Burgundians who had burned her at the stake.

'There has been mention of another person, a large black woman, is she here?' Chub was keen to meet his benefactor.

'You mean our maid Dora,' said Jerry O', 'she is standing right behind you. You can blame her for the metaphysical occurrences.'

Twenty-Three

The Manhattan Criminal Court has an ornate facade. Roman columns stand tall supporting the grand colonnade which flows to the bank of wide glass doorways that lead into the spacious lobby. Lawyers, litigants and witnesses enter through the front entrance. Judges have their own undercover parking area which is in the basement. Jurors are processed through an entrance on the opposite side of the building to the judge's entrance.

The rear of the building is the engine room. The staff access the building through a number of small, unmarked doorways. Police and security gain admission through a separate undercover car park and staircase. Then there are the prisoners. The admissions entry is open twenty-four hours a day. A constant trickle of police cars disgorges their human cargo of manacled malefactors being led by uniform police into the building. They proceed through a narrow-secured vestibule into a wide-open reception area. There are six queues each manned by a police officer. Generally between six and ten prisoners stand in each queue. There is a constant hubbub of noise as the cons call out to each other and police officers give sharp directions or admonishments to their charges.

The three mounted police who attended the scene of Vasco De Gama's roughhouse in Central Park handed Vasco and his opponent to squad car officers who now brought the two men to Manhattan Central for admission and booking. Vasco was surprisingly quiet and orderly. He had a deep respect for the administration of the law. He also was a little overawed by some of the other denizens in the reception queue. There were giant angry gang bangers, small vicious looking Asian hoods and numerous loud shouting prostitutes of both sexes. There were multisexuals, transvestites and bull lesbians. There were hairy legged men dressed as women and svelte pretty girls in three-piece men's suits. It was an ever changing, ever moving mélange of the netherworld of society. Vasco had seen executions in Calicut and strangling on the Ivory Coast. He fought one of the early Morgan pirates in a bloody battle off the beach of Obock at the Gulf of Aden. Despite all he had seen in the past, he was disquieted by the disorderly scene. Vasco, on the other hand, was viewed by the other admittees as just another freak. Perhaps he was a sexual deviant or fraudster, nothing special. His protagonist was not faring so well. The waved pompadour of hair was causing some merriment. 'He's wearing a possum on his head', 'Isn't he gorgeous' and 'what about it handsome' were some of the comments the man heard as he went through the laborious admission process.

Eventually the two men were logged in and placed in adjoining interview rooms. Officer Murray Glick was the arresting officer. Sergeant Max Flanagan was the Officer in charge. Glick reported to Flanagan.

'Ok what have we got here?' said the Sergeant.

'The big guy, Oliver Givens-Cater, is a bond trader. He went for his morning jog in CP and he ran into the little guy in fancy dress. His name is Vasco De Gama.'

'His name is what,' said the sergeant.

'Vasco De Gama, so what,' replied Glick.

'And that didn't give you any food for thought.'

'Food for thought, I don't know what you mean sarge. The guy has a spick name and he is a spick, so what's the big deal.'

'You've never heard the name Vasco De Gama before,' said Sergeant Flanagan.

'Has he got a felony conviction in the Bronx?' asked Glick.

'Ok do not worry about it. What happened?'

'We have some witnesses. They got into a verbal and then the big guy came up and felt the spic's balls.'

'Felt his balls, well what the fuck did he think was going to happen?'

'The little guy went bananas and was belting the shitter out of the Bond Trader until the Mounties turned up and shut it down.'

'Felt his balls, what a dickhead. A guy is walking around Central Park grabbing some other guy by the cojones. What a dickhead,' the sergeant was an old school bog Irish copper. His first sympathy was with anybody fighting with a Wall Street Trader, whom he regarded as fat cat thieves who prey on the vulnerable.

'Witnesses say the grease ball was with a young woman who was also getting into the ball grabber. She was dressed in armor and was angry as a cat in heat who has lost her mate. Anyway, she just disappeared,' said Officer Glick.

'Yeah, that would be right,' said the sergeant, 'and I suppose Mr. De Gama had no identification of any kind.'

'As a matter of fact he has Sarge, he has a valid credit card in his name, a Plaza Hotel Room key card and an old gold coin which he says establishes his bona fides from Lisbon. I wasn't sure Sarge what that meant.'

'No I guess that's true,' replied the sergeant, who stood up ready to meet the two fighters.

They went into Oliver Givens-Cater interview room first. The man was as arrogant, and self-satisfied as Flanagan expected.

'I am the innocent party here, Sergeant,' he said after being introduced, 'that little animal is a feral, and the girl too she kicked me, scratched me and bit me. Do you have her in custody as well? I want her charged.'

'We seem to have mislaid her for the moment Mr. Givens-Cater, but there was something I wanted to ask you,' said Sergeant Flanagan, 'were you attracted sexually to the man or were you just good friends.'

'Sexually attracted, good friends, are you trying to be funny, what the hell do you mean.'

'Well there is independent evidence that you grabbed the other man by the balls and it was after this occurrence that he became angry. If that is true it is, of course, a most serious allegation. He may have over reacted, but the city takes sexual assault very seriously, particularly when the victim is a visitor,' Sergeant Flanagan was quiet and commanding. The bond trader was seeing his situation in a new light.

'What about his clothing, how does he explain walking through Central Park looking like a French Soldier.'

'I think more a Portuguese sailor,' replied Flanagan, much to Officer Glick' surprise, 'I am going to hold both of you over night. There will be a bail hearing tomorrow. In the meantime, I am going to have both of you blood tested for drugs.'

'I have decided, I won't press charges,' said Givens-Cater.

'You might not, but Vasco De Gama may,' replied the Sergeant gesturing to the young constable that they were leaving.

The two police went into the adjoining room where De Gama was sitting quietly at the table. Sergeant Flanagan introduced himself.

'It is an honor to meet you Sir; I am sorry you have had such a bad experience but tell me what happened.'

'It is a pleasure, Sir to meet such a senior man. I can assure you I have been treated fairly by your vassals. When I was in your park this morning a poltroon in a black costume came up to me and snatched my gonad pouch. I became angry and I began flogging him. If I had been carrying my rapier, I would have cut his heart out.'

'I am afraid Mr. De Gama that we may have to hold you here until tomorrow. We also will need to conduct a blood test. I can assure you it will cause no pain,' Glick was confounded by the apparent respect shown to the strangely dressed man by his usually taciturn sergeant.

'Glick,' said Flanagan, 'do you have Mr. De Gama's identity documents.'

Officer Glick passed over a plastic evidence bag, and the sergeant examined the Credit Card briefly.

'Is this yours Sir?'

'Yes,' replied Vasco, 'but I have not yet had the need to use it.'

The sergeant held up the Plaza key card.

'And this is your room card.'

'Yes Your Majesty,' replied Vasco, 'it is where I am staying during my visit to New York. The room is in the name of Wilf – I should say Jerry O'. He is from Ireland.'

'Do you need to contact him, Mr. Da Gama?'

'No I am sure he will find me.' replied Vasco.

The senior officer carefully studied the old gold coin.

'And this coin Mr. Da Gama, what is this?'

'It is my accolade from the King of Portugal. It grants me the title of freeman of the city of Lisbon.'

'And the date of the accolade?' asked Flanagan.

'1503 sir, on the first day of May. I remember the day well.'

Flanagan looked at Glick with a perfectly straight face. He put the credit card, room keycard and coin back into the plastic evidence bag and zip locked it. He gave the bag back to Glick who was beginning to wonder whether the senior officer was losing his marbles.

'Oh and one final thing Mr. Da Gama,' said Flanagan, 'there are witnesses who claim you were accompanied by a small young woman dressed in chain mail or armor. Is this so?'

'Yes that is Joan of Arc. She accompanied me on my walk.'

'Of course,' responded Flanagan, 'I should have realized.'

The two policemen left Vasco waiting patiently to be transferred to a cell. He was unconcerned. He had once been locked up for three days in Senegal by bandits. This would surely be a more pleasant experience.

As Glick and Flanagan returned to the booking department the sergeant turned to Glick and said:

'At least there was someone in the fight dressed as a French soldier.'

Glick failed to understand the allusion. He could not wait for his shift to end to call in at Mulligan's Bar and Grill and regale the drinkers in the squad about his Sergeant's peculiar behavior.

Twenty-Four

CHARLES DICKENS JOURNAL

As an observer, a commissioned observer no less, I watch events unfold and characters develop. It has indeed been a fascinating experience to monitor my fellow visitors cope with the beginning of our great mission.

Jerry O' is his father's son. I can see that the higher the stakes the better our Jerry O' will perform. He may miss his precious golf, his lovely Mary Mags and the perks that, no doubt, go with being the son of the Big Feller. Oh yes, I hear you now, but Paradise, your Paradise is it not the ultimate realization of the equality of the human spirit. Well yes and no, you see this human spirit we are talking about is doled out in unequal portions to a variety of recipients. I would like to think, for example, I have more cultural significance than the man Da Gama, but most surely I have less endurance and aggressive enterprise than he. And our little Joan, she is blessed yet cursed with the most extraordinary naïveté, yet her ferocity and will to trounce, no, slaughter the Burgundians, makes my personal courage quota a mere piccolo of the weakest milk.

However, there is more to this conundrum than mere mortal equivalence. Jerry O', I observe and my reader will appreciate, is no man. I will be perplexing. He is a man but is not a man. Hear me out.

Now I am on earth again I am back to being flesh and blood. I must say I prefer my spirit form. I prefer to know that a blood vessel cannot burst, a boil cannot appear nor a bone can fracture. It is comforting, very comforting. But I have meandered down a shadowy sidetrack. You will note, it is my wont, I have read much criticism of my work. Some say Bleak House is too long or Great Expectations too odd or David Copperfield too innocent. Literature is in the eye of the scholar, just as beauty is in the eye of the beholder. I wrote before to be read aloud. Alas I cannot change my ways. I apologize if I am meandering rather than piercing straight for my target. I now return solemnly to my main thesis and that is that though I am back to being flesh and blood [as are Joan and Vasco] our leader Jerry O' is a mere avatar. Do not think I am being disrespectful. That is certainly not my intent. Rather I exalt his celestial being. Jerry O', in my opinion, has been constructed by the Big Feller to be able to return to Paradise. I may return, if I do not drift into sin. The same caveat surely applies to Joan and Vasco, but not our Jerry O'. You see it is my belief that his form is human, but not his structure. How do I know this revelation? I do not know. It is simply my opinion.

Now let me continue my narrative. The sun shines in the afternoons in my study and this causes me to loll my head and doze. When I wake, I am in a reverie. Thoughts dance about my head like fleet footed Bow Street Runners slipping in and about the crush of humankind as they rush to tackle a purse snatcher in Regent Street.

The party has settled into an odd routine. Jerry O' cogitates and waits. Calliope flits between angel and maid in his oddly discomforting way. Joan has found the joy of television. She watches it constantly. Her eyes burn with interest. She observes what are called reality shows. These purport to exhibit ordinary humans going about their daily affairs. I saw a little of an American production about a family known as the Kardashians. It is an odd name for an American family. I am unable to tell you whether I enjoyed it or not as, for the life of me, I could not understand what was happening. Joan has also recommended to me that I watch a Series featuring English people and set in the county of Essex. I sat with her for a while as she sought to explain the various characters' lives to me. I am afraid that it only highlighted and reinforced the reason why Jerry O' has been sent here. The lives exhibited were not only banal but lumpen. I am not sure whether the persons on show are educated. I sincerely hope not, because if they are not simply cretins, it means that Jerry O's task is mountainous. If they are cretins, it is to be hoped that they represent a de minimis minority of hominids. Perhaps this is why they are selected to appear. Perhaps what I saw was a Twenty First Century version of the stocks. Reality television is a place where clods can be held up to ridicule and where the sour fruit and blackened leaved vegetables thrown are simply metaphoric. I suggested to Joan that she turn to the National Geographic Channel and watch majestic big cats behave harmoniously with nature. Alas, she ignored my entreaty.

I heard De Gama raving about being cooped up. I studiously kept out of his way. There would be no point in exchanging words with the man. I am afraid I did not hear Vasco and Joan leave the suite. If I had, what would I have done. I think nothing. Perhaps informed Jerry O', yes that is what I would have done, I would have informed Jerry O'. And what would he have done, that dear reader is a very good question, just what would Jerry O have done. The answer is clear as burning day. He would have done nothing. Nature would take its course.

Would things have been different if Calliope had been around. Indubitably, but better, of this I am unable to say.

I am sorry to say that when Joan of Arc told us Vasco De Gama was incarcerated I had a sinful moment. I succumbed to the temptation of being excited by the Sea Captain's discomfort. It was not that I wanted him to be hurt or even interned. It was just that spice was added by the sauce ladle to my journal from his misfortune.

Now we are getting somewhere, a member of our party is locked in a cell somewhere in the bowels of a dank New York chamber. Is he surrounded and enclaved with the violent riffraff of the streets or the vicious thugs of the underworld? I wondered if the Nineteenth Century London lock ups were salons of comfort by comparison with the New York prisons of today. Certainly, I was sure the denizens today were no better.

As I write De Gama is still away. Jerry O' seems insouciant. We have, however, now met our first earthly contact. It is another writer. I am pleased with this development. The man Mr. Chub Checker looks like a tippler. This, of itself, does not concern me. I knew Oscar Wilde. He was a tippler. He was also a writer, a great writer. It was not the tippling that made me wary of Wilde. He was a well named man and there were other aspects of his character which displeased me.

I questioned Mr. Checker, not as to his credentials, but rather as to his vocabulary and his urbanity. I am satisfied with the man. [If it is any of my business which it is not], he may not have the elegance of Swift or the gravitas of Trollope, but I am sure he is a cosmopolitan. He is a raffish, heavily lubricated cosmopolitan, but a cosmopolitan no less.

I await with feverish anticipation further developments.

Twenty-Five

CALLIOPE'S EPISTLE

I have been tracking the progress of the authorized correspondent; Dickens and I can see that recording prose is more art than trade. One needs the patience of Job, though he is a fictional figure. You, my epistle master must know this. You may have even written the 'Job' book. He fooled us all our Job. He is referenced in the Christian epistle of James. The Koran claim him as a prophet. Even the Mormons aver to him, referencing him in their 'sacred' texts. It was only a few of the Rabbis who were suspicious. They hit the nail on the head when they claimed the prophets merely used the story to make a point. Well as an angel I will follow suit. I repeat to be a writer one must have the patience of [the fictional character] Job. That is not all, you need an ordered mind. I fully understand your skepticism about my ability to comply with this requirement. Mohammed once said to me after I delivered a message to a surprised Venetian concert pianist, when the recipient was supposed to be Viennese.

"You have a disorderly mind, my Calliope, can you write things down or at the very least think things through".

As it turned out it did no harm. The message that the Big Feller asked me to deliver was to place in the musician's mind the name of a song. It was the favorite song of a handsome noblewoman who would swoon at the sound of it, I think it was Beethoven's 5th Piano Concerto that was to be my mind message. The Venetian piano player completed his rendition to listless applause from his audience of canal squatters who would have much preferred the flamboyant sound of the local hero Vivaldi, played by a quartet, rather than the Germanic sounds of Beethoven. On the other hand, our Viennese artist played his especially beautifully structured Bach to the annoyance of the Noblewoman, who did not take to the pianist or the music at all. As it turns out, the Noblewoman was killed the very next day when her carriage overturned, and she was swept into the marshy reaches of the Wien River. I would have thought I did the man a favor. I can hardly be blamed for him catching syphilis the very next year from a liaison with a whore, or for his subsequent painful death. Not that Mohammed, as such, assigned fault to me. He was just regretful and pensive. Gabriel, of course, blamed me and when he pillories me, he never fails to take the opportunity to mention my mistake.

"And what about the musician, Calliope", he says, "you couldn't even get his country right".

And I reply that it was three hundred years ago, but that does not satisfy him.

I have been busy since I last wrote my [draft - I emphasize draft] verse.

It seems the Big Feller, as ever, keeps a close eye on things and an alert newshound called Chub Checker has become interested in our team. My brief was to keep an eye on Mr. Checker and make sure he stayed on the scent. I had no brief to buy him dinner at the Galleon, but frankly I felt sorry for the man. He eats alone with Billy Booze for company. I thought I would buck him up. I think it worked. He had already heard about the 'black woman' in the taxi, so I just added some mayo to the salad. You can see that I am picking up the local jargon. In this way, I am ahead of Dickens. He still writes from two centuries in the past.

Back in the suite at the Plaza things were going well enough. The only hiccup was when on the first day a butler turned up to look after us. Mr. Gaunt said he came with the suite. I admit I was slightly late in appearing as Dora, but I soon saw him off.

Shortly afterwards I was sent for by Mohammed and I left. I was a trifle uneasy as things had not gone exactly to plan. I took the liberty of seeking a good reference from Jerry O', but I did not press it as he seemed ambivalent.

I knew the wearisome Metatron and his master Gabriel would chide me over my expense account. I regard their pettifogging as one of the small tariffs I must pay to be an angel. It is very annoying and tiresome.

Uriel lightened my load a little with his humor. There do you like that - lighten my load - Charles Dickens would not write that.

Anyway, far from being annoyed with me the Big Feller was full of praise. He said that buying Checker dinner was 'an inspired decision'. They are his words, so Calliope, the bumbling expense cheater, according to Gabriel, has made an inspired decision.

I was briefed extensively about the three human spirits accompanying Jerry O' and I. It turns out Joan is sixteen years, De Gama thirty odd and Dickens is aged forty-nine. They are fully re-formed humans with all the human spirit both good and bad. Jerry O' or Wilfred is only in human form. He has some wounds from his first trip to earth as JC, but I suspect the Big Feller has left them there as a reminder of the inhumanity that humanity can show.

While I was gone, Vasco De Gama got into a fight in Central Park and is now in jail. Why am I not surprised. When next I return to Paradise I am sure Gabriel will blame me for this, but I was not there when it happened. Joan had been with De Gama at the time of the melee but escaped. I suspect that this was with the help of Sandalphon. I cannot prove it and I am certainly not going to ask Joan, but it makes sense.

I returned just after Jerry O' had heard the news of the imprisonment of De Gama and I calmed him. It was my idea to leave him in jail until the bail hearing on the following day. [I can inform you my epistle writer I write this entry just before I head to the Manhattan Court to assist Jerry O' make bail for our Portuguese friend].

Checker rang yesterday after I had calmed Jerry O' and I arranged for him to meet Jerry O' today.

I am happy to say the meeting went extraordinarily well. Checker is an intelligent fellow, though much the worse for wear. I listened to Jerry O' explain the circumstances of our visit. It is unlikely Checker believed him, but there is plenty of time for that. Jerry O' has never been known for sarcasm, but when I put in a sudden appearance, he claimed that I could be blamed for any metaphysical occurrences. This is strictly correct, but I thought it was an unnecessary insinuation.

Now I ponder what to write. I believe I have brought you up to date. I have been looking at an ancient, dog-eared Bible in the Suite. It is published by a group called the Gideon organization. I have noticed that many of the best epistles are in rhyming verse. I know this is a major leap by me into the unknown, but I am going to try. I have decided to leave out De Gama's jailing, not because it may be said not to reflect well on me, but because I suspect it will be of no consequence.

CH 1
And the attending angel was called away,
So the Big Feller could have his say,
In Paradise the course was charted
When the angel heard, he then departed
A human man has found the son
So far he is the only one.

Twenty-Six

Back at the Bear Pit, there was the usual chatter and buzz. The Bulgarian earthquake had been a godsend. The first four pages were full of stories of extreme bravery and adversity. There were human interest pieces about Bulgarian Karaka Chan mountain dogs rescuing their trapped owners and children being dug out of small rock fissures where they had been snared. To balance the good news reportage, there were pieces written about pillaging, raping and looting. A sub-editor had cutely named this piece 'Vulgar Bulgars.'

Chub Checker sat at his desk staring at the wall. He felt a strange necessity, even a propulsion, to proceed with the story of Jerry O', despite the absurd yarn spun to him by the Irishman. Chub analyzed the tale in his mind.

Jesus has returned to Earth from Heaven accompanied by Charles Dickens, Vasco De Gama and Joan of Arc to warn us about our future. Does that seem likely? Jerry O', the Irishman, had spelt out the faults of Twenty First Century society. Goodness knows the man was right, but you would not have to be the son of God to know that earth was a shambles. Turn on a TV set and switch channels for a while and you will soon appreciate what is wrong with us.

You will see vacuous young women seeking to have their tush landscaped or their breasts 'enhanced'. On another channel will be a simpleton overpaid sportsman being interviewed by an over reverent journalist. On another station one will see violence of a kind that would be horrific even to the Huns of Attila and explicit sexual scenes which would have embarrassed the satyrs of Bacchus. However, Jerry O's acute perception of our modern reality did not necessarily make him Jesus revisited. It was true that the actor who played the writer Charles Dickens performed his part well. He even looked the image of some snapshots of the man. The young girl Joan of Arc was equally convincing. There were, of course, no photographic reproductions of Joan of Arc, but she was utterly plausible. There was also the evidence of the strange happenings, such as the self-propelling luggage and 5th Avenue wonder walk, but Chub thought of trying to sell this narrative at the forthcoming editorial meeting. The Bulgarian earthquake would be a mere tinkle of a tremor compared to the explosion that would erupt from the editor-in-chief Bear Grizzard.

Chub was not afraid of his boss, but he wanted to pursue the story to wherever it led. A misstep at the meeting would see Chub banished to City Hall to pursue the never-ending story of the mayor and his so far unproved corruption.

There was the black woman Dora who seemed to come and go like some kind of willow the wisp. What had Jerry O' said:

'You can blame her for the metaphysical occurrences.'

What did he mean by that? More importantly how could Chub run this past the liverish Bear Grizzard. He could imagine his editor-in chief roaring in anger when confronted with Chub's 'evidence'.

'So, she bought you dinner and left! You crapulous fucking pisspot that does not make her a fucking alien life force. The only meta fucking physical thing in this fucking room is your common fucking sense. You are fucked Chub, truly fucked.'

And so, it would go on and in the end Chub Checker would be pacing the corridors of City Hall looking for a story that may or may not exist. Chub appreciated irony and the irony of his present circumstance was not lost on him.

Then came his revelation. Chub was reading and re-reading the police report that Sergeant Flanagan, his source in Manhattan Central, had emailed over to him. Flanagan had been curious when they spoke earlier.

'What's your interest in this whacko, Chub,' he had asked.

'Oh just the fancy dress and the name, I want to find out if HBO are doing a series on great sailors,' Chub replied unconvincingly.

'There was a girl with him. She was a vicious little creature. You wouldn't know who she is,' said the sergeant.

'You mean Joan of Arc,' Chub replied, hanging up on his source. He knew he should not have offered up Joan's name, but he found the opportunity irresistible.

However, this was not the revelation. The revelation was the name Oliver Givens-Cater. If there was one thing Bear Grizzard hated more than Newspaper Proprietors and politicians, it was bond traders. Gangsters in Hugo Boss was Bear's usual sobriquet for this species. And Oliver Givens-Cater was a prince of traders. He owned a multimillion dollar spread on West 110th. He had a major interest in one of the smaller Spice Islands and was a partner in a large cruiser, Rumors abounded about his extravagant lifestyle, his drugs, parties and beautiful women. Yet he was in his late forties and had never married. Bear Grizzard would relish a claim Givens-Cater grasped a handful of foreign testes in Central Park. It would be the cream on his strawberries or the cocktail sauce poured over his beloved Aussie Shrimps. This still left the issue of what to say about Jerry O' and the others, but Chub was formulating a plan.

He rang the Plaza and was put through to the Royal Suite. Dora picked up.

'Miss Dora,' said Chub, 'I have an embarrassing request to make of you. I would very much like to introduce you all to my Editor-in-chief, but he is a difficult fellow. He will need an incentive. I was thinking of dinner. He is also very picky. The Galleon is perfectly adequate in my opinion but Bear Grizzard my editor would not be enticed. His favorite restaurant is called Alle. It is very expensive and serves small serves of French food, which is plated prettily and is extremely fashionable. The trouble is the cost. I have a small expense account, but it is constantly under strict scrutiny. I gained the impression from Jerry O' that money was not an object.'

Calliope was sympathetic to Chub's predicament.

'Don't get me going about expense accounts, Mr. Checker, I spend my life being turned over by

Metatron and that blasted Archangel Gabriel. Sure, we can pick up the tab. Alle you say, is tonight ok.'

'Tonight, will be fine, but Alle is booked out months in advance. We'll never get in'.

'Leave that to me,' Dora replied, 'we will see you there at 8.00 PM.'

Dora rang off giving Chub more food for thought. 'Metatron? and the blasted archangel Gabriel?'

He had no time for further cogitation as he needed to get to the meeting nice and early.

Twenty-Seven

It was a first. Chub Checker arrived at an editorial meeting early. He seated himself at the board table and waited expectantly. It was not long before Joanne Rixti wafted in. She wagged a reproving finger at Chub. He noticed that her nails were now a peach color. He wondered why women changed colors so often. She seemed to be dressed for a yachting party or a night at a fancy Country Club. She wore a dark navy blazer with white piping, a soft navy roll neck sweater and sharply creased white duck slacks. Her navy heels were adorned with silver bling. He thought of making a sarcastic comment to her:

'Admirals Cup Day Joanne' or some such remark, but Chub decided against it. He reckoned he would get it back in spades.

Other editors began drifting in.

Finally Bear Grizzard turned up. He was upbeat. Clearly the reports of the rising death toll from the Bulgarian Earthquake were selling papers.

Chub noticed that Bruce Gotby was absent, his place taken by a pimply stringer.

'Don't tell me Gotby is covering the earthquake,' Chub asked Joanne.

'Well, he is the Foreign Affairs editor,' she replied, 'I believe he is with the other International Correspondents at their base.'

'In Bulgaria,' Chub queried.

'Actually,' she replied with the merest hint of sarcasm, 'in Paris.'

'Figures,' Chub said, 'still at least he is on the right continent.'

'Ok, you miserable bunch of mongrel pricks,' said Bear, 'the first four pages are the quake. Gotby is doing fine work out there.'

'Poncing up and down the Rue St Honore,' said Chub quietly.

'Chub,' said Bear pointing a stubby nicotine-stained digit at Chub, 'what about page five. What about you, Chub, old lush, have you got anything on that rotten thief of a mayor yet. Do not tell me that pixies are doing handstands in the Pierre lobby or sprites are cavorting in Times Square. Tell me what you've got, Chub.'

Chub rose to his feet.

'Boss,' he said, 'I've got your favorite bond trader Oliver Givens-Cater grabbing a male tourist by the balls in Central Park. The tourist became angry and a fight ensued. Both Givens-Cater and the tourist are presently behind bars at Manhattan Central. There will be a bail hearing at noon.'

'Oliver fucking Givens fucking Cater, that is magnificent Chub, this will be an inset on page one. Tell me more, that wanker has been getting up my nose for years with his fancy pants parties and flash cars. Give me the gory details. Tell me about the tourist. He wasn't a pillow biter, I hope. He wasn't looking for it.'

'No,' replied Chub, 'he was a Portuguese tourist, walking with a young Frenchwoman. He was in national garb, but otherwise he was just taking in the sights.'

'National garb,' asked Joanne, 'what exactly do you mean. As far as I know the Portuguese dress in the same clothes we do.'

'Who gives a fuck, Joanne,' interposed Bear, 'you look as if you are just about to sit down for strawberries and cream at Wimbledon and nobody is commenting on your clobber.'

'Except you,' mouthed Joanne.

Bear ignored her and turned to Chub.

'The Portugee wasn't wearing a little frock and garters or lacy panties I hope, Chub.'

'No nothing like that,' replied Chub evenly, 'I have not met the man yet. All I know is what my snitch told me.'

'Well, fuck me dead, what a great front page. A fucking great earthquake in Bulgaria and one of the biggest arseholes in Gotham City grabbing a tourist by the balls. They are both in jail, you say Chub, does that mean the tourist belted the shitter out of Givens-Cater.'

'Yeah, he had to be dragged off him. He was apparently furious.'

'And when are you seeing the Portugee?' asked Bear.

'I will be seeing him immediately after he is bailed.'

'We could put up the money, Chub, I want an exclusive. I want Oliver Givens fucking Chater up in lights. We would have plenty of good file photos of him. We might even get one of him in a blazer and white strides.'

Bear waved vaguely towards Joanne, as if she was his inspiration for the photo idea.

'Bond trader - Oliver twisted. The subbies will have a ball thinking up bylines. Now I hope we have an exclusive, Chub. No sharing of this story. What is the bloke's name whose nuts were swaddled? Do we know anything about his background?'

'I have not researched his background yet, but I have spoken to his—,' Chub thought about this, 'mentor.'

'Mentor, what the fuck do you mean, Chub, what's a fucking mentor?' asked Bear.

'It's just that the Portuguese man is staying with the French girl and this other guy. I think the Portuguese fellow works for the other guy. The mentor is Jerry O', he is Irish.'

'Jerry O,' said Bear, 'what sort of fucking name is that, Jerry fucking O', is he a fucking rapper.'

'No I would say he is a mogul. I met him. He is at the Plaza. I took a snap of him with my iPhone, look'. Chub passed the iPhone to Bear.

Bear looked at the photo and appeared relieved.

'He looks like one of those fucking little leprechauns that run airlines all over the joint. He looks ok.'

'He would like to meet you, boss. He has invited us for dinner. He wants to take us to Alle tonight.'

'Alle, Alle, he wants to take us to Alle,' Bear was excited at the thought, 'the trouble is that Alle is booked out for six months.'

'This does not apply to Jerry O,' replied Chub, 'his servant Dora told me that a booking can be made for tonight. She has suggested Eight PM. I hope you can make it.'

'Alle! wild fucking brumbies would not stop me, Chub I'll be there all right.'

Chub had an idea which he expressed. 'I think Roger Sebastian ought to come along too, in case there is a literature angle and Joanne of course to look into this national costume business.' Chub was thinking of Roger and Charles Dickens meeting, which would be only a fraction more interesting than Joanne being introduced to Joan of Arc.

'The more the merrier,' said Bear, 'if your mate Jerry O' wants to take the editorial staff to Alle for a free dinner who am I to fucking complain.'

Chub noticed that a few of the other editors appeared slightly put out, but they held their peace. Gotby's pimply stringer seemed to be about to open his mouth, but Joanne laid a hand on his arm and he sat back quietly.

The meeting turned to other inconsequential matters, but just before it broke up Joanne Rixti looked over at Chub:

'You didn't tell us the name of the Portuguese man Chub.'

'Mr. De Gama,' Chub replied.

'Not Mr. V De Gama,' Joanne said.

'Fuck, Joanne,' exclaimed Bear, 'don't tell me you know him.'

'No,' she replied, 'but I might know of him.'

'Know of him, I suppose the bastard went to your brother school Harvard and was in fucking uppa, fucking bumma fucking sigma fraternity,' said Bear.

'I doubt it,' replied Joanne, 'and anyway Wellesley's brother school is M.I.T.'

'Well fuck me,' said Bear rising to leave, 'I don't care if it is M fucking T fucking A.'

Chub left as quickly as he could. He wished to avoid any further interrogation from Joanne.

Twenty-Eight

The Number One Banco Court in the Manhattan Criminal Court Complex was known amongst attorneys as the Coliseum. It was the court where all criminal cases commenced. The Coliseum was presided over by Judge Nola Kreuger. She was known amongst the eagles, not altogether affectionately, as Freddy.

Judge Kreuger was a tiny woman with steel grey hair ascending vertically from her crown. A courthouse wag described it once as the inverted toilet brush look. The Judge ruled her court with iron determination and in her pursuit of efficiency she took no prisoners if angered by a recalcitrant attorney or a disruptive defendant.

At any time between Nine AM and Four PM on any weekday, one would see a constant and ever changing stream of lawyers coming and going. Earnest, bespectacled young women from the Office of the District Attorney would joust with pale young men in cheap suits from the Public Defender's office. Occasionally a star would enter the arena. There would be a flurry of activity at the two rear doors and in would come a train of attorneys. There would be young lawyers wheeling trolleys of books and arch folders and four or five others carrying laptops. In the center would be the star. He or she would be perfectly coiffured and dressed in hand made designer threads. One could almost smell the money.

These entrances failed to impress Judge Freddy Kreuger. She treated the stars with the same tough single-mindedness she treated all lawyers. Not that the stars noticed. They were generally so wrapped up in their own self-importance, that they gave no consideration to their physical surroundings.

It was to the Banco Court that Jerry O' went to obtain the release of Vasco De Gama. He was accompanied by Calliope in his persona of Dora. Chub Checker was already in the otherwise empty press gallery when Jerry O' arrived and sat with Dora quietly in the back of the court.

Judge Kreuger was busy as usual dispensing justice. She either granted or refused bail depending on the circumstances. She fixed dates for trial to be heard by one of the other seventy-eight judges who sat in the court complex. She granted or refused applications for adjournment, heard minor interlocutory applications and approved plea deals.

Few judges enjoyed working the Coliseum. When Judge Kreuger took holidays, the Chief Judge could only find a replacement with an inducement of some kind, such as an opportunity for a study trip to Florida or an exchange with an out of state judge. Nola Kreuger, however, enjoyed the work. She was more bureaucrat than jurist and she knew it. She had come from the bowels of the Bronx to be a Superior Court Judge, and she was well satisfied with her achievement.

In her nine years in the Coliseum Judge Kreuger had pretty much seen everything. Each day produced trannies, gang bangers, rev heads and flashers. Mob connected killers mingled uneasily with sex offenders and fraudsters as justice was dispensed. A small army of mini-me clerks with the same haircut as the judge shifted the paper, organized the attorneys and lowered the hubbub. An army of warders brought prisoners and defendants backwards and forwards. Some of the litigants were heavily manacled and menacing, others were frightened as mice. Men were brought from the right-hand cells and women from the left. There were others of indeterminate sex who seemed to come from either door. The prisoners were brought up to the court six at a time. Judge Kreuger would deal with the six men in the cage. Those still in custody after the brief hearing would be removed and then another six would be brought up from the basement cells. While this was occurring, the judge would deal with the women. Germaine Greer would have been proud of the equal opportunity court being conducted. As it happened there were times when there were more women than men, due to the large number of female pickpockets, prostitutes and drug dealers who had taken over significant portions of downtown Manhattan.

Then there were the police. When a name was called a police officer would approach with the Assistant DA who was handling the matter. Both would take their place at the prosecution table. On the other side of the room an attorney would take his or her place at the defense table. If the client was not in custody the client would sit at the table with the lawyer. On the other hand, and more often, the customer was confined and would remain in the steel framed cage with the other five prisoners. The client would stand forward when his or her name was called, face almost touching the steel mesh window of the cage.

Sergeant Flanagan was looking after Vasco's case. When De Gama was called the sergeant sat behind Rose France the young ADA who was handling the case. Jerry O' walked forward and stood just behind the low swinging doors that separated the public gallery from the attorneys pit.

Rose France rose and spoke:

'Your Honor, this is a case which with your Honor's leave we can dispose of today. However, I wonder if you can have the next matter of Givens-Cater called as the matters may be best dealt with together.'.

'Call the Givens-Cater case,' said the Judge. Frequently deals were done which involved two defendants who had imparted misery of one kind or another on each other.

Oliver Givens-Cater name was called, and he stood forward next to Vasco who was holding himself in his usual proud manner.

Judge Kreuger looked over at the Defendants and looked again. Though she had seen all sorts, these two were newbies. She took a minute to open both files and find out the nature of the charges. She looked again at the Defendants, particularly Vasco.

But it was a big day. The Judge had better things to do than run a fashion exposition. She looked down at Rose France the ADA.

However, before Rose France could rise to commence speaking, the rear doors of the court opened and a caravan of attorneys marched in. There were no trollies or law books being carried. The energy was generated by the mass. Even the young men and women on the outer edges of the phalanx were as well suited and feline as catwalk models. In the center was the star. Melvin Van Horn wore a cream suit coupled with a pink and white guardsman striped shirt and a black silk tie adorned with a large pink flamingo. He was a large fleshy man. His tan looked permanent, as if perhaps his daylight hours were spent on the deck of an ocean-going yacht sailing in the Grand Bahamas.

Van Horn and his team arrived at the bar table. There was much tippy toeing and tooing and froing by the party while the seating arrangements were finalized.

Judge Kreuger watched the spectacle unfold with annoyance.

'I guess you act for Mr Givens-Cator Mr Van Horn. Are you quite organized. I am not running a dinner party here. There are no place settings.'

'I apologize Your Honor,' said Van Horn. He articulated as he looked. He had a deep sonorous tone. He spoke slowly and deliberately as if he wanted to personally savor every word he delivered.

'We act for Mr. Givens-Cator. He is a valued client of my firm, and we wish to give him every available assistance we can in resolving the present situation.'

The judge had acute perception. Van Horn spoke of his appearance using the royal 'we 'and his firm using the common 'I'. She knew Van Horn of old. He was your typical high priced over egged Wall Street turkey whose actual ability and perceived reputation would not recognize one another if they passed in the street. She was tempted to use some sarcasm to bring him down a peg, but she had too much work to do to waste time on him. She looked at Jerry O'.

'Do you represent Mr. De Gama?' she asked him.

'No Your Honor, I am an associate of his. I am just here to be of assistance if needed. I am not an attorney.

The judge had visited Ireland the year before with her husband to hike the wild Irish West Coast. She had a soft spot for the Irish. She liked the look of Jerry O'. She liked his lilt. He had been courteous and restrained [unlike Van Horn] and was well dressed in an informal way. The judge had another look at Van Horn.

'A fucking flamingo,' she thought.

She addressed Jerry O':

'You may sit at the table, Sir, next to Mr. Van Horn. What is your name, please?'

'I am Jerry O,' said Jerry.

He sat at the table and took Van Horn's hand from its resting place on the bar table and to the annoyance of the lawyer shook it warmly.

Calliope was concerned that he was separated from Jerry O' and no longer able to advise him. He decided to act. Dora became undetectable, much to the surprise of the person who had been sitting next to her. Calliope moved to the bar table and sat between Van Horn and Jerry O'. Jerry O' noticed and simply moved a fraction. Calliope had taken an immediate dislike to the big white suited attorney, so he entered him for an instant which caused him to suddenly squeal and momentarily spasm.

'Are you all right, Mr. Van Horn?' said Judge Krueger without much concern.

Van Horn nodded weakly. He would seek medical treatment the second this case was over. Was it a tumor, or epilepsy? Did he need a break? A trip, a sail, a ski, his wife or his mistress who shall he take? All these thoughts slipped in and out of the Van Horn id.

'Miss France,' the Judge looked down at the ADA who commenced her submissions'

'Your Honor, Mr. De Gama is a tourist, a visitor from Portugal. Mr. Givens-Cator is a New Yorker. Mr. De Gama was strolling through Central Park with a lady friend when they crossed paths with Mr. Givens-Cator. Apparently, some words were exchanged. In the aftermath Mr. Givens-Cator grabbed Mr. De Gama by the testes. Mr. De Gama became angry and struck back. It is the State's case that the force used by Mr. De Gama was excessive, therefore both men have been charged with assault. Neither party wishes to proceed with a complaint against the other. There are some independent witnesses. They were bystanders, but in the absence of the two protagonists' evidence, the State has concluded that the best way of dealing with the matter is to have both sets of charges dropped'.

'Was there a sexual element to the charge Miss France?' asked Her Honour. 'I am concerned that a visitor to our country should be assaulted in such a highly offensive way.'

'Your Honor,' said Van Horn, 'my client is a highly successful bond trader on Wall Street.'

'Yes,' replied the Judge, 'but that does not give him the right to go around grasping the gonads of tourists. Miss France was there a sexual element to the assault by Mr. Van Horn's bond trader?'

'The State does not believe there was any sexual or predatory element to the assault. It was simply stupidity.' The pert Rose France looked over at Oliver sweetly.

Givens-Cator glared at her.

'And what about the girl who was with this man,' said Givens-Cator interrupting the proceedings, 'she kicked me.'

'Did she break any bones?' asked Judge 'Freddy' Krueger.

'No,' replied Givens-Cator, shaking his head.

'Well, you're lucky,' said the Judge, 'both sets of charges are dismissed. Thank you for attending Mr. O and Mr. Van Horn you might tell your client that in future he should trade only in pearl mollusks such as Ballon or Blue Point and leave other people's prairie oysters alone. Discharge the prisoners. Call the next case.'

Vasco De Gama and Oliver Givens-Cator were both released. Givens-Cator ignored the outstretched De Gama hand. Jerry O' and Vasco left through the rear door. The Van Horn phalanx regrouped to leave, now with the addition of their client Oliver Givens-Cator. Calliope could not resist, so before he hurried off to join Jerry O' and Vasco he entered Van Horn again causing the fancy pants lawyer to double over in pain, before being assisted out of the court by two of his young assistants.

Chub Checker observed the proceedings happily from the still empty press gallery. Van Horn had foolishly identified his client with a juicy job description, and the judge made some lovely bon mots. Chub had an exclusive, oh happy day.

Twenty-Nine

After Jerry O' had left the Plaza with Calliope to bring home Vasco De Gama from the courthouse, both Charles Dickens and Joan of Arc left the Plaza Suite.

They left separately and without consultation.

Joan was first to leave. She had enjoyed her first excursion with De Gama until the pervert American assaulted her fellow visitor. She wanted to see more. She wished to investigate shop windows and take in the manners and comportment of the New York population. It is true that she had some trepidation. The reality personalities she had observed on television were mostly knuckle dragging brutes and trollops. Surely, she thought, all humans cannot be like this.

Charles Dickens was eager to find a bookshop. Were humans still reading his fiction? Who were the modern authors and what was their subject matter? He heard the front door of the suite close and left his study to investigate. He found the place deserted. It would cause no harm, he thought, to take a brief stroll.

Joan walked out the front door of the hotel and after strolling a short distance she found herself in 5th Avenue. She walked slowly. She stopped at store fronts taking in the clothes dummies clad in their finery. Joan herself was dressed in her steel chain mesh halter which she wore over her brown hessian full length robe. She wore a wolf fur hood which attached to the back of the halter by a wooden button. Joan drew some attention, but there were numerous other equally bizarre sights on 5th Avenue on that day. There were men in pants which fell beneath their butt cheeks showing unpleasant hairy cleavage. There were young women who were hardly dressed at all. There were toothless beggars and police on horseback.

Joan watched and wondered. She was most of all absorbed by the middle-aged women who paraded along the Avenue. There seemed to be many who were so emaciated to be skeletal. Joan felt sorry for these creatures. She decided they must be so poor that they cannot afford food. On the other hand, there were both men and women who were so fat they waddled like pregnant ducks and wheezed mightily as they plodded down the street. Joan would have been mystified to find that the thin women were generally rich beyond her wildest dreams, and the blubbery humans were often paupers.

Two men walked towards Joan. It was clear they were talking about her. One was a slight red-haired man wearing a lime green hairy sweater and black skintight pants adorned with bright yellow lizards. His hair was gel spiked to make it appear as if he had just suffered from an acute case of the heebie-jeebies. The other man was as hairless as a seal. He was dressed from head to foot in black plastic and every obvious orifice was embellished by a ring or bauble.

Joan watched the men approaching and readied herself to fight them off. 'Brigands', she muttered to herself. Sandalphon had been following Joan from the Plaza. He clutched her arm and whispered 'they are harmless' to his charge. Sandalphon remained invisible. He was, unlike Calliope, an angel who preferred to remain in the shadows. He was also conscious that his path was tortuous. He served two masters. His heart rested with Joan, but he owed his job security to Gabriel.

The men became near and the red head spoke:

'Oh you gorgeous creature, we just love your style. It is so Ann Sui. Tell us please tell us, who is your designer. He must be French; you are just so chic.'

Joan of Arc did not have the faintest idea what the man was talking about but he did not seem to be an enemy. She did hear the French mentioned and she replied.

'The French burned me, I have no time for the Burgundians.'

'Oh.' the red haired man said, 'the French are so awful. They burn everybody. I suppose they just stole the patterns, but you have not told us who is your designer.'

Joan, thought 'designer', what did the man mean? He must mean the Creator.

'I am with Jerry O.' she replied, 'he is Irish, but he is really the son of the Big Feller.'

'Oh my God Armani.' the man said, 'Jerry O' is the bastard son of Giorgio Armani. Oh, this is too much. I am Ginger Scollop and this is my co-producer Tweak Monk.'

Sandalphon was horrified and thought transferred to Joan. /you have said too much Joan, no more about Paradise, no more about the Big Feller.'

Joan heeded his words but she was angered by the man's false charge.

'You strange fish, withdraw your claim or be dead, Jerry O' is no bastard son. And who is this Armani and why does he claim to be a God. I will cut out his tongue if I find he is circulating such vicious lies.'

Tweak Monk was clearly frightened by Joan and cowered behind his red headed cohort, but Ginger Scollop was undeterred.

'Look we meant no harm and I agree Armani is over rated. All we want is the chance to meet Jerry O'. We love his style. We may be able to do business with him.'

Joan was not sure what sort of business, this pair were talking about, but she decided it could do no harm.

'We are staying at the Plaza Hotel. Jerry O is not there, He has gone to get the Portuguese man De Gama', she paused and looked the two men over carefully.

'But,' she said, 'I think you are both poltroons and you may well be cock suckers.'

'You had better believe it,' replied Ginger Scollop.

Sandalphon decided it was time for Joan to go and he willed her back to the Plaza where she settled down to watch a new episode of Jerseylicious.

Ginger and Tweak were mystified by her sudden disappearance, but were looking forward to meeting Jerry O', the brilliant Irish couturier. They wondered who the Portuguese person De Gama was, perhaps he was Jerry O's lover, or better still, the latest fashion sensation from Lisbon.

Charles Dickens by chance took a different route. In his quest for a book shop, he walked along East 60th Street to Madison Avenue and walked North. He soon came upon a large chain store book shop and record bar. He entered and approached the counter where a scruffy looking acne damaged young man was sorting compact discs.

'Sir,' said Charles, 'I am looking for Charles Dickens' works. Can you direct me.'

Charles was wearing his usual velvet long coat and leggings, but this garb was not particularly striking compared to some of the other oddities that peopled modern day Manhattan.

The young shop assistant thought for a few seconds.

'I do not know any Charles Dickens, but there is a Little Jimmy Dickens who sings Traditional Country Music. You will find him over there in the CD section.'

Charles realized there must be some misunderstanding.

'No,' he said, 'Dickens is a writer. You may have heard of David Copperfield.'

'The magician,' the shop assistant replied, 'try biographies.'

'No Dickens is a novelist. Have you heard of Great Expectations.'

'Ah yes.' said the boy, 'now I remember try TV adaptations. I remember that show now.'

Charles was a patient man, but this young man was sorely testing him.

'Bleak House,' Dickens said.

'Now them I know,' responded acne face, 'they are a Detroit group. Wow man, they are great. Try under Funk.'

Charles Dickens wandered off in confusion. He walked over to the capacious book section of the shop. There were no customers, but a bespectacled young girl was placing books on shelves. She wore a badge which read 'How can I help you. I am Jodie.' Charles approached her and she turned to face him. He read the badge and spoke.

'I am looking for Charles Dickens books Jodie, can you help me.'

'I think,' she replied thinking aloud, ['you will find them under Young Adults, but they might be under School Texts or Popular Classics.']

Charles considered her answer.

'So they would not be amongst your Older Adults section.'

'There is no Older Adults section,' she replied.

Jodie put her pile of books down and led Charles to the innards of the book shop. She found David Copperfield under School Texts. Dombey and Son and Little Dorrit were stored under Popular Classics and Great Expectations was in the General Fiction section. Charles took them all and for good measure bought a CD of the funk group Bleak House. Jodie told him to take his basket of goods back to the counter where Charles used his credit card for the first time. He had been given careful instructions by Mohammed as to its use and Dickens found the transaction easy to conduct.

Charles left the shop and headed back to the Plaza.

The book shop manager had been out to a book fair and when he returned, he asked the spotty shop boy whether there had been much custom.

'Not much,' said the boy, 'except for an old guy who bought a load of books by a guy called Charles Dickens. He was an odd dude he was dressed funny.'

The manager looked through the credit card receipts and found Charles receipt. He noticed his beautiful copper plate signature. The manager looked up Dickens on the web. He found an ancient gravure photo of Charles Dickens in Wikipedia. The manager turned the screen to the shop assistant without comment.

'That's him boss,' the boy exclaimed.

Thirty

The Big Feller was in a contemplative frame of mind. He was sitting at his desk but had swiveled his chair to face the window. He had a view over the garden, but the Big Feller was more interested in the Citadel which dominated the right-hand side of the property.

Necessary but annoying, was the Big Feller's unspoken thought. Gabriel had been back to see him with his miserly accountant Metatron. Gabriel had been complaining about Calliope making a requisition for new clothing for his party and the costs of dinner for eight at a fancy New York restaurant called Alle. The Big Fellow knew little about modern restaurant costs on earth. Cost, after all, was determined by demand. If a human was prepared to pay the cost, then the cost was value. If the cost was too high, there would be no custom. The Big Feller had simply established the law of supply and demand. It was part of nature, and he did not interfere with nature.

There was another issue that Gabriel harped on. That is what angels did they harped. The Creator thought again of the archangel's second gripe. What was it again - Calliope was making decisions outside his brief. And how did Gabriel know this? Gabriel told him Sandalphon happened to be in the vicinity.

The Big Feller did not buy that nonsense. He knew Sandalphon was Joan of Arc's angel. He was, no doubt, acting as either a double agent or an informer for Gabriel.

As the Big Feller told Mohammed, Gabriel could not win an argument with him. The Big Feller ran the show, but the archangel apparently believed that constant carping may gain him some concessions.

Calliope was a bit of a wild card, but he meant well and he always got there in the end. The Big Fellow wished he was a touch more organized and punctual, but you cannot have everything. Calliope had a lot more initiative than Metatron and was not as dizzy as Uriel.

The Big Fellow told Gabriel fairly peremptorily that Calliope was acting within the scope of his instructions though at times he apparently was forced to improvise. He also told Gabriel that he must realize that humans acted upon emotion as often as on logic and Calliope had to take this into account. He ended the conversation by telling his chief angel that everything was going to plan and he was presently well satisfied.

Gabriel and Metatron left in their usual shuffling whispering way, muttering to each other about their nemesis Calliope.

Yes, the Big Fellow said again, they were annoying but necessary.

He left Mohammed to sort out the new clothing and its delivery. He would message Calliope to organize delivery of the gear to the hotel. Mohammed had taken on the task with enthusiasm. For Dickens there was to be a brown velvet coat, with a fancy silk brocade vest, a black silk neck scarf and black and white houndstooth plus fours into which were tucked black silk stockings. Charles was also provided with ankle boots of the finest Spanish leather. Boots of Spanish Leather - the Big Fellow was reminded of the human folk singer Bob Dylan who he enjoyed listening to so much. He had come to like him during the time he said he found God, but the Big Fellow had to admit the Jewish warbler had improved his song writing since he had left religion in his wake.

Vasco De Gama was to be clothed in scarlet. A scarlet tunic, over scarlet pantaloons with contrasting navy silk hose and scarlet patent kid shoes with large gold clasps.

The girl Joan was to be in a new steel mesh chain mail doublet worn above a forest green gaberdine wool ankle length gown. Her shoes were to be new forest clogs carved from a sapling of yellow maple.

Wilfred would be in a new black suit with his usual crisp white shirt.

It was the hats that were causing Mohammed the most concern. He had come in from time to time with fresh designs and swatches of possible material. In the end he had decided on a simple homburg for Charles Dickens, a high scarlet tri-corner with a bunch of white plumage for Vasco and a round white linen skull cap for Joan of Arc with a back gauze veil which trailed to her waist. The Big Fellow said to Mohammed,

"Fine work Mohammed, if the Burgundians had seen the girl in this costume they might have thought twice about burning her at the stake."

Mohammed was well pleased with the compliment and happily contacted Calliope to arrange for the delivery of the clothing.

Thirty-One

Ginger Scollop and Tweak Monk had repaired to Granny's Bar and Trattoria on East 49th Street for a libation to celebrate their chance meeting with Joan of Arc.

'Jerry O,' said Ginger to Tweak, 'what a great moniker for an Irish dress designer. It is just so clever and Chi-Chi. The 'O' is so savvy. Think Jackie O meets Lisdoonvarna.'

Tweak Monk never said much. He claimed this was because he was the weak silent type. The reality was that Tweak Monk was pretty much devoid of original thought. The more he said the more this became obvious. At least he was sensible enough to largely keep stuhm.

The two men worked the fringes of the New York rag trade. They were notionally documentary film makers, but most of their work was freelance photo shoots of unknown or unfashionable designers. Tweak was the better photographer, but Ginger was the front man. His brand of ebullience actually appealed to some of the 7th Avenue pea brains. Still and all they were only a step or two above paparazzi and they knew it.

Ginger Scollop sipped his Tequila Orgasm, which was a violent yellow snot color and was decorated with a paper umbrella fork to which were attached three Maraschino cherries. Tweak Monk made do with a Heineken.

A red-faced bluff man with an unpleasant waxed mustache approached.

'Hi boys,' he said in a surprisingly high-pitched campy voice, 'any big news from your neck of the woods?'

'Karl,' replied Ginger, 'it's good to see you. How is Alle? Still packing them in?'

Karl Kouvousier pulled up a stool and perched between Ginger and Tweak.

'It's high farce really,' he replied, 'we serve sparrow size portions of faux French bullshit fare and the fuckers can't get enough of it. We are booked solid for nearly six months. We put more bums on seats than Yankee Stadium at one hundred times the price.'

'The food is supposed to be better at Yankee Stadium,' retorted Ginger, 'I just love their hot dogs, with pickle, onion and ketchup.'

'You've got it,' said Karl, 'but the money is good. For some reason every fucker who enters Alle sticks a ten dollar note in my mitt. As if the Matre'd has anything to do with the seating plans. It's all done by a computer these days. My only problem is Ally Oop.'

'Gone to his head,' asked Ginger. Alley Oop was the nickname of the Iranian owner-chef of Alle. His real name was Omar Fagdour, but he spoke passable French and falsely claimed a French mother with a fine cooking pedigree. He had written a cookbook, conducted a cooking program on the Food Channel and was the Executive Chef of a small airline. He had rejected the opportunity to take tourists on a cook's tour of Provence, as he sensibly realized the French would quickly spot a fake.

'Gone to his head,' exclaimed Karl, 'Alley Oop is a poncing prancing prick. If I was not making so much loot, I would smack his behind.'

'If you are intent on spanking someone, you might give Tweak and I first right of refusal.'

This comment from Ginger brought hearty laughter from the three men.

Karl bought himself a neat Belvedere Vodka and a round for Tweak and Ginger. They made small talk about the vagaries of the rag trade when Ginger Scollop remembered his chance meeting with Joan of Arc that morning.

'You get the A list in Alle, Karl, have you ever heard of an Irish designer called Jerry O'. He has a great new look. Sort of Ann Sui and dominatrix wrapped up in new peasant. We met his model. Gorgeous little waif of a girl, but tough as all hell. Tweak here was cowering behind my skirt. He was so terrified I thought he was going to do wee wees. This Jerry O' is staying at the Plaza. The girl is staying there with him. He is probably rogering her, but who knows.'

'Jerry O,' said Karl, 'now that is an amazing coincidence. He is booked in tonight with a party of eight. He has booked the fishbowl. It is our private glassed in area smack bang in the middle of the room. It is where we used to put Brangelina when they were in town. The funny thing is that the booking has seemed to come out of nowhere. Up until this morning I thought some lawyer hot shot called Van Horn had it booked it for his wife's birthday and today his booking has gone and Jerry O' has the fishbowl. I guess the arsehole attorney must have cancelled and Jerry O's timing was exactly right. Does Jerry O' do men's clobber? From your description of his women's gear, it sounds fabulous. I am imagining cavorting around a loft in SoHo or TriBeCa with a whip dressed in chain mail chasing somebody on all fours with his bare buttocks pointing to the top of the Empire State. Oh, I can see his face. It is Tweak.'

Ginger laughed heartily, but Tweak simply smiled weakly. He had been whipped before and the pleasure of the moment was subsumed by the angry welts that caused pain for days.

'Would there be the slightest, the tiniest chance of a table tonight,' pleaded Ginger, 'I would adore to meet Jerry O'. I am sure that the model will remember meeting us.'

Karl looked the men up and down.

'I am sure she will remember you two. There are no tables, but I can get you seats at the bar. Turn up about eight fifteen and wear jackets. Now I better get going. If I am one-minute late Alley Oop throws a tanty.'

Karl downed his vodka and left Granny's. Ginger and Tweak decided a celebratory round was in order.

Back at the Royal Plaza suite all was quiet. The four visitors were resting in anticipation of the important dinner they were attending. Jerry O' had brought Vasco home who behaved as if he had done something heroic. Charles Dickens told Jerry O' he had ventured out. He showed the group his purchases. He even played the first track from Bleak House's album, but all agreed that it was cacophonous and unpleasant. Joan did not mention leaving the suite. She was concerned she had said too much to the two poltroons, but the likelihood was they would never be seen again. She hoped as much.

Whilst the group was unwinding, Dora was laying out their clothing in readiness for the evening. She was whistling softly. Dora was well satisfied with her work today. Calliope had gone to Alle and inserted the booking in the system. It was a pleasant surprise for him to realize that the reservation he was undoing belonged to Melvin Van Horn. Calliope had not liked Van Horn or his execrable client Oliver Givens-Cator.

Dora finished her handiwork. She looked at the clothing laid out around the main room. Mohammed had excelled himself in his selection.

Thirty-Two

The Alle staff were readying themselves for the night ahead. The restaurant was in the center of Irving Place amongst the myriad of dining options in the trendy thoroughfare overlooking Gramercy Park. A small army of waiters stood at the chef's bar tasting the specials of the night and learning the spiel required to sell the dishes to customers. Omar Fagdour was their instructor. He was regimental sergeant major as well as master chef. He inspected each waiter to ensure their black aprons were starched and clean, their black and white chalk stripe shirts were pressed, and their black and brown club striped ties were immaculately Windsor knotted. He examined their shoes. He checked their hair. He satisfied himself that there was no facial jewelry adorning anyone. When Omar was sure the team was ready, he sent them to their stations. Each station served eight tables and was looked after by three waiters, a busboy and a captain. There were forty-eight tables which served one hundred and eighty-four people nightly per sitting. There were two sittings. One was at 5.30PM and the other at 8.00PM. The early sitting had to vacate by 7.30PM. The early sitting comprised largely tourists. Bookings were taken and advance payments made from such places as Sydney,

Prague and Casablanca. All were told of the strict dress code. Men had to wear jackets. Jeans were forbidden unless one was a movie star.

Omar Faghdour had escaped from Iran when he was Fourteen. He hitched a leaky boat to Djibouti where he worked for an ancient French crone serving brilliant Provencal food to coarse expatriates from goodness knows where. Omar saved his money and took a flight to the USA. He cooked his way across the country, learning the nuances of taste and preparation.

He now knew to temper his flavors and brighten the colors of the dishes. He realized his market preferred style to substance, and he cooked to his market. Omar Faghdour was a frugal man, so here he was, after humble beginnings, the owner-chef of the most sought-after dinner table in New York. The restaurant was housed in an old livery and stables. It had served its time as a themed Elizabethan restaurant before Omar bought the building. He gutted it. The street front now was a heavy wrought iron fence, behind which was an elegant finely trimmed hedge. Inside the broad gateway was a cobblestone paving yard where cars were dropped off to be valet parked by three muscled drivers. Omar was exceedingly security conscious, so the drivers served as security guards. If thieves struck, the guards were expected to leap into action. Omar was not so much worried about the takings. These days much was pre-paid and the rest were largely credit card transactions. The Iranian was more concerned for the valuables and security of his well-heeled customers in their jewels, finery and Patek Phillipe Watches.

The restaurant was now a large rectangular space. At the front was a cloakroom and a curved oak bar. A black silk screen and reception desk stood between the bar and the main restaurant space. Plush burgundy banquettes lined each side of the room and tables were dotted about the center area. In the very middle of the room was a circular glass enclosed space in which there was one round table. It was called the Fishbowl and was the preferred hangout for celebrities who wanted to be seen but not buttonholed. The open kitchen was at the rear of the room. It lay behind a blue and red travertine bar which shone and sparkled with the understated elegance provided by its subtle in-floor lighting.

The first sitting was uneventful. When the last tourist left, the waiters quickly re-laid tables and polished glassware. The busboys filled water jugs. The chefs prepared appetizers and julienned vegetables. Karl Kouvousier checked and re-checked the bookings and gave instructions to the hostesses and Omar surveyed his domain from the chef's pass with satisfaction. He looked forward to a profitable and smooth evening.

Calliope made sure his charges were on time. He had booked a Plaza limousine to make certain there was no repetition of the unfortunate contretemps he had with the taxi driver on their arrival at the hotel.

The group were at the door promptly at Five minutes to Eight PM and Karl himself showed them to the Fishbowl. There were a few other early birds, and they watched the group make their entry. Omar Faghdour or Alley Oop as he was known when he became angry buzzed Karl on the intercom.

'What the fuck is going on, Karl, you have just seated a man dressed in a red mini skirt and a girl who looks as if she is just about to invade Lithuania.'

Karl had been waiting for the outburst. He was ready for it.

'Chef,' he said, 'the chap in the dark suit is Jerry O' the famous Irish dress designer. The other guests are modeling the new seasons styles. I personally think it is marvelous. The man in scarlet does have a jacket. It is just a short jacket. The girl looks fabulous. I predict next year this place will be full of people wearing Jerry O.'

'I am selling up,' replied Omar, who was still not comfortable with what he saw, but did nothing as the strange menagerie might bring him more publicity, another cookbook perhaps and best of all a worldwide cable series. He went back to checking and distributing the orders that were starting to dribble in.

Bear Grizzard, Joanne Rixti, Roger Sebastian Keats and Chub Checker got to Alle at Ten past Eight. Karl led them to the Fishbowl. Bear slipped a ten-dollar bill to Karl as was customary. Calliope did not know this and consequently Jerry O' had not tipped the Maitre'D. When Calliope saw Bear hand over the money, he quickly palmed a ten dollar bill of his own. Kouvousier suddenly found he had twenty dollars. He had felt the second bill placed in his hand. He turned to see the gift bearer, but there was nobody. He shrugged and went back to his desk.

The Van Horn party arrived at Twenty past Eight. Melvin believed fashionable lateness was a sign of sophistication. His party had spent the last two hours eating canapés and drinking Krug at his Park Avenue three story walk up. It was the lawyer's wife's birthday and tonight's celebration and the exquisite Tiffany brooch he had given her would compensate her for the week she would have to do without him whilst he went fishing off Grand Cayman. He was taking his mistress, but his wife did not need to know this. There was a last-minute addition to Van Horn's Alle party. It was the wealthy Wall Street bond trader Oliver Givens-Cator who had just been cleared of serious criminal charges by dint of the Van Horn brilliance - or so the story was told.

Karl told Van Horn the bad news in his best deferential, but firm way:

'But Sir,' he said, 'you cancelled. I am afraid we cannot accommodate you. We are booked out for months and the Fishbowl is rarely available.'

At first, Van Horn pleaded his case. He tried a vague threat of calling journalists. He became angry. Other arrivals were starting to congregate behind Van Horn and were murmuring about delay and poor form.

Karl moved the lawyer's group to one side preparatory to ordering the party to leave, but unfortunately at that moment Oliver Givens-Cator caught sight of Vasco De Gama and vice versa,

De Gama rose from his chair in the Fishbowl and strode to the edge of the glass wall nearest the bond trader. He grabbed his amply filled crotch and thrust it at Givens Cator. The bond trader began rushing towards the Fishbowl. Karl pressed his security buzzer and two of the guards ran into Alle. Karl pointed at Givens-Cator, and he was taken by the arm pits and frog marched out. He was shouting "and it's the girl;

it's the girl who kicked me". Over his shoulder he could observe Joan of Arc next to Vasco mouthing the words 'cock sucker' at him. The bewildered Van Horn commenced to leave. Calliope momentarily entered Van Horn causing him to scream in pain. His wife and another guest helped him out to his waiting limousine.

Peace was restored. Guests continued to arrive. Chub Checker explained to Bear and the others that Givens-Cator was the pervert who had assaulted De Gama yesterday. Bear was pleased by the turn of events

'This evening is going to be a huge success,' he said, 'I can feel it in my bones.'

At the Chef's pass Omar had seen the scuffle, but it was over in seconds and when Vasco and Joan were teasing Oliver, they had their backs to him.

'Anything I need to know?' he asked Karl.

'No,' replied Karl, 'just an over lubricated man without a booking.' Karl looked into the Fishbowl with fascination. He had taken note of the massive De Gama lump and liked what he saw.

A problem emerged during the ordering. Joan of Arc had been excited to hear that this was a French restaurant. She consequently ordered her meal in French. Unfortunately, the waiter had never been west of the Brooklyn Bridge and did not have the faintest idea what she was talking about. She reverted to English.

'You have frog legs I see,' she said.

'Yes, I mean oui,' said the waiter, ['they come all the way from Brittany.']

'Good I will have this dish, but I would like the whole frog,' said Joan who was used to living rough whilst on the run from the Burgundians.

'No, no, Madam, we only have the legs. We do not have the rest of the frog.'

'So you kill French frogs, cut off their legs and ship them to the New World, nothing has changed.' Joan was satisfied she had made her point.

De Gama was persuaded to have steak and Charles Dickens and Jerry O' ordered without difficulty.

The food arrived. Wine was ordered. Vasco was dissuaded by Jerry O' from swigging the bottle from behind his hand and Calliope whisked about placing the correct utensils in the correct hands. Calliope was kicking himself. He should have realized that the visitors would have trouble with modern customs. Sandalphon was watching from the bar. He shook his head in disgust. Calliope had no attention for detail.

When Vasco finished his T Bone steak, he threw the bones over his shoulder onto the floor. He called the waiter over.

'Where are the dogs?' De Gama asked, 'they should be here. There should be sawdust, where is the sawdust.'

The waiter left the area and sought help from his captain. The captain intercommed Karl who went straight into the Fishbowl. By then Calliope had taken things in hand and removed the bones. Vasco, in turn, had settled down to talk to his neighbor the beauteous Joanne Rixti. Karl saw no bones and left the area.

'You are a fine young trollop,' Vasco said to Joanne, 'I will rut you later.'

'I doubt it,' she replied. Joanne was not categoric, as she too had seen the De Gama crotch lump.

Charles Dickens was intrigued by his companion Roger Sebastian Keats.

'And you are a relative of the young romantic poet?' he asked.

At first Roger Sebastian gave his usual palaver, but Dickens probed.

'So your grandmother was a relative, how then do you bear the name. I take it your grandfather was of another family?'

Dickens was not trying to catch his neighbor out. He was merely interested in tracing the ancestry of the man.

Dickens spoke:

'Pensive they sit, and roll their languid eyes,
Nibble their toast, and cool their tea with sighs,
Or else forget the purpose of the night,
Or else forget their tea- forget their appetite.
See with cross'd arms they sit - ah! happy crew.'

After Dickens finished the verse he waited for a response, but there was none. Roger Sebastian Keats had never heard the words of 'A Party of Lovers' before and if he had he would not have known it was written by his alleged forebear. Charles Dickens was, on the other hand, satisfied. His knowledge of his famous relative had seemed to floor the man next to him. The man seemed so overcome he was lost for words.

Chub, for a change, was drinking in the various conversations rather than just drinking. Joan was also perusing the scene carefully. She had found the food unsatisfying. She decided the frogs must have been underfed little blighters. 'Like the women here,' she noted, as many of the women in the body of the restaurant were gaunt and skeletal.

Bear Grizzard took a deep draught of South Africa's finest Syrah. Time to get down to business.

'I want to talk to you, Jerry O', about the assault in the park when your friend Vasco, is it, got mauled by that prick Oliver Givens-Cator. Fortunately, I had my phone with me so I got a good picture of the fucker running at us tonight. Fucking front page tomorrow - I can see it now - out Alle Out Oliver - it will say. Fucking brilliant. Now what is the deal Jerry O', how much are you asking for the story?'

Jerry O' thought for a moment, he decided there was no point in mincing words.

'I am not an Irishman, Mr Bear, I am not trying to sell a story, I am the son of the Big Feller, I come here to warn you about your world.'

Jerry O' paused to collect his thoughts.

'Son of the Big Feller' thought Bear Grizzard. 'Did Rupert Murdoch have an Irish wife'?'

'Look the girl is Joan of Arc, the fellow in red is Vasco De Gama, the other man is Charles Dickens. We are here from Paradise to warn you.'

Jerry O' had risen and was speaking to the table.

'Your world is in danger of self-destructing, the human condition is corrupt, evil flourishes and good is weakening. This is your last chance. The Big Feller wants to make this clear. That is why the four of us are here.'

'And what about the black woman?' Chub asked.

'You mean me,' said Dora, suddenly appearing for an instant, but only an instant.

'This is a giant truck load of bullshit,' said Bear Grizzard, 'I do not know how you performed your illusions. I do not know nor fucking care how you made the Black woman come and go. I am here to buy an exclusive about that cock sucker Oliver Givens-Cator.'

Joan nodded her head in agreement, 'you are correct that is my view of him too.'

Jerry O' remained on his feet.

'Look,' he said, 'I can do party tricks. Dora can come and go, but I understand you want some tangible evidence that I am not from this earth. I can give you a miracle, but I am not here to turn water into wine. Ask me to do something you believe cannot be done. However, I emphasize, it must be a just and modest wish.'

'Ok,' said Bear, 'put His Honor the Mayor of New York Billy Lowe in jail tomorrow. He is a corrupt arsehole. He has been a thief from the moment he became a union official thirty years ago. He treats the city's money as if it is his personal piggy bank.'

'That is a fair and reasonable request, Mr Bear. It shall be done and in return will you tell my story.'

'Sir, if you put the arsehole in jail, you will be the front page of every paper in the world. But there is a condition that I wish to impose.'

'Yes,' said Jerry O'

'The four of you have a medical examination.'

'The five,' interposed Chub.

'No not the five you fucker Chub, I am not going to make an appointment for a sometime invisible black sheila to see a quack.'

Bear took another draught of the Syrah. He wondered for a moment if he was hallucinating. Could this whole evening be a dream or nightmare.

The restaurant was emptying. The Fishbowl was, of course, soundproof, but it was visible to all. There were two disheveled figures in the darkest corner of the bar. Ginger Scollop and Tweak Monk had watched every moment of the activity within the Fishbowl. They were some distance away and the lighting was diffuse, but they were both shaken when Dora came and went so suddenly. They put it down to the lighting. It must have been a shadow. They had taken in the clothing of the party with mounting excitement. Tweak had taken some photos. They muttered the words 'renaissance kick butt' to one another as this was their best description of Jerry O's creations.

The master chef had seen the last Creme Brûlée through the pass and as was his custom he wandered through the emptying dining room taking the deserved plaudits of the crowd. He walked into the Fishbowl. Joanne, Roger Sebastian and Chub clapped. After a moment Jerry O' and Charles Dickens joined in. Omar noticed that Joan of Arc and Vasco De Gama were not applauding. The chef walked over to Joan.

'Was everything satisfactory?' he asked her.

'I think if you are serving frog, particularly French frogs you should serve the whole frog. If you did, some of the skinny women who eat here may be fattened up.'

Omar looked around for a hidden camera. Was a reality TV show being filmed in the Fishbowl. He saw nothing and found himself in front of De Gama.

'And the steak, Sir, I believe you had the T Bone. Was it to your satisfaction.'

'Excellent.' replied Vasco, 'but you must tell me what type of horse was cooked, was it mare or stallion. I can tell the creature had not been gelded. The taste of a de-balled horse is sour. Also, the hair was removed in a most efficient way. I did not find one hair on the plate. My only complaint is that there were no dogs, forget the sawdust, but there should be dogs and a spittoon. Give a man wine and food and there will be slobber and spittle as night follows day.'

Omar retreated in confusion leaving the door open so Ginger Scollop and Tweak Monk took their chance. They rushed into the Fishbowl. They wore the same clothes they wore this morning, but each had added a moth-eaten blue blazer bought for five dollars each at a Times Square stall. They ran towards Jerry O'. They stopped short of him and bowed their heads.

'Jerry O',' said Ginger Scollop, 'your designs are not of this earth. Can we follow you? Can we be your servants?'

'Good work,' said Jerry O' directing his comment to the faint shimmer of Calliope in a corner of the fishbowl, 'we have our first two disciples.'

Calliope shrugged his shoulders. It seemed there was an unintended consequence. Sandalphon, back at the bar, shook his angelic head in disgust. 'This farce can be laid directly at the wings of Calliope'.

Even Joan was surprised.

'The sself-confessed cock suckers are now our disciples,' she thought the words but did not speak them.

The party left. The Plaza Suite crowd got into the waiting limousine and the journalists, including Joanne Rixti, hopped into a cab. Joanne had decided that she had slept with enough weirdoes without getting involved with Vasco De Gama or worse still, a man who thought he was Vasco De Gama. The massive lump of Portuguese crutch that she had observed was interesting, but not that interesting.

Thirty-Three

CHARLES DICKENS JOURNAL

Much has happened since I last scribbled. I write in my study. There is a pale cool sunlight which provides a slight burnish to the room. Unfortunately, I suffer from a headache. I rarely drink alcohol, but I found I much enjoyed the Syrah from South Africa last night at Alle. It was peppery yet crisp. It rivaled the Shiraz wines from Bordeaux that I have tippled and was a good deal better than the robust but malodorous Italian red wines.

When Jerry O' left to collect Vasco from jail after our friend's unfortunate escapade, I took the liberty of going for a constitutional. Quite frankly, dear reader, I was becoming bored by the Plaza Royal Suite. Luxury, I am afraid, does not become me. In all my years in Paradise I have never for a moment felt the pangs of sadness or regret. I have never felt the sharp laceration of the saber of anxiety or the insistent pummeling of the small blows of boredom. It is only now that I am alone in New York and back in human form that I appreciate the true nature of the glory that I have left behind.

Why, oh why, dear reader can this be so! I look out the window and see milling crowds which encompass every milieu of the human condition. I see traders from Africa, European high castes, beggars and I suppose some thieves. Surely amongst this swarm are stories to tell and personalities to draw and flesh out. But suddenly the metaphoric lightning flash strikes me. It is good will that is lacking from the scene below. I am sad to say that it seems that beggars in Cheapside in 1850 showed more generosity of spirit towards each other than the modern narcissistic men and women who scurry about without consideration for one another. I can but wonder why.

My fellow journeymen are unlike modern man.

The rascal De Gama is, if you like, the exception that does not prove the rule. Joan of Arc is a girl of great character and Jerry O' is a true son of the Big Feller. He will rise to the occasion. I do not know about angels. I generally have little to do with them, but Calliope in his frantic disorganized way means well. That is clear. I gain the impression from Calliope that others within the angelic bureaucratic hierarchy are not so well intentioned. This may just be his reaction to criticism of some muddle he has caused. I simply do not know.

When I left the Plaza, I walked down East 60th Street into the famous Madison Avenue. I was pleased to find a bookshop and music bar.

The first young man I spoke to looked as if he had emerged intact from East London circa 1840. He suffered from the same type of facial blemishes which were then prevalent. He carried himself meanly and his hair was unwashed and unkempt. I was not surprised when it became apparent that he did not know of me. He claimed there was a musical artist named Little Jimmy Dickens who may somehow interest me. I got Joan to later find Little Jimmy on iTunes. Strangely enough I found his music did bear some odd connection. He sings of personal tragedy and unrequited love as I write of the same subjects. His palette, of course, is quite different. His scape is of lost dogs, broken down trucks, drunken farewells and life on the run, while I write of lost jobs, the debtor's prison, stolen love and mixed blessings. Our methods are divergent, our subjects are somewhat disparate, but my best postulation is that Little Jimmy and I may well be distantly related.

I wandered aimlessly around the shop until I came across a poor half demented young woman who is employed by the bookshop owner, perhaps as an act of charity. I could appreciate her state of misfortune as she did not even know her own name and wore a card which read 'Can I help you. I am Jodie'. Half fool she may be, but her knowledge of books greatly surpassed that of the spotty young man I first spoke to.

She told me how the books were arranged. The filing system was strangely artless. My favorite London store Foyle's simply listed all books in the alphabetical order of the author's surname. Jodie explained to me that there was a 'Young Adults' section, a 'School Texts' section and a 'Popular Classics' department. Surprisingly there was no division for 'Older Adults'. I can but wonder, have older adults read all they need or has reading been eliminated from their avocations. Perhaps the watching of television is the preferred pursuit of 'Older Adults'.

Yet poor Jodie was able to find some of my books. David Copperfield was listed under 'School Texts'. This must mean children learn it. I am not sure what they would learn. The book is not a deep read. It was serialized and sold on the streets of London as simple entertainment for the common folk. I am happy to say it was hugely successful. It made me a small fortune, though all in grubby pennies. But who I am I to wonder why it is read by children. I wonder more as to who the recipient of the royalties is. Is it a relation - Little Jimmy? - or has copyright simply died with me. On the other hand, there are no royalties receivable in Paradise. Best that I forget earthly rewards, dear reader. I have only been back on earth for a few days, and avarice already attacks me.

I was pleased to see Dombey and Son and Little Dorrit were stored under 'Popular Classics'. These words make for a formidable combination. 'Popular' denotes success and 'Classics' must mean masterly or first rate. Only Great Expectations was in the 'General Fiction' department. This seems to be the section where otherwise unclassifiable books are lodged. Great Expectations was sandwiched between a book called 'Why Carrots, not Zucchini' by a Doctor Heather Dick and a tome named 'The Young Cannibals v The Young Vampires' written by Douglas Dickenson. The former book seemed to be based on the unlikely theme of comparing the qualities of carrots and zucchinis and the latter was a fictional tale of a war between an army of cannibals and a battalion of vampires. I opened both books briefly. They are both composed in trite and facile terms. The best that can be said for them is that their titles accurately depict their contents.

I purchased copies of my books and a CD by a group named Bleak House. This musical disc was purchased on the recommendation of the acne faced youth who I first met in the shop. I should have known better. His appearance accurately reflects his recommendation. The music turned out to be bleak indeed.

I came back to the Plaza with my purchases. I proudly showed them to my cohorts. We then readied ourselves for our excursion to the famous restaurant Alle, where Jerry O' was going to lift the stakes, to use racing parlance.

We rode in a grand limousine ordered by Calliope. At first sight the restaurant grounds were most impressive. It reminded me of some of the old London Pubs in Camden Passage and Piccadilly that I used to frequent when I was last on earth.

I was, however, most disappointed by the interior. What could have been a wonderful shadowy gas lit red carpeted interior was a large open space. Also, to my immense surprise the kitchen was in full view of the customers. It was only in the poorest soup kitchens or hospital cafeterias of my time that cooks were to be seen. After all their art, I thought, is the skill of the cut, the mix and the plate. I was wrong. Today the visual construct of food seems to be as important as the taste. Give me a Yorkshire Hot Pot or Corned Beef and a baked potato. Down with pretty plates and stacked delicacies, I say.

But dear reader, let me narrate the strange events of the night. We were seated in the oddest room. It was a glass space within the main area. I was told that people known as celebrities receive rite of passage to book this room. The girl Joanne, who I found to be a most amiable and well-bred young woman, told me celebrities were people who were famous for being famous. This is a bizarre notion, but it is the present way of the world. At each twist and turn of this trip I understand better the Big Feller's unease at his creation.

I have mentioned Joanne to you. The beast De Gama made a sexual suggestion to her in the most profane and obvious way. She naturally rejected him but did so with a degree of friendly nonchalance that was quite disarming. If such a remark had been made to a lady of good breeding at the Cafe Du Paris in my last visit to earth, the woman's father would have had the man horse whipped. I have found I have a soft spot for De Gama, so horse whipping may be too great a punishment for the crime. Perhaps a severe dressing down would be sufficient in the circumstances.

The editor Bear Grizzard is a foul mouth. He is a man of Chaucerian nature. He drinks like a fish, swears like a trooper and may well partake of other sins of the flesh. He is Antipodean. That explains it. However, under the bluster and the profanity lies a keen mind and I suspect a generous soul. Methinks Bear Grizzard is a good man.

It was a privilege to meet a relative of the great poet Keats. We discussed his forebear and the interesting chain of relationships. I fear his grandmother may never have married. This would explain why the Keats name survives with Roger Sebastian. I understand his nervous reticence. His guilty secret may be exposed. His grandmother's otherwise perfect reputation may be sullied by an admission. I was I think too pushy. I regret it. I know some of Keats work and I spoke a verse of A Party of Lovers. Roger Sebastian was so overcome he could not speak.

Chub Checker I know and like. He is our conduit. Tonight, he was a quiet conduit as he absorbed the significance of the faith Jerry O' has in him.

But let the narrative continue. Suddenly we have a dramatic scene.

A large angry man ran at our glass wall. De Gama pushed his pudenda pouch at the man in a most aggressive way. I did not know, at the time, this man was the debaucher who attacked Vasco in Central Park. I must say I would have thought this would have been a good reason for the Portuguese to hide his testes rather than thrust them at the man. The restaurant clearly has a fine system to deter vagabonds, as the large angry man was removed in seconds. To add to the drama of the moment, another member of the lecher's party appeared to have a seizure at the door. It was an exciting introduction to our meal.

The ordering and eating provided me with some fodder for my story. I hesitate to criticize the girl Joan. She was burned at the stake. She ordered a frog. Personally, I believe, she should have been given a frog - not just the legs, but the whole frog. De Gama threw food around and called for dogs to clean up the mess and a spittoon to hawk into. This was quite out of place, but he is a creature of his time.

Jerry O' made me proud when he bravely told the Americans who he was and why we are here. They do not believe him - yet.

Thirty-Four

CALLIOPE'S EPISTLE

Dickens is resting. He is no tippler. I noticed at Alle yesterday evening he drank two glasses of red wine. Today he perspires and his eyes are reddened. He has, nevertheless, worked busily. He has written quite a long chapter of his diary which I have just read.

I am surprised by it. Dickens fails to mention the most important event that occurred last night. He has not given it a thought, but it is there, at the forefront of my mind. It would be the first thing I would want to epistolise.

Sir, I assume you are a man, but can I assume that? For all I know you may be a woman, O Biblical scholar. I withdraw my 'Dear Sir' and replace it with 'Dear Person.'

I first want to say I have mulled over my examination of the Charles Dickens manuscript. I conclude that I owe no apology. We are both chronicling the same events. I understand my document is unrequested and informal. I understand his is the official version, but in the past the scholars have had to sift through the rubble of records and diaries to write their gospels. But surely the rubble must be complete. That is my point. Dickens journal is incomplete.

It may be that you Dear Person simply laughs at my pathetic jottings You may describe them as unnecessary or worse pathetic. You see I know that and Dear Person, I accept it. Underneath my wings and my shimmer, I am a realist. But now I see you are becoming angered and impatient. What, you ask, is this great event Charles Dickens has ignored?

The appearance of disciples, the appearance of disciples and yes, I will say it again the appearance of disciples. The earth moved, chandeliers fluttered like leaves, windows rattled noisily because disciples appeared. I re-read what I just scratched down. I am very pleased with what I have written. Dickens is rubbing off and I am starting to wax poetic. And 'wax poetic' oh dear person can you forgive me my newfound literacy. I hope so.

So, there was Jerry O' telling the journalists the 'big' news as to who his group really were, but then out of the blue come our disciples. Now I grant you I have seen more likely disciples. The man Ginger Scollop looks like his name and Tweak Monk appears somewhat sinister, but Jerry O' seemed pleased enough and that is the main thing. After all he is the son. He will be the bearer of the revelations. I wonder if that is what I can call them. Could my little first draft, be the precursor of a Book of Revelations. We will see.

Vasco's court appearance was interesting, and I have pondered whether it is worth inclusion in my writings. I conclude it can be simply worth two lines. I realize this will impose an additional stress on me by having to make those lines rhyme, but I will try it.

Our warrior bold was jailed but saved
After being clutched by a man depraved
As they say now - that works!

I was most worried when Jerry O' sat near the front of the court and I was separated from him and unable to help. I know, you say, you are just the angel and a disorganized one at that. You are a cheeky devil more than a humble angel. But, in the first place, there are no such things as devils, cheeky or otherwise. Secondly and most importantly, Jerry O' [Wilfred] may be his father's son, but in his present human persona he seems innocent and even unworldly. I am sure this is the Big Feller's wish. He after all created the persona. Do not get me wrong, Jerry O' is every bit his father's son. He will do as he is bid with grace and substance, as he did when he came to Earth before. We do know that one day he will be back at his father's side and I will be back at my desk in the Citadel under the eagle eyes of Metatron and Gabriel. I am not so sure about the others. Not that it is any of my business, but I wonder if the sins of the flesh may consume Vasco De Gama.

Will Joan slit a throat or two. Will Dickens want fame and fortune. And what will be the consequences? I hear you Dear Person say 'mind your own business' and I will, but I have come to like the three visitors [even De Gama] and I wish them well.

Jerry O' took me to court as Dora and I confess it was my decision and mine alone to vanish and plonk my invisible self at the front table. I wanted to help. The lawyer Van Horn is a grotesque man. I could not resist briefly entering him twice to cause him discomfort. I am sure he has spent his life discomforting others.

I appreciate that dear person, you are not going to be sympathetic to my complaints of petty tyranny and overbearing bureaucracy from the Citadel, but I want to record it. I have my own plant at HQ. The angel Uriel is my friend and confidante. Uriel is a good snooper. He hides his light under a bushel of jollity. He is keeping me informed of Gabriel's continual harping on about my spending and my alleged failure to account. It is a never-ending story. It turns out that Gabriel and the hand wringer Metatron have gone to the Big Feller with a ridiculous diatribe about my alleged misdeeds. Now I know the Big Feller has a soft spot for me, but I also know that I am obligated to do my best. And I do. Sometimes I fall short, but it is never for want of trying. I assure you of that. Uriel told me by angel message that when Gabriel and Metatron got back to HQ, they were livid and spent the rest of the day whispering sour somethings into each other's ear. 'Great news,' I messaged back.

I have a few apprehensions about my organization of the dinner at Alle. I needed to book the Fishbowl. That was well within my instructions, but I really should have stopped the Van Horn party from making their fruitless trip to the restaurant. Though it is doubtful, amongst the Van Horn party there may have been a good person or two. Given my time over, I would have gone to Van Horn's office. I would have entered him again for a longer period and suddenly appeared as Dora claiming I was the mother of a black man wronged in the past by the lawyer. I am sure he has left a trail of wronged black men as well as white, brown, yellow and brindle. If I had done this the unfortunate scene at the restaurant would have been avoided. Van Horn would have been so overcome he would not have ventured out, other than for medical testing. I suppose it could be said that the actions of the debaucher Givens-Cator and the vulgar response by Vasco was a dramatic moment which heightened the interest of our journalist guests. I could say that, but it is an excuse. I noticed the sneak Sandalphon lurking again. He pretends to be watching over his saint, but he is a spy for Gabriel.

Lack of attention to detail, I know that is my failing. I should have known customers tip the Matre'd. My afterthought of dropping money in his hand from an invisible source was a silly mistake. At least the limousine ride went well enough. I made no mistakes there.

I was proud of Jerry O,' He spoke the truth with careful authority. The reporters did not believe him. I could see that. I appeared as Dora briefly to make the point. I concede this was not in my brief, but I thought Jerry O' needed a spur. I confess it did not work.

It would have been easy for the Big Feller to get Jerry O' to move a mountain or walk on water, but life on earth was not meant to be easy, as the human writer George Bernard Shaw once said. There I go again with my newfound literary talent. One day Charles Dickens may steal into my lair and secretly read my journal. I only jest, dear person, of that I assure you.

So what do we have? We have my earlier two lines of poetry, we have the declaration of Jerry O' and we have the entry of two disciples into our narrative. I will commence with my earlier lines and add some new musings. But before I try to rhyme my epistle, I have remembered something. Fortunately, my diary is private and cannot be used against me. You see when I was summoned back to Paradise by the Big Feller, he gave me explicit instructions to warn Vasco, Joan and Charles to be mindful of the fact they are humans once again, with all the temptations that go with that state of existence. Have I warned them - no - why not, because I forgot. I have been so intent on getting the details in order that I forgot the main instruction I was given. Oh woe is me; I will immediately repair my wrong.

Here is my verse, I do not include a reference to my misdeed.

CH.1 V. 5
Our warrior bold was jailed but saved
After a clutch by a man depraved
The son told listeners of the truth
An antipodean man said 'strewth'
Two disciples come with visage meek
One called Ginger the other Tweak.

Thirty-Five

Jerry O' slept well in Paradise. Here on Earth in his newly minted human body, he was unable to sleep. Back at the Plaza and after the important dinner at Alle he sat on his huge King bed and contemplated the future. Calliope had wafted in swishing and shimmering, but Jerry O' sent him away. Calliope had his instructions for tomorrow and Jerry O' needed time to think. He needed time to gird himself for the challenges ahead. He never engaged in the fruitless task of self-analysis. It was a futile exercise. It changed nothing.

Jerry O' realized that as the son of the Big Fellow he was in a remarkable position. He is not the creator, but he is the son of the creator. He is more powerful than a saint and much more powerful than the former inhabitants of earth who have been accepted in Paradise. He is even more powerful than angels. They must obey his commands. Yet for all that Jerry O' knew he had no direct power at all. His strength was passed to him by the Big Feller. Without the Big Feller he would have no power at all. Not that Jerry O' had any difficulty with that. His life in Paradise was - well life in paradise. It could not be more perfect. Jerry O' had only made one trip to earth in the past and that was as Jesus. That trip had been so important that the Big Feller had left the nail marks in Jerry O's unearthly body as a reminder to all what had happened to Jesus. He had made that trip to turn humans onto the right path. It did not seem to have worked that well.

It is true that the Big Feller had tried before to enlighten earthlings. He had sent many prophets with messages, but they were simply good men and women with a story to tell and some additional powers that the Big Feller had imparted. Each had been accompanied by an angel. They were all in Paradise now and lived in Prophet's Corner a gated community with a lovely view over the Seventh Universe. The residents' committee meetings were supposed to be interesting affairs. Moses was the current president, but his committee of Isaiah, Jeremiah, Ezekiel, Abraham, and Mohammed the Prophet often disagreed about even minor matters. Their arguments were always civil and decent, but the prophets were hard heads. The Big Feller told Jerry O' that the prophets were left with a residue of power. They had all performed great work. 'They laid the foundation for you.'

'Not that great', Jerry O' used to think ruefully, 'I was crucified.'

Jerry O' may not have been questioning the Big Feller's judgment, but the thought crossed his mind as he sat on his bed at the Plaza that the Big Feller could have used a prophet to spread his message now.

But he accepted that he must stop grumbling. He must put aside his reservations. He had a task, so important that his father could only entrust it to his son.

Jerry O' missed Mary Mags. He missed his daily golf. He missed his lattes at the Paradise Espresso with old friends like the writers Matthew, Mark, Luke and John. The four authors were all still writing, but each had taken up a musical instrument and often played at sing songs and picnics. Matthew had turned to crime fiction. This was difficult as there was no crime in Paradise. He found the Grillabies on Pluto perfect subjects. They were subhuman in form and substance and most of them had committed the criminal calendar before they entered adulthood. The Grillaby detective was hard to write but Matthew depcted him as being depraved, just less depraved than his fellow Grillabies.. Mark was still working on updating the Bible. He said it was like painting the Saturn Bridge. Luke was working on the true story of Plato and Socrates. The philosophers were willing, almost too willing subjects. This left John who was, like Jerry O', an avid golfer and had written a book called The Outer Game of Golf. The reader was supposed to sit inside himself and watch his swing from inside out. Jerry O' read the book, but he preferred a mirror as a teaching tool.

Jerry O' could hear some sounds from other parts of the suite. He could hear grunting and farting. That would be Vasco De Gama. He heard from another room some soft whistling. He went to investigate. Joan of Arc was sitting in an easy chair with her feet on the windowsill watching the never ceasing New York traffic.

'Are you feeling all right, Joan?' he asked.

'I hardly ever sleep,' she replied, 'I just like watching the lights.'

'We have a big day tomorrow,' said Jerry O', but without any conviction. Joan had shown she could look after herself.

Jerry O' retreated. He could not hear anything from Charles Dickens room. The scribe would no doubt be out like a light. Jerry O' had never seen him so animated than tonight at dinner.

Jerry O' wandered back to his room and again sat himself down on the edge of his bed pondering the days ahead.

Last night before bed, Calliope told the three human visitors he had instructions from the Big Feller to remind them they were back in human form. He told them they ran the risk of losing their places in paradise if they fell victim to temptation. Jerry O' thought this homily was somewhat belated, but he supposed it was better late than never. The instruction, however, did not seem to take the three by surprise.

Jerry O' turned to consider his first earthly contacts.

The newspapermen were skeptical of his claims, but so they should be. Jerry O' accepted his story was astonishing and implausible. It was more; it was simply unbelievable. Yet it was true. Jerry O' wondered why his father had not allowed him to perform some extraordinary miracle which would have caught the attention of the world. Why not turn off Mt Kilauea or perhaps permit another miracle. Instead, he was going to have to find a way to put the Mayor of New York into jail. From Jerry O's research it is where the man should be. He was corrupt and debased. However, it would not follow that the world would know that the man was imprisoned because of a supernatural phenomenon.

Jerry O' appreciated he would have to be patient. Charles Dickens was everything he expected. He writes his diary daily. Jerry O' was sure his jottings would be an accurate and perceptive account of the trip. Joan of Arc was a great girl. She was tough and self-possessed. He could imagine her leading a French Army into battle - but as a strategist for the team. Jerry O' wondered. Then there was Vasco De Gama. Jerry O' sighed. The Portuguese sailor was a rambunctious man. Jerry O' wondered how he made it to Paradise in the first place. 'It must have been touch and go' he thought.

Finally, there was the angel, Calliope. He meant well and the Big Feller had a soft spot for him, but Jerry O' speculated that the Archangel Gabriel would certainly have been a superior calculator and organizer. Gabriel is not a people angel, but he is better prepared than the Peloponnesian Army was when it invaded Thrace. However, the bottom line, was that the Big Feller had chosen Calliope and Jerry O' knew he would have a reason and a very good one.

The man Chub Checker had been oddly quiet tonight, but Jerry O' guessed that he was either convinced or close to being convinced that the party were not earthlings. The man Keats seemed to Jerry O' to be a pompous ass. He was open mouthed, almost gasping for breath, when he heard the Jerry O' revelations. Finally, there was the girl Joanne Rixti. She seemed unconvinced. At least she rebuffed the gross overtures of De Gama. Jerry O' hoped he was more talk than action. Otherwise, he would be a detriment to the undertaking. It would seem extremely peculiar to onlookers if the Creator, or God as they called him, had sent to Earth a fornicator.

Jerry O' thought about the editor Bear Grizzard. As Dickens said, his manner of speech was Antipodean. There were few Australians in Paradise. The only one that Jerry O' remembered talking to was a new saint called Mary who sounded Scottish and certainly did not use profanity. Despite the cursing, Jerry O' considered Bear Grizzard to be a formidable person. He respected him and believed that he would be a man of his word.

Jerry O' turned on the TV. On a Twenty-Four `Hour News Channel the Mayor of New York was giving a press conference. He was pontificating about his ambition to rid the city of corporate crime. Tomorrow would be another story.

He surfed channels until he reached the Fashion Channel. To his surprise his two new disciples Ginger Scollop and Tweak Monk were being interviewed by an extremely tall and painfully thin young woman wearing the tiniest of miniskirts and the highest of heels. Ginger was talking:

'We had a thrilling evening,' he was saying, 'we met the man who will be the most important new face in our world this generation. He is Irish and his name is Jerry O.'

'Ok boys,' said the interviewer, 'what's his angle.'

'Heavy metal meets peasant comfort meets vivid color, if you know what I mean.'

'You've lost me guys,' the girl said shrugging her shoulders.

'Here Kelly,' said Ginger 'we will give you a tiny taste.'

He handed over two photos which were then shown on the screen. They were close up photos of Joan of Arc and Vasco De Gama taken inside the Fishbowl at Alle Restaurant from somewhere in the bowels of the restaurant. After the photos were removed from the screen the girl, Kelly, resumed her interview:

'Well, we have just seen the first pictures of models wearing designs by the brand new Irish sensation Jerry O'. Will he take New York by storm? Will he be just another fragment of flotsam in the big catwalk of life? But thank you Ginger Scollop and Tweak Monk for your sneak preview. Do you like that - a sneak from Tweak. We love new fresh hoopla. This is Kelly Bamwoo saying goodnight to you. We will be back tomorrow night at Two AM with another edition of Hot Goss.'

As the screen faded you could hear Ginger Scollop calling out, 'and we are disciples.'

Jerry O' was mystified by the experience he had just endured. His strange disciples were already speaking for him. How did they get on TV? And what was this business about heavy metal, peasant comfort and vivid color? What did they mean? And why was the girl saying that he designed Joan and Vasco's clothing? As far as he knew Mohammed arranged what they wore.

Still they told the peculiar tall girl that he, Jerry O', was going to be the most important new face in the world of this generation. If everything went according to plan at least that would be correct.

There was a knock at the door. It was Calliope in his Dora body.

'Everything is ready for tomorrow, boss,' she said happily before leaving Jerry O' to wait for the morning to arrive.

Thirty-Six

The Mayor of New York the Honorable Billy Lowe had a spacious apartment at the rear of City Hall. He also owned a Five Million Dollar duplex in Tribeca and a beach front three story classic weatherboard at Cape May on the Jersey Shore. Billy Lowe had done well for a former hotel bellman.

He climbed the steps of the Hospitality Union ladder to be its national secretary. From there he entered the New York State Legislature and now here he was at the zenith of his ambition - the Mayor of Gotham City.

On the morning after Jerry O's fateful dinner at Alle, Billy Lowe woke from deep cocaine induced slumber. He turned over and noticed he was alone. He remembered his wife Muriel was at a fat farm in Maine. Billy used to say, sometimes to her face, that she was so gross she was dressed by Armbruster the tentmaker. Muriel tried two or three times a year to lose her flab, but after a week back in the Big Apple, the Dunkin Donuts, Hot Dogs and Magnolia Bakery Hummingbird Cupcakes replaced her layers of blubber. Billy also recalled his mistress the TV anchor Kelly Bamwoo was absent. He remembered she was doing her sad little gig on the Fashion Channel. She would now be drinking absinthe in one of the all-night bars in Greenwich with the crew while toasting each other for the pathetic and jejune scuttlebutt they had shared with the minuscule audience they attracted at Two AM. Billy had got Kelly the job. He did not mind her absence. Her childish prattle was annoying. It was her carnal skills that Billy found pleasant.

The Mayor heard a sound at the end of the bed. He raised his body and noticed he was not completely alone. His cocker spaniel Charlie was lying on the bed. The dog was awake and expectant. He watched his master vigilantly. Billy's moods were notoriously fickle. He sometimes was happy to see Charlie and at other times became angry that the pooch had found his way into the bedroom.

'I see you've snuck in again, Charlie,' the Mayor said cheerfully.

Charlie barked happily. He would not be shouted at or kicked this morning.

Billy Lowe rang down for breakfast. It was delivered by his PA and occasional bedmate, the loyal Arnold Prink.

'Call a press conference at 10.00AM, Arnold, I have something important to say - and bring a table and dog biscuits. I want Charlie there with me,' Billy said to Arnold as he munched on his toast.

'What's it about, Your Honor,' replied Arnold who was careful to be formal with the Mayor at all times other than when he lay on his stomach naked with his legs splayed whilst the Mayor rogered him.

'You will find out,' replied Billy, waving Prink away. And the truth was that Billy Lowe did not have the faintest idea why he was calling a press conference. On the other hand, he knew he had to call one. Calliope had done his job well. Billy was inculcated.

Calliope knew this morning's extravaganza was going to make or break their mission. For once he had made a list and ticked off all his boxes.

The press was notified. Dora had rung the networks, syndications and newspapers to advise them that the Mayor would be making an important announcement at 10.00AM. She had told them to bring cameras and film equipment. She emphasized that the statement would be breathtaking. She also rang the police commissioner and told him to bring a large squad, including anti-riot police. Dora even took the time to go down to Wall Street and tell the unkempt Occupy crowd that it would be in their best interest to attend.

Arnold Prink began getting calls soon afterwards from all and sundry. He fielded them by telling the truth. He did not have the remotest clue as to why the press conference was being called, but he guessed it was something very serious. 'I would call it historic,' said Arnold to disbelieving journalists.

At about Nine Forty-Five the crowd began to gather. The Occupy gang was the first to arrive. They were hoping some bones were going to be thrown at them. The Standard team was there in force. Bear Grizzard was in the front row flanked by Joanne Rixti and Chub Checker. The Police Chief was a reluctant attendee. He had heard enough of the mayor's bullshit in the past to last several lifetimes. He had put Sergeant Flanagan in charge of security, and the Sergeant was standing to one side next to the mayor's rostrum.

Arnold Prink, the Mayors Aide, was not sure what was to occur, so he had placed a microphone on a rostrum at the top of the steps of the grand front entrance to the City Hall building facing Broadway. He hung the city flag of vertical tricolors of blue, white and orange charged in the center by the city seal on the wall behind the mike. He had also followed orders and placed a small wooden table next to the microphone. He was not sure as to the table's purpose and, to be on the safe side, he covered the table with a burgundy tablecloth.

As the journalists gathered on the steps, passers-by stopped and joined the throng. By Ten AM there were several thousand people gathered.

Billy Lowe readied himself. After showering he found his clothing laid out. He saw nothing odd in the fact that he was to wear a white toga with a blue sash, a laurel wreath on his head and chunky leather Roman sandals. He saw nothing peculiar in the fact that he was applying bright red lipstick and a line of black mascara on his forehead and a spot on each cheek.

Far from being uneasy, he examined himself in the mirror with palpable satisfaction. The mayor was still a fine-looking man. Late middle age had weathered him, but he was trim and tanned. He affected a ponytail but otherwise carried himself with what he considered to be quiet dignity.

After finishing his self-examination Billy placed a smaller laurel wreath around Charlie's neck and then led the dog down the wide staircase, through the majestic lobby and out the front doors. Charlie was wagging his tail furiously. He was pleased to get the attention. In his other hand, the mayor carried a small brief case which he had found next to the bedroom door as he left. He knew the valise was important, but he knew not why.

Billy Lowe made his way to the microphone and raised his arms to quieten the crowd who had begun murmuring and laughing when they saw the mayor in his strange finery.

Finally, the crowd was still, and Billy Lowe began what was to be the last speech he ever made in his public life:

'Friends, New Yorkers, countrymen, be quiet or I will cut off your ears,

I come to bury Charlie's bones not to eat them,

The evil done is grave and must be cured - crime is rife, sodomy is blatant.

So my friends I hereby dissolve the New York House and Senate and I banish the Governor of New York State to Toledo, Ohio.

I declare myself to be Billy Brutus, the ruler and potentate of the boroughs of New York. I will raise the taxes on Millionaires to Ninety per cent. The money collected will be distributed to the poor of the city. Every freeman will receive Ten Thousand Dollars.'

There was loud cheering from the Occupy crowd. Billy continued.

'And we must have a Consul.'

Billy leant down and picked up Charlie. He placed him on the small red covered table. The mayor waved over Arnold Prink and whispered in his ear.

The astounded aide gave him the bag of Rover Doggie Bites he was carrying.

Billy Lowe resumed his speech. The crowd was silent. they could not believe what was happening. Two rumors were spreading. One was that the Mayor was going to announce a revival of A Funny Thing Happened on the Way to the Forum and soon the cast would appear. Others speculated that Billy was about to announce that New York and Rome would become sister cities. Billy resumed his speech, raising his toga clad arms again to gain attention:

'Friends, it is with great certainty and comfort I appoint my dog Charlie to be Pro Consul of New York, and I rename him Gaius Ceasar. Gaius do you accept the appointment.'

The Mayor held up a Doggy Bite and Charlie barked gleefully.

'See Gaius accepts the appointment,' Billy announced.

'But there is more to say my subjects, oh yes there is much more. It is I who need forgiveness and remission of my crimes. I need my Pro Consul to grant me a Nolle Prosequi to absolve me from any charges. I must first tell Gaius what I have done and then seek his clemency and mercy. I have cheated on my wife many times. I have also spread the beef curtain of my assistant Arnold Prink. I have awarded tenders without proper formality, but most of all I have misused, no stolen, City funds. My larceny has been of mammoth proportions. I have embezzled Thirty Million Dollars.'

The Mayor paused and bent to his knees.

'Do you absolve me Gaius from all my treachery,' Billy held out a Doggy Bite and Charlie barked again loudly.

You see, my people, the Pro Consul has acquitted me. I have the evidence with me. It is in my case. I will now eat it.'

The Mayor took a piece of paper out of his case and began masticating it.

'All right,' said the Police Chief to Sergeant Flanagan, 'I've heard enough arrest him.'

The Sergeant and four of his men clambered up the steps. They manacled the mayor and led him away. As he left one could hear him still speaking.

'O judgement! thou art fled to brutish beasts,
And men have lost their reason.... Bear with me.
My heart is in the suitcase there with Gaius,
And I must pause till it come back to me.'

Kelly Bamwoo, Billy's mistress and non-prime time TV hostess, downed her Absinthe and looked incredulously at the flickering television screen in the little bar in Greenwich.

'Silly prick,' she said to the crew, 'that fucking blow will do your head in.'

Arnold Prink had his head in his hands. He was sobbing. Journalists surrounded him and were firing questions at him.

Back at the Plaza Royal Suite Jerry O' sat in a semi-circle with his team watching a wide screen HD TV.

'Well done Dora, excellent work,' he said to Calliope who was sitting in his Dora skin.

At City Hall Bear Grizzard turned to Chub Checker.

'Ok, Chub,' he said, confirm those medical appointments.

Thirty-Seven

The Mayor of New York, the Honorable Billy Lowe, was still in his Calliope induced fugue state when he was transported at the Manhattan Criminal Court and Justice Centre.

The New York Police Chief was not sure what to do with him. The Chief had political aspirations himself. The Mayor was an important man, a former heavyweight union boss with impeccable labor credentials. Discretion was the better part of valor. The Chief delegated the responsibility for looking after Billy to Sergeant Flanagan.

The FBI were sniffing around. The Chief was keeping an eye on this development. If given the opportunity he would pass the poisoned chalice, of the mad mayor, to the federal agency. On the other hand, the DA had a nose for notoriety. If he thought the case of Billy Lowe would advance his career he would fight the Feds for it.

About an hour after being detained Billy came to. More accurately he no longer believed himself to be Billy Brutus, dictator of New York. He did, however, remember in vivid detail his extraordinary performance on the steps of City Hall. He could not explain it. Billy now felt healthy and primed. He thought of last night.

He had drunk no more than two or three snifters of Hennessy Cognac. He had snorted two lines of coke after dinner, but purely for medicinal purposes. He had not taken a lover. Billy's wife was away, Kelly Bamwoo was working and the thought of pork swording Arnold Prink had not appealed to the Mayor. Billy had slumbered dreamlessly and without interruption. He wondered if he had been somehow poisoned. He wondered if the blow was contaminated. The former was unlikely. He and Arnold Prink had both eaten the same meal. He could hardly complain if the latter was the cause.

The Police Chief had not been sure what to do with the Mayor, so he placed him in an interview room in the care of a soapy social worker. After Billy had become accustomed to his reality, he asked the social worker to contact his attorney, Melvin Van Horn.

'And tell him to bring some clothes for me,' said Billy who now felt quite ridiculous in his toga and laurel wreath.

The social worker rang Sergeant Flanagan who made the call.

Soon enough the lawyer arrived in a rush.

'We'll get you out of here before you know it,' said Van Horn, 'I have arranged for an early hearing today. You must have been drugged or suddenly taken ill. That can happen.'

Van Horn was an expert on mystery illnesses. That very morning a team of New York's finest doctors had poked every crevasse and orifice of the Van Horn body and scanned every inch of his innards to determine what was causing his sudden and painful convulsions. Nothing was found.

Billy Lowe was dressed in a conservative suit and brought before Judge Nola 'Freddy' Krueger, who was, as usual, the duty judge.

Judge Krueger tried the matter as an urgent application. She decided to hear it in camera, bearing in mind it was the mayor she was dealing with, and she was not sure what the application was about nor who was bringing it.

Rose France of the DA's office arrived in court. She presented with a small file and an assistant. Melvin Van Horn made his usual grand entrance accompanied by his usual retinue of lick spittle associates and camp followers. Billy Lowe was brought down. Van Horn immediately took up the cudgels.

'Your Honor, our client the Honorable Billy Lowe, Mayor of this city, is being held against his will without charges being laid. It is the grossest false imprisonment I have encountered in my thirty years of practice. This morning my client had an unfortunate.' Melvin looked for the word, 'episode.'

'Yes, I saw some of it on television,' said Her Honor blandly.

'I am glad Your Honor, because you must have concluded there has to be a medical reason for the Mayor's actions. We intend to have a team of the finest medical practitioners in the city examine the mayor to search for the cause of the problem. We therefore ask Your Honor for a Writ of Habeas Corpus to release the mayor.'

'Ms. France,' asked the judge, 'why are you holding Mr. Lowe? As I understand it no charges have been laid against him. If that is the case, there may be force in Mr. Van Horn's argument that his client is being unlawfully imprisoned.'

'Your Honor,' replied Rose France evenly, 'we are holding Mr. Lowe for questioning. This morning during his—performance he admitted stealing large amounts of money from the city. The Police seized a case load of documents which the mayor had begun to eat. Our preliminary investigations reveal that the documents indicate that over Seven Million Dollars has been transferred in a clandestine way from City Bank Deposits to accounts in the Grand Cayman Islands in the name of Mr. Billy Lowe. We can further say that Mr. Arnold Prink, the mayor's PA is a co-operating witness. We have spoken to Lowe's wife, and we are disposed to accept her claim that she knows nothing of the fraud perpetrated by her husband. Of course, there is much to be done. We have only just started to forensically examine the material. Currently, we seek leave to serve and file twenty eight counts of fraudulent conversion against the Mayor in the sum of Four Million Dollars. More charges will follow. They will include charges of anal rape. The victim being Arnold Prink.'.

'Yes, Mr. Van Horn'? the Judge seemed quite chuffed by the turn of events. She had always thought the mayor was a self-satisfied rooster, but a sodomite and a fraudster they were surprises.

Your Honor.' replied an indignant Van Horn, 'when Ms. France handed us those documents it was the first intimation, we had that there were any charges to be laid against our client. We need time to obtain instructions and carefully examine the charges.'

'Of course, Mr. Van Horn, naturally you will not be caught short. But the real question I must determine today is what we do with Mr. Lowe in the meantime. I expect you are asking for bail.'

'Oh yes bail is sought, Your Honor, this man is the Mayor of New York. His family is here—.'

'Yes I understand,' said Judge Freddy Kreuger, 'let us see what Ms. France has to say. She may not even be opposing bail.'

Rose France was on her feet in an instant:

'The State opposes bail most strongly. This Defendant is a serious flight risk. He has access to vast sums of money sufficient to enable him to escape from the jurisdiction.'

'Bail,' thought Calliope who was lounging invisible in the back of the court, 'that is one thing that is not going to happen.' Calliope had stayed close to the mayor since he arrived at the Manhattan Court Centre. It was his brief to keep Billy Lowe under lock and key. The fine points of American Jurisprudence were not within Calliope's purview, but he could see this was a fair judge who was considering granting bail to the mayor. Calliope acted to inculcate Billy Lowe once more.

The response was instantaneous. The Mayor ripped off his jacket and shirt and stood up with his arms thrown wide apart:

'Where is Gaius Ceasar?' he called out, 'where is the Pro Consul of New York? I am here before you as defendant, therefore I cannot act in my capacity of Billy Brutus. Before the Court acts it must be properly constituted under the authority of the Pro Consul Gaius Ceasar.'

'Who exactly is Gaius Ceasar?' said the Judge who had only seen excerpts of this morning's performance.

'It is his dog,' said Ms. France in her usual matter-of-fact manner.

'He is a dog no more,' roared the Mayor, 'as Billy Brutus dictator of New York I have appointed him Pro Consul of the City. While I am unable to rule, he is my deputy and protector. He must validate this court's authority. He will then release me and order my captor's to be publicly placed in stocks and stoned.'

The Judge leant back in her chair and considered the matter. A couple of the Van Horn lickspittles had taken the mayor by the arms and propelled him back to his seat at the bar table. 'Either this arsehole was stark raving mad, or he was setting up a brilliant defense of insanity.' In the end, Judge Kreuger decided, it did not much matter:

'The Defendant will be held without Bail,' she said, 'there will be a psychiatric assessment by two doctors. One is to be appointed by the State and one by the Attorney for the Defendant. The reports shall be filed with the court within twenty-eight days. The case shall be adjourned for six weeks. Each side therefore will have two weeks to consider the reports before the adjourned hearing.'

Calliope was relieved. In six weeks, the mission should be ended.

When Billy Lowe heard his fate, he left the table and began crawling around the floor. The lickspittles had been holding Lowe, but their attention was diverted when Van Horn suddenly doubled up in anguish and howled in pain. Calliope retreated after entering Van Horn to watch the closing act of the Billy Lowe show.

As the Mayor crawled around under the bar table he intermittently hoarsely barked. In between barks he called out 'it is I who is now the little dog, chain me, whip me, feed me dog food.'

Police arrived and carted off the still barking and wailing mayor.

A tall bespectacled man entered the court and walked to the prosecution bar table:

'Your Honor,' he said, 'I am James Butterworth from the Federal Department of Justice. I have just received instructions from the FBI. My instructions are that this is a federal matter as money has crossed State lines. We wish to interview the Mayor.'

'I suggest you bring plenty of doggy bites,' said Her Honor as she swept up her papers, in preparation of adjourning the court. The Judge looked over at Rose France.

'Ms. France, I recommend that you enter earnest negotiations as to who will bear the responsibility of the carriage of the case. If the issue is not resolved by the two of you, I will resolve it. In other words, if the little dogs cannot agree, the big dog will make the decision.'

With a twirl of her gown and a slight grin the judge left the court.

Thirty-Eight

Our four visitors gathered in the lobby of the Plaza on the morning following the fall from grace of the Honorable Billy Lowe Mayor of New York. Curious bystanders stood discussing them sotto voce. One brave teenage girl approached Joan.

'Like I wonder if you would give me your autograph,' she asked, thrusting out a pen and a scanned photo of Joan, no doubt lifted from the web cast of Kelly Bamwoo's late night TV show.

Joan looked at it in surprise.

'What does this girl want from me?' she asked Jerry O' in her thick French accent.

'Sign it,' said Jerry O'. He thought this over, 'or leave your mark.'

Joan took the photo and pen and signed it Joan D'Arc.

'Do you think I do not know the Garamond lettering, Jerry O'. Do not forget I defeated the English in the Loire at Patay. We killed Two thousand five hundred of their best warriors. How do you think I gave orders, by the puff of smoke or the wings of pigeons. I wrote in copperplate Garamond, Jerry O'.'

'Oh my God,' called the teenager, 'what a cool name for a model. Joan Dark. Oh my God, it's just sooooo cool.'

Fortunately their driver turned up and herded the group to a waiting nondescript black van. Calliope hopped in last and spread himself out in the back row. He remained invisible. He suspected it would be a difficult day. He was not wrong.

The vehicle took the Lincoln Tunnel and crossed from New York into New Jersey. The driver took the Turnpike and exited at the Success Road exit. He drove South until he reached the town of Lacey. He turned West and travelled along a rural narrow avenue until he arrived at their destination.

The Plus One Medical Center was located at the end of a winding tree lined lane way. The Center itself was a modern cement sheeted, glass fronted block. When the vehicle stopped and the group alighted, they were met by a group of white coated men and women.

'Hi.' said the man at the front of the group. 'I am Dr Sneider. I am the leader of the team. Follow us and we will get you comfortable.'

Jerry O' had told the others that Bear Grizzard was having the four of them medically examined. Jerry O' said that this should not be a matter of concern. He knew the other three were back in their human bodies. Jerry O' was not so sure about himself. This was not a matter he had brought up with his father. When he last visited Earth as Jesus, he was in a body that looked human but was capable of resurrection and eventual evanescence. Of course, way back then there were no medical examinations carried out on behalf of Herod or Pontius Pilate. Jerry O' knew very well that today he was in a vastly different world.

The four were shown into a large reception room where Chub Checker was waiting. He was sipping coffee with relish, largely because of the Irish Whisky he had added from his flask. He greeted the visitors warmly.

'Welcome Jerry O', and you too Charles. Joan, we have a TV for you to watch in between your tests. Vasco, I hope you are over your unpleasant incident with Oliver Givens-Cator. The doctors assure me that the tests will not be too intrusive, but I guess you understand that before you have the paper's full support we must be satisfied that you are the real deal. My boss Bear is a tough old bird, but he is a man of his word. I am fully expecting you will be front page news tomorrow. Jerry O' this will mean your mission from your dad can take off.'

Charles Dickens was nodding his head with approval. He enjoyed the journalist's use of idioms. He liked the rhythmic New York timbre.

Joan and Vasco got the general idea, and Joan was pleased to know she would have the chance to watch some television. The Only Way is Essex was on at noon, and she was keen to see whether Arg could get back with Lydia. Vasco was not sure what to expect. His experience with the medical profession in the past had been restricted to treatment meted out by his fleet doctors to hapless crew members. They generally died or were maimed by the treatment.

It was only Jerry O' who was uneasy. He was not sure what to expect.

'And Dora,' said Chub, 'where is Dora?'

'She is not to be examined,' said Jerry O' with finality.

'Ok, ok,' said Chub, 'I guess she is not part of the deal.'

Calliope was put out. Chub was no doubt interested in getting Dora examined, but really what a try on. Calliope thought for a moment of entering Chub briefly to give him some momentary pain, but he was a friend, so he decided against it.

Four doctors entered the reception room, and the visitors were ushered away. Calliope flitted around the four examination rooms making sure all was well.

Charles took to his medical examination like a senior citizen getting his free annual checkup from Kaiser Permanente. He removed his clothes, bent over, opened his mouth and had his MRI with apparent pleasure.

'Fine equipment,' he said to his doctor, 'very advanced no doubt, oh yes I see the purpose. What an eye opener this is.'

Joan of Arc was mistrustful, but being the plucky girl that she is, she took the prodding and poking without complaint. Her doctor was a sharp featured elderly woman with a matter-of-fact manner. There was, however, one occasion where minor trouble erupted. After Joan had stripped off and was lying on the examination bench the doctor looked her over and said:

'I see you do not shave. You do not shave your legs, Joan, this is unusual.'

'Shave my legs, what kind of nonsense is this. I have never heard of such a thing. This is why we wear hose,' Joan was indignant at the woman doctor's foolishness.

'Well these days girls not only shave their legs, but also their—,' she pointed at Joan's private place, 'it is called a Brazilian.'

'Their twats,' exclaimed Joan, 'they shave their twats. Why do they waste time on such a stupid pursuit. I fought the English and the Burgundians. I defended myself against treachery. I spoke to Gods and Saints. I did not have the time nor inclination to shave my twat.'

The Doctor was sorry she had mentioned the subject.

Vasco was examined by a tiny Asian doctor with thick spectacles.

'Do you use leeches,' asked Vasco, 'the chinks were supposed to be good with leeches but the Portuguese quacks killed more patients than they saved.'

The doctor assured Vasco that no leeches were used. The examination progressed smoothly until the doctor endeavored to perform a prostate examination. When he inserted his fingers into the De Gama anus the Portuguese sailor screamed in anger and began chasing the Chinese doctor around the room.

'What a world this is, first a lecher grabs my balls in the park and now this yellow libertine sticks his fingers in my arse under the pretense that it is medical treatment.'

Calliope was quickly on hand to quieten Vasco, but the doctor was shaking like a leaf.

'I have seen enough,' he quavered.

Soon Vasco, Joan and Charles were back in the reception rooms comparing notes. Dickens tried to assure De Gama that the prostate examination was above board, but Vasco was not convinced.

Joan asked Charles if he shaved his legs or the hairs around his penis, but Charles said he knew of no such customs.

'It is called a Brazilian,' said Joan of Arc, 'it must be a custom imported from the Americas. Where your people travelled,' she said looking pointedly over at Vasco.

But Vasco was still nursing his aching arsehole, so he ignored her.

There was no sign of Jerry O'. His examination had finished and he was resting on his examination bed reading an old copy of Golf Digest he had found in the reception room.

The doctors were conferring with Chub in the Boardroom of the Center.

'You have a document signed by each patient waiving privilege?' asked Dr Sneider.

'Yes,' said Chub producing the four letters.

'Ok,' said Sneider, 'this is the wash up. Dickens is relatively fit. He is a human being. He has broken no bones. Joan is a small young teenager. She is a virgin, though the examining doctor did not feel it necessary to raise this subject in the circumstances. She has had several broken bones, including a fractured right ulnar. This injury would have been caused by a severe fall. She is not groomed as a young woman of today.'

'Meaning?' asked Chub.

'She has very hairy legs and armpits and elsewhere,' said Sneider, 'but this proves nothing.'

'And then we have De Gama,' the doctor paused, 'he is also of young middle age, but his body has seen much trauma. He also became aggressive when a prostate examination was conducted.'

'I can imagine,' said Chub, 'but you had a speech pathologist examine them. What was the verdict?'

'It is her conclusion that each of the three patients talk in the patterns of the century they claim to come from, but this is not conclusive. They may be very good actors.'

'Academy award winners,' suggested Chub.

'I guess so,' said Sneider, 'but the man Jerry O' is in a completely different category.'

'Yes?' asked Chub, he was beginning to wonder if this story was going to have legs.

'Jerry O' has no brain,' said Sneider.

'A Democrat,' quipped the woman doctor.

'No really, he has space, where the brain should be. Notwithstanding the absence of a brain, he functions perfectly well. We tested him using advanced psychological testing and he exhibited superior thought skills, motor processes and patterns of understanding. In other words, he has a brain, it is just not traveling with his body.'

Chub was trying to soak up this information. He needed a drink. The story had more than legs, it had big rubber jet propelled wheels.

'There is more,' said Dr Sneider, 'he has no heart.'

'A Republican now,' said the woman doctor.

'No he has perfect heart function. His blood pressure is sound. His body works perfectly. But like the brain, the heart is not in his body.'

'I want these tests to remain completely secret.' said Chub.

'We are doctors,' said Sneider, 'we are bound by the rules of confidentiality.'

'And you better be,' said Chub.

The driver was called. The four tourists were collected and set off back to the Plaza. Jerry O' had read the Golf Digest from cover to cover. Joan had seen the second half of her 'Essex' show. Arg and Lydia remained estranged. Charles was his usual curious self, and the De Gama arsehole was now free from pain.

Chub rang Bear Grizzard.

'Good news, boss,' he said, 'Jerry O' has no brain and no heart.'

'Fucking hell,' said Bear, 'he is a newspaper proprietor.'

Chub rang off, but before he put the phone down he could hear the editor shouting 'Hold the front page.'

Thirty-Nine

There was a grungy taproom called The Monkey Bar downtown in the basement of a rundown building across the road from Studio 54. The building was scheduled for re-development, but the precarious state of the economy had so far wasted two developers and put the present owner in a holding pattern. The building was rat infested. The basement bar was similarly infested, but by human rodents. The detritus of the New York Fashion industry gathered during the long afternoons to muckrake, drink booze and share drugs and bodily fluids in the washrooms.

On the afternoon of the Mayor's disgrace, there was a larger crowd than usual in The Monkey Bar. The noise levels were high, and the tittle tattle levels were higher still.

Ginger Scollop and Tweak Monk were squeezed into a greasy booth with Kelly Bamwoo and Arnold Prink. They endlessly trawled the fertile ground of the Mayor's fall into the sea of infamy. Kelly and Prink had something in common. They had both often been comprehensively shafted by the Mayor. Prink's poking, of course, had been metaphorical as well as physical and his claim was that the physical copulation was against his will.

Arnold Prink told the trio that he was now a police witness. The Governor of New York had installed an administrator and one of his first actions was to suspend Arnold Prink on full pay.

'I can never show my face again; I might as well be dead. I still cannot understand what happened to him. As far as I know the blow was fine. I did not see any X or Ice around. He seemed all right last night.'

Ginger was sympathetic. Her Hot Goss television hour rated spectacularly unsuccessfully and was gauche in the extreme. She was not particularly insightful, but even Kelly knew her future may be entangled with that of Billy Lowe, the ex-Mayor.

Ginger Scollop waited for the conversation to peter out. He had something important to say. Eventually Arnold Prink began to softly weep. Ginger comforted him.

'Do you have any drugs Ginger,' she asked, 'some blow or uppers, even Horse would do.'

Ginger had his opportunity and he took it.

'My life of drug taking is over, Kelly,' he said portentously.

'I don't give a flying fuck whether you inject a needle up your arse or sniff crack, Ginger,' retorted Kelly, 'I want to buy drugs for Arnold - and me too.'

'No you misunderstand me, Kelly,' said Ginger, 'since meeting the Irish designer Jerry O' I have felt somehow different inside. I feel that I must follow him. He will somehow save me.'

'You know Ginger,' added Tweak Monk, 'I have not wanted even a toke since yesterday. I thought I must be coming down with something.'

Both Kelly Bamwoo and Arnold Prink were mystified by this turn of events.

'For fuck's sake, Ginger,' said Kelly angrily, 'he is a threads man not a fucking faith healer. What is wrong with you.'

Though Ginger and the mumbling Tweak continued to try and explain the strange affect meeting Jerry O' had on them, it was useless. Kelly was vehement, she wanted drugs. She began trawling the bar. She was prepared to pay with money or in kind.

Ginger followed her and took her arm.

'Come with me, Kelly,' he said, 'we shall go to the Plaza and see if we can find Jerry O'. I will be a true disciple.'

Ginger nodded to Tweak who collected the still sniffling Arnold Prink and the strange quartet made their way up the stairs. Ginger flagged down a cab and five minutes later they were deposited at the entrance of the Plaza.

As luck would have it as they alighted, Dora was leaving the building accompanied by Vasco De Gama and Joan of Arc. She had agreed to accompany them on a constitutional whilst Dickens scribbled and Jerry O' contemplated his arrival on the world stage tomorrow.

Tweak saw them first and grabbed Ginger's arm and gesticulated.

'Oh my,' said Ginger, 'it is Jerry O's models. We have met the girl. We have not actually met the man, but I know his name is De Gama.'

Dora saw the quartet at the same time. She knew exactly who they were. She had observed the two 'disciples' last night. Kelly was the skinny tall girl on the television and Prink was the buttocks lifter who worked for Billy Lowe, ex-Mayor of New York. Her first thought was to scramble. She could herd her troops back into the relative safety of the Plaza lobby. On the other hand, the two strange creatures from Alle last night had been appointed disciples by no less than Jerry O'. So instead, she walked with Vasco and Joan towards the arrivals.

'Hello,' Dora said, 'I am Dora, maid and assistant to Jerry O'. This is Joan D'Arc and Vasco De Gama.'

'Oh I know,' said Ginger Scollop, 'we met Joan yesterday, but we did not get her name and Vasco, we have not formally met.'

Tweak muttered something unintelligible in apparent agreement.

'But Dora,' Ginger continued, 'you seem familiar. Haven't we met before?'

'No,' said Dora with authority, 'we have not met before.'

'I would like you to meet my friends Kelly Bamwoo and Arnold Prink,' said Ginger, 'Kelly is a TV presenter. She has a fashion show. What do you think Kell? Aren't these two just the bees-knees? You have got to admit. Jerry O' has something really, special.'

Both Joan and Vasco were dressed in their usual costumes. Though they still got curious glances from passersby, the Plaza staff were now used to them. Joan had taken on board the strange reactions of her examining doctor earlier. This afternoon she wore no hose. Under her tunic, she wore just short pantaloons. Her thin legs were bare.

'Can I ask you something personal, Joan?' said Kelly.

'You may ask,' replied Joan, 'but I might not answer.'

'I notice you do not shave your legs. Is this part of your look?' said Kelly.

'Nobody shaves their legs,' said Joan, 'and we do not partake of the Brazilian.'

Kelly was worried. Her pudenda had been cropped yesterday. She wondered how long it would take to grow out.

In the meantime, Arnold Prink had perked up at the sight of Vasco.

'Oh, yes, Mr. De Gama your clothing is so innovative and exciting. I cannot wait for Saks and Bloomingdales to have it on show.'

Kelly had forgotten her quest for drugs. She was contemplating a follow-up piece to her interview last night with Ginger and Tweak. She joined in.

'Mr. De Gama your clothing is truly fresh and brilliant. How would you describe yourself?'

Vasco knew he should respond. He did not have the faintest idea what the woman was talking about. She was no beauty. He thought she looked like a stork, but at least she was a female stork.

'I am what the English call a gay blade.' Vasco remembered an English pirate called Morgan being once described this way. It somehow seemed appropriate.

'Oh did you hear that,' said the delighted Prink, 'Vasco is pink.'

Vasco wondered what in hell the man meant, pink - what did this imply. He noticed Kelly was looking at him apparently fascinated. He decided not to simply ravish her. He would play the gentleman and compliment her.

'You are a scrawny wench,' he said, 'but I believe we should rut.'

'He is a bi,' said Arnold.

Vasco turned to Joan and whispered, 'what does the man mean by - bi – Joan?'

Joan thought for a moment. She looked at Dora for support, but she was looking over at the gates to Central Park, her attention diverted. She had seen Sandalphon hiding behind an iron pier.

'I think it means - two – Vasco,' she whispered back.

'Bi,' said Vasco, 'I am more than Bi.'

'Oh, just listen,' said Arnold Prink. 'he must mean animals. What sort of animals do you rut, Vasco, farm animals like sheep or dogs, but not cats, surely not cats?'

Vasco listened closely to the strange man. It took him a moment to realize the full import. He took hold of Arnold Prink by the shoulders and threw him into the large rhododendron shrub which bordered the concourse to the lobby.

'This weasel accuses me of rutting animals. Is every New Yorker a debauched fornicator. I can see why the Big Feller is so upset. I will now kill this man.'

Vasco started striding towards the hedge where Prink was cowering. Dora was back on the job. She stood between them.

'The man misunderstood you, Vasco,' she said in a placatory tone, 'he means no harm. I do not think Jerry O' would be pleased if he had to extract you from prison again.'

Dora waved off the small crowd which had gathered. She collected her brood and they retreated into the lobby of the hotel. As they entered the building Joan of Arc, repeated her comment from the night before to no-one. 'They may be disciples, but they are surely cock suckers.'

Sandalphon was still behind the pier. He shook his head in disgust at the travesty he had just witnessed.

Ginger, Tweak and Kelly Bamwoo consoled the shaken Arnold Prink. A cab was hailed and they repaired back to The Monkey Bar. Kelly was the first to compose herself.

'I will never shave my legs again,' she called out loudly causing the Montenegrin cab driver to intone a silent Serbian curse.

Forty

The New York Standard animal pit was humming. The sub editors were glued to computer screens. The editors were all in their cubicles. They were either talking and gesticulating to minions on the phone or perusing copy which had come down the line.

The city editor Gordon Robert Checker, otherwise known as Chub, was collecting his thoughts. He was due to visit Jerry O' shortly and wanted to make sure his pitch was on the right key and his delivery was true.

Bear Grizzard had met with Chub and Joanne Rixti, upon Chub's return from the medical examinations of Jerry O' and his cohorts.

'We go full steam ahead,' said Bear, 'but the details of Jerry O's medical tests shall remain in this room with just the three of us. So, to fill you in Joanne, Vasco, Charles and Joan are normal humans. Well perhaps not normal, but everything is pretty much in place. Jerry O', on the other hand, has no brain and no heart. And Joanne do not say he must be an editor in chief.'

Joanne did not comment. She just looked at Bear in astonishment.

'The doctors cannot work out how Jerry O' talks, walks, thinks or even breathes, but he does. The only explanation is that his brain and heart are somewhere off site. Now I know this is beyond our belief, but it is a fact. I am going to simply tell the troops that Jerry O' is not human. I guess there may be complaints, but they are going to have to do what they are told. It is my head on the block.'

Chub noticed that not one profanity had so far passed the lips of Bear. He decided to test the waters.

'That sounds fucking good, Boss.' he said.

'Cut out the language, Checker, there is a lady present.'

'Oh, I can only see Joanne,' said Chub.

Joanne shrugged her shoulders, but Chub could see that she was also amazed by the foul-mouthed Bear's newfound delicacy.

'How about Billy Lowe's Brutus act, what about that?' Chub knew journalists were a cynical and distrustful bunch. They would want more than Bear's word to take the tale seriously.

'Leave that to me,' said Bear.

'I'm going to have to come clean' Bear continued, 'but I believe it will be OK with the Big Feller.'

Chub looked at Joanne who raised her eyebrows.

Bear set off down to the reporter's floor. The sub-editors were summoned. The whole motley group gathered in a circle. Bear stood in the break of the sphere. He was flanked by Chub and Joanne. He called for silence.

'Now I want you to listen carefully. Very carefully - because tomorrow morning we are going to break the biggest story for two thousand years. We are going to tell the world that we have a visitor from heaven. And he is not just some wandering spirit. It is the son of the Big Feller'.

There were murmurings amongst the crowd. Bruce Gotby, the Foreign Affairs Editor was back in town. He was dressed in khaki camouflage pants and jacket and a black peaked cap. His skin wore the yellow pallor of a cocaine sniffer.

'And just who.' he asked in a patronizing way, 'is the Big Feller?'

'The Big Feller is God, get it God you fucking nose tippling wanker', Bear paused for effect. His propensity to curse had apparently returned. 'And the son who we will call Jerry O' has brought Joan of Arc, Charles Dickens and Vasco De Gama with him.'

'Of course, I should have realized,' intoned Gotby softly.

Bear ignored him and turned to Chub.

'Ok Chub fill the arseholes in with some meat.'

'The story starts three days ago,' said Chub, 'four people walked across 5th Avenue in the afternoon. They simply set off into the traffic. The traffic stopped dead. We have CCTV photos. Now I know that this is not very compelling. You each will have the still photos in the folders that will be distributed. You can see that three of the visitors are dressed in old fashioned costumes. We have blown up the figures. There are photos around of Charles Dickens. The man walking across 5th Avenue is the image of Charles Dickens. There are paintings and images of Joan of Arc and Vasco De Gama. Compare the images. The fourth man goes by the name of Jerry O'. He has an Irish accent.'

'He looks like the President of Ryanair.' said Bruce Gotby.

'I think the Big Feller's intention was to leave that general impression,' interposed Bear mysteriously.

Chub looked at the group, while he collected his thoughts for his next installment. He noticed Dora had suddenly appeared and was standing next to Gotby at the rear of the crowd. She was whispering in his ear. His complexion appeared to visibly change from yellow to mandarin. He shifted from toe to toe in a nervous manner. He even seemed to have developed a right opthalmic tic. Dora shook her head at Chub. He took this to mean that he should leave her out of the story. This would be tricky as the appearing and disappearing woman was an important part of Chub's narrative.

'The party checked in to the Plaza. Their luggage was strange. Joan of Arc's case looked as if it was Five Hundred Years old. It was the same with the others. Their luggage fitted their persona. They also checked in a live rooster.'

A young woman journalist hesitantly spoke:

'But I have seen Arabs check in goats. Apparently New Zealanders occasionally bring sheep.'

'There is more,' said Chub, 'much more. Just hear me out. Vasco De Gama went for a walk with Joan of Arc in Central Park. De Gama was sexually assaulted by a bond trader. There was a fight. Joan joined in. It finished up with Vasco De Gama and the bond trader Oliver Givens-Cator being arrested.'

There was a murmur and a couple of whistles. Givens-Cator was a well-known and much disliked man.

'I became fascinated by the story, so I got myself into see Jerry O'. He told me that he comes from Paradise. He said it was the place we call Heaven. Each religion has a different name for it, but there is only one place. He said his father, the creator, who he calls the Big Feller is worried about humanity. He has observed small dangerous countries which have developed weapons of mass destruction. Wars are continually fought, with each side claiming to have God on their side. But worse the human condition has been corrupted by narcissism. Both sexes are obsessed by worldly goods, appearance and most of all themselves. The new technology only encourages this folly. I made a note of all he said. Of course, I was still suspicious. I had no proof. The next thing that happened was the court hearing. Both sets of charges were dropped. The next day Jerry O' invited me to dinner. I took along our Managing Editor, Joanne Rixti and Roger Sebastian Keats. They can tell you what they saw themselves, but if Dickens Joan and De Gama are actors they all should have a sideboard crowded with Oscars. During the evening Mr. Grizzard asked Jerry O' to explain why he was here. Jerry O' told him. Mr. Grizzard asked for a miracle to prove it. Jerry O' said he was not prepared to indulge in party tricks but would be prepared to offer something tangible. Perhaps I can ask Mr. Grizzard to explain.'

Bear was animated. He also seemed to have regained his vulgarity. 'I asked Jerry O' to have our esteemed Mayor jailed the next day. He agreed and it happened. You all saw that silly fucker appointing his dog to be consul and trying to eat evidence. Well, you fuckers, I am satisfied that one way or another my Irish friend Jerry O' was responsible. Joanne, Roger - anything to add.'

'You will hear more from Chub, but I am satisfied Jerry O' is not from Earth,' said Joanne.

'I had a long talk to Charles Dickens and speaking as a scholar of English verse he was entirely convincing. I must also say both De Gama and the girl Joan did not act as if they were modern humans,' Roger Sebastian Keats recalled ruefully De Gama throwing food around and Joan of Arc's anger at not being served whole French frogs.

'Medical examinations have been conducted on all four visitors,' said Bear Grizzard, 'De Gama, Dickens and Joan of Arc are humans. Jerry O' is not human. I am not going to say any more about this phenomenon. I do not want the man to be turned into a freak or to undergo more tests. The medical evaluation provided indisputable evidence. Chub Checker is going to see Jerry O' now to sign him up for an exclusive. We have been selected to spread his message, but we may as well legal it. Joanne, I want you to organize a hideaway. Tomorrow the Plaza will be too hot. Every fucking news hound in the world will descend on the place. See if you can find a nice big spread in Jersey or perhaps the Catskills. Have a chopper at the ready. Employ Security Guards. Get a chef, preferably one who can cook whole frogs. Roger Sebastian, I want you to look after the historical angles. Chub has obtained a history. Use it. It seems that each of the accompanying humans bear the age of their greatest achievement when on the planet before.

Joan is sixteen. This was her age in 1429 when she led the French Army to victory against the Burgundians at Orleans. Some say she was merely the standard bearer, but this view is wrong. Joan was a fighter and master tactician. De Gama is thirty. This was his age when he arrived in India in 1498 with the Portuguese fleet. Dickens is forty-nine years old which was his age in 1861 the year of the publication of Great Expectations his finest novel. I think that about covers it.

'I will never snort cocaine again,' said Bruce Gotby out of the blue, due to his minor inculcation by Dora who had now vanished.

'Bruce,' said Bear Grizzard, 'I don't care if you poke it up your arse. Just do your fucking job and look after the Foreign Affairs angles. The Vatican may be interested to hear their main fucking man has sent his son to New York not Rome and that little fucker in North Booga who wears the one-piece fucking pajamas may be diverted by the news. You have got plenty to do Bruce get to it'.

Bruce commenced to leave when Roger Sebastian Keats piped up:

'What about the black woman who suddenly turned up at the dinner?'

Bruce Gotby turned sharply back.

'Dora, you mean Dora, laughed Bear Grizzard, 'well that's a whole other story, but Roger Sebastian mate, my guess is we have not heard the last of Dora. Now Chub you had better get on your fucking bike. There is a paper to write.'

Forty-One

Chub Checker hopped a cab to the Plaza. As he alighted, he was surprised to see his former City Hall snitch Arnold Prink being supported by a tall spindly woman as he meandered unsteadily from the hotel portico. The woman was being assisted by the two disciples Ginger Scollop and Tweak Monk. Chub watched them enter the cab from which he had just alighted which then set off in the direction of Times Square. Chub hoped the four of them held their peace as the Montenegrin taxi driver with his odd nervous facial tic and the heavy steel crucifix hanging from his rear-view mirror seemed edgy.

Chub Checker made his way via the private lift to the Plaza Royal Suite where he pressed the buzzer. The door was opened by Dora.

'Nice to see you again,' Chub said, 'we must have a long talk one day, before you disappear.'

Dora thought of doing her disappearing act immediately just to serve the reporter right, but she knew Sandalphon was hanging around and decided she would provide no further grist for Joan of Arc's personal angel's mill. Earlier in the evening Dora had observed Sandalphon shimmering around the entrance to Central Park when Dora, Vasco and

Joan had met up with Ginger Scollop and his misfit friends. No doubt the skirmish that occurred would be part of Sandalphon's presentment against him. Gabriel and Metatron would love the yarn. Dora merely ignored Chub, other than to call out to Jerry O' that he had a visitor.

Jerry O' ushered Chub into the sitting room. The others were not in evidence. Chub sat himself down in an armchair facing Jerry O'. Chub was not surprised to observe that Dora had disappeared.

'Jerry O',' commenced Chub, 'we are going to press tonight. The paper will be on the streets just after dawn tomorrow. I have an agreement for you to sign. It gives me exclusive rights to your story. I have capped the agreement at Twelve months. Is that ok?'

Jerry O' agreed. He would have no golf swing left if he had to be on earth for twelve weeks let alone twelve months. As for the exclusivity agreement, Jerry O' thought it was appropriate. Chub was the only news man who had shown the presence of mind to pick up on the story. He should have the rights. He did have a proviso.

'Vasco, Charles and Joan are not, I trust, included in the agreement. It would be my opinion it would be impossible to police. It would be like herding cats.'

'We understand,' said Chub, he and Bear had discussed this and agreed that the Standard would have enough trouble trying to close the gates on Jerry O'. The paper would still have the front running on the others. They decided not to be greedy.

'We also think that you will have to leave the Plaza tomorrow. The place will be overrun by reporters, priests, politicians and other sinners. Joanne is setting up a nice rural retreat for you. We will have a helicopter ready at six am. We are also arranging for private security.'

'We will be ready,' said Jerry O'. He was pleased with the plan. He remembered Pontius Pilate two thousand years ago and his unholy alliance with King Herod. He wanted this trip to be less bloody and more contemplative.

'Will Dora be joining you?' Chub asked.

'Dora is always with us,' said Jerry O' impassively. Chub knew when to leave well alone, so he changed the subject.

'Can I run through some features of the story with you, Jerry O'? You have told me you come from Paradise. This is the Muslim word. Christians use the word, Heaven. Others say Nirvana. Our view is that we should use the word, Heaven. Is this ok with you? We can say you call it Paradise, but we want to make sure the readers know what we are talking about.'

Jerry O' nodded his agreement. He could see the sense in the journalist's argument.

'As I understand it, this is the second time you have been here. Can we call it the second coming? Look I know Jerry O', the term has significance for a Christian. I have done some research, and I wanted to run this past you. The gospels talk of a sudden and instantaneous coming. Your mission seems more guarded and specific. Also, I have seen no gospel which speaks of you returning with other people.' Chub was suitably deferential, but he was speaking with a degree of insistence.

'It is not the second coming Chub, it is a warning from the Big Feller that if human nature does not change, there will be no second coming, as there will be no earth for me to come to. You must understand my father does not interfere with nature. He gives humans the opportunity to work with and not against nature. Animals and plants are attuned to nature. Humans seem intent on defying it. This is the message I bring from my father. I want the whole world to hear and see my message. That is my goal. Charles Dickens is my diarist. Vasco De Gama is my guard and Joan of Arc is my strategist. You have asked about Dora. All I will say is that Dora is our link to my father. You will probably learn more of her later.'

'Is she an angel?' asked Chub.

'No comment,' replied Jerry O' in his charming Irish lilt.

Chub had other questions, but there was copy to be written. He left the Suite and cabbed it back to the Standard.

Bear Grizzard was with the sub-editors mulling over headlines and sub headlines.

'We've got it,' he said, 'Jesus Rides Again - two thousand years ago the son of god was here. Well now he is back for the second coming and you will hear his story firsthand only in this newspaper. We have interviewed Jerry O'. We can say he is not a human being. He says he is the son of God and comes to us from heaven. We believe him. How does that sound, Chub?'

'Pretty good, boss,' replied Chub, 'but you are going to have to leave out that stuff about the second coming. This is just the dress rehearsal.'

Forty-Two

At six am sharp the next morning two black Audi Q5 SUVs pulled up at the front entrance of the Plaza. Our four travelers were herded quickly into the front vehicle, and it drove sharply into the empty street. Inside the hotel Joanne Rixti was attending to the account. Porters brought the luggage from the Royal suite down to the lobby under the watchful eyes of Dora. It was loaded into the second Q5.

The gift shop of the Plaza was just opening. The owner was cutting the wires of packages of the morning newspapers. The New York Times was aptly placed on the left in its own purpose-built stand. 'Not that we sell many' thought the owner grimly. The Post was placed on the bottom shelf next to an assortment of dailies from the Wall Street Journal to the Washington Post. The Standard was the last package opened. The owner cut the wires and carried the bundle to the shelf. The Standard would sit between the Brooklyn Eagle and the Jewish weekly Der Blatt. He set down the package incuriously. The owner was more interested in the latest NFL action than current affairs or the endless intrigues that C grade celebrities got up to. However, this morning something caught his attention. He picked up the

Standard. There on the front page were the four creeps who had been wandering around the hotel for the last three days. The owner put on his glasses and read the paper. Calliope watched. It was his first chance to see public reaction to the story. The owner of the stand read the first four pages of the Standard thoroughly. Page five dealt with the other news of the day. The owner, an orthodox Jew, put the paper down and stood in the lobby chanting:

'Barukh atah hashem elokayno melekh haolam.'

Soon the porters had gathered, and the duty manager came striding over purposefully.

'What is he saying?' asked a young porter.

'Blessed is the Lord, our God, the King of the Universe,' said Dora happily, who had just materialized. It seemed the newspaper report was working.

Calliope left the hotel and made her way to White Lake in the Catskills where Jerry O' and the others would be housed.

The Audi Q5 carrying the group drove to the East River and the four visitors alighted at the Manhattan Heliport. A Bell 206L Long Ranger Chopper was waiting on the tarmac with its rotors whirring. Moments later they were all aboard. The helicopter rose sharply and swung over the river on its way to the foothills of the Catskills.

Bear Grizzard was in the front passenger seat when Jerry O' and the others boarded. He wondered how the three ancients would cope, but they all seemed quite relaxed. Then again Dickens was an inquisitive man. A helicopter ride was yet another experience for him to mull over. Vasco De Gama had fought off pirates in three oceans. He was unlikely to be phased and as for Joan of Arc - she had been burnt alive.

Bear had copies of the Standard with him. Without comment he handed them out to the four.

They read silently. Jerry O' and Charles Dickens quickly got the drift. Vasco and Joan had been given some elementary English reading and writing skills to go with their accented language capabilities. The finer nuances may have been lost on them, but the meaning was clear. The four realized they were outed; life would now not be as before.

Charles Dickens was fascinated by the way that the Standard compartmentalized the story. He recognized the skill the journalist exhibited in the distillation and dissemination of the facts.

Jerry O' was struck dumb. The big picture was now revealed. He was going to have to sell the Big Feller's message to two billion humanoids ranging in intelligence from super gifted individuals to morons who were just about on a par with the subhuman Grillabies on Pluto.

Bear Grizzard had put his career on the line. He wrote the front-page header. Photos of the four visitors accompanied the lead story. Bear had focused on the fact that Jerry O' was not a human being. He said he was the son of the creator. Bear wrote that he was not going to release the details of Jerry O's physical fettle for reasons of privacy, but a full-scale medical examination had been conducted of all four space travelers. He went on to say that psychological testing indicated that the three humans were Charles Dickens, Vasco De Gama and Joan of Arc respectively. Grizzard spoke of Jerry O's mission, and he stated it was on the orders of the Big Feller. He wrote that this was how Jerry O' referred to his father. Grizzard faithfully recorded the Big Feller's disquiet about human behavior. Bear had written his piece in a bland and simple way. He laid out the consequences for humans if they failed to take heed of Jerry O'.

'We face destruction of our world,' he wrote.

Chub Checker had written the whole of page two. He concentrated on the circumstances that had occurred since the group's arrival in the Big Apple. He wrote of the walk across 5th Avenue. He illustrated this with a photo. He wrote of the arrival at the Plaza, the luggage and the rooster. He described the fight in Central Park. With relish he named Oliver Givens-Cator and mentioned his despicable snatch at the De Gama testes. He wrote of the court appearance of Vasco. He described the dinner at Alle, with all its drama and weirdness. Chub decided to leave out the appearance and appointment of the two 'disciples' as he was not sure of their significance. Perhaps Jerry O' was merely trying to be pleasant. After all the two oddballs seemed to think, for some unknown reason, he was a dressmaker. Chub also left out all mention of Dora. She was a complete mystery to him. Jerry O' had not denied she was an angel. But if she was a heavenly creature, she was not at all what Chub would have expected God's messenger to be like. She hung around bars, frightened cabbies and may well have interfered with the check-in process at the Plaza. She was a strange one. Chub finished his story by stating that Jerry O' was not in town to heal the poor, damn the rich or stop volcanoes. His miracles would relate only to trying to save the human condition from itself. However, to demonstrate his power he had brought down the Mayor of New York, or more exactly, he caused the Mayor of New York to engineer his own downfall.

Bruce Gotby took up all of page three with a stunning summary of how foreign affairs would be affected by the arrival of the son of God. On one hand warring countries may unite, but on the other they may see the event as simply a cunning CIA plot or worse still a Vatican inspired intrigue. He wrote of the likely competition amongst organized religion to own Jerry O'. Yet other religions may simply try to debunk the whole story. Since meeting Dora briefly, the Gotby nose had not felt the inhalation of white powder. Bruce was shaking a little, but he somehow felt relieved and pure. It was the best work he had ever done.

Roger Sebastian Keats and Joanne Rixti shared page four. The Arts editor commenced with a striking admission. He stated his real name was Derek Pigsley and he was the son of a couple of Leeds touts. He wrote that he took on the name Keats for affect and to claim a false relationship with the long dead English poet. Strangely Bear Grizzard was moved to near tears when he read the article by the Arts editor. He hugged him warmly and said, 'Good work, mate, fucking good work.' It seemed that Bear's inclination towards profanity had not entirely vanished. Keats went on to say he had met and had a lengthy conversation with Charles Dickens. He said that Dickens was the real thing. Keats said he would stake what was left of his reputation on his assessment of Charles Dickens.

Joanne Rixti had found the time to describe the fashions of each of the travelers. Jerry O' wore either Armani or Paul Smith. His shirts came from the great Jermyn Street shops such as Gieves and Hawkes. His shoes were from Loake. He was the epitome of a successful Irishman. But no tie, the successful Irishmen never wore a tie. Charles Dickens was clad in conservative Nineteenth century dress. Vasco De Gama in his best finery was a Portuguese grandee and Joan dressed as one would have expected. She was clothed as the young peasant girl who led her army, against the mighty British and the vicious Burgundians.

The Bell chopper reached Woodstock, the home of the music festivals. It went up country and commenced its sharp almost vertical descent. It landed on a circle of cement with a red painted circumference within a large green field. The field was fenced and there was a thick high hedgerow which blocked the view from prying eyes. Two more black Audi Q5's waited. There were two men per vehicle. They were dressed identically in black combat fatigues. Each man carried an automatic rifle and wore a cross-sling shoulder holster carrying a silver handled Glock.

'Part of our security team,' said Bear Grizzard.

The helicopter disgorged its occupants. They entered the SUV's which made their bumpy way across the field and out through solid wood electric gates onto a narrow one vehicle cement driveway. They snaked their way between heavily wooded hedgerows into a large open red tiled forecourt. Four more security guards were waiting, two on either side of a large steel door. The door had an incongruous inlayed etching of a pair of cartoon wood ducks with over large heads. One duck wore a thick mustache and the other had frameless spectacles. In front of the door was Dora accompanied by Chub Checker.

'Where are we?' said Jerry O'.

'We are staying at Little Pink in White Lake New York State. We are in the foothills of the Catskill Ranges. As you can see it is a large property. It is one hundred and thirty acres. There are security guards guarding the perimeter. There is an electrified fence. It used to be a safe house for US intelligence until the Seventies when a rock musical star bought it and stepped up the security. The Standard is renting it for as long as we need. Jerry O', there are fine communication facilities. You will be able to converse with anybody on earth with a computer. Charles, there is a great library. It includes many books you have written. Vasco, you will be glad to know there are dogs. They are of the Cao de Agua breed - Portuguese Water dogs. Joan, we have a fine French chef, but I am afraid she has no access to whole frogs. There is however a TV room with a large high-definition screen. I have been able to get hold of the second series of 'The Only Way is Essex'. I do not believe you have seen it. You will be able to catch up with the latest adventures of Arg and Lydia.'

Jerry O' and the others entered the pink three story wooden building. They were chatting to one another happily.

Sandalphon was in the hedge directly opposite the peculiar front door. He had read the Standard. Despite himself he was impressed. Though he was loyal to Gabriel and Metatron, his first loyalty was to the Big Feller, closely followed by his doughty little charge Joan of Arc.

Forty-Three

CHARLES DICKENS JOURNAL

The seasons of New York's rural landscape are clear and defined. I suppose I should have noticed rust-colored leaves in Central Park. Alas, my writer's eyes were obscured by my thirst for all things new fresh and exciting. Now, here in my bedroom in Little Pink, I can see a landscape of green turning to brown. Autumn must be approaching fast.

But my dear reader, let me not be diverted by my window shopping of nature's blessings. I have much to tell you.

I am seated in a stuffed armchair. It is so soft that when I first lowered myself into it, I felt myself disappearing within its generous folds. You must be wondering how Dickens can write his modest meanderings when he is so comfortable. It is a fair question. But I use my iPad.

When we arrived together at this estate and were shown to our respective rooms, the girl Joanne Rixti came to my door with the electronic tablet that has become my new scribblers' friend. I use an 'app' [what an apt name] called Pages. I still print my work. Joanne explained that I can print at Little Pink using what she calls 'WIFI'.

So, I sit deep in the tweed cloth of my chair. I face the window and type my stuff. I am no expert on the 'qwerty' keyboard, but strangely enough the brief delays caused by my search for letters has somehow helped me cogitate. If only I had this instrument when I wrote my 'modern classics', my tomes would have come more readily to the streets of London. The term 'modern classics' is self-deprecatory my dear reader, of that I assure you. It refers to my categorization on some modern book shop shelves. I struggle with these thoughts. I trust I am not already being induced to avaricious aspirations. I brought joy to lives, by my books, I must never forget that this is my finest legacy. Yes, I made money, but I deserved [most of] it.

I take you back to the fine restaurant Alle. This is where I must begin this chapter of my journal. Jerry O' promised a miracle, but not a magician's trick or a re-design of nature's will. He agreed to have an important man jailed on the morrow. I wondered at the time just how he would accomplish this. I knew Calliope would provide the toil. Jerry O's plan executed by the cavalier Calliope worked a treat. At the time I watched the horrible Mayor metaphorically self-immolate, I reflected whether the irony of the situation occurred to anybody but me.

You see, dear reader, I compare Billy Lowe with Herod. Think it over. Think of the pact of the Jewish King and his instrument the Roman Pontius Pilate. Then ruminate on 'Billy Brutus,' as the venal mayor called himself and his wagging foolish dog who he christened Gaius Ceasar. The causticity is truly palpable. Paradise is no place for irony. But here amongst my twenty first century human relatives I see sardonicism at every turn. One needs to simply watch the reality television productions to appreciate how the human condition has deteriorated and is awash with unearned self-esteem and narcissism. I know all humans are not as jejune and shallow as the 'reality 'performers, but dear reader, they watch them, yes they watch them. That must tell you everything.

I saw the mayor's ignominy from the comfort of the Plaza Hotel. One should generally not take pleasure at another's misfortune, but the mayor deserves every barb and arrow that pierces his thick skin of infamy.

The important Chaucerian journalist Bear Grizzard must have been well satisfied by the exposure of Billy Lowe, and he arranged for our little band to be medically examined. I was fully expecting the appraisal to take some days. I imagined that the quack would draw blood. I expected to be clothed in flannel, fed salt, have my feet washed in methylated spirits and spooned molasses. However, there was no calomel nor jalap, I saw no medical chest and there was not a lancet nor a clyster in sight.

To be wholly truthful I found the evaluation enervating. Modern science is truly amazing. My body was pulsed and stimulated. It was wholly immersed in a great machine. I could watch my innards on a computer. I am glad to say everything is in working order. There was a commotion next door when De Gama claimed to have been molested. I received the same treatment. The white gloved doctor did test the inside of my rectum for nodules. He prepared me well and the test was only fleetingly painful.

Chub Checker is still our closest associate in the new world. I continue to be impressed by his syntax. I do not however believe he is our organizer. He reminds me a little of our wayward angel Calliope. They both mean well, but they lack method. Strangely Calliope, as Dora, seems to discomfort our Chub. I am not sure why this is so. It deserves further consideration. I will look for answers. This is what a scribe must do.

The trip to Little Pink was a truly jolly adventure. I had never travelled by air before and the Bell 206L Long Ranger [yes, I obtained its correct nomenclature] is a magnificent beast. I am sorry I did not spend more time viewing the ever-changing scenery as we sped across New York State, but I was fascinated by the morning paper handed to me by Grizzard. The first four pages were solely devoted to our arrival.

Page One was written by the senior man, Grizzard. This is as it should be. His writing is crisp and aseptic. The reader will be left to ponder. Oh, and how will they ponder. And what will they ponder.

Chub Checker has faithfully recorded details of our visit on Page Two. It is surprising just how much the man has discovered. He is truly a master of commentary.

I do not know Mr. Bruce Gotby. He is the Foreign Editor. His writing is descriptive and quite marvelous. I will tell him so if I am ever fortunate enough to meet him. I am sure he is a man of substance. It will be fascinating to see if any of his predictions come to pass.

Page Four was partly devoted to Joanne Rixti's fashion column. She writes clearly but I am not particularly interested in compositions about the cuttings of swathes of cloth. I was more interested in the jottings of my new friend Roger Sebastian Keats. He reveals that his life is a lie. He claims to be a Mr. Pigsley from Leeds. Those of you who know my writings, appreciate that I people my books with hay loads of characters. It is why I sometimes use a glossary or index to help readers identify a name. Remember my readers used to read me weekly by installment. There were times when a character would be described and then disappear for weeks. Hence the need for a memory jogger. I have the impression that I wrote of a Mr. Pigsley. Was it in Nicholas Nickleby or perhaps

Little Dorrit. The name Pigsley certainly sounds germane. But I am not sure. I have thought carefully of Keats' confession, and I simply do not believe it. I think he writes his clap trap to give more life to his piece. He did not need to take this step. Without any chicanery by the man his writing is colorful and visionary. Dear reader I believe Roger Sebastian Keats has embarked on an elaborate literary trick. A practical joke, if you like, and taken the name of one of my old characters. I like his whimsy.

When the helicopter disgorged us at Little Pink, we were taken to our new quarters. I suspect we had better get used to them. Not that this will be difficult. The house is quaint. It is painted a bright shade of pink. Its decor smacks of make-believe. I asked Bear Grizzard who had designed such a place, and I give you his exact response:

'The architect was Peter fucking Pan, and the Interior Decorator was Tinker fucking Bell.'

This, of course, cannot be true as Peter Pan and Tinker Bell were fictional characters created by the early Twentieth Century writer J. M. Barrie. I have seen his work in the library in Paradise. I have not met the man, but I believe he has a house with a rose garden in Paradise Meadows in the Fifth Universe. I believe that Mr. Grizzard used these names with Chaucerian expletives to make his point. Our Little Pink is a chimera of a house. Dear reader, do you detect further irony. I do.

Forty-Four

CALLIOPE'S EPISTLE

Many things have happened. I think I have done well. Sandalphon still hangs around. He says he has no option because he is looking after his Joan of Arc. From what I have seen she is perfectly capable of looking after herself. Sandalphon is compiling a dossier. I am the target.

This is more than an epistle. It is my defense to Gabriel and Metatron. They will babble on about expenses, dockets and receipts. I have few receipts. That is the problem.

Sorry!

I must take my punishment like an angel, but I still say I have done well.

After we got back from the restaurant, I shimmered in to see Jerry O', but he waved me away. Jerry O' has come into his own. I was frankly worried John [or Matthew, Mark or Luke]. Jerry O' has been here before. He still has the nail marks to show for it. I thought he may be showing human emotions whilst encased in a human frame. I was wrong. He was just thinking. Gabriel claims I do not think. He is wrong.

I write this epistle. Surely, I must be thinking. Tell me epistle writer, does thin air produce epistles. I hear your answer, well I think I hear it - thought produces epistles. Tell that to Gabriel.

We are now on the cusp of our adventure. We are all here in rural New York State in the house known as Little Pink. I love the house. I wish I could take it home with me. I wish I could consult the other John - the builder and get him to transplant it for me. However, as you know, angels live in the Citadel unless traveling as heavenly spirits on a mission. I guess I cannot have everything.

Presently I pose as Dora. I walk the corridors of Little Pink in a purposeful way. The man Chub Checker keeps out of my way. He does not know what to make of me. I fascinate him, but my frequent comings and goings unnerve the poor fellow. I will let him sweat it out for a while. There are more important things to do.

Remember! Make a list! Think before you act! These are my goals.

I saw those strange disciples on television. I should mention this. Disciples sometimes are referred to in epistles. Mentioned in dispatches, if you like.

For some reason they think Jerry O' is a dress designer. The two men Ginger Scollop and Tweak Monk were interviewed by a long thin girl called Kelly Bamwoo. I got a shock when I saw her because I have seen her before. I conducted surveillance of our target, the

Mayor Billy Lowe. I think John [or whoever] I am getting the hang of modern language. I saw a blue ray film called Tinker, Tailor, Soldier, Spy. The title bore little relation to the film. There was not a tinker nor tailor to be seen and for that matter there were few soldiers. There were however a lot of spies. I have learned their jargon. I think it will assist my epistle. As a secret agent I have no need to employ lamplighters or devise a legend. I can appear and disappear at will. This is a huge advantage for a spy.

But back to the girl Kelly Bamwoo - she is a paramour of Billy Lowe the hapless mayor.

One of the less appetizing parts of spying is watching the target. I saw the profligate mayor copulate with his goober of an assistant Arnold Prink. Later the same evening the mayor performed the same act but, to put it delicately, in a different cleft of Kelly Bamwoo. The twerp, Prink, now claims his rogering was not consensual. The man is lying. He howled like a banshee, with great pleasure, throughout the whole sickening performance. Prink is an acquaintance of our friend Chub Checker, but I believe he is simply a source of information and not sexual gratification to our reporter friend. Nobody, however, got more pleasure from the evening than Gaius Ceasar, the dog formerly known as Charlie. He barked and wagged his tail throughout both deeds. I put a stop to the noise by appearing briefly as Dora. This frightened the Doggy Bites out of him.

Prink is an associate of our two disciples. That troubles me. They are odd bods. I will keep an eye on them.

The unmasking and humiliation went to plan. I will go as far as to say it was a great success. Unfortunately, I know little of the New York legal system, and I had to go back to court in the afternoon to as lawyers say - seal the deal.

The medical examination of my friends was largely uneventful. I had to quell De Gama's momentary rage when an Asian doctor was checking his prostate. My guess is the Asian will in future order blood tests for this procedure.

Checker, the inquisitive reporter, wanted me examined, but Jerry O' rightly pointed out I was not part of the deal. Do you like my mastery of the vernacular. All I can say that if they got a shock when they examined Jerry O', they would have keeled over if they tried to inspect me. They would have found no heart, no brain, no nothing.

I should also mention I saw the disciples walking with the two recipients of the mayors, shall we say, endowments outside the Plaza. Nothing any of them said or did gave me any cause to be well disposed to them. The lecher Prink openly discussed Vasco's sexual proclivities. The Portuguese man reacted badly. I intervened.

Our newspaper friends have been diligent. Upon Jerry O's instructions I attended the editorial conference. The Foreign Editor, a munchkin called Bruce Gotby, was scornful and patronizing. I appeared as Dora and told him quietly that his cocaine filled nose was about to fall off. I encouraged him to feel his nose disengaging from his face. He quickly became a changed man.

So here I am at Little Pink. I am ready. I am willing.

But I see Chub. I smile warmly. He leaves in a hurry. He asked Jerry O' if I was an angel. Jerry O' did not deny it, but Chub is not sure.

Our epistle must - no please I do not mean must - let me say 'might' - yes let me say might deal with the girding of our loins for our future experiences. I of course, mean 'girding our loins' in a totally innocent sense.

CH 1 V.6
The mayor is out of work,
Because he went berserk,
He rots in a cell,
For citizens,
This is just as well,
Now the son is ready waiting,
Earths future contemplating,
Later he will tell the world.
how their future will unfurl.

Forty-Five

The New York Standard has the third largest circulation of all Gotham City newspapers. It has a digital service which provides free news bites and sells an App that not only has all the news but many interactive features as well. The Standard is owned by Tiger Television Network. This multinational company owns television and radio stations and newspapers in thirty eight countries. It has had a checkered history. It was founded by a Missouri entrepreneur in the Sixties. It was bought by an Arab company in the Seventies and sold to the Japanese in the Eighties. It went back to America in the Nineties briefly, but since 1999 it has been owned by a Chinese company. The Chinese owners generally keep out of the hair of editors, but in each office is a CEO who is nothing more nor less than a human abacus.

Bear Grizzard sat behind his desk at eight am waiting for the call from his CEO. Chub Checker was with him. He had been ferried back to the Standard HQ leaving Joanne Rixti in charge of the brood. As expected, Bear was summoned to the top floor executive suite. Gary Lusich the CEO was pacing the floor holding a copy of the Standard.

'What on earth do you think you are doing, Grizzard? This story is total crap. We will be the laughingstock of the media industry. I have already had the Chinese on the phone. They want your head on a platter, without even hearing your take on it. You should have run this past me. It is hard enough to sell papers at all without you writing crap about visitors from outer space.'

'They are not visitors from outer space, Lusich. It is the son of God traveling with Charles Dickens, Vasco De Gama and Joan of Arc. And since when have you shown the slightest fucking interest in editorial content. You are a fucking accountant. Do you realize that our first edition today has sold out. When was the last time that happened. It was September 11, that is how long ago. I am making the bloody Chinese money.'

'Today, you are making us money, but when the shit hits the fan and we are shown up as charlatans, what then Grizzard, what then I ask you?'

'Look I can prove Jerry O' is not from earth.'

Bear Grizzard had brought his medical evidence with him. He showed Jerry O's report to the CEO.

Lusich read it. Then he read it again.

'I see,' he said, 'but this does not prove he is the Son of God.'

'It proves he can talk and breathe, but he is not a human being. Does that help?' said Bear.

Bear had not wanted to provide this information to his CEO. Lusich was a creature of his ultimate employers who were Chinese money men and technocrats. Once the Board knew what they had, Jerry O' would be pulled apart like a Meccano set. The

Chinese would want to build one. On the other hand, if Bear was fired, the mission would be jeopardized. So, here is a turn up for the books, Bear Grizzard the terror of the reporter's pool, is worried about bringing the Creator's message to the world. Bear was an intelligent man; he saw the incongruity of his position.

'I want to see this man, person, thing,' said Lusich, 'the Board will want to fly here.'

'Listen hard Lusich and listen fucking good,' said Bear Grizzard grimly, 'Chub Checker has an exclusive agreement with Jerry O'. You even tell the Board about Jerry O' and you will not even see Chub's rear taillights; he will be gone so fast.'

He paused and walked over to the flabby CEO pointing a finger deep into his upholstery.

'And me too, you fucking arsehole, get that.'

Lusich was about to launch into a tirade. This was his forte. Why has that fool of a journalist Checker been given the rights over the greatest story of the Century, but Lusich paused. He had no cards to play - yet.

'Ok,' he said in a placatory way, 'you have forty-eight hours to get the agreement signed over to Tiger. After that I will move. Checker works for Tiger. He has no rights.'

'Yeah, right,' said Bear and left the office and the plush executive floor to return to his den.

When he was back behind his desk, he told Chub of the situation. What would the abacus do? He would ring the Chairman of the Board - unless. Chub rang Little Pink and asked to speak urgently to Dora.

While Chub Checker was haltingly explaining the problem to Dora, an excited Arnold Prink was sitting in Melvin Van Horn's capacious lobby. He had a story to tell and a proposition to sell.

Two hours later Van Horn and his retinue plus one entered Judge Freddy Kreuger's Court in Manhattan. Her clerk had been informed the attorney had a brief but extremely important urgent submission to make about the former Mayor of New York, Billy Lowe.

'I have got a busy day, Mr. Van Horn,' said Her Honor, 'this had better be good.'

'Oh, it's good Your Honor, have no fear of that. It goes to the whole issue of the arrest and incarceration of my client. It is a matter of human rights'.

'I did not think Human Rights law was your field, counsel, but get on with it,' said Judge Kreuger dryly.

'Your Honor, I have present with me Mr. Arnold Prink. He is the former aide to the mayor. The mayor is here on video link.'

'This is the Mr. Prink who has accused the mayor of rape,' interrupted the judge.

'Yes, that is so, but Mr. Prink instructs me that he wishes to withdraw the charge. I will call him briefly.'

'Any objections Ms. France?' said Judge Kreuger to the ADA Rose France who was pretending to be disinterested in the strange new turn of events.

'No, Your Honor,' she replied coolly.

Prink was called.

'Tell Her Honor what you know,' said Melvin Van Horn.

'Your Honor I am an acquaintance of two men a Mr. Ginger Scollop and a Mr. Tweak Monk. They have informed me they are disciples of a man they call Jerry O'. The Standard has a report about this man today. It is stated categorically that he is not human and he is the son of God. It further states that he influenced the mayor's conduct and caused him to implode. I have met two of Jerry O's associates and it is my belief that they are Vasco De Gama and Joan of Arc'.

'Any questions?' asked Her Honor.

'Is the moon made of blue cheese?' asked Ms. France in her winsome way.

Arnold Prink looked nonplussed and Melvin Van Horn rose angrily to his feet.

'It's OK Mr. Van Horn, the question was rhetorical,; interposed the judge.

'I have no further questions,' said Rose France.

'Yes Mr. Van Horn, what exactly is your application?'

'It is my submission that my client Billy Lowe was acting under the influence of a supernatural force when he erupted. His arrest and subsequent imprisonment were therefore unlawful. I ask for his immediate release.'

'I can inform counsel that I have also read the report in the newspaper,' said Judge Kreuger, 'I will make no comment on its veracity other than to say you are lucky I have not been turned into Judge Roy Bean. Anyway, even if you are right Mr. Van Horn, your client was trying to eat evidence, which as I understand it, tends to incriminate him in serious corruption offenses. Have I got it right, Ms. France?'

'As each hour passes, Judge, more charges emerge,' replied the demure Rose France.

'Your application is dismissed, Mr. Van Horn, what about the rape charge Ms. France.'

'After hearing and seeing Mr Prink, Judge,' said the ADA, 'I will be recommending the charge be dismissed. It seems very likely he and Mr. Lowe are a fine couple.'

'Well, Mr. Van Horn, you seem to have had a win, call the next case,' said Her Honor.

The Van Horn wagon train left the court. The ex-mayor, who had seen the show on television, was taken back to his cell muttering to himself. Calliope was in the back of the court watching. He was well pleased by the outcome, but he had important work to attend to. He resisted the temptation to enter the pompous lawyer Van Horn to discomfort him.

Calliope re-appeared in the Standard CEO's office. Lusich being the human abacus that he was sat at his computer writing up the notes of his meeting with Bear Grizzard. He finished the document and saved the file as 'alien 1'. He emailed the Chinese Managing Director to his personal email address. He attached 'Alien 1'. Calliope made some changes to Alien 1 before it left.

The managing director of Tiger Television Network was finishing a ten-course banquet dinner at the best Mandarin restaurant in Shanghai when he received the email. He was enjoying a fine Hennessy Cognac and eating fortune cookies, but being the company man that he was he read the email and opened 'Alien 1'.

He spoke and read good English. His MBA was from Harvard. He read and re-read the attachment. He rang Bear Grizzard.

'Grizzard,' he said, 'it is the M.D. here. You are to be the new CEO of TTN in USA. Your tenure starts now. I will arrange for Lusich to be escorted from the building now. I will send you a copy of his gross correspondence to me. You will see why I have acted so promptly.'

Moments later Bear Grizzard received 'alien 1'. It read:

'You are a slope eyed arsehole. I suggest you piss in your short soup, shit in your chop suey and pour both dishes over your head and call them curls.'

Bear Grizzard looked out his window. A shocked Gary Lusich was being pushed out the front door of the building by two guards. He carried a small box containing his belongings. He seemed to be in pain as he doubled over as if suddenly struck with force. As he hailed a cab, he realized he had no memory of anything that had happened this morning. What had he done? Why was he fired? He sat in the taxi on his way to the Lower West Side weeping loudly. The Montenegrin taxi driver listened silently. This place was full of weirdos. First, there was the Black woman who appeared out of nowhere demanding a receipt, then last night there was the girl passenger calling out loudly that she was never going to shave her legs again and now this. The driver muttered a nearly silent imprecation at the madness of his adopted city.

Calliope was busy in Bear Grizzard's new office erasing the original 'Alien 1' and its attachment.

Forty-Six

Bear and Chub were fielding telephone calls. Journalists rang for comment. It was clear that they recognized that the story was more than the revelations themselves. Bear Grizzard and Chub Checker were players.

Both were asked about the sudden departure of their CEO Gary Lusich. They were queried about the Arnold Prink court appearance that morning before Judge Kreuger. Most of all they were asked about the 'evidence' that Jerry O' was not human. There were lots of ancillary queries. Where were the visitors being housed? What was the story of De Gama, Dickens and Joan of Arc? Why were they here? Where did they come from? Could it all be a hoax? It was not April fool's day and so it went on.

Chub was the front man. He bore the brunt of the attack. He answered every query, saying everything and nothing. Bear took the editors and advertisers. He was diplomatic and sure. His message was simple. Wait! all will be revealed.

There was no response from government. Nor could there be. Bear, however, knew somebody at the CIA would be monitoring the situation. He warned Chub that their phones would probably be tapped and that there was likely to be surveillance. There was stony silence from organized religion with one exception. In Idaho an obscure denomination known as the Church of the Holy Peach claimed Jerry O' was their savior. The leader of the church was a former dot.com bankrupt called Manfred Melt. He was all over the cable news channels claiming the cult was expecting Jerry O' and they wanted him to be immediately released into his care. Bear ignored him.

Both Bear and Chub were also phoned by friends and acquaintances. Were they ok? Had they flipped their lids? Did they have jobs lined up after the excreta hit the blower? The two journalists were polite and non-committal.

Roger Sebastian Keats, down in the bear pit, was becoming a celebrity in his own right. He regaled other Arts honchos with tales of his friendship with Charles Dickens. The BBC had rung wanting him in London to feature in a documentary about his life story. It was to be called 'Pigsley to Keats, by Dickens'. Far from ruining his career, Keats admission as to his deceit made him a celebrity. The documentary was to feature Charles Dickens as a social commentator on Roger Sebastian Keats' life. Roger Sebastian was wildly enthusiastic, but at least he had the sense to tell the BBC producer that she must wait until he had approval from 'higher powers.'

Bruce Gotby kept an eye on foreign news services, but if the story ran at all, it was simply retailed as a human-interest odd ball anecdote. They had heard it all before. He did receive a call from the Portuguese News Agency asking for an interview with Vasco De

Gama. Bruce refused. He said he would have to run it past the State Department. This was a lie, but it built some bricks on the thin veneer of reality surrounding the strange events.

Joanne Rixti was busy at Little Pink. She had conducted a briefing of security and had personally toured the perimeter of the property to look for weaknesses. Her charges were comfortable. Dickens was writing. Vasco was in the home Gym doing push-ups and Joan was watching series Two of The Only Way is Essex. Jerry O' was just waiting. Dora had befriended Joanne. The journalist liked her new buddy but wondered at her habit of suddenly seeming to be missing only to appear again in a puzzling and unnerving way.

There were others trying to worm their way into the story. Three black gang bangers claimed they had an altercation with Jerry O' and the others four days ago in 42nd Street. A Montenegrin Orthodox Priest alleged his brother was a New York cabbie who was frightened by a large Black women traveling with the group. His brother was still driving a cab but was under daily psychiatric care.

These stories were either sold or given to small time Web News mongers. Chub kept up to date with them. When he read the blog about the Black woman. He smiled ruefully. 'Dora, that bloody Dora'.

A Front Office Manager of the Plaza named Clive tried to sell an account of the check in of the four at the hotel, but his garbled account of self-operating computers and trolleys and live roosters in cages made no sense even to the most addled journalists.

Three TV news shows and fourteen newspaper journalists tried to contact the ball- grabbing Bond Trader Oliver Givens-Cator, but his phone was off the hook as he was an in-patient at a Clinton, Texas facility for the treatment of sexual addiction.

Melvin Van Horn had been in a meeting with his PR firm most of the afternoon trying to nut out the best way of getting some favorable coverage for himself. His advisers were firm. You have nothing to gain. Keep a low profile. This advice went against the grain, but Van Horn accepted it. He had not suffered from any sharp attacks of pain recently and it seemed to be related to stress. The attorney decided to take a lengthy vacation alone.

Billy Lowe, the former mayor, was busy composing a letter to Ms. Rose France ADA asking for mercy. When she received the letter, she immediately filed it after stamping it with the seal 'no action required'.

The 5th Avenue video had leaked and was being shown interminably on every news outlet. Other videos had surfaced of the walk which were sold and being shown continually.

Still more videos emerged.

The fight in Central Park had been captured. Givens-Cator could not totally escape publicity. At least, however, nobody had definitively captured his ball grab.

Alle Restaurant was a great news source. From the chef down to the Matre'd and the waiters every last moment of the quartet's visit was analyzed and discussed. Linguistics experts had been engaged by network producers to discuss the vocal patterns of the visitors with anybody who had encountered the group. Historians learnedly pontificated about the eating habits of the four. Joan of Arc's request for whole frogs and Vasco's demand for dogs to eat the bones were both dissected and scrutinized.

A very stupid young man from the Times fresh out of Yale even rang Judge Krueger for a comment. Her PA told the man that if Her Honor made a comment to him, it would be 'thirty days' for contempt. He hurriedly rang off.

Finally, the Montenegrin Taxi Driver rang the Standard. He said he had seen signs the world was coming to an end. First a black woman materialized in his cab. Then last night a woman had been calling out strange things in his cab. She was saying she would never shave her legs again. And now today he had carried a man from the Standard office who was crying like a baby. He finally said that perhaps the Muslims were right and America was the Great Satan. The Standard cadet reporter who took the call was polite, but unimpressed. The CIA monitor, who was now bugging the newspapers phones, moved quickly. The Montenegrin was traced, arrested and flown to Guantanamo Bay before the sun had set that night on Manhattan.

While monitoring TV coverage, Bear Grizzard chanced upon the day's broadcast by Gavan Rowntree, who was the premier talk show TV presenter of his generation. This description of Gavan Rowntree came out of the presenter's own mouth. His show was called Straight Talk and the sub text was 'come inside the spinless belt, if you dare'. Rowntree who made self-righteousness an art form was already announcing that the Standard was both irresponsible and foolish in publishing the story of Jerry O'. It was contemptuous of Christians. It fed into the prejudices of others [who he did not name] and would only serve to bring America into disrepute. Rowntree went on to say that he would not bother asking Jerry O' on to the show, as Jerry O' would not have the courage to attempt to withstand his rigorous cross examination. As for Dickens, De Gama and Joan, Rowntree categorized them as jobbing actors who were not worth talking to. Bear rang the Producer of Straight Talk.

'Hi Bear Grizzard, here,' he said, 'does Rowntree have the balls to take on the Son of the Creator.'

'You are joking,' the Producer said, 'Gavan will eat him for breakfast.'

'No really.' said Bear, 'yours will be Jerry O's first and probably only TV appearance. We want the whole show. We also will bring Charles Dickens, Vasco De Gama and Joan of Arc. Can you clear your decks?'

'It's a done deal.' said the excited producer.

The time of arrival was sorted out and Bear hung up. The CIA monitor rang his controller. He told him that the freaks are appearing on Straight Talk tomorrow.

'Good.' the monitor replied, 'we'll be there.'

Bear informed Chub of the development and Chub was ferried over to Little Pink to prepare the four visitors.

Strangely, nobody heard a murmur from Ginger Scollop, Tweak Monk or Kelly Bamwoo. They spent the day in Tweak's filthy one room apartment eating pizza, drinking rot gut chianti and talking endlessly about the meaning of life - and Jerry O'.

Unsurprisingly, Arnold Prink left the city for San Francisco, 'where boys are boys and so are girls,' he said to his last remaining friend. He travelled by bus and carried with him a small dog in a wooden box.

'What's its name?' the driver asked him as he stored him carefully in the live pet compartment.

'He used to be known as Gaius Ceasar,' said Prink, but I call him Charlie.'

Forty-Seven

Straight Talk is recorded each weekday at a purpose built studio in Brooklyn. Gavan Rowntree owns the building. He also owns the company which packages Straight Talk. He employs the staff and a subsidiary company is the distributor. Straight Talk is shown on one thousand nine hundred and sixty five stations in sixty three counties. It is the most popular talk show in the world. It is simulcast on internet radio and to subscribers on web TV.

Gavan Rowntree believes he earns every cent of the seven million dollars he earns per episode. Rowntree has total control over content, advertising and guest selection. He is a rude, abrasive man who does not suffer fools or superior intelligence gladly. His method of interview is to ask a long-convoluted question which is really a statement and ask for a brief answer. He has a vile temper and if he becomes angry, he will shout at a hapless guest. If he receives a non-responsive answer he is undeterred. He will then either abuse the interviewee or ask the next question as if the guest has answered responsively. Many politicians refuse to go on Straight Talk, but more are prepared to wear an emotional flak jacket and accept the Rowntree assault in the interest of gaining exposure.

Chub briefed his team before they left for Brooklyn. Charles Dickens listened carefully and seemed to appreciate the dangers ahead. Vasco and Joan listened, but Chub got the impression they did not get it. Jerry O' was unworried. Dora was present, but it seemed to be common ground that she would not be at the shoot.

The helicopter took the group to the studio and parked on the rooftop heliport. The appearance of Jerry O' had been advertised the evening before on radio and television and a small group of people had gathered on Ocean Boulevard outside the studio. There were some reporters and TV news crews. There were a few religious cranks. The odd local had also turned up. Right at the front were Ginger Scollop, Tweak Monk and Kelly Bamwoo who had come by train from Manhattan.

The producer of Straight Talk and three or four gophers were waiting for their guests. They were hurried into the cavernous depths of the office block which housed the Rowntree empire and the large studio where the show was recorded.

Gavan Rowntree was in his executive suite reading the research his associate producers had put together. Every few moments he would harrumph in disbelief. In his thirty years of broadcasting Gavan Rowntree had never read such a steaming pile of hog's crap. Son of the Creator, we will see about that and as for the turds in the body of the main heap! Gavan could not wait to show them up for what they are. Gavan's only misgiving related to the question of causation. The four dickheads were pretenders, but why, that was the question - why?

Rowntree had a flash whizz bang intercom, but he preferred the old-fashioned method of summoning staff.

'In here now,' he shouted.

His four researchers and his two P. A's who had been huddled in his ante room came rushing in. The Rowntree shouted decree was a daily occurrence. They gathered around his desk like curs at the heels of a wolf hound.

Rowntree shook his thick shock of black wavy dyed hair and flicked a corner of his bushy dyed indigo mustache. He was a tiny man, no more than five foot three. He compensated. The floor on his side of the desk was built up by two feet. The set itself was thirty inches higher on the right and Gavan Rowntree always sat on the right. His shoes were built up; his hair was high waxed and his hand crafted Zegna suits were cut long and narrow.

He shouted at his frightened gophers.

'Why are these fuck-knuckles here, nobody tells me. This research is nothing but second-rate arse wipe. Any shit beetle can copy newspaper articles and photoshop excerpts of videos. What I want to know is why? Get that you fuck-wits why?'

The group looked at one another and back at Rowntree in abject terror. These meetings were often a blood bath. He occasionally fired people and often brought producers to tears, even sometimes one of the women producers. The Associate Producer job on Straight Talk was akin to being a Christian waiting in the wings of the Roman Coliseum. Lions surely await you and the only question is when.

Peaches Globby, the newest and least frightened of the team, spoke up. Peaches real name was Relena

Vodanovich. She had escaped from a miserable village near Minsk to make her fortune in the USA. She was a girl of considerable fortitude and ingenuity. Her looks helped. Peaches was six foot four. She was stick thin, with the longest legs in Manhattan. Her hair was as golden as the richest ingot and her lashes were as long as baby's fingers. Her manner was that of an ingenue but underneath lay the steely resolve of an assassin. Peaches was not frightened of Gavan Rowntree.

'There are a number of theories.' she said, 'some say they are promoting a product or TV show. Others say they are Al Queda operatives here to foment religious trouble. Still others say they are Holy Roman plants sent by the Vatican to promote their failing numbers.'

'I am not interested in fucking theories, Peaches, stop wasting my valuable, very valuable time. I ask you arse holes again. Why are they here/'

Peaches looked at the other staff. They all looked away.

'Well, fuck you too,' she said in her odd, affected Bronx drawl plus Minsk drone, 'Jerry O' is said to be not human. It may be the truth. He may be from heaven. If this is so he is now in hell.'

Peaches waited for the explosion, but there was none forthcoming. Gavan Rowntree leaned back in his black Italian leather chair and closed his eyes.

'Out.' he shouted, 'everybody out.'

The staff left. Peaches walked tall, well taller than even usual. She led the others like the ornament on the prow of a large steamer, proud as punch and ready to face the largest wave the world could throw at her.

Gavan Rowntree subsided. He was not worried. Why should he be, after all Gavan Rowntree was the master of Straight Talk and Straight Talk was the most watched talk show on the planet.

The make-up department proved to be the source of some difficulty. Jerry O's skin did not seem to accept the liquids or powder applied. The make-up simply vanished, leaving no trace on his face.

Calliope had been in Rowntree's office watching the meeting. He had not intervened, though he was strongly of a mind to enter and hurt the presenter. After the meeting he went to see how the group was taking to make up. He intervened. Jerry O's face suddenly glowed. The make-up artist was now content.

'It's probably because he is Irish,' she told the girl at the next chair, 'they have very pale skin. It takes a while for the cream to work.'

The next-door cosmetician was having her own problems. Vasco De Gama was making a spirited argument that no powder or cream should be applied.

'I am a warrior seaman,' he said, 'I am no poltroon.'

Calliope calmed him down.

Charles and Joan were more amenable. Dickens wanted a full explanation of every substance applied.

'For my journal,' he said.

Joan asked her grease painter if the substances applied were the same as the make-up applied to Lydia in The Only Way is Essex. When she was assured that all make-up artists used the same equipment Joan enthusiastically complied with every request to move her head this way or that.

After leaving make up, the group made their way to the Green Room for tea and biscuits. A few of the assistants were already there. They would pour the tea hand around the biscuits and make conversation. It was too late to try to garner information as the interviewees would go direct from the Green Room to the main set.

Peaches Globby found herself handing a cup of coffee to Vasco De Gama. He looked her up and down with interest.

'You are the second young wench I have met on this trip who looks as if she has been stretched. The other scrawny damsel was a TV presenter named Kelly Bamwoo. I asked her to rut, but my request was forgotten when I was insulted by a man she was with named Arnold Prink.'

'Well, fuck you too,' said Peaches for the second time this morning, but Arnold Prink, where had she heard this name. Then she remembered. It was claimed that Jerry O' had caused the demise of the mayor. Arnold Prink was the mayor's personal assistant and bum boy. And now this doughty little man claimed to know him.

Vasco was reeling from Peaches comment. Could she be offering herself to him. If so, she must be a harlot. Vasco did not much care for harlots. Too many of his men had died from syphilis carried by Indian whores. On the other hand, this woman was well dressed and apparently working for the television company.

'If you are offering me a rut, I will need to know your price and whether you are clean and free of crabs and syph.'

Peaches laughed with pleasure.

'Vasco, my dear little sailor-boy, I don't charge. If I want a fuck, I have one. Also, the only crabs I like anywhere near me are whole Chesapeake Blue Crabs cooked in Chili Sauce.'

Vasco was trying to absorb this information. It was difficult.

Peaches interrupted his reverie.

'But how do you know Arnold Prink,' she asked, 'and Kelly Bamwoo is she the girl on that pathetic TV show spruiking fashion trends, and anyway she is much shorter than me?'

Vasco thought this over.

'Prink was with the wench Kelly Bamwoo and Jerry O's first two disciples Ginger Scollop and Tweak Monk. He insulted me. He is lucky to be still alive.'

Peaches was well pleased. She took Vasco's hand and led him out of the Geen Room.

'Let's rut,' she said.

Joan had found a producer who had worked in England. She was happily talking shop about Series Two of The Only Way is Essex. Jerry O' was making small talk. He was asked about his clothes. Paul Smith, he said, opening his coat and revealing the bright mauve and heather lining. Charles Dickens was surprised to find the Green Room was painted off-white. He told a group of producers that the origin of the term Green Room dated back to mediaeval theaters when the stage was on the edge of the green and the cast remained on the 'green' until they were called on stage. The producers were so obtuse they did not use the opportunity to quiz Charles about the depth and origins of his knowledge.

Charles finally exhausted the subject and decided to investigate the rest of the building. He walked out of the Green Room and entered a long corridor. He walked aimlessly until he heard noise. There was muffled screaming coming from a door marked Storeroom. He opened the door and to his surprise there was Vasco De Gama and Peaches Globby. Vasco's plus two's were round his ankles. He was standing three steps up a step ladder. On the other side of the ladder was Peaches. Her long thin bare legs were wrapped around the waist of the Portuguese sailor like a spider capturing an insect. Her arms were spread out wide. She was leaning back and half screaming and half calling out as the Portuguese man humped her heartily.

As Dickens hurriedly shut the door he identified the girl's cry.

'Rut me Vasco,' she was moaning between her yelps of pleasure.

Charles hurriedly made his way back to the Green Room for a fresh cup of tea. About five minutes later a bell rang.

'Time,' said a harried young producer putting his head in the Green Room doorway.

The party made their way to the brightly lit set. Dickens noticed that Vasco was already seated. He thought perhaps he had seen a mirage in the storeroom, but then he noticed Peaches Globby chatting to another young woman. She had a glow, which Charles recognized from long ago. Dickens wondered whether Vasco's re-entry to Paradise would be thwarted by his fornication. Charles hoped not. He had come to quite like De Gama.

Peaches was still whispering to the other young woman.

'Guess what,' she said, 'I just fucked Vasco.'

'How was it?' said the other girl.

'It was great for me and Vasco said it was his best root in five hundred years.'

The hum of voices in the studio ceased immediately when Gavan Rowntree entered and sat opposite his four guests who were now lined up on uncomfortable wooden chairs on the left side of the bench table which was the centerpiece of the set. Rowntree did not speak. He just looked straight ahead. Occasionally he pursed his lips or hummed. He was exercising his voice. He also occasionally swung slightly in his plush leather swivel chair.

Joan sat furthest from the camera, next to her was Vasco De Gama. Jerry O' sat on the end with Charles between he and Vasco. Rowntree sat opposite Jerry O'.

There was a countdown from ten to one by the director in the booth above the studio. Gavan Rowntree spoke.

'Hello world, this is Gavan Rowntree, your host of the most watched show on cable television Straight Talk. Come inside the spinless set if you dare. My guests today are Jerry O', who claims to be the Son of God and his three friends who call themselves from the right Joan of Arc, Vasco De Gama and Charles Dickens. I would not normally interview charlatans, but these four swindlers have already attracted worldwide coverage. I will therefore question them and like hundreds before there will be no spin allowed.'

Calliope took hold of Rowntree's chair and swung it violently around in a circle about half a dozen turns. Rowntree was shouting.

'Stop this, I will find out who is responsible you will never work in television again. Cut the take, cut the take.'

The Director spoke to Rowntree via a mike into the presenter's ear. 'We are live Mr. Rowntree, we cannot have clear air.'

By now Rowntree was stationary once again. He commenced again.

'I don't know if you are responsible Jerry O'. My guess is you have bribed one of my staff but let me proceed. What part of Ireland are you from?'

'All of it.' answered Jerry O'.

'If this interview is going ahead, I want straight answers. Where do you come from?'

'I am from Paradise,' responded Jerry O'. 'it is the place Christians call Heaven and others call Nirvana. I am the son of the Big Feller. He is the Creator of the seven universes. I have come to earth to warn humans that they are at risk of destroying their planet. Your society is corrupted, your clerics are mostly charlatans, and your politicians are mainly imbeciles.'

'Now look here Jerry O',' said Gavan, 'it is easy to come here in your flash suit with three people in fancy dress and claim to be the Son of God but we do not accept spin here.'

Once again Calliope spun Gavan. This time he turned in the other direction. He was shouting and screaming. Many on the set were openly laughing. The spin stopped as suddenly as it started.

'I am not the king of talk television for nothing,' said Gavan, 'despite your sorcery I am going to continue the interview. Who are the three jobbing actors with you?'

Charles Dickens was enjoying himself. He appreciated that Calliope must be pulling the strings or more accurately spinning the chair. Joan did not like the look of Rowntree, but so far, she remained quiet. After all she had a pleasant time in the Green Room discussing her favorite reality TV show. Vasco was another story. He had sown his oats. He was enervated. He was also alert to the contemptuous tone taken by Gavan Rowntree.

'I am no jobbing actor, you sniveling poltroon,' he said, 'I am Vasco De Gama of Portugal. I have been honored by the King. I have conquered three seas. If you were on my ship I would use you for bait. A shark or dolphin would spurn you, but if you are lucky a swordfish may find you suitable. It would pierce you first then throw you in the air then eat you. I would enjoy the spectacle; my sailors would line the sides of the ship cheering the swordfish on. It would be a sight to see.'

The production crew of Straight Talk were delighted by the picture painted by Vasco and clapped in appreciation. The friend of Peaches tapped her on the shoulder.

'Did you get his phone number?' she asked.

Gavan Rowntree may have been a pompous man, but he was no fool. He needed to take control. He would take control. He would humor the troupe of magicians, because that is what he now thought they were. Later when control was achieved, he would step in for the kill. He signaled an ad break and looked at his notes. There seemed to be only one significant hook. He would use it. The ad break finished. A countdown occurred. The show re-commenced.

'Welcome back world, I hope you are enjoying today as much as I am. We live in a dangerous world. It is important to have some levity.'

Calliope had been standing behind Rowntree. Later he would explain he misunderstood. He thought the man meant levitate.

Calliope lifted Gavan Rowntree from his chair. He held him about six feet in the air. Rowntree was still in a sitting position. His little legs were kicking furiously revealing Mickey Mouse socks. He was shouting 'put me down, put me down'.

Jerry O' understood what was happening. 'Let it go, Calliope,' he said, at which the Angel dropped Gavan Rowntree. He fell like a stone. It was fortunate he only suffered a Monteggia fracture of the right arm. Still, that was painful enough. The ulna and radius were both fractured and the ulna had penetrated the elbow joint.

Later Jerry O' would also have some explaining to do. He now agrees that the words 'let it go' were not felicitous. 'Put him down' would have been better.

The director moved to an ad break when Rowntree hit the ground. By the time the two staff medicos had tranquilized Rowntree and wheeled him to the waiting studio ambulance the show had re-commenced.

Without discussion Peaches Globby was now behind the desk in the old Rowntree seat.

'Hi I am Peaches Globby. Welcome back everybody, unfortunately Gavan has had a drop, but not a ratings drop and I am your host for the rest of today's show. Now first Jerry O', who is Calliope?'

Calliope appeared as a shimmer and pulled up a chair next to Peaches. 'I am Calliope', she said, 'I am an angel. I have accompanied Jerry O' and the others from Paradise. There is another angel here called Sandalphon. He is Joan's angel. She gets her own angel because she is a saint.'

'Is Sandals here?' said Joan, oh there he is.' She waved to a corner of the set. The staff turned to look but nobody could be seen. Sandalphon was livid with rage at Calliope's folly. 'Wait until Gabriel hears of this,' he said to himself.

Calliope then vanished. Peaches was undeterred.

'Jerry O' tell me why you differ from other humans. This is the claim of the Standard. It is said you are not a human,' Peaches was in fine fettle.

'I am missing some human organs,' said Jerry O', 'my father controls my brain and my heart from Paradise. It is only when I am on earth that he exercises this control. It was why I was able to rise from the dead when I was last here as Jesus of Nazareth. When I am in Paradise, he does not control my golf swing.'

'So, you like golf,' Peaches asked.

'I love it, but it is difficult to master. I have only been playing the game for two hundred years.'

'Tell me again why are you here Jerry O'. What is the purpose of your visit?'

Jerry O' was ready:

'Humans must renew their faith. The churches should be doing this, but they are beset by corruption, pedophilia and terrorism. Humans at first were little more than simians. You resembled our annoying sub-human Grillabies on Pluto, who incidentally continue to fight endlessly amongst themselves. As time has passed you have evolved. Your capacity for learning has increased by a hundred-fold. Your life span has more than doubled due to great men and women mastering ways of curing illness and disease. Others have grasped the significance of diet and exercise and taught you ways to extend and improve your conditions. Nature itself has also evolved as you learn how to use your environment. Yet for all this you somehow never learn. Let me speak of the small things first. They may seem unimportant but are symptomatic of the whole human enigma. It starts with the children. The teachers are often ignorant themselves. The basic tenets of learning are no longer being taught. The parents are often of no use. They treat the children as if they are small adults. Childhood itself is being denied the next generations. These children, unless something is done, will grow up to be even worse than the foolish, narcissistic baby boomers who are now teachers, lawyers and world leaders. Large canines which were bred over centuries to be hunters and runners are being cooped up in tiny enclosures called yards and kept as trophy pets by humans. The dogs are becoming as neurotic as their owners. Tribes of half-educated people called counsellors now are paid by you to give half-baked advice as to how you should live your lives. Though the middle classes in your first world wring their hands endlessly about the state of the planet, they drive huge petrol guzzling vehicles called SUV's and talk constantly on portable phones. There is a new cult of celebrity which involves humans seeking fame for its own sake even if it is for a fleeting moment. As part of this odd phenomenon people use computers and phones to constantly inform the world of what they had for breakfast, where they are standing and other minutiae. Your sun provides an important vitamin, necessary for your well-being, but you hide from it and pay people to spray fake tan on your bodies. However, what I have just detailed to you is small potatoes compared to the more important dilemmas facing humanity. Some of the priests are pedophiles and the churches have either failed to act or covered up the evil. Some Muslims claim that they must eliminate all Christians and create an Islamic caliphate across the world. In pursuance of this object, they encourage young men to act as suicide weapons in the belief that they will be transported to Paradise where they will find fifty virgins waiting for them. Though it is difficult to comprehend there are takers to this monstrous offer. There are whole societies where the starving outnumbers the fed and the homeless outnumber the housed. Wars still break out constantly. Yet you do nothing. My father created a whole system of nature and allowed it to evolve without his interference. This will continue. However, he sends me as his messenger with a warning to humans. The priests must be taught to be good as well as pious. The Muslims must drag themselves into the new century. The first world must re-learn the basic tenets. Children must be allowed to be children. Hypocrisy must be exposed and then excised from the human condition. There is much to be done. So, I warn you that if human nature does not change, there will be no earth. You must understand my father does not interfere with nature. He gives humans the opportunity to work with and not against nature. Animals and plants are attuned to nature. Humans seem intent on defying it. This is the message I bring from my father. I want the whole world to hear and see my message. That is my goal. Charles Dickens here is my diarist. Vasco De Gama is my guard and Joan of Arc is my strategist. Calliope is our angel. He is our contact with the Big Feller. I mean my father. I hope this makes things clear.'

'And will you act to achieve your goal,' asked Peaches, who seemed perfectly at home and attuned to the situation.

'I will not freeze volcanoes or dam floods, but tomorrow I will send a clear message to the world. It will be unmistakable,' said Jerry O'.

'You talked of Grillabies on Pluto, so there are other life forms in the universe,' asked Peaches.

'Grillabies are sub-human. They constantly bicker and fight, but they are incapable of blowing each other up. If they could they would. I am not at liberty to talk of other life forms, except to say that there are seven universes.'

'Can I turn to your friends, Joan,' Peaches said, 'are you really Joan of Arc?'

'Of course,' replied Joan, 'and I do not shave my legs and I have never had a Brazilian. My pudenda is hairy. I was burned at the stake, but I killed many English and foul Burgundians. I do not know if any of the British were from Essex. If they were I may have thought twice.'

Even Peaches was bemused by Joan's remarks.

'And Charles you are the writer, Peaches felt she was on safer ground.

'I have much to report,' replied Charles, 'I have seen some strange sights since being here.'

Peaches remembered the storeroom door opening and a man looking in. It was Dickens. She decided to move on.

'Charles we are running out of time today, but my guess is that you will need a series to do justice to your talent. Now Vasco when did you die?'

'Christmas Eve 1524, my sweet skin and bone wench,' said Vasco.

'Geez,' said Peaches friend to nobody in particular, 'it was his ONLY root in five hundred years.'

Peaches had a thought.

'Jerry O' I have heard you have two disciples. Can you tell me more?'

'Yes, there is Ginger Scollop and Tweak Monk, but I am hoping that there will be more. I am expecting that the Big Feller will allow me to select twelve apostles. I thoroughly enjoyed my last meal with the previous set – but not the aftermath.'

Ginger was slipped a note while Jerry O' was speaking.

'I have an invitation for you, Jerry O'. Constitutional Golf Club in Bethesda, Maryland has asked you to be its guest for a game this afternoon. It is one of the country's best courses. It is very exclusive. At least one ex-president was refused entry.'

Jerry O' noticed Chub in the rear of the room nodding his head.

"I shall be delighted", said Jerry O'.

'And paradise,' Peaches asked, 'can you describe it?'

'Paradise is as it sounds as I am sure my friends will agree. But it will remain a mystery for humans until they enter,' Jerry O' looked at the others who all nodded in hearty agreement.

Forty-Eight

'Funny little man, that Gavan Rowntree,' said the Big Feller to Mohammed. They were walking in the grounds of the Big Feller's house in Paradise. They had sat together and watched Straight Talk in the Big Feller's study. The Big Feller had imported the telecast by wave transference and showed it on his whiteboard wall for Mohammed's benefit.

'Wilfred did you proud Big Feller. He certainly gave the humans something to think about,' responded Mohammed.

'I'm not sure that Calliope should have dropped the man - from such a height, but the result certainly worked in our favor. The girl Peaches was a more sympathetic interviewer. She let Wilfred tell his story.'

Mohammed nodded.

'I am surprised Gabriel has not already been over here wringing his hands. But I spoke too soon. Here he comes.'

Gabriel and Metatron were marching across the lawn towards them.

'Ah Gabriel and Metatron,' greeted the Big Feller warmly, 'Mohammed and I were just talking about Calliope's fine work in New York. Pity he injured the chap, but in the end it all worked out. When Calliope gets back just remind him to be a bit more careful when he decides to levitate humans. We don't want the hospitals full of Calliope's victims. Also, Sandalphon should be down there keeping an eye out for young Joan. I hope he is supporting Calliope - to the hilt, Gabriel - to the hilt. The team is about to get into top gear. It will need your support.'

Gabriel was nonplussed. He nodded his head and wandered off with his assistant. Mohammed could see their heads were close together and they were whispering to each other.

'Plotting,' suggested Mohammed.

'No doubt,' replied the Big Feller equably, 'but remember my old friend, it is all part of the nature of things.'

The Big Feller and Mohammed completed their constitutional and retreated back to the sunlit study. Reports were starting to surface from Earth about Jerry O'.

The Vatican had issued a press statement to the effect that if there was a holy visitor he would only enter through the gates of a Roman Catholic cathedral. The statement went on to say the story by Jerry O' was a hoax either perpetrated by an enemy of the western world or a mischievous prankster. Surprisingly the document did not address any of the substantial concerns raised by Jerry O'.

'Typical of the Holy Romans,' said the Big Feller, 'for some reason they think they are the sole font of religious knowledge. They should stick to banking.'

'And sexist,' said Mohammed, 'the bishop writes of a 'he', what about a she. I would like to see what Joan or Florence Nightingale would say.'

'What about St Columba of Spain. She fought the Moors in Cordoba until they beheaded her,' replied the Big Feller, 'a blood thirsty lot your forebears.'

'It takes two to tango,' said Mohammed obliquely.

The Grand Ayatollah of Iran also issued a statement. He went on Al Jazeera TV. He was dressed in his white robes, and his great bushy beard flew about as he screamed in his guttural tongue. As he spoke one could observe gobs of spittle flying about striking his courtiers who stood beside him occasionally flinching.

'This is yet another sign of the fall of the great US Satan. These strange creatures dressed in ancient garb expect us to believe that there is a second coming. It is a lie. They are charlatans. On the other hand, much of what the Irishman says has merit. Strangely however his criticism of modern society is criticism of his own culture - the debased west. God is great, Islam is the only true faith. Mohammed is great, Jesus is good. Fifty virgins await those who die in our great cause. God is Great, God is Great.'

'Do you think he means me?' asked the Big Feller.

'I doubt it,' replied Mohammed, 'and it is a different Mohammed he is talking about. He is talking about Mohammed the Prophet. But I don't like this business about the fifty virgins. Do you think the Muslims are going to try to kill Jerry O's team?'

'I doubt it,' said the Big Feller, 'but I hope Vasco does not put any store in his nonsense about those fifty virgins. We don't want him changing sides.'

The Archbishop of Canterbury's office stated he had no comment to make.

'Typical of the old snob,' said the Big Feller, 'he would not be satisfied unless a saint appeared at his window dressed in silk and ermine accompanied by four snow white angels playing Hark, the Herald Angels Sing on flutes.'

The Av Beth Din of Israel ignored the story.

'He is a cunning fellow our Chief Rabbi. He is waiting for the Mossad to confirm the story,' the Big Feller knew plenty about the Mossad. Gabriel had wanted to study their methods of surveillance and even made a request of the Big Feller to send four angels to a Mossad conference to be held in Cannes. 'Have the Mossad agents the power to dematerialize, Gabriel,' the Creator had asked Gabriel. The angel said, 'no, of course not.' The Big Feller sent Gabriel packing saying:.

'When and if the Israeli spies can appear and vanish at will we will give further thought to angels attending expensive conferences on the French Riviera.'

Various minor church orders were sending out mixed messages. The fool Manfred Melt, head honcho of the Idaho based Church of the Holy Peach, was still claiming Jerry O' as his own savior, however he was no longer alleging that the Standard was somehow holding Jerry O' hostage. Melt's statements now took the form of a plea to Jerry O' to contact him. It was wretched.

No government commented. The Big Feller knew the statement from the Ayatollah was akin to a government decree and if the Vatican called out 'mouse' the Palazzo del Quirinale would send over a herd of rat catchers.

'Nothing from the US,' asked Mohammed rhetorically.

'Not yet, but they have hacked into the Standard Newspaper computer and have read Jerry O's medical report. This will intrigue them. I hope that Jerry O' marks his golf balls carefully. This afternoon he will be playing golf with three spies.'

'What do you expect the Americans will do with the information?' asked Mohammed.

'Apart from telling Israel, nothing yet,' replied the Big Feller, 'But this afternoon we will up the ante. Would you mind asking Peter the Fisherman over for tea.'

Mohammed left to get Peter.

Peter the Fisherman had been the leader of the apostles. He was Wilfred's best friend when Wilfred was last on earth as Jesus. He now ran a string of skiffs in the Appollean Sea catching snapper and tuna by the tonne. He lived his life in Paradise on the sea. It was his home. Mohammed picked him up at Peter's Pier [named after him] and drove him back to the Big Feller's home.

'Come in, Pete,' said the Big Feller, 'it's good to see you. Your tuna catches this year are better than ever. I have never tasted more delectable sashimi.'

Peter thanked the Creator, but he was a trifle uneasy. He was so used to being on the water, that he was unsteady on shore. He had no land legs. He, of course, knew Wilfred was back on earth. Peter decided he was welcome to it. Peter's experiences were a distant memory, but a memory, nevertheless. Wilfred had given Peter great responsibility, and he had let him down, not once but three times he had denied him. When Nero eventually caught Peter and was going to crucify him, Peter insisted that he be hung upside down when the torture was applied to him. It seemed the least he could do to rectify his wrong. At least he would be crucified in a less dignified way than his friend Wilfred. But now what, surely, he would not be asked to go back. He doubted Wilfred would want him.

'It's not about those pearly gates,' asked Peter, hoping that some query had been raised about gates that never existed. He knew humans thought he guarded the gates, when they were simply a product of the fertile imagination of a gospel writer in the Book of Revelation. He once ran into John who had written the book and queried the reference, but John simply said the gates were allegorical, whatever that meant. Michaelangelo's mural of the gates did not help to dispel the illusion, but at least that was up here behind reception in Paradise.

'No Peter, I am afraid not,' said the Big Feller, 'Wilfred is back on earth. He is going to appoint some apostles. You will be the leader.'

Forty-Nine

Bear Grizzard was sitting in his new executive suite with Chub Checker, Roger Sebastian Keats and Bruce Gotby watching a replay of Straight Talk. It had become within minutes, the most watched single episode of a television show in the history of the medium. From big screens in the food courts of huge shopping malls to private homes, sports bars and shanties in Somalia crowds huddled in front of monitors. Desk top computers, lap tops, phones and pads were all focused on Jerry O' and his unique performance.

In addition to the endless repetition of the program, commentators of varying disciplines and knowledge were commenting on every aspect of the show. Unfortunately, of course, the main emphasis was on the antics of Gavan Rowntree and his eventual unfortunate injury.

Peaches Globby was becoming a super star. She insisted that the production staff had nothing to do with chairs spinning or the host levitating. She was already being compared to Barbara Walters and Diane Sawyer.

Bear watched Peaches being interviewed by a rival network. She sat perkily on a stool. She wore the shortest of skirts and her long bare legs were exposed only fractionally less than Sharon Stone in

Basic Instinct. The interviewer's eyes seemed drawn like a magnet to her southern cleavage, but each time he realized it, he would lift his head like a gobbling rooster about to forage.

'No wonder they call America, the land of opportunity. This tart is a fucking illegal from Minsk. Peaches Globby! What a fucking name, pardon my French.'

Bear had background checks done on Peaches. Her history was easy to trace. Grizzard still used expletives, but he had now taken to apologizing for uttering them.

Bruce Gotby was watching developments around the world closely. Every contact in every city was being canvassed by his reporters. Every favor he was owed was being called in.

'Our spooks have loose lips,' he said, 'just about every world leader now believes we have an alien on our hands.'

'He is no fucking alien, sport,' said Bear, 'he is who he says he is.'

'Alien is not my word, Bear,' replied Gotby, 'I am with you. However, the problem is that a nasty person like that tiny turd in North Booga in the one-piece pajama suit is likely to make a play for Jerry O.'

'Make a play for him,' asked Chub Checker.

'Buy him or kidnap him,' replied the Foreign Editor.

'Or try to kill him,' added Roger Sebastian Keats.

'The best of British luck if they try that,' said Bear.

'Do we have him safe and sound,' asked Bear.

Chub nodded:

'At this moment Jerry O' is on his way by our chopper to Maryland for his golf game. He does not know it but the US Air Force has two Blackhawks tailing him,'

'And the others!'

'They are with Joanne. Those two wanky disciples are fielding job offers. I have told them they are better off doing one good interview with Meghan Kelly.'

What Chub did not say because he did not know it, was that Calliope was winging his way to Maryland on the tail of the military choppers.

Joanne Rixti was at that moment sitting uncomfortably on a shiny red vinyl chair at an office within the bowels of the Fashion Channel. The chair felt vaguely sticky, but Joanne hoped it was just her imagination. Kelly Bamwoo was not in evidence. She was busy preparing for her evening's performance of Hot Goss.

Ginger Scollop was sitting at the other end of the office speaking into the microphone of a miniature web cam. Next to him were the three visitors Charles Dickens, Vasco De Gama and Joan of Arc. Tweak Monk was fiddling at the controls of a small black computer interface which was connected by USB to a large monitor. A huge black man with a shiny bald pate was on the screen. The web cam at his end was incompetently managed which resulted in the monitor being dominated by the black man's face. It looked huge and out of proportion to his shoulders which was the only other part of him one could see. The picture was also unbalanced to the point that his left ear was out of shot. This did not seem to worry our three visitors who sat watching the man patiently.

'My idea,' he said, 'is for Vasco De Gama to hunt African pirates. We will fit him up with a sailing ship and a crew. We will, however, provide him with modern weapons so he will be able to catch and kill the pirates.'

'How long will this take to organize?' asked Ginger Scollop who seemed to have acquired some much-needed gravitas.

'It will take about six months to organize finance for the show and another year to build the ship and employ crew. To be on the safe side I would say we need two years.'

'Can you do it in two days?' asked Ginger.

'Don't be ridiculous,' said the man.

Ginger signaled to Tweak Monk who disconnected the man.

'All right who is next,' said Ginger.

Vasco had been fascinated by the proposal. He had excitedly sat up. When the man was unplugged, he leant back unhappily.

'But Ginger,' said Vasco,' give me any ship, give me any ten men and I will hunt down and execute these buccaneers.'

Ginger Scollop ignored him. He was focusing on the next pitch. It was a well-known Hollywood producer. She was a middle-aged woman. Her face was leathery and heavily lined. Her long straight hair hung in plaited dirty braids. She wore rings on every finger and had another circular ring through her nose.

'A sorceress,' muttered Joan of Arc, without any rancor.

Ginger beckoned to Joan who sat next to him facing the camera.

'Voila,' said Ginger, 'here we have Joan of Arc. You could film her today as narrator of her own story. It would be your exclusive. Later you could employ writers, engage your actors, build your sets, do your location scenes and film the show.'

The leathery woman inspected the monitor at her end.

'But it has been done, Ginger,' she said, 'Milla Jovovich and Leelee Sobielski have done recent versions of Joan. The first Joan was filmed in 1928 starring Renee Jean Falconetti.'

'But here you have the real Joan of Arc,' exclaimed Ginger.

'I am afraid,' said the woman, 'she does not look the part. I will always think of Ingrid Bergman as capturing the real Joan of Arc.'

'This is bullshit,' said Ginger, gesturing to Tweak to disconnect.

Joan was angry.

'What is this, about some person called Bergman capturing me. I have never been seized by any such creature. And who was that witch and why does she have a ring through her nose. The Burgundians had eunuchs who wore such rings. Is she a female eunuch?'

'Female eunuch, now that is a really great name,' said Tweak.

'It's already been done,' replied Ginger, "ok, who is next".

A heavy-set man in a pinstripe suit was the next prospective customer. He had a deep baritone and spoke in a London Home Counties accent.

'We are looking for a new Charles Dickens novel. We are ready to advance One Million British Pounds.'

'Keep talking,' said Ginger Scollop, ushering Charles over to take Joan's chair.

'It should be no more than sixty thousand words. We want some raunchy sex, a hideous crime, an Arab terrorist and a handsome hero.'

Charles was trying to comprehend what the man was saying. Did he really say one million pounds. Could such a sum exist? Then Dickens thought of the man's requirements. Could he really expect him to write explicit fictional scenes of copulation? It was going to be hard enough to catalogue Vasco's real life amorous adventure with the lanky girl this morning, let alone ask him to make up such a tale. And hideous crimes and Arab terrorists, how could he write of such nonsense? Handsome heroes now they are another matter. Every one of Dickens books had at least one such character. But sixty thousand words - it would take that many words to set the scene.

'I could write you a short tale of a handsome man and unrequited love. I am only here for a short time, but I could put down ten thousand words today. But there will be no fornication, crime or Arab terrorists.'

'I will pass,' said the man in the pinstripe suit and exited the system.

Kelly Bamwoo entered the room.

'We are ready to film,' she said. Kelly was going to do a piece on Vasco and Joan for tonight's edition of Hot Goss. Charles was not unhappy to be excluded from this facile exercise.

Kelly was followed into the room by a sweet young girl with lips of the brightest red and shapely well-muscled tan legs. She carried a clip board.

Vasco stirred with anticipation. Earlier in the day he had asked Kelly if she would rut and she had surprisingly told him she was going to wait until she was married, but this girl, she was gorgeous. The newcomer gave Vasco a flirtatious come-hither look which the Portuguese profligate recognized instantly. He was on his feet:

'Can we rut?' he asked the girl.

Kelly intervened before the girl answered.

'I do not think it is wise she is a trannie,'

'A trannie what is a trannie?' Vasco murmured to Ginger.

'There is a dick under that dress, Vasco, a trannie is a man dressed as a woman.'

Vasco cursed furiously in Portuguese and gestured with his fist at the new arrival.

'It is no wonder Jerry O' has come here,' he said, 'this earth is sinful beyond belief. If I had not known and put my hand up the girl's dress, I would have found a cock. It is lucky I did not, as I would have twisted it so hard it would have fallen off.'

'I notice your legs are shaved,' Joan remarked of the newcomer, 'is your twat shaven as well. Do you have a Brazilian?'

The trannie left the room. She was shaking and ashen faced.

Joan and Vasco followed Kelly into the studio. They were seated on a moth-eaten couch. Kelly sat behind an adjacent cheap pine desk.

There was a single producer sitting at a tired looking black console. He gave a thumbs up to Kelly.

'Welcome to our special early edition of Hot Goss. Today we have two wonderful visitors from the past. The brave and beautiful Joan of Arc is here accompanied by the great Portuguese adventurer Vasco De Gama. But our interest is in their clothing. You can see their chic and unique style but let me try to describe their outfits. Joan has managed to pull off the new masculine trend with ease. Her metallic jacket is well fitted and shows off her lean figure. Matched with her natural tresses Joan is the quintessential modern pre-Raphaelite goddess. Vasco stands solidly behind his choice to wear fur. With his heavy fur collar balanced out by his weighty pantaloons Vasco mirrors the latest runway Pirate trend - aka Captain Jack Sparrow sans eye make-up and hair beading. Joan tell me the back story of your metal jacket. Tell me why you choose this garment.'

Joan thought for a moment:

'The jacket wards off most attacks by sword, but if the swordsman faces me a direct thrust can pierce it. The jacket also affords me some protection from the mace, but the foul Burgundians carried maces adorned with spiked balls. My shield was my best defense against these abominable instruments.'

'Well, thank you, Joan,' said Kelly Bamwoo, 'now Vasco why the fur.'

'My furs are from the great black bear. I prefer the black to the brown. The black is the more uncommon. My furs are especially good because the bears are skinned alive and the pelts are therefore in one piece and capable of being trimmed to suit without stitching or joins.'

At the offices of PETA [People for the Ethical Treatment of Animals] the staff were watching Hot Goss in horror.

'My God did you hear that.' said the Director, 'alert the troops that creature will not get away with this.'

Joanne Rixti rang the Standard and spoke to Bear on speaker phone. Chub, Bruce and Roger Sebastian were present. They had all watched Hot Goss. Joanne was checking in.

'I thought that went well,' she said ruefully.

Fifty

The helicopter carrying Jerry O' landed in the West car park of Constitutional Golf Club in Bethesda, Maryland. The park had been cleared for the occasion. There were a few grumbles from the Members Lounge. The last time there had been such an interruption to the use of the grounds was when Boris Yeltsin was scheduled to play with Bush One. As it turned out the Russian was so inebriated when he arrived that he never left the spike bar, where he drank the best part of a bottle of Stoli to Bush One's liter bottle of Club Soda. Constitutional was the ultimate toffy club. Even its web site was inaccessible to non-members. In recent years the members had blackballed two three-star generals, four congressmen and a senator. This was apart from the ex-president who failed to make the cut. Sometimes a Constitutional member will compare his club with Augusta National. New money, the Constitutional man will say of the National types, all glitter and no class.

The CIA had sent a team to the club carrying a portable X-Ray screener. It was placed at the front door. The spooks claimed it was there, only for the day, for reasons of national security, but members scowled and quarreled with the CIA operatives.

'The thin end of the wedge.' was the most common complaint, which surprised a fairly stupid assistant golf pro as he passed. When he got back to the pro shop, he examined carefully the latest 56 degree loft Callaway sand scraper, but he was unable to detect any decrease in the density of the iron.

Three spies calling themselves unimaginatively, Brad, Sean and Matt, were scheduled to play with Jerry O'. The CIA Ordinance staff had fitted them out in golf clothing which was supposed to make them appear to be Constitutional members. They fooled nobody. Not only was the car park out of action and a Heath Robinson machine placed in the foyer, but there were spies dressed up like extras in Caddyshack on the course.

Jerry O', of course, knew they were spooks. He shook their hands warmly and in his rich Irish brogue joshed that he hoped their surnames were not Pitt, Penn and Damon. The spies looked guiltily at each other and laughed uneasily.

Jerry O' happily walked through the X-Ray machine. It was the latest whizz bang MRI plus metal detection device. The operator was the head of the nuclear medicine department at Mark Hopkins. For the occasion, he was reluctantly dressed in a black jacket with the logo Constitutional Security on the left breast. When Jerry O' walked through the machine, the doctor signaled Brad. 'It had a glitch, ask him to walk through again.' Jerry O' walked through a second time followed by Brad. This time the doctor called Brad over in an agitated manner.

'It is working all right, but he does not show up at all,' he said.

Brad shrugged. Such problems were well above his pay scale. This would be the only time he ever played Constitutional, and he was going to make the most of it.

Jerry O' was fitted out with clubs and clothes.

'Great,' he said delightedly, 'new Clevelands, I have read about them in Golf Digest, and would it be possible to try the new Titleist driver, wonderful and a Ray Cook putter too, thank you so much.'

The four took a cart each. Calliope had plopped himself down next to Jerry O'. Above the course the Blackhawks circled, keeping away the eighteen news and television choppers which were seeking to get a glimpse of the match. The perimeter was guarded by a squad of marines. Inside the clubhouse, the Director of the CIA was in the Golf Club Board room with a surveillance team monitoring the First Hole with a Drone. He had spent the best part of the morning fending off complaints by the angry retirees who otherwise played the Devereux Emmet Blue Course and who had been banished to nine holes only on the Gold Course with a noon finish.

The four golfers were all reasonably proficient. The three spies played weekly at the golf course on Andrews Air Force base.

Jerry O' was hitting the ball well. The tartan plus fours and navy Ballantyne sweater fitted perfectly and the clubs were well balanced and easy to swing. Calliope was impressed. He resisted the temptation to move Brad's ball the milli-second before his club connected or shift Sean's ball into the bushes after a particularly fine drive. Calliope asked Jerry O' if he would like some assistance, but Jerry O' was insistent that he would play the course on its merits.

The four men had the opportunity to have some conversation.

'Are there good courses where you come from?' asked Matt.

'Oh yes,' replied Jerry O', 'we have some great designers. A chap called old Tom Morris laid out Paradise Pebbles and a man named Alastair Mackenzie designed Paradise National. They are our best courses. They are a bit beyond me though. I have not been playing that long.'

'How long?' asked Sean.

'Only two hundred years,' replied Jerry O'.

He had the honor at the Eighteenth and he struck his new Titleist driver lustily. The hole is a five-hundred-and-thirty-yard par five. It has a subtle bend and there is water behind the green.

All four were on the fairway. Their second shots were also useful. Brad went slightly right but was longer than the others. Sean and Matt had played conservatively. They had both struck six irons. They were in the middle of the fairway but were well back from the green. Jerry O' was usually conservative, but today he decided to take a chance and use his driver off the fairway. He had a good lie, and he struck the ball cleanly. His ball landed beside the one-hundred-yard marker. He was well pleased.

The other three all made the green with their third shots. All four were between twelve and fifteen markers. They had decided to play scratch matchplay. Jerry O' was one down to Sean, two up on Matt and three up on Brad. Jerry O' could see Sean's ball was about thirty feet from the hole. The green was tricky, but Sean was a competent putter. Jerry O' decided he needed to put his ball very close to give him a chance of birdying the hole and perhaps squaring the match.

Jerry O' lined up carefully. He had a practice swing and stepped up to hit his wedge. He struck the ball cleanly, but two events occurred.

Sean was first to see the boat on the lake beyond the green. 'There's somebody on the lake,' he said, 'jeez he's fishing.'

Sure enough there was a small dinghy in the middle of the lake and in the boat was a man with a long beard dangling a line overboard. He waved happily at the approaching golfers.

Marines and spies emerged from bushes and trained guns on the man.

'Don't shoot him,' said Jerry O', 'I think I know him.'

The second event was that Calliope took hold of Jerry O's golf ball. He carried it across the green and over the water. When it was above the boat he dropped it sharply onto the deck.

The four carts made their way to the side of the green.

'I think it is still mine,' said Jerry O' as he was further from the hole than his three opponents.

He took out a sand wedge and walked across the top of the water towards the boat. As he approached, he called out to the fisherman.

'Peter, it's great to see you, have you caught anything?'

'Just a small white ball, Jerry O'. I understand that is what I am to call you.'

Peter stepped out of the boat and walked on the water to Jerry O'. This was not within the power bestowed on a human form and Calliope held Peter up as he made his way to Jerry O'. The two men hugged warmly.

Jerry O' called out to his fellow golfers from the lake:

'I think I have a shot.'

The three spies were too staggered to reply. However, the Club President who was sitting with the Director of the CIA said 'this is outrageous. The ball is in a hazard he must take a drop and a one-shot penalty.'

Peter and Jerry O' walked back to the boat. Jerry O' gingerly climbed aboard and stood on the small deck. Peter supported the boat by holding the stern firmly.

Jerry O' wasted little time. He lined up the hole and swung. He made thin contact, but Calliope went to the ball's aid. He flew it low across the green and landed it about four feet from the hole. It rolled ever so slowly down the slight left to right camber and fell leisurely into the hole.

'You need to hole yours, Sean,' said Jerry O', 'but it was too late Sean, Brad and Matt had taken off running towards the club house. They were document analysts and I T technicians. This was too much.

Jerry O' and Peter left the boat and walked across the water to the shore. By the time they strode onto the green they were surrounded by marines.

The CIA director was already there. He introduced himself to Jerry O'.

At least six marines had recorded the whole scene on their phones. They continued recording as Jerry O' spoke:

'I would like to introduce you all to my friend Peter the fisherman. He has come down from Paradise to help me. He was with me last time I was here. He will be my first and my chief apostle.'

The club president turned up in a golf cart. He walked into the lake. He was going to remove the offending boat. When he was up to his neck he began shouting for help. Two marines dived in and carried him out. They looked back at the lake. The boat was gone.

Fifty-One

The videos of Jerry O's hole in one went viral. There were four versions on U Tube taken from different vantage points by quick thinking marines. The two best were illegally sold to network television.

The films were shown repeatedly. Different spin was used to keep the watcher interested. Religious scholars opined about the second coming. Art experts compared paintings of Peter the fisherman on the lake at Constitutional Golf Club with ancient masterpieces depicting St Peter. They did not seem to appreciate that a Fifteenth Century painting of a man dead for fifteen centuries may not necessarily be much of a likeness. The Golf Channel analyzed the Jerry O' golf swing. Experts agreed that he did not swing as flat as modern day golfers. They agreed he had good hand to eye co-ordination. He needed better course management, said one golf commentator.

'At home in Paradise,' said Jerry O', who was watching the show at Little Pink, 'Calliope is not in the cart with me.'

After the game at Bethesda, Jerry O' was taken back to the Catskills. Strangely enough the press had not yet located the whereabouts of the group.

This is not to say Jerry O' was not now famous. He was the most talked about man on earth. Churches were filled with people praying and proclaiming their faith. Manfred Melt the cult leader of the Church of the Holy Peach was now in New York. He attracted a huge and unruly crowd in Times Square when he made an impromptu speech declaring that he was the leader of Jerry O's church on earth.

Peaches Globby, the presenter of Straight Talk, while Gavan Rowntree recovered from his injuries, later interviewed Melt and in a brutal no spin cross examination exposed the man as a blatant fraudster. More Pontius Pilate than sky pilot was her clever conclusion. The expose did not stop Manfred. He was seen later on the Comedy Channel reiterating his claims.

After a quiet dinner and a restful night, the travelers plus the new arrival Peter the Fisherman, assembled in the drawing room at Little Pink.

Some guests had been invited. They all sat around the large comfortable room weighing each other up.

Jerry O' took charge.

'Today is the beginning of the end of our mission,' he commented, 'humans now know who we are and why we are here. It is up to them as to how they now react. The Big Feller does not interfere with nature and that includes human nature. There are followers, there are doubters and there are disbelievers. This is the nature of things. There are those who seek to take advantage of our arrival. There are those who have placed their heads in the sand. The Vatican and Canterbury ignore us. The Jews wisely watch and wait. The Buddhists in China are untroubled as they are sensible enough to search for their nirvana whilst they still live on earth. On the other hand, snake oil salesmen like Manfred Melt of the Church of the Holy Peach seek to use our arrival for their own gain.'

'Manfred Melt is a different proposition from the young woman on Straight Talk. Her ministry would be the Church of the Unholy Peaches,' murmured Charles Dickens, but nobody took any notice of his riposte

'Today,' continued Jerry O', 'I select eleven new apostles. Yesterday my old friend Peter the fisherman arrived from Paradise, and I appoint him to be my first and chief apostle. Please welcome him.'

There was warm applause. Jerry O' continued addressing the gathering.

'Naturally my three colleagues Charles Dickens, Vasco De Gama and Joan of Arc will be apostles. Charles, I want you to appear today on Straight Talk. Peaches Globby will interview you.'

'I will do that,' interposed Vasco.

'It is my belief that you already have done that,' said Jerry O' dryly.

'Charles, I want you to give your perspective of our journey. Advise the audience. About the only things that must remain our secret are details of life in Paradise. It is for them to want, not for us to sell.'

Jerry O' turned to Vasco:

'De Gama you have other fish to fry. You have a dangerous and important mission. You will accompany Calliope across the ocean.'

Chub Checker looked around nervously but neither Calliope nor Dora were in evidence.

Vasco De Gama in turn wondered how it could be possible that frying a fish would be dangerous let alone important. Unless it was a white shark and it was alive when you sought to fry it. Vasco pondered this prospect. One would need a very large pan, was his conclusion.

'And Joan,' Jerry O' said, 'you will travel too, but your angel Sandalphon will be with you for company and shall protect you if required.'

Joan nodded and smiled at Sandalphon who was leaning against a wall anxiously brushing his wings, invisible to all but Jerry O' and Joan of Arc.

Jerry O' paused and took in the expectant faces.

'I hereby also appoint as apostles Bear Grizzard, Chub Checker, Joanne Rixti, Bruce Gotby and Roger Sebastian Keats. Bear you are to deal with business moguls, press tycoons and the US government. At this moment we are being 'protected' by four Blackhawk helicopters which circle Little Pink and only serve to bring attention to us. The alleged field exercise being carried out in the Catskills by Special Forces and Marines may frighten squirrels and retirees but do little else. Call them off. Calliope and Sandalphon can if required do the work of a battalion.'

Vasco and Joan were obviously put out by this comment and Jerry O' gestured towards them

'And Vasco De Gama is as brave a man as ever lived and Joan of Arc is certainly the most fearless girl in the history of this planet.'

The two intrepid adventurers seemed satisfied by Jerry O's praise.

Jerry O' continued his speech:

'Chub Checker you are to be our eyes and ears. You will keep us informed of public reaction. Joanne, I would like you to be our modern social commentator. Perhaps you may care to appear with Charles on Straight Talk. It may also help to save him from temptation.'

Chub and Joanne nodded in agreement. Charles Dickens was unimpressed. He believed he was perfectly capable of withstanding any advance Peaches Globby made towards him. Charles did not appreciate that Jerry O' had spoken tongue in cheek.

Jerry O' continued:

'Bruce Gotby, would you mind keeping an eye on our world leaders. I have been reading your work. I am impressed by the breadth of your knowledge and the strength of your contacts. Finally, Roger Sebastian, you are to be our conduit to the modern world of arts, music, food and literature. I would offer you the opportunity to appear on Straight Talk with Charles and Joanne, but you should bear in mind that Ms. Gobby is a relentless interviewer who will no doubt interrogate you about your past folly.'

'I will happily appear Jerry O',' said Roger Sebastian.

'Fine,' said Jerry O', 'you will be a valuable addition.'

Jerry O' went over to a couch where his remaining three guests sat:

'My final three apostles will be Ginger Scollop, Tweak Monk and Kelly Bamwoo. Your job is to be cool. In other words, you are to help sell our message to the youth of the world. As you now appreciate, I am no clothes designer, but the garb of Joan and Vasco has already provided you with inspiration. I suggest you look for what is apparently called 'a hook'. Design a piece of clothing that will take the world by storm. Make it simple. I want it on the market immediately.'

Kelly, Ginger and Tweak high fived each other in excitement.

'There is one other important piece of news,' said Jerry O' gravely, 'this morning we have been served with legal proceedings. Several diverse organizations have combined to seek an injunction restraining me from claiming to be the son of the creator. It is claimed I am causing a public nuisance. They argue I am guilty of chicanery. The organizations are being represented in court by our old foe Melvin Van Horn. I must leave soon for court. I am going to represent myself. I will ask Chub Checker to explain the intricacies of the case to you'.

'A number of special interest groups have combined,' said Chub, 'they represent pet lovers, gay and lesbians, women's groups, environmentalists, film actors and producers, anti-smokers, children's rights groups, some fundamentalist Christian organizations, climate changers, bicycle riders and atheists. The only group that I believe they have not accepted is NAMBLA, which is a pedophile organization. These groups have vast resources. I have told Jerry O' he needs an attorney, but he insists on representing himself.'

'Thank you, Chub,' said Jerry O', 'I will have Calliope as my second chair and Vasco will be in the gallery. After the case they will leave together for their hazardous journey,'

Jerry O' did not seem in the least overawed by his forthcoming trip once more to the halls of justice.

Peter the Fisherman was looking at his sandals and vowing to himself that he would never again deny his friend as he had done three times in one night two thousand years ago. He was looking forward to the challenges ahead.

'May I accompany you to the court of law,' Peter asked.

'Certainly,' replied Jerry O', 'but you will find Judge Kreuger a much more terrifying proposition than that pompous old prefect Pontius Pilate.'

Fifty-Two

The application for an injunction was devised after a hastily assembled meeting of the various interested parties at the offices of PETA.

Strangely some of the attendees seemed to have taken on the physical characteristics of the organization that they represented. Others were readily recognizable as representing a particular group. The Director of PETA was a large hairy woman who looked like a great shaggy malamute sled dog. The cyclist was thin as a whippet. The film actor was flamboyant. The atheist was miserable. The Christian was so happy one expected him, at any moment, to burst into a hosanna. The National Organization of Women was represented by a scrawny, henpecked-looking man. The children's rights movement was looked after by a teenager. The gay man wore a pink sweater, white silk slacks and was daubed with rouge. The lesbian. by contrast, was clothed in a fine three-piece houndstooth man's suit set off with a club striped tie. The environmentalist was clad in green, and the climate changer had wet hair. In all they were a mixed bag. The only non-attendee was the anti-smoker who had sent his apologies as he was ill with a sore throat.

The first problem was caused by, none other, than Arnold Prink. The former mayoral aide was now the San Francisco based president of NAMBLA. He wanted his organization to be included in the team. A fundamentalist Christian objected strongly when he discovered the meaning of the acronym.

'The North American Man-Boy Love Association, I cannot believe such a body can show its face. If this twerp stays, I go,' he said pointing a finger at Prink. Others were of the same mind and Arnold Prink left with his metaphorical tail between his legs.

After considerable argument a consensus was reached. The cyclist walked out when it appeared to him, he was not being shown proper respect and he had to be coaxed back. At another point the film actor broke into tears at some barely perceived insult. The environmentalist was a master of straying from the point under discussion which led to the pink-sweatered queen calling him the green herring. But eventually a vote was taken, and Melvin Van Horn was appointed to represent the group and take immediate action.

So it was that documents were electronically filed and served and on the stroke of high noon Melvin Van Horn with his complete legal team strode into Judge Freddy Kreuger's courtroom in Manhattan. Her Honor was having a rare day out of court, but the Chief Justice himself had requested her to hear this urgent application.

'It sounds like a judicial nightmare,' he said, 'but if anybody can handle it you can, Nola,' he said.

The judge entered the courtroom and surveyed the scene. Word had spread and reporters competed for space in the public gallery with Christians, atheists, dog lovers and the other special interest groups. It was standing room only.

Judge Kreuger acted quickly. She cleared the court of journalists. They were dispatched to the court communication center where they could observe the hearing on closed circuit. She rejected an application by a network lawyer to film the hearing.

'Certainly not,'she said, 'this is not a circus.'

But looking round the room at the assorted menagerie of human detritus she was not so sure.

When the room had settled down, she called for appearances.

'I appear for the applicants,' intoned Melvin Van Horn in his best baritone. Jerry O' silently warned Calliope to leave the lawyer alone. This was wise as the angel was about to give the attorney a sharp dose of discomfort. Jerry O' rose to his feet:

'I am Jerry O' and I appear for myself.'

Judge Kreuger remembered Jerry O'. Though she gave him a formal warning about appearing without an attorney, it was Her Honor's opinion that the Irishman would at the very least hold his own with Van Horn.

'I appear for the Federal Government,' said Rose France who had been demurely sitting at a small side table.

'I object', said Melvin Van Horn in an outraged manner, 'the government is not a party to this litigation. It has no right to be here.'

Rose France was on her feet, but the Judge waved her back to her seat.

'Let us proceed and if Ms. France wants to intervene at some stage, she will no doubt be prepared to declare her interest. Yes Mr. Van Horn, tell me what you are seeking, who you represent and how you claim each has an interest in the litigation.'

'Certainly, Your Honor, we seek an urgent interlocutory injunction restraining Mr. Jerry O' from claiming he is the son of God.'

'Stop there,' said Judge Kreuger turning towards Jerry O', 'are you claiming to be the son of God?'

'Well, Your Honor,' he replied, 'I don't call him God. I call him the Big Feller, but he did create the seven universes including the one where this earth spins.'

'We can take that as a yes, Mr. Van Horn, you may proceed.'

Van Horn resumed his submission:

'This man is creating a public nuisance by his utterances. The claim he makes is patently false and is causing general consternation and disorder. As we speak there are crowds outside this court shouting his name.'

Melvin stopped theatrically and, it was true, one could just hear the chorus 'Jerry O'. Jerry O' being chanted outside the building.

'We would argue that his behavior,' continued the lawyer, 'is a threat to the stability of this city, if not the whole world.'

'But' said Her Honor, 'even if this is so, what has it to do with your particular clients.'

Van Horn smiled. He thought the Judge was clearly on his side.

'Let me quickly run through them, Your Honor. PETA is concerned because Jerry O' travels with a man who claims to be Vasco De Gama who wears the fur of an endangered bear. We acknowledge it is no crime to impersonate a dead hero, but the wearing of fur is abhorrent to PETA.'

'And what exactly has this to do with Mr. Jerry O'/' queried Her Honor.

'We submit that the man who calls himself Vasco De Gama and the other two freaks who call themselves Charles Dickens and Joan of Arc are the servants or agents of Jerry O' and he is therefore vicariously responsible for their actions – Ahhhh.'

Calliope had heard enough, 'freaks' Calliope would show him 'freaks'. The angel had sharply penetrated Melvin Van Horn.

'Are you all right, Mr. Van Horn?' asked Judge Kreuger.

'Yes, Your Honor,' said the lawyer, 'just a passing spasm. I will continue. Gay and lesbian groups are now being persecuted because of the vile heresies that are being spread by Jerry O'. He claims that traditional values should apply to modern men and women. The Climate Change Forum and the National Environmental Association are being pilloried because of this man's claims that his father is the creator of the universe. Cyclists are being forced off our roads by the crowds. Atheists are being assailed, but so are some fundamentalist Christian groups. In a nutshell, this man is not only an imposter but an imposter preaching doctrines which are past their use by date. We live in the age of political correctness, and we should be proud of it.'

'Yes, I think I get it, Mr. Van Horn,' said the judge, 'what you are saying is that public order is at risk by the preaching of Mr. Jerry O' and your clients are particularly vulnerable. But Film Actors, the Anti-Smoking League?'

'Film actors are threatened by foolish public complaint, caused by Jerry O', about the level of sexual content and violence in movies. It is a matter of free speech. As for my client the Anti-Smoking League, it complains because the man pretending to be Charles Dickens smokes a pipe openly and is therefore a bad example. There are other of my clients who express a more general concern. For example, I also act for Move Up. Org which is a liberal think tank and the Young Conservatives Association, a Republican group'.

Judge Kreuger interrupted him:

'A liberal think tank and the Young Conservatives Association. Both bodies sound as if they are contradictions in terms but proceed Mr Van Horn.'

Melvin Van Horn had heard the sound of the attorney's corral swing gate. He turned to see Arnold Prink approach the bar table. Before Van Horn could speak Prink addressed the Judge.

'Your Honor I am Arnold Prink. I apologize for being late, but I seek to be heard. I am the president of NAMBLA. My members are being cruelly vilified by Mr. Jerry O',"

'I am not familiar with the acronym, Mr. Prink,' said Her Honor who remembered the mayoral aide's last unfortunate appearance before her and was well aware of NAMBLA.

'The North American Man-Boy Love Association,' responded Prink.

'So, your organization promotes sexual relations between adult men and under age boys, would that be a fair categorization, Mr. Prink.'

'Yes, very fair, Your Honor'.

'Mr. Prink I will give you thirty seconds in which to leave this court, otherwise I will issue a bench warrant for your arrest on charges of conspiring with others to commit sexual perversions on minors.'

Prink rose and began hurrying away. Calliope struck just before he left the room. Prink doubled over and cried in pain as he exited.

'It must be catching,' said Her Honor.

Rose France had risen to her feet.

'It is my respectful submission that now may be an appropriate time for me to be heard. I believe that my submission may assist in expediting the determination of the matter.'

'I object,' said Van Horn furiously.

'We will see what Ms. France has to say. If I find she has no locus standi I will simply expunge her submission from the record. Proceed Ms. France.'

'Your Honor, I will first call Mr. Jerry O' to give brief evidence. Cross examination can be stayed until I finish my submission. I am confident that it will not be necessary.'

Rose France called Jerry O' to go into the witness box.

'He does not use the word God, Your Honor, may he be sworn according to his appellation of the Creator.'

Judge Kreuger nodded. Melvin Van horn snorted in disgust. Calliope restrained himself.

'I swear by the Big Feller that the evidence I shall give to this court shall be the truth the whole truth and nothing but the truth.'

Jerry O' put the Bible down. It was his favorite book. He was pleased to swear on it.

Now Mr. Jerry O', I have only two questions,' said Ms. France in her pert way, 'one is are you the son of the creator of earth?'

Yes,' replied Jerry O'.

Secondly are you a human being?'

'No,' said Jerry O'.

'You may leave the witness box, witness,' said Rose France. 'Your Honor I wish to tender a document. It is a medical report which confirms that Jerry O' is not a human. I would ask that you keep the contents of the report confidential. It is a matter of national security.'

'From Mr. Van Horn too?' asked Her Honor.

'Especially Mr. Van Horn,' replied Ms. France winsomely.

Melvin was about to create a storm of protest, but Calliope entered him causing him to reel backwards in pain.

The Judge read the document in silence. When she finished, she folded the paper and handed it back to her orderly who returned it to Rose France.

My submission Your Honor,' said Rose France, 'is that this court only has the power to act against a person or a corporation. Jerry O' is neither.'

'Mr. Van Horn, assuming Jerry O' is not a person, in a legal sense, then Ms France's submission must be correct.'

Melvin Van Horn was exhausted. He just nodded in agreement as he prepared to undergo a new spasm. However, Calliope remained still.

'Application dismissed.' said Judge Kreuger briskly as she swept out the rear door.

After she left, Calliope pulled up a chair next to Van Horn and appeared as Dora.

'Courts cannot act against angels either,' she said to the startled attorney as she pushed him in the chest with a pudgy black finger.

Fifty-Three

The Standard headline was arresting.

WELCOME JERRY O' AND YOUR 12 APOSTLES

Throughout the length and breadth of the cities, hamlets and villages of our planet we welcome the son of the Creator to Earth. The apostles have been named, and we are proud to announce that your humble Newspaper is well represented. Your message is being delivered. Take heed fellow humans. Our destiny is at stake. It is up to us all to mend our ways and take to heart the message.

We list the apostles below.

PETER THE FISHERMAN	-	back from Paradise to lead the Apostles.
CHARLES DICKENS	-	returns to Earth to keep a record of the odyssey.
VASCO DE GAMA	-	Great sailor from Portugal and head of Jerry O's security.
JOAN OF ARC	-	triumphant reappearance as chief strategist.

BEAR GRIZZARD	-	our editor-in-chief who is in talks with world leaders.
CHUB CHECKER	-	journalist, who will gauge public reaction.
JOANNE RIXTI	-	journalist and modern social commentator.
BRUCE GOTBY	-	editor, following world reactions.
ROGER SEBASTIAN KEATS	-	arts and literature monitor.
GINGER SCOLLOP	-	designer, specialist in youth affairs.
TWEAK MONK	-	youth affairs, graphic artist.
KELLY BAMWOO	-	youth fashion presenter of HOT GOSS.

The story was fleshed out from every angle. Bear had spoken to the British Prime Minister who used the opportunity to try and lift his flagging fortunes. He was cautiously supportive of Jerry O' without conceding he was a visitor from Paradise. A few minor dictators were prepared to go on the record. Some were dismissive others more cautious. Business moguls applauded the message but not the credibility of the source.

Chub found that the public was much readier to take sides. The special interests represented at the hearing before Judge Kreuger were lined up firmly against Jerry O'. He was variously described as a fraudster, magician or actor. Vasco was taking great heat from PETA and NOW [National Organization of Woman] was scornful about Joan of Arc. The President of NOW said it was close to blasphemy for this actress or stooge to present this sham. Joan of Arc was a symbol of the woman's movement, and her name should not be sullied by this hairy legged girl. Chub hoped Joan did not read the NOW remarks as she was not likely to take them well.

Joanne Rixti was also finding that the politically correct were all lined up against the visitors. It appeared that organized religion was having a hard time accepting that the Big Feller was the Creator and Jerry O' was his son. It was at grass roots, however, that the message was tearing through society. Churches were packed all day. The streets were full of well-behaved Jerry O' supporters and local halls were home to meetings of old and new God Botherer's who prayed to the Big Feller for salvation. Some were even sincere.

Bruce Gotby was worried. Iran was stirring. The Ayatollah was decrying Christian values. He described Jerry O' as a monstrous vandal of truth and civilization. He said the Great Satan, being the USA, would be brought to its knees and its lap dog Israel would be expunged from the world. Pakistan and India were squabbling over borders. The Russian Bear was awake and angry, and the desperately poor Greeks were still railing over the failure of their currency and their inevitable slide into the abyss of financial ruin. Jerry O' seemed to have only stirred the pot.

Roger Sebastian Keats was surprised to find that Jerry O' was a dirty word [or words] in Arts circles. He correctly deduced that the reason was that Jerry O' had argued in a speech that morning that all human achievement should be judged on merit. This would put in jeopardy the thousands of subsidies, scholarships, bursaries and grants handed out to inept and undeserving artists and writers by governments of all persuasions.

It was the youth of the world who were united. Jerry O' and his apostles were symbols of a new beginning, but more importantly they were cool. It was this chord that Ginger, Tweak and Kelly realized must be tapped into. But how?

What would be the 'hook'?

It was Kelly Bamwoo, the fashion 'guru', who came up with the solution. Her star had risen, since her interviews with Vasco and Joan and her appointment as an apostle. Hot Goss had been picked up by a worldwide cable network and her new web site was getting over a thousand hits per minute.

'Who is the most reviled man in the world?' she asked Ginger Scollop and Tweak Monk during a 'brainstorming' meeting at the offices of the TV network which had taken up Hot Goss.

'That singer who lip synched,' suggested Ginger.

'President Biden,' was Tweak's helpful offering.

'No,' said Kelly, 'who has killed millions of people and who is immediately recognized by his costume.'

'Colonel Sanders,' said Tweak.

Kelly ignored him.

'Moon Moon the dictator of North Booga,' she said triumphantly, 'he is a mass murderer and has been for yonks. He makes his own special fashion statement. It is strange but cool.'

'You mean the little fat fucker in the one piece pajama suit. How can you say that look is cool.' Ginger was skeptical.

'Well, it is so uncool it is cool, but I have a hook. What if we called the suit Moon Jam Jams and we put a trapdoor in the back.' Kelly paused and waited for the inevitable response.

Tweak and Ginger laughed and Ginger asked the question.

'For easy access?'

'No, for mooning. What I suggest is that we put the pants on the market now. They are so easy to make they can be on the streets by tomorrow. They can be in different colors and cloths, but each suit will have a trapdoor. We shall tell the youth of the world that we may not have guns or bombs, but we have the people power to show Moon Moon what we think of him, by wearing our Moon Jam Jams on the day after tomorrow. On the stroke of eleven am New York time the youth of the world will open its trapdoors and moon Moon Moon. Just imagine fifty million keisters facing North Booga and fifty million voices calling out Moon Jam Jams, Moon Jam Jams.'

'You know,' said Ginger,' it could work'.

Within an hour the suit was designed. and Kelly was web casting the message to the world. Within two hours, four thousand factories from China to Bratislava and from Lima to Anchorage were making the suits. FedEx and DHL were readying every plane in their fleets to ferry the suits around the world. Queues were starting to form outside clothing stores which were already advertising Moon Jam Jams in one hundred and sixty major cities.

Jerry O' had been informed and he seemed insouciant. Charles Dickens had expressed some reservations.

'It is rather indelicate, Jerry O',' he said.

'That it is, Charles, but we are dealing with modern youth. As Kelly has told me. We must be cool. That is all that counts to them.'

Charles was not convinced, but he let the matter rest. He appreciated as a chronicler, the exposure of massed gluteus maximus to Moon Moon would make good copy.

In North Booga Moon Moon was told the news by his Head of Security. The dictator was livid with rage at the mass insult devised for him.

'Prepare the bomb,' he said, 'I want it on its way to New York tomorrow. I want it to hit the Empire State Building at the same moment the wad of buttocks appears.'

The security chief agreed, but he had his reservations. The country only had one bomb and one rocket. The prospect of aiming the rocket to hit a building in New York was absurd. It would be a miracle if it landed on the continent it was aimed for. As for meeting earth at a particular time – that was a fantasy.

Fifty-Four

CHARLES DICKENS JOURNAL

Much as I am enjoying my sojourn back on earth, I must confess I miss Paradise. I appreciate the certainty of my old life. I enjoy the regularity that Paradise bestows. Let it not be thought, however, that I regret this opportunity. In my past life I chronicled the lives of the English. I tried to find their very spirit. I believe I was sometimes successful. Ebenezer Scrooge existed in some form or another in every borough of every county in England, just as every family has an Uncle Pumblechook. I did not invent these people. I simply wrote of them and named them. In the world that I have re-entered, human nature itself has not changed. It is rather the culture in which the human nature breeds that has undergone a metamorphose. Methinks, it has coarsened and roughened. This is, in a way, surprising as communication is now sophisticated and instant. Yet humans do not use these rapid technologies to refine their words. Instead, they instantly inform

EVERYBODY, yes EVERYBODY of the slice of pie they have just placed in their mouths, the color of their mittens and the sound of a passing train. Why, I know not why.

I was pleased to hear Bear Grizzard has been appointed the senior manager of his company. I have come to enjoy the bluff Antipodean's common sense. For some reason I suspected that Calliope had a hand in the meteoric rise of Bear, but I am probably thinking unworthy thoughts. Calliope is such a disconcerting angel, that I tend to blame him for any unforeseen happening.

The brave early reports from the Standard Newspaper certainly spread our message widely. It also brought out from under rocks every citizen whose paths crossed ours. Yet I stop for a moment. If I was in Cheapside with Jerry O' in let us say 1850 and Jerry O' announced he was the son of the creator, what would happen? He would be pelted with rotten tomatoes, that is what would happen, and if afterwards his situation was verified, what would then happen? The same tomato throwers would be lining up to give interviews to The Times for a penny. Nothing, therefore, has altered.

My friend Roger Sebastian Keats has become very popular. I am pleased. His confession that he really is a Pigsley not a Keats was courageous. I have enjoyed our literary conversations, and I am flattered by his knowledge of my body of work. It is engaging.

I am marking time. I know that, but I am reluctant to write of our encounter with the world of live television. The reasons will become obvious. But I suppose I must scribble of my experiences.

We all arrived at the studio, /and our faces were made up. I understand this is because of the artificiality of the bright lighting in the room where the film is 'shot', yes that is the word used by the employees. De Gama put on his usual song and dance claiming he is a warrior seaman and not a poltroon. Our fine Vasco seems to have forgotten that when he lived last his peers [and Vasco too I suggest] applied rouge and powder liberally to dampen the smell of their sweat.

When I was 'made up' I went for a meander. I heard noise and opened a door. To my horror there was De Gama in congress or conquest with an extraordinary looking young woman who is blessed by the name of Peaches. I say conquest because there was no act of love blossoming between these two creatures. I would describe it as vigorous lasciviousness. My only question relates to the issue as to who was the conquistador. De Gama may have been thrusting, but I suspect Peaches was the puppeteer, pulling the Portuguese sailor's strings. I wonder if his act of lechery will close Paradise to Vasco. Though I cannot excuse him and will never forget the extraordinary vision, nevertheless, I believe he is at heart a good brave man. I sincerely hope and pray he is given the chance to prove this before his second judgment day.

The interview itself turned out to be enormously entertaining. Gavan Rowntree, the interviewer, was a pompous ass of a man. He was eager to try and show us up. He was quite rude and unpleasant. Calliope was useful. He spun the man twice then levitated him. It is unfortunate that he dropped him quite so hard as to break a bone, but I must concede there was not a teary eye in the room as Rowntree was carted away. The woman Peaches took over and proved extremely proficient. An ounce of hay and an apple is more likely to make a horse compliant than a whip across the haunches.

I have returned to Little Pink to write. I watch television. I can see our story unfold. The walk on water was a masterstroke. The arrival of Peter the Fisherman has given us a rock of strength. I am sure he will never deny Jerry O', as he did to Jesus three times in the past.

On one view the twelve apostles may appear to be an odd bunch, but Jerry O' has chosen well. The journalists are building the framework. The three youths have come up with a scheme that they believe is 'cool'. This is the master word of the generation. Our finest compliment was to call a man a 'gentleman', but now he simply must be 'cool'. Their scheme does not bear repeating. I will probably have to discuss it, but it can wait. As it is I have been as salacious as I care to be in one chapter of my journal. I will simply say their plan is ribald.

Joan and Vasco have already played their parts before the world. I have commented on Vasco's bravery, but Joan is a fine and steady lassie. She accepts no nonsense and deals with offense swiftly. I expect that her hated Burgundians were rightly frightened of her. Both Vasco and Joan will, I am certain, play important parts in the days ahead.

And I, well I am of no use physically. I simply try to give wise counsel, but only sparingly. I know my purpose. I do not veer from it. I am simply the recorder.

Fifty-Five

CALLIOPE'S EPISTLE

I have many advantages as an angel. I can travel through time and space instantly. I can vanish, now that is a great convenience. But I have responsibilities as well. And never have I had a mission with such responsibility. I accept I have made mistakes. Gabriel says and Metatron repeats that I have an impulsive nature. They say angels should be thoughtful and controlled. I accept they are correct, but on the other hand, my editor [can I call you that dear John, Matthew, Mark or Luke], I think if you have read this much of my musings you must be at least interested in my writings. I hope so.

Lawyers make pleas for clients who are admitting guilt to a crime. At times when writing these notes, I feel like that client. There will be accusers, make no mistake of that. Gabriel and his miserable lackey Metatron will truly be avenging angels. I can call evidence to rebut their claims.

Jerry O' will be supportive. Joan of Arc will help and surprisingly the mole Sandalphon is turning from finky to funky. I will call the spy as my witness. I will ask him to support me and I think he will. Dickens will sit on the fence. He writes with conviction, but lives in confusion. Vasco would support me, but Vasco may not make it back to Paradise. Not that Vasco is a Judas. Far from it, but the pleasures of the flesh may be his undoing.

I am sorry John [or other], I have digressed. There is much that has happened since my last installment. I have been rushing hither and thither. The world is aware of us, and the humans are skittish and nervous. The lowest humans are about as advanced as the smartest Grillaby from Pluto. They function but use raw emotion to act rather than logic. I often see the old Greeks Plato and Socrates hanging about the Big Feller's gardens walking and eternally arguing about metaphysics, literature and the body politic. They would not be attracted to the Grillaby like humans. I can imagine Plato looking over his new pince-nez and saying to Socrates:

'Evolution was supposed to advance our tribe not regress it.'

I hope you like my word picture, epistolian, as I never sleep, I have had the chance to read up about words and thoughts. If I wasn't an angel, I would like to be a writer - like you Sir, yes like you!

When Chub Checker phoned Dora and told her [me] of his problem with his employer Mr. Gary Lusich, I consulted Jerry O' and he waved me away.

'Look after it, Calliope,' he said, 'I have total confidence in you.'

So I fixed it. I agree that it was a robust solution, but his desk was cleared in a flash. Gabriel may argue that my touch should have been softer and my solution defter, but I am confident if a complaint is made I will not be censured.

I then rushed to the court to watch Melvin Van Horn perform. He is much over-rated, particularly in his own mind. A great loss would be made if one bought Van Horn at the price that he puts on his own head and sold him off at market price. I mostly resisted causing him discomfort. Judge Kreuger and Ms. France had already done that.

I have heard enough from lawyers in the last few days to know that there are good arguments and bad arguments. I know one cannot turn a sow's ear into a silk purse.

Here is my sow's ear. I know that my behavior during the TV show Straight Talk will come under scrutiny. I cannot shy away from this. Jerry O' instructed me to put the host Mr. Gavan Rowntree under pressure. Spinning his chair was great fun and I am afraid I got carried away. I thought Rowntree asked to be levitated. I misunderstood. He used the word 'levity', and it is very similar but has a different meaning. Jerry O' did not actually tell me not to levitate the man, so I believed it was within my brief. However, I certainly should not have dropped him quite so sharply or from such a great height. I did not mean to hurt him or to break bones. In fairness, though, I argue it was the way he fell.

Anyway, here is my silk purse. My appearance as a shimmer before the new host Peaches Globby worked a treat. It was quite unrehearsed. I sought no approval, but it is still being talked about by humans in their homes and bars. Sandalphon was very angry, at first, to be exposed, but I have been talking him round. I know his report to Gabriel will mention my misdemeanor, but I think he now agrees that I did not commit a felony. There you see, my reader, I am learning the words of the law.

But now to my highlight, now to an event that will certainly play a part in my excerpt. You will, of course, my master scrivener decides if there are other scraps amongst my writings that are useful or whether there is a pearl in the snow.

I will not dwell on the game of golf. It seems to me to be a puzzling and pointless pastime. But the joy of seeing Peter the Fisherman was the finest moment - so far of our journey. Peter stood tall like the great man that he is. I am sure he will be a true leader of our apostles.

One can argue that the apostles are a queer lot, but then again they are representative of modern humans. What is vital is that they are spreading the message. True they do it in odd ways. I have heard young Ginger Scollop and his friends are organizing a worldwide 'moon' [showing bare buttock cheeks] to rail against an evil dictator. I am not sure what good this will do, but it will certainly be watched on earth.

I finally attended yet another court case. I did not give service to Wilfred when he was last on earth as Jesus, but from what I have heard from Uriel [who was there] the case was a travesty and the judge a beast. Judge Kreuger is tough and strong, but oh she is fair and that is what counts. I did my best to behave but, as usual, I strayed slightly. I should not have entered the court as Dora. I know that, but the man Melvin Van Horn is a great provider of temptation.

And talking of temptation I must mention that Vasco succumbed to the lusty charms of a tall thin woman. This must be mentioned by me, but if Vasco makes it back to Paradise you may decide to hold the story - to protect the guilty.

CH. 1 V.7
The world now knows the son is here
To give good counsel as the seer
Peter the Fisherman on a boat
Apostles all must stay afloat
The judge gave justice at the trial
Jerry O' surprised her for a while
A word of caution about damnation
If apostle succumbs to earthly temptation.

Fifty-Six

'We have our apostles, at last, Mohammed,' said the Big Feller to his trusted aide. They were fishing in the Venusian River. They never seemed to catch any fish. In fact, they would have been surprised if they did. It was a good opportunity to sit and talk and reflect on Wilfred's mission.

Mohammed did not comment which the Big Feller took correctly as some minor opprobrium.

'You are not sure of the quality of our apostles my friend,' asked the Big Feller..

'It is difficult for me to try and appreciate the reason that millions of human hind quarters are to be bared and waving in the wind,' said Mohammed.

'Well, they won't be exactly bared,' replied the Big Feller, 'they will be viewed through an open trapdoor of their Moon Jam Jams.'

'I see,' said Mohammed, though he did not see.

'There is a complication,' said the Big Feller, there is a large meteor the size of Jupiter which is now passing from the sixth to the seventh universe. It will travel towards the planet Earth, but it is about seven degrees west of its orbit area. In other words, Earth is safe, but the scientists on the planet will not know this. They will be confounded and frightened.'

'And may well blame Wilfred,' said Mohammed.

'True,' responded the Big Feller, 'but this may work in his favor. Presently humans are split over Wilfred - I should call him Jerry O'. Some believe him to be my son. Others see him as a magician or trickster and there is a third group who regard him as a force for evil. It is up to him and his apostles to persuade humankind to mend their ways.'

'And if he cannot do so?' asked Mohammed. He had laid down his line and was looking carefully at his master.

'Well I am afraid,' said the Big Feller dryly, 'this may well be the second coming. I am not going to send my son down there every few years to try and sort out their troubles.'

'It has been two thousand years,' replied Mohammed.

'Yes, not long at all,' the Big Feller also laid his line down. He pulled out his curved pipe and filled it with tobacco. He lit it and took a deep puff.

'You see, the thing is Mohammed, I set the Earth up as a bold experiment. I gave humans the opportunity to evolve. I hoped their transformation would cause the seven deadly sins to be expunged from their character. I have not interfered with the system of nature. I have let it adapt. Plants and animals come and go and the humans have developed. Unfortunately, the changes are merely superficial. Their nature is jejune. I dread to think what old Socrates and Plato make of it'.

'Or Michelangelo,' interrupted Mohammed.

'Exactly,' said the Big Feller, 'or Michelangelo.'

'So the end result will be—,' Mohammed tailed off.

'Either they heed Jerry O' or they don't. If they do not listen to him, they will succeed in blowing each other up. Fortunately, they do not presently possess a bomb capable of breaking up their planet.

'What do we do now?' said Mohammed.

'Gird our loins,' said the Big Feller, 'here comes your favorite angels.'

Sure enough, Gabriel and Metatron were flitting across the bank.

'Ah, it is good to see you Gabriel,' said the Creator, 'I expect you have heard the good news.'

'No,' replied Gabriel, 'I have heard no good news.'

'Peter the Fisherman is on Earth as Chief Apostle. Calliope has seen to it that humans are aware of Jerry O' and the team. A great blow for peace will be struck when the young humans bare their buttocks in the face of an evil dictator. Very inventive, wouldn't you say.'

'I am afraid I would have to say that such a sight is likely to be deleterious to my angels' equilibrium,' said Gabriel.

'I do not know what you are talking about, Gabriel, but if the sight of a few million tushes will offend your army tell them to avert their eyes.'

Gabriel knew he could never win an argument with the Big Feller`, but it was what he did. It was part of life in Paradise. He changed tack.

'Can we assist the mission in any way,' he asked the Big Feller.

'What to make sure the keisters blossom,' asked the Big Feller.

'No, I was thinking more of providing a force. I can muster our troupe. Calliope and Sandalphon are alone down there. We could help.'

Mohammed was enjoying the repartee. As if Gabriel gave two hoots about how Calliope was coping, but the Big Feller rose and took hold of Gabriel's wings in a warm, friendly way.

'That is good of you my Archangel,' he said, 'prepare them, just in case.'

Gabriel and Metatron left clucking away to each other. They were no doubt discussing summoning Angels from the other universes, organizing ordinance, arranging for wing clipping and preparing the paperwork.

Oh one thing, Gabriel,' called the Big Feller. Gabriel and Metatron turned and hurried back.

'Get your hands on as many school buses as you can. I mean the human kind, not the Grillaby kind from Pluto. Earthly buses are yellow and run on petrol.'

The two angels rushed off in confusion. But Metatron was meticulous. He would do as he was bid.

'The Grillaby kind?' Mohammed asked, 'I did not know Grillabies have school buses.'

'They have plank boards on hand hewn misshapen wheels pulled by pigs. I think, we should do better than that.'

Mohammed shrugged his shoulders. He was not so sure. A race of people who were prepared to let the universes see where the sun never shone may well deserve to be carried about on planks pulled by hogs.

Fifty-Seven

The set of Straight Talk was more crowded than usual. Every staff member who could get into the studio was jammed in. Charles Dickens sat quietly on a couch between Roger Sebastian Keats and Joanne Rixti. Opposite him perched on a stool was Peaches Globby. She wore a bright red and yellow patterned wool sheath. She reminded Charles of a huge skinny parrot. Between the host and guests was a large hanging white screen. The countdown commenced:

'Today folks we have a rare treat for you. In the studio is Charles Dickens. He comes to you direct from Paradise. As you are all aware he travels with the son of God, Jerry O'. Also here are the chronicler of our great city Joanne Rixti and the noted arts columnist Derek Pigsley also known as Roger Sebastian Keats. Welcome all.'

Roger Sebastian Keats was bristling, but Charles put a hand on his arm and spoke:

'Thank you very much Miss Globby but we call the Creator, the Big Feller.'

'Good Charles I will remember that, but today we have another special guest who comes to you from London, England. It is the Archbishop of London, Sir Rupert Dugong. Sir Rupert is a noted Dickens scholar, but he is a skeptic. Charles, Sir Rupert believes you are perpetrating a hoax. What do want to say about this charge?'

'I am not sure what I should say, Miss Globby, I am who I am. I respect the archbishop. I am sure he is a fine man, but if he is trying to discredit me, it will be to no avail.'

Charles did not like confrontation, but as it transpired, he had nothing to fear. Calliope had been very busy overnight. He had stopped off in London.

The archbishop had woken in the Cathedral residence feeling odd. He sensed contentment but aberration. He dressed in the clothes laid out for him. He put on a long white robe and a white skull cap. He placed his feet into leather sandals. A book was next to the clothes. He ate the breakfast laid out for him by his housekeeper and called for his driver.

He set off to the studio carrying his new Koran.

The Diocese Jaguar drove him to the Chelsea studio where the Straight Talk cross overs were filmed. The technicians had the satellite booked and the studio set up.

The chauffeur had been a little surprised by the archbishop's garb, but he had driven enough church dignitaries to know that they loved dressing up. The studio staff were all atheists or worse and they did not know the difference between an archbishop and a lorry driver. The cross over occurred from London to New York. Peaches Globby was momentarily stunned but she soon resumed her composure. She had researched the British clergyman. It was Dugong all right but dressed in Arab thobe and taqiyah. Peaches wondered if perhaps Sir Rupert was being ecumenical. Peaches learned quickly. She was fast on her feet.

'Sir Rupert, I want to ask you about your clothing, are you not wearing an Arab tunic and cap.'

'Yes and I have my Koran.' The archbishop raised his book triumphantly.

'But why,' asked Peaches Globby.

'I have had a revelation,' said Sir Rupert.

Uh, uh I expect our Calliope has been at work, was Charles Dickens first thought. He was correct. Roger Sebastian and Joanne both looked at Charles for guidance, but he was giving nothing away. The archbishop sonorously continued:

'I have appreciated that I have lived my liturgical life wearing a blindfold. I have been wrong. I now understand that Jesus was a prophet, but not the son of God. No that was Mohammed.'

Charles hoped he was not referring to the Big Feller's factotum.

'Jerry O' is the son of Mohammed,' continued Sir Rupert in his plummy English accent, 'and this explains why he calls his father the Big Feller. It is why he is so reticent about using the word God, but he gives the game away, you see, by referring to their trek from Paradise. Paradise is where Muslims go. I hereby renounce my faith I will turn my cathedral into a mosque. I will lobby my government to introduce Sharia Law. In the interim, I will make some Church law. Women must not, in future, speak unless spoken to first by their husbands and must obey their husbands every whim. No woman may be educated without permission from her father. Marriages shall be arranged. I shall broker the marriages. The price of a healthy woman under the age of twenty-five years shall be fifty thousand pounds. Between twenty-five and thirty-five the price shall be twenty thousand pounds. If they are over thirty-five the price shall be negotiable. All women that are arranged to be married shall be virgins. If the woman is found not to be a virgin the money shall be refunded upon request. My fee is ten per cent but is not refundable. There shall be prayers five times a day. Alcohol is forbidden, but all men must smoke. Orange hair is preferred. Oh yes and women priests will be stripped of their priesthoods.'

Sir Rupert paused. Peaches took the opportunity to take back the initiative.

'But what will your parishioners think?' she asked.

'My Parishioners will do what they are. bloody well told.' replied the archbishop.

Charles Dickens decided to enter the conversation.

'I believe you query my credentials, sir?' he asked.

'Query your credentials, query your credentials, of course not. You are Charles Dickens the novelist. You wrote bourgeois romantic tripe about Christian families in Britain in the Nineteenth Century.'

Charles was offended, but his annoyance was directed more at Calliope whom he correctly deduced was responsible for the man's remarks.

'And terrorism, are you supportive of terrorism?' asked Peaches.

'Terrorism!' exclaimed Sir Rupert, 'of course I am against terrorism. For goodness's sake I am an Englishman.'

By now the Canon of the rectory had arrived at the Chelsea studio and during the first advertising break he ushered the archbishop away. Sir Rupert was not eager to go. He was enjoying his time in the sun.

The Canon drove the archbishop back to the Cathedral. By then the inculcation was wearing off. Sir Rupert was surprised to see that there were two groups of demonstrators waiting for him. There were hundreds of Muslims chanting and holding up signs reading Ayatollah Sir Rupert and a lesser number of mainly women parishioners who were calling for his head. The Canon helped the archbishop into his residence and he retired to the comfort of his bed whilst his doctor was summonsed.

Peaches resumed her interview with Charles Dickens as if nothing had happened.

'Sir Rupert claims that Jerry O's father is named Mohammed, what have you to say about that?'

Dickens thought this over.

'I only know the Creator as the Big Feller. I know a Mohammed, but he has no son.'

Dickens was pleased with this answer. It was exhaustive but inscrutable.

But Peaches had not finished.

'Do you have any idea why Sir Rupert should suddenly become a Muslim?'

'Yes I do as a matter of fact,' answered Dickens, 'but I am not telling you.'

Back at the Standard offices Chub Checker watched the show with the other Standard apostles.

'The man is a natural for a series of documentaries, I just wish he was staying on earth.'

The interview continued but Peaches had kicked her goal. The Archbishop of London had become a Muslim and Peaches got the story.

Fifty-Eight

Sandalphon, Joan of Arc's angel, disliked Kandahar. Angels, of course, simply thrive no matter the environment. They create their own space. However, Sandalphon is a sensitive heavenly spirit. He may not be affected by the foul smell and execrable appearance of the run down bombed out little city in Afghanistan in which he found himself, but he still sensed that he was not in a good place.

Calliope gave Sandalphon a full briefing before he departed with his ward Joan of Arc. The assignment itself was well within Sandalphon's powers. The angel generally served Joan and his other master Gabriel well. He carefully balanced his obligations and responsibilities between his doughty little human mistress and the imperious oversight of the chief angel Gabriel. He rarely saw or was tasked by the Big Feller. He saw plenty of Calliope, too much, but he had never received orders from him before. Despite himself, Sandalphon was beginning to respect Calliope. What he lacked in attention to detail he certainly made up for in daring. Sandalphon would have done things differently, but he accepted that the tactics seemed to be working. Jerry O' wanted the world to know of him. Well now they did and that was p0artly due to Calliope.

At present Sandalphon and Joan were sheltering behind a stone fence watching rebel soldiers firing rockets at a small, ragged Taliban force. The rockets all missed their mark. The rebel's aim was haphazard. Occasionally the Taliban would in return fire off an ancient mortar held by two scruffy warriors. Their aim seemed to be better. Not that either side suffered injury. It all seemed to Sandalphon a bit of a formality. Right on five pm the rebels shut up shop and retreated. In turn the Taliban turned to face East, crouched on the ground and wailed their evening prayers. They were a shabby threadbare group. They ranged in age from young boys to old men. They all wore black hessian robes and black turbans wrapped around their cotton caps. Their dirty feet were encased in either sandals or stolen American army boots.

Sandalphon inculcated the twenty-seven Taliban men and when they came to their senses they had been tripped to a Quonset hut in Tel Aviv. They were sitting in a bunch drinking green tea.

Joan ordered the men to their feet and commenced to rehearse them. Three hours later she was satisfied with their work.

'Ok guys we are ready to perform.' she said.

A small Jewish fellow smoking a big cigar and wearing a wide striped bookies suit walked in.

'Meet Mr. Goldberg,' said Joan, 'he is our producer. Show him what you can do.'

The men performed. Goldberg clapped happily.

'It will be a hit,' he said.

Shortly afterwards a film crew walked in. The indomitable Peaches Globby had organized it.

Straight Talk was going to stream the show. She was beamed to Tel Aviv.

'Tell me what is happening over there in Israel. Is that the Taliban I see?'

Goldberg replied:

'Joan of Arc who has come to earth with Jerry O' has auditioned these fine young men to perform in our forthcoming Broadway production called Taliban the Musical. It has been written by two young Jewish New York writers. It tells the story of a group of Taliban fighters who are ordered to go to New York to kill Americans. They are told for each kill fifty virgins will appear. One of the men misunderstands his orders and thinks he has been ordered to kiss Americans. Sure enough he walks up to a Man on the street in Manhattan and kisses him. Fifty virgins appear. He rushes back and tells his friends who in turn kiss New Yorkers. Each kiss and fifty virgins arrive.'

Peaches intervened:

'You are going to need a pretty large cast.'

'We are going to have a big chorus line, Peaches. Going back to our storyline, the men give up their hatred of the USA and start a dance club called the Talibanarama. The men we have here today are the real Taliban. They are going to be the stars of the show. Let me introduce you to the Mullah Omar.'

'Hello Peaches.' said the Taliban man, 'today we were fighting Americans and tonight we are singing and dancing. Our teacher has been Joan of Arc, and our new friend Mr. Goldberg is our producer. God bless America.'

He repeated the cry and the other Taliban dressed in their sinister black gowns and turbans joined in.

Joan walked up to an upturned packing case and climbed on to it. She waved a baton and the Taliban lined up in front of her. The doors opened and fifty young girl dancers came in. They were dressed identically in bobby sox, billowing bright blue dresses and white silk polo shirts. They each had a bright ribbon tied to their ponytails. The men started to sing and do a simple up and back two-step. The girls formed circles and began to dance in step with the music. Goldberg had put on a tape recorder and music accompanied the song.

The tune sounded suspiciously like the old Harry Belafonte song The Banana Boat Song and the chorus was catchy and simple and went something like this.

'Hey Mr Taliban, Talibanarama,

Me like kiss, no wanna go home.'

The Standard apostles watched the cross.

'Taliban the Musical, what do you make of that Keats?' asked Bruce Gotby.

'It has all the hallmarks of a hit,' the arts commentator replied.

He was right and the show would have been a hit if it was ever performed, but alas the cast was never going to get to strut the boards. Fate would intervene.

When the link was broken the CIA arrived and escorted the men to a small Gulfstream jet plane which took them to Guantanamo Bay. The fifty girl dancers went back to their day jobs as Mossad spies. Mr. Goldberg returned to his employment as Israeli minister for the Arts.

When the Sandalphon inculcation wore off the Mullah Omar found himself in a cell with a man unknown to him. He introduced himself.

'I cannot believe it,' he said, 'one minute I am happily fighting rebels in the hills outside Kandahar and the next minute I find myself singing and dancing in a Jew Quonset hut, and now they take me here.'

'I know how you feel,' the other man said, 'I am from Montenegro. I escaped to America and became a taxi driver. A black woman appeared out of nowhere in the front seat of my cab, then a tall woman said she would never shave her legs again and a businessman cried inconsolably. For this they send me to Guantanamo.'

The Mullah became silent. He was clearly housed with a madman.

Joan and Sandalphon were back at Little Pink.

'That was great fun Sandals,' said Joan, 'I hope we can do it again.'

Sandalphon hoped not, but he remained silent.

Fifty-Nine

Vasco De Gama was not altogether excited by the task allocated to him by Jerry O'. It did not sound dangerous to him. He failed to appreciate that Jerry O' meant that the danger was to the De Gama future if there were any more shenanigans.

'You are to visit Portugal, Vasco,' said Jerry O'. 'You are to tell the populace that they must mend their ways. I do not want any brawling. You are human and can make whatever decision you like about yourself, but I do not want our mission put in jeopardy by a melee caused by you. I would also prefer if you avoided the sins of the flesh, but that is a matter for you. Calliope will accompany you, but not I hope to save your skin.'

Calliope was in his Dora body with Vasco at Little Pink when Jerry O' gave them his rare homily. Calliope expected this mission would not be without tribulation.

In the meantime, the pace was quickening. The Standard-On-Line was now the busiest web site on earth. Chub and the others churned out stories as they came to hand. The revelation of the Archbishop of London was the cause of much confusion. The National Organization of Women was meeting twice daily. The women of NOW were torn. On one hand they had a natural antipathy towards Christians and denounced them at every opportunity. They preferred Muslims who they said were unfairly characterized as terrorists. On the other hand, the Archbishop's comments about women were intolerable. He asked for women to be obedient. If he had his way women priests would be banned. The acute irony was lost on the group of social workers, minor politicians and other unemployables who made up the committee of NOW.

The unveiling of the Taliban song and dance troupe was a great hit. A rapper had already released a cover version on ITunes and a Country and Western version was due for release this.

Moon Jam Jams were selling by the million. Every clothing manufacturer on earth was making the suit as fast as they could. Committees had sprung up to co-ordinate the MOON SHOT as the trapdoor opening event was now being called. Some music had even been written to accompany the bash. It was recorded by a Chicago funk band and was called The Bare-Arse Polka. There were queues to buy Moon Jam Jams throughout the world. From Bloomingdales in New York to shanty stores in Mogadishu the youth of the world lined up to buy their one-piece suits with rear trapdoors. Economists watched the phenomenon with amazement. It seemed that Moon Jam Jams may be the catalyst to lead the world out of the ongoing financial stress that plagued the Western World. Certainly, the Greeks were profiting from the exercise. An Aegean entrepreneur had come up with the first edible Moon

Jam Jams. The Fetta flavor was extremely popular. In Ireland a company was manufacturing green Jam Jams with a shamrock on every trapdoor. They were selling like Irish shortbread.

In North Booga Moon Moon was becoming angrier by the minute. His nuclear physicist [kidnapped from Pakistan] who was alternately starved or lauded was working like a beaver trying to get the poorly constructed rocket [adapted from a Scud missile] to support the one nuclear bomb the country possessed.

'Talk about a lose-lose situation', the Pakistani thought as he drilled holes in the rocket housing.

Manfred Melt, the crooked leader of the Church of the Holy Peach had given up trying to get to Jerry O'. He had seen the Archbishop of London's performance on Straight Talk and he now professed that he too was a Muslim. He dyed his hair orange, began smoking heavily and banned women from his presence except to be his servants or concubines. His following dissipated. He was picked up by the Police alone and wailing on Mott Street outside a Turkish Restaurant and committed to a Mental Institution. His next-door neighbor in the asylum was the disgraced Mayor of New York, Billy Lowe. They had much to discuss.

The institutional churches remained isolated from the hysteria. The Romans made occasional forays into the media with various savvy priests giving oblique commentary about the unlikely nature of Jerry O's story which they compared with traditional Catholic theory. The Ayatollah saw the whole shebang as manna from Paradise. Unfortunately for him ordinary Iranian citizens were as caught up in the hysteria as the rest of the world. The Coptic Christian Church in Teheran was inundated by applicants to join.

The Chinese were momentarily puzzled but soon got over it and set about copying Moon Jam Jams at a blistering pace. It was only the Jews that hunkered down and said nothing. As one rabbi said to his friend:

'We have seen it all before. Our King Herod got involved when that Jesus turned up and look what happened to us then.'

His friend agreed.

Vasco flew to Lisbon in a jet plane supplied by the CIA. Though the spies did not know it, Calliope was resting on the back seat. Joanne Rixti was onboard. She had two roles. She represented the New York Standard and the Apostles.

When the aircraft arrived at a small private strip in the foothills outside Lisbon, it was met by a US junior diplomat. The Catholic Church protested that the Portuguese Government should ignore the visit. As the government ministers were all devout Roman holy rollers, they agreed. They did not count on the power of Twitter. Joanne tweeted that Vasco De Gama would be speaking at the Triumphal Arch in Comercio Square at eight PM. This was clever timing. It coincided with the end of the daily Portuguese siesta. The Cabinet met hastily. Should the police or army try and break up the expected crowd? Should the President attend? Wisely it was decided that co-operation was the best way to go.

At eight pm Vasco and Joanne arrived at the square accompanied by his CIA guard and an invisible Calliope. The President was waiting to greet him.

'Good evening, Sir, I am Don Pedro la Rosa President of Portugal. Welcome to our country.'

Vasco was unimpressed:

'But where is the King. I answer only to the King. I served the Aviz and the Aviz-beja dynasties. I am the follower of Emmanuel and before that John the Second. Where are their progeny?'

'I am afraid', said the President, 'the Monarchy was deposed in 1910 and were sent into exile in Brazil.'

'Well I must go and get them and bring them back to their rightful place,' Vasco De Gama was losing his temper at this low caste man claiming to be president.

Don Pedro, however, was a sensible man. He accepted that he was in the presence of an odd creature. He persisted:

'No the present heir Dom Duarte is here in Lisbon. He is the Duke of Braganza. We accord him respect, but we are a Democracy - like America.'

'Like America,' Vasco was scornful, 'I have just come from there. It is full of riff raff from every corner of the globe.'

Vasco surveyed the crowd. It was later estimated at between four hundred and six hundred thousand. There was no loudspeaker system. The crowd was silent with faces raised to the column where Vasco was now perched.

De Gama looked down at the President:

'Sir I see many faces that are not Portuguese in origin. Where do your immigrants come from?'

'They come from Africa and Arabia,' said Don Pedro, 'and we have many Rumanians.'

'You have gypsies,' answered Vasco, 'I used to kill them.'

Joanne Rixti was standing beneath the column. She was shaking her head furiously and gesturing for Vasco to make his speech. Calliope took the page out of Vasco's pocket and placed it in his hand. Vasco read his prepared speech. It had been written for him by Jerry O' and edited and translated into Portuguese by Joanne Rixti using Google.

'Friends,' he began, 'your world is corrupt. Your rulers are corrupt.'

The crowd began booing and jeering Don Pedro. Hs security detail became alert.

'Not all rulers,' added Vasco, 'do not boo your leader. True Portuguese would be respectful. Those booing are probably the gypsies. Citizens be good to one another. Bring up your children to respect authority and to live with courage and dignity. Be courteous to your neighbors. Remember that money is the means to the end and not the end itself. Use your phones and pads. Do not be used by them.'

The crowd respectfully passed on his words from row to row.

Calliope had heard what De Gama said about Rumanians. He could not resist mingling with the crowd to hunt them down. As Vasco spoke an occasional muffled squeal would come from the crowd.

After the speech Vasco left for Big Pink. Crowds lined the roads to the airport. Many Moon Jam Jams were worn, but no trapdoors were opened.

On the flight back Joanne Rixti sat in a comfortable leather recliner near the front of the plane sipping a gin and tonic. 'What a trip!' But Vasco had not mentioned once about wanting to 'rut' her. Joanne was vaguely vexed by this, though she doubted she would have accepted such an advance.

Sixty

The general populace of the Earth first became aware there was a large meteor headed in its direction shortly after the twelve apostles had gathered at Little Pink for a confab.

Jerry O' praised his followers:

'You have done well. The humans seem to be listening. I am not sure whether it will work, but we have done our best. The Big Feller is pleased. I am to return to Paradise. Peter the Fisherman, Joan of Arc and Charles Dickens you will travel with me. There is some difficulty involving Vasco De Gama. I think the modern terminology for his situation is that the jury is still out. The remainder of you shall remain on Earth to live out your lives. Be true to your principles and one day we will meet again in Paradise'.

Vasco De Gama was saddened by what he heard, but he understood. He had acted like an old bull, angry, rampaging and rutting. He would just have to take his medicine. He thought for a moment of Peaches Globby. There was an upside.

Jerry O' continued.

'We will meet tomorrow morning for our last meal. It will be at Alle. I have booked the Fishbowl. The owner has promised secrecy. I want you all to attend. The meal will take place immediately after the Moon Shot. We will callit The Last Brunch. We will then depart.'

Phones began ringing and the journalists began picking up.

'There is a meteor,' said Chub Checker, 'it is as big if not bigger than the Earth itself. Scientists are tracking its approach. According to most scientists it will miss us but only by a few degrees. A few, however, claim we are doomed. There is now even more unrest.'

'Actually, it is now tracking to miss us by seven degrees,' said Jerry O', 'I have been informed of the meteor by the Big Feller. It is much bigger than Earth. It is the size of Jupiter.'

'The less reputable news services are blaming you Jerry O,' interposed Bruce Gotby, 'do you want to respond?'

'No,' said Jerry O' quite vehemently, 'it is nothing whatsoever to do with me. The Big Feller does not interfere with nature. The meteor is there by dint of the force of nature. We will ignore its presence.'

Jerry O' turned to Sandalphon who was one of two shimmers standing near the open bay window.

'I forgot to say thank you to you Sandalphon. You did very well in Afghanistan. It was very good work.'

Bear Grizzard whispered to Chub:

'Who the fuck is Sandalphon?'

'I do not have the faintest idea,' said Chub.

Joan waved towards the shimmer:

'Good on you Sandals. We are a great team. You are a cool dude.'

When Joan spoke to Sandalphon he shimmered from white to gold for a moment. It was enough for Bear to notice.

'Geez I need a stiff drink,' he said to nobody.

'And you too, Calliope,' said Jerry O', 'your work has been fine. However, I have to say questions are being asked by Metatron about your unauthorized entry of Rumanians in Portugal. You had better start preparing your defense. But tell me why you did it.'

'I was just trying to help,' said Calliope who had materialized as Dora.

'All right, just who in the fuck is Metatron?' Bear whispered to Chub. He paused for a moment before continuing.

'On second thoughts don't tell me.'

Sixty-One

Moon Moon had left his palace and travelled in a motorcade to his underground nuclear facility. His harried Pakistani fission specialist was waiting for him with his team. There was no competition by the young assistants to stand anywhere near their boss. It was better to hang back. Any mission by the team was likely to be a disaster because of the wretched state of the equipment.

'Is the rocket ready to be launched?' asked Moon Moon of his fearful Pakistani scientist.

'It has been prepared with the utmost diligence. Nothing more can be done,' said the Pakistani.

'I did not ask you to wring your useless hands or make lame excuses. Is the rocket ready to be launched?'

'It will do all that it is capable of doing,' said the Pakistani scientist. He knew it did not matter much what he said. If the mission was unsuccessful, he would, if he was lucky be quickly killed. In the unlikely event the mission was successful Moon Moon would inevitably take the credit.

Preparations were put in train. The countdown began. The rocket zoomed away with a satisfying burst of energy and soon was lost in the glare of the afternoon sun.

'How long will it take to get there?' asked Moon Moon.

'Twenty one hours forty-seven minutes,' replied the Pakistani with a confidence he did not feel.

The US intelligence services had monitored the lift off by satellite. Israeli Mossad agents had a Pakistani double agent in North Booga who was reporting that the rocket carried a nuclear bomb. He further reported the rocket was programmed to hit Manhattan.

Bruce Gotby, the apostle and Independent foreign editor knew the whole story within fifteen minutes. He reported his information to the rest of the editorial staff.

'It is Moon Moon's only bomb. Its chances of making it to New York are remote, but if it blows it will do a hell of a lot of damage. It is three times the size of the bomb which decimated Hiroshima. The air force is tracking it. They could destroy it at any time, but the problem is that it is passing over land. If the bomb explodes anywhere near the ground, it may cause harm. It is traveling due west and will be over land until it gets to the North Atlantic. Its course takes it right across Europe. The Pentagon have decided to let it get past the Azores Islands and then it will strike. There is no land mass between the Azores and our coastline save for Bermuda and that is a long way South.'

'But surely', said Bear, 'if they blow it up in midair it will be harmless. By the time the radioactive shit hits the ground it would be dissipated.'

'True,' replied Gotby, 'but the USA is so much in the bad books of the rest of the world that if a chipmunk was made slightly nauseous by a speck of nuclear waste, the green movement would be all over us. There would be writs, threats and protests. I am told there is not going to be a problem by waiting to strike. But my information is totally classified and off the record. The government is worried there may be panic.'

Bear and Chub and the others grumped about the exclusive that could not be printed, but in the end they knew they would have to grin and bear it.

Other apostles were out and about. Peter the Fisherman had accepted an offer from Omar Faghdour the owner of Alle Restaurant to go deep sea fishing off Martha's Vineyard. A full complement of journalists accompanied the boat and marveled at Peter's dexterity with a rod.

Joan of Arc was modeling some new chain mail outfits at Neimann Marcus under the tutelage of Kelly Bamwoo with a hovering nervous Sandalphon never too far away.

Vasco and Charles were watching the Young and the Restless on cable back at Little Pink. Vasco was excited by the romantic plot, but Charles was horrified by its absurdity.

Jerry O' was sitting in his room waiting. He knew the climax was nigh.

Ginger Scollop and Tweak Monk were hard at it organizing the Moon Shot. Reports were arriving from all corners of the globe that assembly points were being publicized, musicians gathering and the press preparing. The United Nations had been totally ignoring both Jerry O's activities and the

Moon Shot, but as the event gained momentum, it was felt something should be said. Moon Moon had few friends, and they were simply friends of necessity, but they had made representations to the UN Security Council that the moon shot was a degrading and intemperate attack on the leader of North Booga which, after all, was a member of the General Assembly of the United Nations. The Secretary General of the Council, who was a cannibal from North Carziland, wrote an open letter to the New York Times complaining bitterly about the proposed Moon Shot. He said the Moon Shot was a contemptible act of scandalous depravity which was designed to humiliate a great statesman. Ginger Scollop was asked by the Times if he wished to comment. Ginger described the letter as dopey and said the Secretary-General must have munched on a rabid child. Ginger went on to say that the Occupy Moon Jam Jams movement was considering a permanent picket of the United Nations with teams of mooners opening their trapdoors on the hour twenty-four hours a day. After this statement from Ginger Scollop was posted online, the Secretary-General of the UN Council relapsed into silence.

In Paradise the Big Feller sat in his study with Mohammed watching developments.

'You know,' he said to Mohammed, 'this Moon Shot business gives a whole new meaning to the old saying 'giving cheek, Mohammed.'

The Big Feller paused and re lit his briar.

'And that Moon Moon fellow, he could have turned the other cheek.'

Mohammed was not sure what the Big Feller meant by these remarks, but he could see the Big Feller was being humorous so he laughed dutifully anyway.

Sixty-Two

'I will start with the steak, followed by the porridge and after that I will have the fruit,' said Joan of Arc to the Alle waiter.

The Last Brunch had commenced. The apostles were seated in the Fishbowl in the center of Alle. Waiters hovered. Jerry O' was yet to arrive.

Omar Faghdour the ever-vigilant owner-chef was at his vantage point at the kitchen pass overseeing his troops.

Sandalphon was shimmering just outside the Fishbowl, but Calliope was nowhere to be found. Joan's angel assumed he must be with Jerry O'. He was correct.

Jerry O' and Calliope had been conferring with the Big Feller by thought transference. The Big Feller congratulated them.

'Both of you have done all that is required of you,' said the Big Feller, 'it is now up to the humans and nature too.'

Jerry O' was not too sure what the last bit meant - 'and nature too', but he guessed he would find out soon enough.

The Big Feller said his farewells. Jerry O's mother Mary and his wife Mary Mags were both looking forward to having him home again, playing his golf and having tea with the family.

When Jerry O' and Calliope, appearing as Dora, turned up at the Fishbowl the waiter was asking Joan if she was sure she wanted to order her meat dish first.

'Of course,' she said determinedly, 'an army marches on its stomach. I always eat the heaviest food first and leave the lightest until last. This way one can march longer. It is only commonsense.'

Joan seemed surprised that anybody would question her ordering.

Vasco was wolfing down oysters. He used no implement. He simply picked up an oyster, opened his mouth wide and emptied the mollusk straight from the shell down his gullet. The juices ran down both sides of his jaw as he swallowed. Occasionally between oysters he would unleash his long red tongue and slide it around his lower face mopping up any remnant of juice which had not already dripped on his tunic. Charles Dickens sitting opposite tried not to watch, but he found his eyes were drawn to the tableau. Dickens noticed Vasco's other hand rested on Joanne Rixti's thigh. She did not seem to have noticed or if she did was unmoved by it.

'Welcome to the Last Brunch,' said Jerry O', 'my apostles I want to thank you for your valuable work. The Moon Shot was a massive event. By its very nature it has caused the traditional churches to sit up and take notice. They claim to be offended by what they saw, but it is simply hypocrisy. The priests, mullahs and holy joes have caused more wars than they have saved souls. Let them learn from the upturned buttocks of the youth of the world.'

The Moon Shot had just occurred. Estimates varied as to the turn up, which was an appropriate description of the event. All networks covered the cheek show worldwide. On the first stroke of the hour millions of trapdoors opened in Moon Jam Jams in every city, town and hamlet from Tocumwal to Timbuktu. The Bare Arse Polka was played by a reggae band in Jamaica, a Peruvian Whistle combo in Lima, a full Symphony orchestra in Vienna and a kettle drum bluegrass duo in Paris, Texas. Moon Moon himself watched the split screen coverage on CNN in alternate rage and joy. On one hand the contempt he had been shown was beyond his belief. On the other hand, he was assured that the rocket and nuclear bomb was still aloft and speeding through the sky on its way to slice the Big Apple into little pieces. His Pakistani nuclear physicist was not confident but keeping his peace. The rocket was still in the sky. He knew that, but it seemed to have suddenly got itself into a holding pattern somewhere in the vicinity of Messina in Sicily. This was inexplicable to him, but he was certainly not going to pass on the news to Moon Moon. He simply hoped there was a glitch in the drive train of the rocket which would self-correct in its own time. Both NATO and USA forces were watching the rocket but were avoiding action as it was circling over a heavily populated land mass.

Chub, back in Alle, had enjoyed his brunch. He was going to miss the excitement of the last few days and his new companions. But then he noticed that a chair was vacant at the table. He counted the apostles.

'Jerry O',' he said, 'there are only eleven apostles here, one is missing.'

And he was right. There was a hush in the Fishbowl as Jerry O' commenced to count his squad.

He did not finish the count. Omar Faghdour, the owner chef and new best friend of Peter the Fisherman heard the front doors of Alle being bashed by fists and hammers. The restaurant was officially closed until evening. The Last Brunch was a special event. There should be no customers hanging around. Omar ran from the kitchen clutching his best cleaver.

He was swept aside by the onslaught which had now broken down the front door. There were angry and vitriolic butch lesbians, PETA members with barking, shitting leashed dogs, gay men in their new Vasco De Gama look alike outfits designed by the apostle Ginger Scollop and the odd remnant of the Occupy Moon Jam Jams contingent with nothing better to do wearing their one-piece pajamas. There was a lone cyclist pursued by a baying vicious Pit Bull Terrier. The environmentalist and the climate change freak stood back as onlookers and there was no sign of the anti-smoker who was still sick or the film star who was a habitué of Alle and did not want to fall foul of restaurant management. The main attackers, however, were an unlikely combination of atheists and Christians who seemed to be the angriest and wildest. The strange assortment of fervent humanity rushed at the Fishbowl, throwing their arms and legs against it.

Omar had run back to the rear waiter's exit door of the Fishbowl.

'Quick,' he said, 'follow me.'

Jerry O' and nine of his apostles followed Omar. Joan took up a fighting stance and was preparing to attack when her angel Sandalphon unceremoniously removed her.

'You are the strategist,' said Sandalphon in explanation, 'not the street fighter.'

Joan was angry, but there was nothing she could do about it.

Vasco De Gama was left on his own to meet the attack. He gathered himself, wiped off the remaining oyster liquid from his chin and found Joanne's Rixti's thigh was no longer there to be rubbed. He noticed the poltroon Oliver Givens-Cator was amongst the invaders. Vasco had not forgiven the swine who clutched a handful of the De Gama family jewels. The turd Melvin Van Horn was also in the crowd. He was surrounded by his usual team of smoke blowers and bum crawlers. Vasco had no weapon but was undeterred. Whooping with excitement and rage he ran to the front entrance of the Fishbowl to attack the hordes of the Politically Correct.

Jerry O' and the ten remaining apostles (now including little Joan of Arc under the wings of Sandalphon) were shown out the back door.

'I am sorry,' said Ginger Scollop, 'it is my old friend Tweak Monk who has betrayed us. We were all offered money by Melvin Van Horn to disclose where we would be after the Moon Shot, and I guess Tweak succumbed.'

'Oh heaven, oh paradise, Jerry O',' exclaimed Peter, 'will I renounce you three times once more, as I did before.'

'Don't be melodramatic Peter,' said Jerry O', 'I think you learnt your lesson last time. I do not expect you want to be crucified upside down by Oliver-Givens-Cator and Melvin Van Horn.'

This quietened Peter the Fisherman.

'So,' Charles Dickens commented as they entered the black bus waiting in the rear lane way of Alle, 'we have a Judas. I suppose it is not surprising.'

Calliope was ready, willing and extremely able to help out Vasco De Gama in his battle. Vasco was alone against a veritable battalion of muffin munchers, dog nuzzlers and pillow biters. The Portuguese warrior needed help.

Alas, Jerry O' warned Calliope off.

'Your job is to stay with me, Calliope, for once in your life do what you are told.'

And Calliope did as he was bid.

Vasco was still fighting. Though he was on his own against a large crowd, he had a home ground advantage. The main entrance to the Fishbowl was a single doorway and the back entrance had been locked by Omar when he departed. Secondly the PETA dogs had turned on the lesbians, who were already angry with the cowering queens. Vasco was simply standing in the doorway swiping whoever dared to show his/her head. If a dog attacked Vasco kicked it good and hard. The poltroon Oliver Givens-Cator and the greedy attorney Melvin Van Horn were now well back in the crowd. Oliver Givens-Cator had seen Vasco was the enemy and he was loath to engage him. Oliver looked around for the dangerous young woman, but she did not seem to be present. Oliver was still anxious. The man was bad enough, but the girl was an absolute menace.

Vasco was sorry Givens-Cator was not within range. He would have liked to grab a handful of the Givens-Cator knacker packer and twist it off. Vasco would have enjoyed force feeding the contents of the marble bag to Melvin Van Horn.

It is testimony to Vasco's will to conquer that he was able to absorb these thoughts whilst fighting single handed against this strange army.

But then the jolt struck Manhattan.

The attackers fell away as the thunderous sound of the earth quaking hit home. Lesbians were thrown backwards onto the floor; dogs turned and ran with their owners howling in support as they tried to keep up. The gay blades cowered in corners with their heads in their hands. The odd Occupy Moon Jammers who had only come along for something to do, dusted themselves off and headed back towards Wall Street.

After the first quake, the earth seemed to roll from side to side until it once again settled down. There was an eerie silence, until New Yorkers figured the occurrence (whatever it was) had finished. Then motors roared into life. Conversations re-commenced and the general hubbub of Manhattan life re-commenced.

Ordinary citizens had their TV's and radios turned on looking for answers, but none were yet forthcoming.

The US Government well knew what had eventuated, but it was still considering what should be passed on to the populace. In North Booga Moon Moon also knew, but he was too busy searching for his Pakistani nuclear scientist to find out why his rocket had behaved in such an eccentric way.

The rocket and attached bomb after circling Sicily for some hours had suddenly dived sharply and almost vertically into the heart of the Mt Etna active volcano. It travelled through the flames and was not halted until it struck the Earth's crust at the twenty-five-mile mark. The bomb exploded. The Earth was shifted slightly off its axis eight degrees by the blast. The enormous quake was felt throughout the world. When the underground mushroom cloud of fission had reached its equilibrium, the planet settled and began re-spinning.

Later in Paradise, the two Greek philosophers Plato and Socrates discussed the event interminably. They could never agree as to causation or effect and in the end, they had coffee with Aristotle and Isaac Newton to seek answers.

'What happened was like a spike going through a golf ball,' said Newton, 'when the spike penetrated the rubber completely it struck the hard center and the ball itself became off center.'

Aristotle, who was no nuclear scientist agreed adding:

'It makes a big difference as the earth was spinning at the time.'

The four men then went to the nearest Golf Driving Range, bought a golf ball and pierced it with a sharp kebab fork. They threw it and rolled it in several different ways. The experiment was inconclusive.

The Big Feller saw the drama unfold. He instructed Jerry O' to head home immediately and contacted Gabriel who was drilling angels in the forecourt of the Citadel.

'Go Gabriel,' said the Big Feller, 'send your army to gather all those humans deserving of eternal reward and bring them to Paradise. Collect them in the School Buses. They will be useful up here.'

The Big Feller could see that the planet earth spun off its axis by Moon Moon's explosion was now directly in the path of the giant meteor which was hurtling into the earth's solar system.

On earth there was disagreement by scientists as to the consequences of the explosion within the bowels of Mt Etna and its relationship to the meteor. Some said the meteor would still pass the earth without incident. Others said the meteor would break up once into the earth's solar system. There would be damage, injuries and deaths, but it would not be catastrophic. Few claimed the earth would be destroyed. However, there was nothing that could be done even if the latter thesis was correct. The meteor was bigger than the planet. There was no earthly weapon that could harm the meteor. Surprisingly the various sects that preached the end of the world regularly were silent.

The angels set forth on their round-up. The collection of souls was a job they knew well and performed faultlessly. Metatron kept count.

'I am afraid,' he told Mohammed, 'there is a final tally of about five hundred and fifty thousand humans. This is above the original estimate. Quite a few earthlings seem to have turned their life around in the last few days. The Big Feller will need more housing.'

Mohammed passed this information on to the Big Feller:

'We will need more housing. What do we have in the way of modern builders up here?'

'None,' replied Mohammed.

'But we have some carpenters,' replied the Big Feller, 'of that I am sure. I am afraid Wilfred's golf game will have to be put in mothballs until we have housed our newbies.'

The angel Uriel was looking after Manhattan. He found Vasco De Gama alone in Alle drinking Puligny Montrachet and eating oysters.

'Come,' said Uriel, 'we have not much time. The earth is going to be hit by a meteor any second.'

'No,' replied De Gama, 'I have sinned while here in thought and deed. There are other more deserving souls.'

'Don't be silly, De Gama,' said Uriel, 'you have played your part. You are expected in Paradise. Get on the bus outside.'

De Gama did not need much persuading. In the street was a yellow bus which was almost full. De Gama helped a small, emaciated man in a wheel chair with a withered body, black spectacles and big ears on to the vehicle.

The bus took off and joined a fleet of over ten thousand yellow buses in the sky traveling out of the earth's solar system. Vasco and the small, wizened man were looking out the back window of their trolley when the explosion occurred.

The meteor struck the planet Earth which was engorged in a mighty blaze of flames and a massive scattering of debris. Skyscrapers were dislodged from their foundations; ships were torn from the sea and jumbo jets fell apart like poorly made Lego set pieces. In a few seconds the planet was gone. There were particles of matter, forming small parcels of space junk, blowing around, and the solar system itself disintegrated.

The little wizened man turned to Vasco:

'I was right you know,' he said through a small mouth microphone which was fitted by tubing to his chest. 'I knew there would be a Big Bang, but my timing was out. I shall have to amend my my theory.'

The man kept rabbiting on about the Big Bang all the way to Paradise, making Vasco a trifle sorry he had loaded him on to the bus in the first place.

Sixty-Three
RETURN TO PARADISE

Peter the Fisherman was back with his fleet fishing the Apollean Sea. His friend Omar Faghdour from Alle Restaurant in New York has opened a seafood restaurant on the pier. He has called it Tin Pan Alle Tuna and his seared Ahi with a Lilikoi Coulis has been praised throughout Paradise. It has even been given five stars by the new restaurant critic of the Paradise Post Joanne Rixti. His Maitre'D Karl Kouvouisier looks after the guests with great aplomb assisted by a man called Clive, who when on Earth, was a front desk clerk at the Plaza Hotel in New York until traumatized by a malfunctioning computer.

Bear Grizzard is the new editor of the Post with Chub Checker as his assistant. Joanne Rixti is reporting on local affairs including writing her reviews of cafes and entertainments. Roger Sebastian Keats is the Arts editor. He found his old alleged relative, but the poet Keats knew the whole story of Roger Sebastian's fictional history and insisted on calling Roger Sebastian Mr. Pigsley. Their association was short lived.

The Post also has a legal reporter Judge Freddy Kreuger. There are no disputes or crimes in Paradise, but Socrates and Plato are often in to see her with arcane questions of canonical interpretation and the angels are always fighting amongst themselves and sometimes require sessions of mediation. Judge Kreuger secretly wonders if the Big Feller will send her over to Pluto to sort out the squabbling Grillabies. It will be a breeze for her after dealing with such creatures as Mayor Billy Lowe, Arnold Prink, Oliver Givens-Cator and the attorney Melvin Van Horn.

Bruce Gotby is covering the Grillaby conflict on Pluto. He has not actually been to Pluto. His source is a garrulous angel.

And talking about that angel! Calliope was severely reprimanded by Gabriel for using his imagination. His punishment was an assignment to report on the state of the struggle between the rival gangs of Grillabies to the Big Feller. This suited both Calliope and the Big Feller. Calliope found the Grillabies stupid, but much more predictable than humans. The Big Feller liked Calliope's off beat yarns of the ongoing battles.

Ginger Scollop and Kelly Bamwoo are designing clothes. Paradise has never seen brighter colored garments nor more imaginative styling. However few Moon Jam Jams are being worn in Paradise and certainly none with rear trapdoors.

Charles Dickens Chronicle has been a great success. He is planning on a series of new novels based on his experiences amongst twenty first century humans. The Biblical scholar John has commenced a Third Book of Revelations based on the Second Coming of Wilfred. John often consults with Dickens, but the novelist has noticed that the scholar seems to have had a second source for his Revelations. Charles wonders who it could be.

Vasco is back happily swallowing swords. He and Joan of Arc have become firm friends, and she often drops in to watch Vasco perform and have a chat with him. Her angel Sandalphon was in Gabriel's bad books for failing to inform the chief angel sufficiently of Calliope's malpractice until Joan intervened. Gabriel withdrew his charge. Joan was just too formidable.

Wilfred, nee Jerry O', nee Jesus, oversees the new building projects in the seven universes. He still plays golf, but his game has deteriorated, as he is not able to get in enough practice. His superintendent of works is a former New York policeman Sergeant Flanagan who is firm yet polite with the many tradesmen employed on the vast project. Wilfred also has the assistance of a fine young interior decorator. Her name is Rose France. She used to be an assistant district attorney. She enjoys her new occupation. She does not have to deal with the likes of Melvin Van Horn.

The Big Feller and Mohammed sit on the lawn of the residence having a cup of oolong tea and discussing the state of the universes. They watch the new gardener at work. He is a provisional, having recently arrived with the other earthly immigrants. The man was a Montenegrin who had escaped to New York to start a new life as a cab driver. He had been bundled off to Guantanamo Bay after a series of mishaps.

'He seems a good chap.,' said the Big Feller.

'Excellent,' replied Mohammed, 'he is just getting over the traumatic time he had in New York. He told me that Gitmo was fine, but New York was terrible. He claims a black woman materialized in the front seat of his taxi when it was already filled with screwballs, on a later journey some mad girl kept calling out that she would never shave her legs again and finally some businessman sat in his taxi sobbing like a baby.'

'I see,' said the Big Feller, and he did.

Just then Wilfred appeared lugging his golf clubs. It was his afternoon off.

'You know we will have to do something about those Grillabies on Pluto,' said the Big Feller.

'It's getting worse?' asked Mohammed.

'Oh yes much worse. Calliope informs me they are fashioning explosive weapons. Admittedly they are not very powerful, but they are killing each other. Perhaps we should send someone over to Pluto to sort it out.'

The Big Feller looked over at Wilfred who was now reaching the house.

'Not Wilfred,' said Mohammed.

The Big Feller took a sip of his tea and leaned back in thought.

'I guess not,' he said to Mohammed, 'perhaps I will just let nature take its course.'

Sixty-Four

CHARLES DICKENS JOURNAL

I write this, my last chapter, back in Paradise. Of course I am glad to be home, but my experiences on Earth have provided me with a fund of anecdotes and information. I have a whole new treasure trove of material.

But let me first tell you of my meeting with the revelation writer John. Mohammed summonsed me over to see him shortly after our sudden return to Paradise. I was just a smidgeon annoyed. I wanted to settle back to my old life, I did not need nor want an emissary telling me I was needed, no not even needed, wanted by John the Revelator. I thought I was the chronicler of the journey. It turns out my version is to be the informal and easily read account. Again, I serve the masses and I am happy with my lot. I thought John would be more the philosopher than the journalist.

I was wrong. John is a sifter of facts and a master of detail. He leaves nothing to chance. And why should he. It is his version which will be the authorized and permanent account of the journey. He is a humble man, our John, he is not what one would expect of such an important literary and religious figure. I was surprised by his knowledge of the journey. I was also surprised by some of his insights. I suspect that there is another chronicler, who fills the gaps and wallpapers the grains. It cannot be Joan. She is a doughty miss, but she is no reporter nor scribbler. Jerry O' was too busy and reflective to write a diary and, in any event, his mind echoes that of his father. So, this leaves De Gama. Still waters run deep and often waterfalls run shallow. I concede I may have misjudged the man. I still remember my sight of him coitus non-interruptus in a closet at the shooting of Straight Talk. Was our Vasco a secret recorder? I asked him - well as good as asked him at the small party the Big Feller gave to welcome us home. It was exciting to see De Gama. I was not sure he had made it back to Paradise. There was a question in my mind as to whether he would be admitted. I took him to one side during the soiree and asked him the question:

'I have to ask you Vasco,' I commenced, 'have you recorded your experiences on earth?'

To my surprise he became belligerent:

'A Portuguese gentleman never boasts of his conquests,' he said, 'my rutting is my business. I did not take you for a poltroon Dickens. You surprise me.'

Now perhaps one can take this at face value, but I think not. Vasco De Gama is himself full of surprises. He sought to put me off the scent.

My narrative recommences with my appearance on Straight Talk with Joanne Rixti and Roger Sebastian Keats. I was expecting to be challenged by the Archbishop of London Sir Rupert Dugong, but he appeared in Islamic garb and professed he had changed his faith. I believe Calliope our sometimes helpful and always wayward angel may have somehow caused Sir Rupert's downfall. I expected my credentials to be challenged, but not my skills as a chronicler. Instead, Dugong told me I wrote 'bourgeois romantic tripe'. I doubt that this was the archbishop's real view, as he had spent his life studying my work. I blame Calliope. I doubt Calliope has read Dombey and Son let alone my denser work. I think the flighty angel had programmed the archbishop so as to further embellish and give credence to his narrative.

The interviewer Peaches Globby may have been a trollop, but she surely was a talented cross examiner. After Dugong was spirited away, I spent the rest of the interview fending off her questioning. I do not believe she made the cut to get to Paradise. It is a pity as though strange in appearance and immoral in her ways she would surely be an asset.

My journalist colleagues all have arrived and are thriving. Bear Grizzard and Chub Checker asked me to meet them for a cup of oolong tea at their new offices. I can only try and report accurately Bear Grizzard's words. I assure you they are not mine:

'Now listen here Charlie, you old fucker, how about a weekly column for our humble little newspaper. Let's call it 'What the Dickens'. Just your latest meanderings about the world we live in. Nothing fancy, no bullshit, just jottings. Pat him on the back, Chub old son, Charlie here looks fucking bemused.'

I have taken the job. I enjoy writing of the sword De Gama swallows, the paintings Da Vinci produces and the jokes De Luise tells. What I have just written is illustrative of my column. Bear calls me a "fucker", yet I do not find this moniker uncomplimentary. He calls me Charlie. I have never been referred to by this diminutive. However, I revel in the informality of the man. His profanity is heartwarming and welcoming. I know I am his friend.

I should perhaps tell of the last day of Earth. There was the strange buttock exposure by millions. Yet it served its purpose. The last brunch was orchestrated by Jerry O', of that I have no doubt, but the desertion of Tweak Monk and the arrival of the angry hordes - I am not so sure this was in the plan.

And the bomb descended into the abyss of the volcano and shortly afterwards the meteor struck and destroyed the planet. What can I say. I will leave it to John the Revelator and his other unnamed (Portuguese?) source to flesh out the circumstances.

I now spend my days writing of my experiences whilst back on earth. My first new novel is called ARNOLD PRINK. It is the story of a snide minor bureaucrat who was in a steeplechase of temptation and fell at every brush hurdle. My next novel will be named THE MAYOR. The lecher Billy Lowe, former Mayor of New York, is my inspiration. I have other novels lurking. I was served in a cafe in Manhattan by a man who spoke and acted as if he was not quite human, but not quite inhuman. He reminded me of what I have read about the sub-stratum species of Grillabies who live on Pluto. I found out the waiter was from a country called New Zealand. I will do more research, but perhaps the Kiwis, as they are called are distantly related to Grillabies.

But as I leave my chronicle I conclude by congratulating the explorer Jerry O'. He may be only the son of the father, but he is truly his father's son.

Sixty-Five

CALLIOPE'S EPISTLE

I have faced the music. I have been dressed down by Gabriel and punished by being sent to Pluto to report on the war between the two competing factions of Grillabies. I must say they are hard to tell apart. They are all short and squat creatures with bulbous stomachs and arms that practically trail on the ground. Their clothing is largely strips of primitive canvas type material which is draped across their bodies. They speak in a guttural tongue. They communicate, but with difficulty. Their language is, to be kind, unsophisticated. They use primitive implements, grow crops of weeds and kill animals for food, but their manners are disgraceful. I have seen a Grillaby from the Gank tribe scratch his backside and then pick up a haunch of bear meat with the same hand and eat it. The leader of the opposing Woob faction often eats his ear wax. On the other hand, this may be a trait of leadership. When I was last on Earth I saw on television a former Australian Prime Minister do the same thing.

I report to the Big Feller of the ongoing struggle between the Woobs and the Ganks. They are both as bad as one another. I have resisted the temptation to enter them as I entered the Rumanians whilst in Lisbon with Vasco. Gabriel made a big song and dance about that, saying it was unauthorized penetration of innocent bodies. From what I heard Vasco say about Rumanians, there are no innocents amongst them.

I have met my epistle writer. It is John no less. He was most kind. He read my epistles closely. He said my work was to use his word - admirable. However, he told me did not want me to write more. John said he already had to absorb the Charles Dickens chronicles and though Dickens could write, he was very wordy. I can tell you reader that I do not intend to write any more epistles. The reason will become obvious.

I am pleased that Charles Dickens is now writing full time. His job as front office manager is now redundant as earth no longer exists, so there are no new arrivals. I will leave it to Dickens to report to John the Revelator about the Last Brunch and the fight and subsequent flight. I should however tell you the sight of the thousands of school buses in the sky above the planet earth was an amazing spectacle. And then to see Earth disappear in a few puffs of steam - I cannot describe it. There you see I admit it; I cannot describe it.

But why must my last epistle be between you and I, why is it secret? I will tell you my reader now but promise me that it shall remain concealed.

Just before the earth came to an end, I thought of the angry and quarrelsome Grillabies. Then I thought of some humans that I had come across on my recent visit and I acted. I know this could be the end of me if Gabriel finds out, but I am destined to act on impulse. I have taken four humans and placed them on Pluto. Not that they are deserving cases, far from it.

I plucked Oliver Givens-Cator, Billy Lowe, Arnold Prink and Peaches Globby and deposited them amongst the Grillabies. Well not quite amongst them, but in a forest of nettles where the new arrivals could see their co-inhabitants. It is the Calliope social experiment. I have told nobody. The Big Feller is all knowing, but he has not mentioned the matter to me, let alone admonish me. I assume he is content or at least tolerant of my actions.

I thought of bringing the lawyer Van Horn with me, but I decided not to. The last thing Pluto needs are lawyers, particularly a pesky one like Melvin Van Horn. I also considered Gavan Rowntree, the television talk back ranter, but if Pluto does not need attorneys, it needs loudmouthed opinionators such as Rowntree even less.

Peaches Globby mind you is neither angry nor quarrelsome. She is just self-centered, pushy and sluttish. The former Mayor Billy Lowe is a depraved, loathsome creep, Arnold Prink is a lying troublesome wretch and what can I say about Oliver Givens-Cator? I will use the De Gama word. The man is a poltroon.

It has been interesting to see how the humans and Grillabies have interacted. The only human contacts the creatures have had in the past was when I once appeared as Dora to see their reaction. Both tribes went rushing away as fast as they could shouting 'Molvag, molvag' as they went. Molvag is the Grillaby word for demon.

It is only early days, but a storyboard is emerging.

Givens-Cator is a disappointment. He remains in the woods alone.

He whimpers like a child and lives on tiny unpleasant tasting berries. I may be imagining it, but his arms seem to be growing longer.

Arnold Prink has been taken into custody by the Ganks. Peaches Globby is also with this tribe. Peaches made a successful play for the king and is now his favorite concubine. I believe she is angling to be queen. She was dismissive of Prink's false claim that he was her friend, and she has seen to it that he is either being regularly rogered by tribesmen returning from foraging or is having his arms stretched and his belly distended by dribbling Grillaby women..

The former Mayor of New York Billy Lowe sought by sign language to enamor himself to the ear wax eating Woob monarch. Unfortunately, his sign was mistaken for a disgusting insult. Billy Lowe is on the run. At least he has company. He has hooked up with a Woob woman who was expelled from the tribe for shitting in her husband's rat stew. The two travel at night and lie in hiding during the day. They seem well suited.

I remain out of sight. I am going to let nature take its course. You see I am learning. Where will the story end - well I guess that is another story.

THE END

About the Author

The author has practised as a barrister, KC, judge and Law Professor over a career spanning 50 years. He has been awarded an Order of Australia medal for his service to the law. He is also a musician and songwriter. He is the Jazzer in the Rocker & Jazzer band that has recorded several albums, and he has co-written numerous songs that have been covered in the USA and Europe. He has written published textbooks, a memoir REFLECTIONS OF TINY VICTORIES and a number of novels including MONKEY MAN and HITLER'S BARBER that are available in print.

www.ingramcontent.com/pod-product-compliance
Lightning Source LLC
LaVergne TN
LVHW050915080826
845145LV00001B/98
9780646736761